THE EVOLUTIONIST

ALSO BY RENA MASON

East End Girls

THE EVOLUTIONIST

RENA MASON

for Rob

Memories are the key not to the past, but to the future.

—*Corrie Ten Boom*

CHAPTER ONE

My book club is killing me. The demands my friends make of me feel like stabbing daggers, leaving open wounds from which my life continuously seeps. The frame of mind I have to be in when I'm around them stretches the thinning boundaries of my will. Between the oppressive heat of Las Vegas, and the endless nightmares I've suffered through, these last few weeks of summer have been especially hard to endure. Every day I have to draw deeper inside myself to find that happy place and smile.

The ladies at the book club—my friends—would never understand that my life has been in a downward spiral in ways I couldn't control with shopping, cocktail parties, prescription medications, or a spa getaway.

I've known little to no violence my entire life, yet I'm almost certain I can dismember a body in less than an hour. No. There isn't any way I could possibly explain to them what I've experienced. I can't get a grip on it myself, yet I feel it slipping away.

Driving past the Catholic school, along the main road from our neighborhood fills me with bloodguilt now. It's a trip I make four to five times a day to take my son to his classes, home again, then soccer and errands, and there is no alternate route. The setting sun's orange glow creates a halo behind the large cross in front of the high school. Remorse sinks into my gut and churns up acid. Lost in thought, I drive over a jagged stone. A loud crunch comes from under one of the tires sending an icy jolt up my spine. In the rearview mirror, I see the broken pieces quaking. This never would have bothered me before. I shouldn't know what the cracking and splintering of bones sounds like, or the dull popping feeling they make when they break underneath the thick flesh of the people I know—by my own hands.

Yet I do.

I pull up and around Cally's circular driveway and park next to Gail's car. Gail likes to get a head start with the wine at these little get-togethers, ever since her husband filed for a divorce. I'm barely in the doorway when Cally shoves a book into my abdomen. "Here," she says. "Open it."

Cally holds a fierce gaze over me, and I'm forced to use my one and only poker face. She stands over me at 5'9, giving her an unfair advantage she plays well and far too often. Nervous perspiration makes my palms stick to the slick book jacket.

Dammit—Cally wins again.

Only in Vegas can a harmless book club turn into

a cutthroat competition. I'm not sure when they got so brutal. Maybe the time Jordan hired a private chef to come and cook for us. We had finished reading a cookbook with short stories about travels at the time, so it didn't seem that outrageous. However, Tara, Jordan's best friend, would not be outdone. The one she hosted had aestheticians who gave us all facials and makeovers—supposedly keeping with the theme of the *Lipstick* book. It doesn't really matter how it began; I just know the absurdity is out of control. Their intimidating tactics of outdoing one another only reinforces why I don't volunteer to host any book club parties. The rest of them all seem to be clamoring for it lately anyhow.

I cow to Cally and read the description on the back of the book. It could be an advertisement for rehab. Words like *epic*, *journey*, and *triumph* are highlighted to trick the wide-eyed into paying for a new life—or in this instance—a book about someone else's new life.

"Sounds great, doesn't it?" Cally asks.

"But the last book was a memoir. You promised we'd read something new this month."

"Oh, you'll love it. Go get a glass of wine," she leans in close then whispers, "before Gail drinks it all." Cally grabs my arm and tugs me toward the foyer. "Don't look over there. She'll know we're talking."

"How's she doing?"

"Not so good. He wants everything. Go over there and see if you can get any more info out of her. Oh! And

I've got some great news. But it's a surprise. You'll have to wait. Now go on." She turns me back around and nudges me forward.

Cally's kitchen is an Italian Renaissance masterpiece complete with hand-tooled cabinetry imported from Sorrento. When she decided to renovate, she didn't ask me to design it for her *de gratia*, which I was thankful for, but she did ask for my opinions at least two or three times a day for about a year. My friends know I handed my clients over to my business partner when I retired from interior design, but it never stops them. Cally and her husband Bill remodeled their entire house after an Italian palazzo owned by her family in Florence. It's been in several home improvement and luxury sales magazines. One of the perks Bill gets for being the producer of a local news channel.

Gail has her bony hip pinned against the center buffet island. There's a full glass of red wine in one hand and a piece of pita bread in the other. She smiles sweetly when she sees me. I step in to give her a hug, and like a true socialite she keeps both arms up to avoid my silk blouse. In return, I don't get close enough to mess up her hair or makeup. Something Cally taught me.

"It's good to see you," I say behind her ear.

"You too," she says. "I like your shoes. Louboutin?"

"No, Laurent." I step back to look at hers. No doubt *they* are Louboutins.

"So…how's the wine?"

"Ah, it's good." She brings the glass to her lips and downs a hearty swallow. "I was sure you were going to ask me how *I* was." She smiles a more genuine smile. "I can't tell you how sick I am of hearing that question." She swirls the little bit of wine left around in her glass and stares down into the vortex of Cabernet.

"Oh, I'm sure."

"Sorry. I should've known better. I forgot you're not like us. I mean you didn't grow up here," she quickly adds. "Which is why you're nicer." She looks up at me and winks.

"No, but I'm your friend, too. We all just want to be sure you're all right."

"Well, I'm fine. And when they ask you what I've said, that's what you can tell them."

"You know me well enough to realize I don't play those games."

"You're right. I guess I'm just…in a mood."

"That's understandable." I pour myself a glass of white, take a sip, then turn to face her again. "You look really good."

"You sound surprised."

"Maybe I am, a little. Not in a bad way though. I mean…you doing something new?"

"No. Nothing." She looks away. "So, what's the next book about? You didn't seem too enthused when you stepped in here."

"It's another memoir."

"Oh God, help us. That explains the incense and Turkish throw pillows on the floor."

"She'll never outdo the monogrammed sailor hats. Remember those?"

We erupt with giggles, careful to keep our glasses steady. A mix of wine and spittle leaks down from the seam of her lips. "Stop," she grabs a napkin from the counter, then dabs her chin. "Maybe we'll get saris this time."

"Jon would just love that, but he thought the sailor hat was kind of cute, too."

Gail's demeanor goes flat. "Oh," she says. "How's that gorgeous husband of yours doing? And Patrick…how's he? Seems strange I see him at soccer practice but don't really know how he is *actually* doing. You probably feel the same way about Justin though. Some days I can't believe how fast our boys are growing."

"He's good. They're both good. How is Justin, by the way? How's he handling everything that's going on with you and Steven?" Suddenly, I hear a high-pitched drone. "What is that? An alarm? Does Cally have something in the oven?" I glance around the kitchen and all of the ovens are off, including the microwave.

"What's what?"

"That noise. Don't you hear it? The TV…"

We simultaneously turn and look into the family room. The massive, blank, flat screen on the wall is impossible to miss. Gail's eyes move back to me. "What's it sound like?"

"Like an alarm, I guess, only not as loud."

"Strange, I don't hear anything." She raises her glass and takes another sip but keeps a keen eye on me. She lowers her glass. "Are *you* all right? You *do* look a little tired."

"I'm fine, really. Busy with soccer, holiday plans—the usual stuff."

"Maybe it's the lighting in here that's making you peaked. These cabinets are so dark and gloomy." A look of disgust supplants her prying stare. "There could be a bulb that's about to go out. Sometimes they make a weird noise, you know, like a buzz. Could that be what you're hearing?" Gail looks up and eyes the kitchen. The lights are all fine.

"It's gone now. Probably a side effect from listening to my iPod too loud."

"Yeah well, no doubt you've *heard* what Tara's up to? She's a real piece of work."

"Who? Tara?"

"No. Cally."

"Okay. I'm confused." Now it's my turn to gulp the wine. I empty the glass before Gail continues with what I'm sure is the latest bit of hot gossip.

"You know Cally has never really liked Tara, but now she's waiting for her at the door like a puppy."

"You're not making any sense."

"Maybe she hasn't told you yet. She'll probably wait until I leave."

"Oh no, here we go," I mumble.

With the sloppiness that accompanies haste, I pour myself a refill while Gail huddles against me and whispers, "You know Tara's husband, Paul, has good friends in Hollywood. Well, they're thinking about starting one of those *Housewives* shows here. They've asked Tara to help choose the other women. Need I say more?" She looks at me with a raised brow.

"Oh God, you don't think Cally wants me to…"

There's no need to finish the sentence. Cally always includes me in her cockamamie schemes. This book club for one. "I couldn't."

"I don't think you have a choice. You know how pushy she is. I'm sure she wants in, and I'm sure she wants you in. And I know because of the divorce, I'm out."

"I can guarantee you there's no way in hell I'm doing it." My heart races at the mere thought. "I've got to talk to her about this, now."

Gail holds me back. "No. Don't let her know I told you, she'll be pissed. Just wait till I go. Please."

"Don't worry." After a deep breath, I back down and then empty my glass with one tilt.

Tara and Jordan finally arrive. Jordan's booming voice and Southern accent fills the entire house. After several minutes in the foyer, they join us in the kitchen. "Stacy. You look fabulous," Tara says.

"And so do you," I tell her. I learned a long time ago she greets everyone this way in order to get a reciprocal response. Even with long, amber hair, green eyes, and the body of a supermodel, she is insecure. I will never understand it.

"You look good too, Gail," Jordan says, like an afterthought. It's her way of being nice, but it never comes out right. She is older than the rest of us, by how many years she will not divulge. Her hair is jet black, short, and she gels it into little spikes. I think her hairdresser encouraged the *edgier* look, but it suits her rough, dominant personality.

Gail raises her glass as if to toast then takes a sip without uttering a sound. Cally nudges Tara with her elbow; she could not have been any more obvious. Poor Gail. A divorce could've happened to any one of us. Already a marked woman and because of something she has no control over. *No way will they ever find out what is happening to me.*

The tension is grating my last nerve. "Excellent," I blurt out. "Everybody looks great. Now let's fill our glasses and get this bitch started. Some of us would like to get home tonight."

They all look at me with surprise. It's not often that I speak up, but I can't stand to feel what everyone's thinking, but nobody's saying, anymore. It's all over me, digging in, and I want nothing more than to shake it all off.

"Honey, speak for yourself," Jordan says with a loud Texan twang, "Samuel's gone for the next four days, and I plan on spoiling myself rotten."

She just saved me from pulling my hair out in front of them all.

"And that's different from when he's here?" Tara says.

"Oh, aren't you just the comedienne," Jordan says. "Stacy's right. Let's pour up then plop ourselves down on those pillows. Gad. That looks uncomfortable over there. Really Cally, what were you thinking?"

"Get over it Jordan. The cultural ambience will get you in the mood."

"Hell, in the mood for what? Is it a Kama Sutra story we're going to be reading next? Now that'd be something, wouldn't it girls? I could scare the hell out of Sam when he gets back and work the moves on him." She shimmies her hips and bellows rowdy laughter that resounds, and we all laugh together.

The moment ends almost abruptly with gentle coughs and then an awkward silence. A palpable uneasiness clings to every molecule in the air, making it heavy around us. It's the weight of a storm that will never come. These women have been insincere friends for far too long to change things now.

One by one, we head over to the cushions in the middle of Cally's family room floor. She hands everyone a copy of the book. "All right ladies, you're going to love this. It's a memoir about a woman who gives up everything then tours nearly every top luxury spa in the world before finding herself through transcendental enlightenment.

"Don't glare at me like that Stacy. It got really good reviews. But maybe the floor pillows weren't such a good idea." She rubs her lower back.

"Sounds good to me," Jordan says. "Does she list the best spas at the end of the book? I'm definitely going to need one after sitting like this." She giggles and flips through to the back pages.

Cally walks over and closes the book in Jordan's hands. "You've got to read it from the beginning."

"Whatever," Jordan says. "Now be a dear, and help me up off this tombstone you call a floor."

Cally reaches down and pulls Jordan up. The rest of us stand on our own.

"Well," Gail says, "I have to go."

"So soon?" Cally says.

Gail gives Cally a hug and glares over at me. Then she walks toward the foyer.

"It's time for me to leave too," I say.

"You can't go yet," Cally insists. "There's something important we need to discuss."

"We can do it tomorrow. I'm exhausted." I turn around to walk with Gail, but she's already made it to the foyer.

Cally grabs my arm and stops me in the hall. "You *really* should stay," she says.

"Do I look tired to you?"

"Actually, you do look a little pale. Go on home and get some rest. I'll talk to you tomorrow." She grins like a little girl with a secret. "We'll get some coffee in the morning after yoga. Don't forget."

I catch up to Gail before she leaves. Books in hand, we walk out to our cars. "Looks like you got out of it tonight," Gail says.

"You're not being fair. You've been friends with Cally since…well, forever."

"Exactly," she says. "Night." Then she gets in her car and backs down around the driveway.

Reluctant to wake Jon, I tiptoe into the bedroom, but the light of the moon reveals an empty bed. After I've been in the shower for several minutes, he steps quietly into the bathroom.

"How was it?" he says.

"Oh, you know—the usual—in-depth, comprehensive discussions on Hemingway, symbolism, pointillism, and transcendental meditation."

Jon bellows out laughter that reverberates around the thick, glass shower door. He walks up and peeks through a patch that isn't fogged over. "So, what is it I can expect to see you entrenched in these next few days?"

"Another chick memoir."

He leans in and puts the tip of his nose against the glass. His dark brown eyes striking, even through the steam. "Hmm…sounds riveting. I'm glad guys don't have book groups."

"Maybe you should start one."

His sensual smile accentuates his robust lips. "No thanks. I'll stick with the occasional poker night."

"You're so unoriginal—especially for Vegas."

"Unoriginal, yes, but easy—and that's what guys want—easy."

"You coming in for a little easy?"

"Unfortunately, no. I've still got some work in the office."

"That's unfortunate indeed." I press my soapy breasts against the shower door.

He leans down and licks the glass in front of each one. "I'll try not to wake you when I come to bed. Unless I see that you need me to."

"Gee, thanks," I reply. "That was great, let's do it again soon. And don't stay up too late."

I pause and listen, but he's already gone.

Two bodies are all I can fit into the shopping cart. Any other day, I could arrange four hundred dollars of bulk food items into a Costco cart without breaking a sweat, but this cart is too small. It must have come from the corner drugstore up the road. I felt fortunate when I found it about a month ago, but now it's a pestering obsession. It doesn't matter how many times I rearrange the makeshift body bags—two remains the maximum capacity.

The day I realized everyone was dead, I forced myself to venture out beyond the cul de sac. I went as far as the other gated neighborhood nestled around ours. Amidst the decomposing corpses that lay strewn across the sidewalks and roads, the empty cart stood alone, a glistening Excalibur jutting out of the pavement. I knew I needed it. The epiphany came when I was crouched next to the cart, busy untangling the foul mess of outstretched human limbs still clinging to its wheels—remnants of the last survivors unwilling to let go of their treasure. Little did I know then the cart would be so essential. And become such a nemesis.

My neighbor's wife was a petite woman, and it's not hard to break and bend her body in half after the incisions. I pull apart one of those black, oversized leaf bags, then slide it over her body, and tie it off, tight. Careful not to tear the plastic, I lift one end onto the lower rack of the cart. With firm, gentle nudges side to side, I maneuver her carcass until it is all the way on.

My neighbor's husband; however, will require a little more breaking down. He was a tall man with a thick build. I'll need the sledge hammer and axe from the garage.

Walking past Jon's car, I catch my reflection in the tinted glass and stop to look. I have on the stupid apron Cally gave me for a hostess gift. It used to be white and read, *I only drink on three occasions: breakfast, lunch and dinner.* There was a picture of two wine glasses toasting above the words. Something is smeared all over it now; it's hardly recognizable.

Peering down at my chest, there is blood in every form imaginable. Layers and layers of bone bits, tufts of hair, and stringy meat are caked to the front. Deep creases traverse the midriff, exposing where I've repeatedly bent down or over. Just below that, the blood is brighter, fresher.

There are bigger, heavier pieces of flesh that slide before they fall off then disappear. Down by my left knee, the iris part of a torn eyeball stares up at me.

I know you.

Heinous scenes flash before my eyes, and I gasp and gasp and gasp, expanding my lungs until they burn. My mouth opens wide, and I scream a scream that shatters nightmares.

CHAPTER TWO

Loud screams launch me up into the darkness. Before I can scream again, Jon coils his arms around me with a python's embrace. "Stacy! Jesus. This is insane."

"So real…so real." I struggle to break free, but it only makes him constrict more. When I'm too exhausted to fight back and barely able to breathe, my muscles slacken. He loosens his grip. "I'm sorry," I whimper. The sobs begin and then the babbling. "Oh God…damn nightmare. So real…"

Mumbling and crying, my face starts to glide around on his forearm. It's dripping with tears, saliva, and mucus. "You'll be all right. We'll talk tomorrow." He kisses the side of my head. The weight of his arms lifts from my shoulders. Then he scoots back and settles in to his side of the bed. "I've got to get up early. I've got meetings all day. Please. Lie down. Try to rest."

"It *is* morning," I mutter. When there's no response, I snatch the covers up then fall back into my pillow. Jon shifts over to my side, then spoons against me; his body next to mine is everything that is safe.

The alarm clock goes off too soon. There is something infinitely cruel about waking up to *Let It Be*. The nightmare images still crisp. Jon gets up, but I can't yet. I close my eyes and fall back asleep. Before he heads downstairs, he wakes me up.

After a while, the odor of burnt crumbs from the toaster floats upstairs. When he's done with his usual quick breakfast of a single toasted bagel, he comes into the bathroom with coffee. He sets one cup down on the counter next to me while I'm on my vanity bench, putting my hair into a ponytail. He leans against the wall behind me, sips coffee from his cup and watches me.

"Were you able to get a decent amount of sleep?" he says.

I regard his reflection in the mirror. He looks handsome in the dark gray suit and teal chevron tie. It's nice he doesn't ask me what to wear anymore, but I couldn't have made it any easier—his closet is almost all color-coded.

"Yeah, eventually," I tell his mirror image. "Sorry I woke you. Did you get back to sleep?"

"No, but that's okay."

"You lie." I twist to face him and grin. "You were snoring again before my head hit the pillow."

He rolls his eyes and then swigs some coffee.

"Jon?"

"Yes, dear."

"Don't. You know I hate it when you say that."

"What, honey?"

"Seriously, what am I going to do? It's been nearly three months. It's not getting better. It's worse, and I'm *so* tired."

"You want me to ask around? Maybe some of the other docs' wives see therapists. They might have some recommendations."

"Absolutely not! Are you kidding? Oh my God, please don't mention what's been going on with me to people at work. You haven't already, have you?"

"Christ, give me a break."

"I just don't want anyone to know."

"And I'm not going to tell them."

"It's a small-town-in-a-big-city mentality here, and it's not the *in* thing to have a shrink on speed dial like it was in the eighties."

"What are you going to do then? You're losing sleep and so am I. Let's face it—when you don't sleep—I don't sleep."

"That's why I'm asking you what you think I should do. You're supposed to be the doctor. What about sleeping pills? Cally takes them. Couldn't you bring home some samples?"

"You've got to be kidding. I could lose my license. Falling asleep isn't your problem anyway. You need to get to the root of the nightmares and why you keep having them. I've tried giving you my advice. Why don't you ask Cally, or one of the other girls?"

"No way. They'd love to hear something's wrong. In

less than a week, we'd be getting a divorce because you were having an affair with a stripper."

"Hmm…" He raises an eyebrow and curls the upper corner of his lip into a sly smile. "You know Dr. Wagoner only dates strippers. Well…and porn stars."

"Gross! I shook his hand at last year's fundraiser."

Jon laughs and nearly spills his coffee. "Look, I've got to go. Promise me you'll do something."

"Promise. I'll Google it. If I make an appointment with a shrink, I want to be damn sure it's someone no one knows."

"Good luck with that."

"Yeah, tell me about it."

"Have fun at the gym. Tell Cally I said hello and that we should get together soon for cocktails, dinner, or whatever. I haven't seen Bill in a while, and I'd like to set up a tee time. I'll be home late tonight, and don't forget to name this year's fundraiser—everybody's asking."

"I won't."

Jon steps up behind me, leans down, and kisses my temple. "I love you."

"Love you, too."

After he leaves, I sit and stare at the spectral reflection in the mirror. I don't understand what is happening and why now, but I can see that these nightmares are slowly sucking the life out of me. Between them, my friends, and family, I'm amazed I've held it together this long.

"Patrick Troy. Get up. What do you want for breakfast?" I barge into his room, walk over to the shutters, and clank them open. Rays of desert sun beam through the slats, making his blanket-wrapped body look like a giant striped burrito. He has the comforter pulled up over his head.

"I'm not hungry, Mom. I'll eat something later." He grumbles.

"Fine, but you need to get out of bed. Now."

I flick one of the toes sticking out of the blanket roll when I walk by. He curls it and pulls both feet in as if a house had just fallen on top of him. I can't believe he's a teenager. Walking downstairs, I suddenly feel much older. I finish my coffee then stretch on the family room floor. Patrick gets downstairs, wolfs down several donuts, and then chugs some milk.

"Mom, I've got practice today."

"I know. What time's the game Saturday? I think I'm snack mom."

"Eight, but I'll ask Kyle."

"All right, let's go. I don't want to be late for yoga." On my way out, I step into the laundry room and grab my mat, purse, keys, and iPod. In the garage, I get a bottle of water from the other fridge. "You've got *all* your homework and books, right?"

"Yeah, Mom," Patrick says in that *ohmygod, you're so annoying* tone that all teenagers seem to master so well.

He attends Trinity Lutheran, which is only five miles from the house, but traffic during drop-off and pick-up is a standoff between the moms. We have all been herding to the same place for years, but it is still important to be the first one in line. Ridiculous, but for the most part I've learned to just follow the herd. This *is* Summerlin—a little Stepford in some ways, but in more ways—not.

The battle continues for a good parking spot at the gym, but I surrender. The air is cool in the morning, and I don't mind the walk unless it's summer. Cars in the lot range from Rolls to Rovers. Fab Freddie's Carwash even offers a detailing service while you work out, but after tips it ends up costing a hundred dollars. I've only done it a handful of times.

Check-in requires a laser scan of the index finger, which is a little over the top. Then someone on staff says good morning and hands me a clean towel. After several miles on the treadmill, I'm ready. The classrooms are up the stairs, behind the smoothie bar and café.

"Morning, Jenna," I say with exuberance on my way to the other end of the classroom.

"Namaste," she whispers softly. Jenna is the instructor, and yoga is her life. Which is good for the rest of us, I guess.

The girls are all smiles this morning. We four tend to cluster toward the right front corner of the room. We try not to talk during class, but it doesn't always work out that way.

"Hey Stacy," Tara says. "You look pale. Are you sick?"

"No. I feel fine." There's no escaping the reflections of reality in the walls of mirrors, though. I'm a ghost.

"You're in need of spa day, that's all. Let's do it. Cally, you set it up," Tara says.

"Why do I always have to set it up?"

"Cause you get the best deals," Tara says.

"Whatever," Cally says. "Next week after yoga then."

"I didn't mean right now," Tara whines. "I have to check my planner."

Cally looks over at me then rolls her eyes.

"I saw that," Tara says.

"Knock it off, ladies," Jordan says "Jenna's fixing to start."

"You look better than you did last night," Cally whispers.

"Thanks," I say.

"Shush," Jordan whispers. "I'm tired of getting in trouble for talking."

"You're kidding, right?" Tara says.

Jordan holds up her hand to block any further comment. Jenna watches us giggle with eagle eyes. She doesn't start the class until we've quieted.

Yoga was another one of Cally's ideas. Then it was body pump classes, Pilates, and private tennis lessons. There's no lack of motivation however, in a city always full of fresh, young bodies made for sin.

My nose starts to run when I'm Downward-Facing Dog. I sniff hard to keep it in, but it's flowing like water. When I raise my head and look in the mirror, jagged lines of crimson dissect the lower half of my face. Cally gasps and reaches for her towel. I grab mine from my mat and press it against my nose.

Jenna stops and comes over. "Are you all right?"

"Yeah. It's just a bloody nose. I'll clean up in the bathroom." I straighten myself out and stand up.

"Good idea," Jenna says.

I look over at Cally, and she nods at me. I know she'll get my stuff if I don't come back.

Half of the towel is soaked with blood by the time I reach the bathroom. I flip it over to the dry side, pull a bunch of tissues out and wet them. I take the towel away and wipe the mess from my face. It has not stopped. Two thin trails of warm blood move over my lips and down my chin. I'm mesmerized by it, watching the drips splatter into little suns in the white porcelain sink. Then I feel dizzy, faint. I grab hold of the sink. Darkness spreads inward from the periphery of my vision. Before it all goes black, I hear the same high-pitched alarm from Cally's house last night.

The shadows recede to the corners of my eyes. The squelch intensifies and so does the volume. It's so loud now, like one of those TV emergency broadcasts, but blaring straight from my head. I let go of the sink and cover my ears, which doesn't help. The sound must be coming from inside me. A deep breath, about to scream…it stops.

All I hear now is the muffled sound of running water. I lower my hands and look down into the sink. The drips have stopped, too. "Shit." I grab a wad of paper towels and clean up again.

Things might be getting worse, but still, I won't tell Jon about this. When it comes to me, he takes his *doctoring* overboard, and the last thing I need right now is to spend hours at a hospital being tested for this, that, and the other. Maybe his suggestion about seeing a shrink isn't such a bad idea. It would be good to talk to someone about everything that's been happening.

Around eleven, the girls come down from class and see me waiting in the lobby. Cally hands me my things.

"Stacy, honey, you really do look tired. You sure you're all right?" Jordan says.

"Yes, everything's fine. I mean, I've been busy planning the surgery center fundraiser, along with the usual daily grind stuff, and then there's the holiday plans…"

"Ugh, why'd you have to go and remind me about Thanksgiving?"

"Speaking of *daily grind stuff*," Tara says. "Don't forget my dinner party this weekend. Be there at six. I've got to go. See you later. Give me a call, Cally. Bye."

"Bye Tara," Cally says.

Jordan gently touches my arm, says goodbye, then follows Tara out the door.

"Honestly, Cally, do I look *that* bad?"

"Of course you don't. I can't believe you're even listening to them. They're walking, talking synthetic twigs with big tits." We both laugh out loud. *Geez, I wonder what she says about me when I'm not around.*

"I don't remember a party invitation. Are you going?" I say.

"I don't have a choice. It's another one of her Botox parties. Why do you think she's been telling you that you look so bad? If she gets at least three people there to pay for the shots, I think she gets a free one. She's so tacky. Believe me, if it weren't for our husbands being in the same business, we would *not* still be friends. But you're all right now, aren't you? It's so dry here. I get bloody noses all the time. Let's get some coffee. I've still got that great news to tell you."

When I get to the coffee shop, Cally is seated at a table for two in an area surrounded by empty ones. Two paper cups are atop a little round granite table, steam rising from their mouth holes. "Thanks for the coffee," I say.

"It's nothing. Caramel Macchiato, right?"

"Perfect."

"Great. Now, have a seat."

I sit down and get a sip in before she starts talking. Cally is at the edge of her chair about to explode into what I imagine will be her most impressive pitch to me yet.

"All right what is it?" I say.

"Geez, I don't know where to begin. You should've stayed last night so you could hear Tara talk about it. But okay, you did look tired. So anyways, Paul's good friend is one of the higher ups in the production company that does those *Housewives of Wherever* shows. And he contacted Tara about doing one in Vegas. They want her to pick some women for them to interview. But there's another producer who also has friends in Vegas who's rounding women up too. Which is a total bummer, but then after they make their selections, they'll film a test pilot or whatever, to see if it flies. And if it does—which I'm sure it will, come on it *is* Vegas—then they'll start up a show, and we'll all be famous. Oh my God, I'm so excited." She grabs my hand and squeezes hard.

Cally looks like she's on the verge of a heart attack. "Breathe. Really, I've never seen you like this before. You're absolutely wild."

"And I should be. And so should you. It's a great opportunity."

"For what?"

She lets go of my hand. "To be a star, silly."

"Oh, no. Maybe for you, but not for me." I should have known what this was all about. Gail warned me, but this morning's yoga event left me unprepared.

"But, Stacy," she whines. "They want real life drama between friends, and that's exactly us. We're like Sex in The *Sin* City."

"Not at all."

"You know what I mean."

"Really, I don't want any part of it. You be the star. You don't need me." The last thing I want in my life right now are cameras filming me spiraling into a mid-life crisis.

"Well, we're still waiting to hear about the other group of friends being chosen by the other producer. It's not a sure thing, but I told Tara you'd be up for it."

"What?"

"It's not for sure. Honestly, I don't think we'll get

picked. And it'll probably take a year before anything gets rolling. Please. Just say you'll do it for now. We're like a team you know—partners."

"You mean Tara wouldn't agree to take you on unless it was the four of us."

"Maybe, something like that." Cally turns away and looks out the window. She pretends to watch traffic, but it's her way of sulking.

"Fine. Whatever."

"Really?" She focuses back to me. "Thanks, Stacy! You're the best friend, ever." She rises out of her chair, stretches across the table to give me a hug, and almost knocks her coffee over.

"Yeah, you too. Look, I'm gonna take my coffee and run, if that's okay. I've got some stuff to do before pick-up and practice."

"Wait a minute. You haven't told me what Gail said the other night."

"Nothing, really. She asked about Jon and Patrick."

"You didn't talk about Steven? About the divorce?"

"She didn't say a word, and I didn't ask."

"Great. Now I'll have to take her to lunch or something to find out what's going on. She seems to be drinking more. Did you notice?"

"I think I'd be drinking more, too, if I was her. Why is it so important for you to know?"

"What do you mean? She needs to talk about it. It's for her own good. We're her friends, and we have the right to know what's going on in her life."

"Not if she doesn't want to tell us."

"Oh, she'll tell me all right. But it's going to cost me a fortune in food and wine."

"Okay I'm leaving now." I stand up and grab the car keys from my purse.

We say our quick goodbyes, and on my way out, it dawns on me that I've never had a bloody nose before. I wonder if it's related to the alarm sound I'd heard at Cally's last night. Maybe these are signs of physical exhaustion. I don't need a doctor to tell me that.

CHAPTER THREE

Thunderous quiet rolls out when I open the door. Most people say they love peaceful silence, but this feels lonesome and unsettling. Sometimes when I'm home alone, I'll leave the TV on all day with the volume set to low. The Science Channel usually—there is a calming quality I find in the narrators' monotone voices.

The constant fall of desert dust is set aglow by the noon sun, beaming through the kitchen windows. It's hard not to think of the radiant particles as fallout. On some days, it has a taste.

Arizona Tan, which is the same color as yellow straw, coats the kitchen walls and family room. It's bright and airy. Neutral colors in the granite countertops work well to hide the fine layers of dust that build up overnight. Simple lines and clean symmetry have always been my personal preference; although I'll admit, I did not mind designing over the top Rococo or Baroque style rooms for some of my clients.

I grab the phonebook out of the cupboard next to the double ovens. It's been almost two months since I've been able to Google anything. I can't seem to enter Jon's office upstairs without feeling doom.

Desperate to prove it had no significance, I went in there after one of my nightmares that involved Jon's surgical anatomy book. His mutilated body flashed before my eyes, then my frantic search through his library to get it right. It was a crazy notion, but the book was on the shelf precisely as I had dreamt it. Hesitant, I pulled it down slow and careful. Then in a fit to get it over with, I flipped to the pages I'd remembered so clear. It was horrifying. Everything was exact. That day, I spent hours crying over the pages. Not wanting to bother Jon, but really, not wanting him to think I was crazy, I kept it to myself. In every nightmare involving the book since then, I've noticed water damage to the pages I'd sobbed over.

The phonebook impacts the counter with a thud, jogging me back to the here and now. I've never liked the inky, oily smell or tissue paper feel of phonebooks. Thumbing through the chalky pages makes my fingertips raw.

For a psychiatrist, a large advertisement obviously means either desperate or popular and neither will work. Toward the end of the section, I find the list of names in fine print. *That* is what I need—*new ones*, those that can't afford big spreads. Scrolling down, I avoid names that sound even remotely familiar. Then a shrill, electronic tone pierces my left ear. It switches to the right. The intensity lessens. I push my finger against the cartilage of my outer ear and close off the opening, but it's still there. The sounds are like a hearing test, only louder. *Not again.* And with that thought, it suddenly stops.

With a little more fervor, I continue eyeing the names. A single droplet of blood falls onto the page. "Dammit." I hold the length of my finger up under my nose and scurry to the bathroom. After pulling a wad of tissues with my free hand, I move my finger away. There's no blood around my nostrils. A quick scan of my face reveals nothing. It's perfectly bare—almost too bare, and too pale. I slam the wadded tissues into the trash then tromp back to the open phonebook more determined than ever. First I need a psychiatrist, then maybe, eventually, an ENT doctor. Ugh, this is going to be a nightmare…*for my nightmares*…how ridiculous.

My eyes are instinctively drawn down to the sunburst of blood left on the page. All of the rays are evenly proportioned outward, except for one. A single line of red extends straight into one of the names—Dr. Thomas Light, M.D., Psy.D. "Perfect." I jot the name and number down on scratch paper then slam the phonebook shut. At least now I have a name. I'll call when I get the chance. I'm tired.

After a sandwich, I lie down on the couch. My eyelids open and close in sync with the louder commercials. Moments later, I'm running down a corridor between mammoth columns. Brilliant murals adorn the walls; they flash by as I rush past. Sheets of long, sheer fabric drape down from the ceilings. They billow with warm breezes across the halls.

Children run with me. Our giggles echo and bounce around the great expanse. My bare feet slap against the cool stone floors. It's a game of Hide and Seek. A voice calls out, and we scatter like bugs. Heavy gold bangles jingle around my wrists and ankles. I duck and take cover behind a fountain, then wait. Impatient, I rise to look for the seeker. There is no one in sight. My eyes focus onto something in the pool below. A sudden gasp escapes me. My reflection—I'm a child, too. A girl, I think, perhaps ten or twelve-years old. Something about my hair doesn't look or feel right. I'm wearing a thick, coarse wig, and it moves.

"Bah!" The seeker grabs me from behind, and we both fall back, I onto him. I scream and struggle wildly, until he lets me go. He sees my fear and bursts into hysterical laughter. The other children quickly surround us. They cackle like a pack of hyenas.

The youngest, smallest child stops laughing, steps toward me and reaches out her hand. Her face is familiar. I know this one. Then they all stop laughing. The fountain thunders behind me, as my eyes sweep over their faces. I know them all. Her little hand is warm and soft. She helps stand up, then smiles wide, exposing missing teeth. The seeker roars into laughter again, and the others follow. The little girl starts to giggle, too and I along with her.

I wake up laughing—happy. But when I stop, the children's laughter continues. A bitter chill races up the length of my spine. I sit up on the couch, turn the TV off, and listen. The laughter rolls past, as if it were caught in an invisible current. I get up and quickly follow the sound upstairs. When I get to the master bedroom, I open the doors, then stick my head in, and listen. They're not in here, but then the laughter intensifies. They are in the office…

Standing at the door with the lever in my hand, I can't seem to find the strength to move. *Stop it.* Their laughter gets even louder. I push the lever down and throw open the door. A gust of air blows out, and the laughter stops.

"Hello. This is Dr. Light."

"Hello. Um, my name is Stacy Troy. I'd like to schedule an appointment, please."

"Yes, of course. Is there a specific day or time that you'd like to come in?"

"No. Not really. Whatever works best for you."

"How does nine o'clock Friday morning, sound?"

Crap, my day planner is in the car. "I'm sorry, Dr. Light. Can you hold a minute? I've got to check my calendar." I set the phone down, run out to the garage and back. I have lunch with Jordan on Friday. I can't cancel, it's for the fundraiser. "I'm sorry Dr. Light. Friday won't work. Do you have any other days available?"

"This Thursday, at ten."

"Yes. That'll work. Perfect. Thank you."

"I'll see you Thursday then, at ten. Do you need directions?"

"No. Thanks. Oh, but do I need to bring anything? Medical records?"

"No. Just your insurance information. You might want to come a little early. There will be plenty of paperwork to fill out. I'll also need some time to jot down your health history. Come prepared to answer a bevy of questions."

"Okay, so Thursday, around nine forty-five. I'll see you then."

"Goodbye, Mrs. Troy. I look forward to meeting you."

"Bye."

He seems harmless, and now I have an appointment—something tangible. What a relief, and before I forget, I put it in my day planner. For all things secret, I draw pictographs. The Roman numeral X for ten and a light bulb for Dr. Light. It's silly, but Jon has occasionally gone through my day planner. Not that I have anything to hide, but some men will never learn…women just know these things. Once in a while though, I'll misinterpret my own code. If I forget what this means, I hope I don't go to the hardware store and buy ten light bulbs.

"Grab the stuff from the back. Coach might need the extra balls." *Rumor has it, he does anyway.* Patrick doesn't see my grin. Poor Coach. Cally should heed the term, "Too much information," more often when she gossips. I really didn't *need* to know about Coach's sex life. Even though I brought a magazine, I know I won't get the chance to look it over. Cally and Gail are already here, sitting under the skeleton of what's considered a tree in the spring.

During the summer months, the few leafy branches that provide shade are a treasure fought over and well-guarded. Creatures of habit, we flock to the same tree, even in the fall. The constant smell of desert dust pervades the air.

I watch Patrick hobble with the overstuffed bag of nets, pylons, and balls. He drops it next to Coach then runs over to Cally's son, Kyle, and Gail's son, Justin. They've all been friends since kindergarten, and now they're all fifteen going on sixteen. We joke around about how they'll be driving soon, but there's always a lull when the joke is over. That's when we remember it's just another reminder of our age.

"Hello, ladies." I pop open the canvas chair Jon and Patrick got me for Mother's Day. It has "Soccer Mom" embroidered on the back—*yea*.

"Hi Stacy," they chime together.

"You guys have a good day?" I say.

"Bill cancelled lunch with me, so I went and got a mani and pedi. You like the color?" Cally spreads out her fingers and toes. "It's called Rapture."

"Yeah, it's nice," I say. "What about you, Gail? How was your day?"

Cally looks over and waits eagerly for Gail's response. "It was good."

"Speaking of lunch…" Cally says. "It's been a while since you and I have gone out, Gail. Let's do it."

"Sure, Cally." Gail turns her head to me, and winks. There's something different about the way she looks. Her eyes…they lack a certain luster they used to, and her face is sullen.

"You sure you're fine?" I say.

Cally stops her jabber to listen.

"I'm hanging in there, but it's not easy. Justin's been so angry lately—acting out."

"Do you have him seeing anyone?" Cally says.

"He's been seeing Hannah Ross since the separation. Have you heard of her?"

"Yeah," Cally answers. "She's supposed to be the best child psychologist in town. Ellie, what's-her-name's daughter, from grade school, sees her for an eating disorder. You remember her, don't you, Stacy?"

"I have no idea who you're talking about."

"And what about you, Gail?" Cally asks. "You should be seeing someone too."

"I've had several appointments with Dr. Goodwin. He's got me taking something… there's an X in the name. I can't remember."

"He's got a decent reputation, too," Cally says. "You're headed in the right direction." Then she looks over at me, and we exchange sideways glances. I remember seeing his full-page layout in the phonebook. Definitely not someone I would have considered for myself. I'm pretty sure Cally told me his wife caught him having sex with one of his patients on his office desk. It was to everyone's advantage to keep their mouths shut. As long as his reputation for being a good shrink upholds, it doesn't matter how bizarre their personal lives get. He will always have clients, and she will always have friends.

Practice doesn't end soon enough. The boys jog over. "Let's go, Mom," Justin says, then walks off.

"Well, I guess that's my cue. I'll see you guys later." Gail gets up quick and follows Justin to her Seven-Series Beemer.

"Patrick, you've got to separate our stuff from Coach's." I toss the car keys to him, and he reaches out and snatches them from the air.

"Go and help, Kyle," Cally says. As soon as they're out of earshot, Cally scoots closer. Gail hasn't even pulled out of the lot yet. "Hey, that was nice work. It must've been killing her to keep all of that in. Don't you think?"

"Not at all. You should take her out to lunch anyways."

"I will. I will. And what about the shrinks? Hmm…" Cally strains to make a facial expression.

"What are you doing?"

"I'm trying to make a quizzical brow." She sighs. "I've really got to lay off the Botox. Anyways, I wonder if she gets a family discount."

"You're wrong on so many levels."

"I'm just realistic. I told you she needed to talk about it, and she did. I'm sure she feels better."

Patrick and Kyle are in the car listening to music with the volume turned up all the way. They are thrashing their heads around like a couple of idiots. "We better get going, before they decide to drive off." I get up and close my chair.

"That might not be such a bad thing," she says, which makes me laugh.

Catty as she gets sometimes, Cally is one of the funnier people I know. We giggle about how silly the boys look while we gather up the rest of our stuff. Then we head for the cars.

"See you tomorrow," I say.

"Bright and early." She smiles.

Kyle gets out, Patrick moves over to the passenger side. I get in and turn down the volume. An earsplitting shrill supersedes all other sound. My jaw clenches. I grip the steering wheel and wait for it to subside.

"Mom, you okay?"

The harsh noise goes away as quickly as it came.

"Yeah, I'm fine." I reach down and turn off the radio. I've heard enough sound for one day.

CHAPTER FOUR

Blood-tinged syrup hangs from the bottom of the cart like strands from a spider's web. It pools in the gutter, and forms a bodily fluid gelatin. There is no rain hard enough to wash away the stains. There's no weather at all, not anymore. No nights, no electricity, or battery power. Something happened. Everything stopped working. The sky became a perpetual red dusk. Maybe it's a mirror image of all the spilled blood.

The bleeding disease was only the beginning. Within a few months, thousands of people went to sleep and never woke up. They were found dead, soaking in crimson pools. It would happen overnight, during naps, any period of sleep—bodies would seep blood. Scientists were baffled. No cure could be found. A few months more, and the death toll was in the hundreds of thousands. It was a pandemic that led to more war. The air was rife with gun smoke and the odor of rust. As people quickly died off, the global wars diminished to local fighting and looting. Madmen ran the streets pillaging any and all drugs that would keep them awake, and killing anyone who got in their way. In the end, some even resorted to removing their eyelids hoping the mutilation would ward off slumber. They were Earth's dying days, and the complete collapse of humanity.

My work here is almost done. My last two neighbors from the cul de sac are in the cart. Bishop Almeida is a private Catholic school. It was built three years ago, a block away. There is a large metal cross planted firmly in front. The icon can be seen for miles around—a beacon for sinners. It makes me feel better about dumping the bodies there. The school was so close, we gave Patrick the option of attending, but he preferred his Lutheran school.

Within the storehouse of implements once called our garage, the long barbecue lighter sits among an assortment of screwdrivers in one of the toolbox drawers. Jon had so much crap shoved in there it took me forever to find the right tools when I first got started. Rather than look through the toolbox when he needed to fix something, he would go to the hardware store and buy everything new. When he was finished, he would add anything left to the tool box. Poor man is dead, but I still find myself nagging him. Jon and Patrick are at the bottom of the pile. I stacked the other bodies on top of them so I wouldn't have to see them anymore.

The lighter slides down into the apron pocket easy. I grab the axe and red gas can and balance them carefully around the bags in the cart. It is stuffed solid, which makes it bulky and awkward to push. I wonder what people would think if they saw me coming down the street, pushing a shopping cart full of body parts in my designer plaid rain boots, a bloody apron, welder's gloves, and goggles.

The mound does not seem as large as it should, being made up of over twenty-five bodies. No animal tracks; they must all be dead too. I haven't even seen a cockroach, which scientists said would survive a holocaust. Next to the mound are piles of empty bags.

This will be an epic funeral pyre, symbolic of my affection for the people whose bodies I used to create it. They have been soaking in the gasoline from all of their cars. The caustic smell sort of helps to curb the stench.

After removing the gas can and axe, I unload the last two of my neighbors. I'm careful not to look at their faces, as I swing the can upwards. Gas spills out everywhere. Even on me, but it makes me smell better too. Their souls will rise up through the red sky. They are my only call for help—a human smoke signal to God.

The mound ignites into a roaring fire. I push the cart and jump out of the way. Flat on my back, looking up at the sky, endless swirls of black smoke rise and curl upwards. The flames are raging, the heat so intense, I feel myself burning—My God, I am burning. The apron is on fire!

Frantic and patting my chest is how I wake up. I have the comforter pushed down to the foot of the bed. Sweat trickles between my breasts. My nightshirt is drenched. I'm amazed Jon is still asleep. Careful to keep it that way, I slip out of bed, then gently close the door when I get in the bathroom. My shirt peels off as if I were shedding a second skin. I wring it out then lay it over a towel bar. One shiver and I'm suddenly trembling all over, waiting for the washcloth I threw in the sink to soak up warm running water. Jon would surely wake if I turned on the shower. When I'm done cleaning up, I put on a new nightshirt then creep back into bed. My side is cool and damp, so I wiggle over to Jon and snuggle against his back. Gently, I pull the comforter up.

For the rest of the night, I mimic the rise and fall of his breathing patterns. When his alarm goes off, I pretend I'm asleep. There's no need to make him worry. Only two days until my appointment with Dr. Light.

He brought me coffee a while ago, then left.

At my vanity, I drink lukewarm coffee, but I'm not sure how long I've been sitting. I scan the room for some wall space. We really need a clock in here. My watch is in the closet.

"Hey, Mom. What's up?" Patrick shuffles into the bathroom. Awake and dressed for school.

"What time is it?"

"Almost time to leave."

"Already?"

"Yeah."

"Then why are you here and not getting your backpack ready?"

"Will you show me how to fix my hair again? The messy way."

"See, I knew you'd be back. Hand me the gel."

Patrick tosses the tube at me, and I let it fall to the floor. "*Mom.*" He picks it up and then hands it to me. I put a dab in the palm of my hand, then rub it into my other, and tousle his hair.

"The idea is to make sloppy look effortless. Get it?"

"Yeah, Mom. I'm hearin' ya."

"Kay now, get out. I've got to get dressed for Pilates."

"I don't *get* how you have to get dressed to go work out."

"You will."

"Whatever. Thanks for the hairdo. I'm lookin' all good now." He pretends to slick his hair back while he stares at himself in the mirror.

"Out."

"I'm going. I'm going," he says, as he struts out the door.

"Be ready. I'll be down in a minute." I put my hair into a clip, put some eyeliner and lip gloss on. Grab my watch then head downstairs.

"Mom, we can't leave now. It's too early."

"Fine. I'll finish my coffee then. Turn up the news, please. Anything going on?"

"No. Just the end of the world."

"What?" My heart nearly skips a beat. "What do you mean?"

"Relax, Mom. It's just sunspots. They're saying it could interrupt your cell service. And that would be like the end of the world—for you."

"No way. You use your cell phone much more than me."

"I text, and that's totally different."

After Pilates, the girls and I meet up for coffee in the old part of Summerlin. We get our drinks at the café next to a clothing boutique we frequent and then head over to shop. Jordan and I are the first ones there. Nothing screams *I AM WOMAN* like sipping coffee while perusing the latest fashions.

"Now these are a sweet pair of jeans," Jordan says. She's got them pulled away from the rack with one hand, eyeing them up and down. With the thumb and forefinger of her other hand, she pinches then tweaks the dark, little spikes of hair above her ear.

"They're cute," I say. "How much?"

"Not bad. Two-forty, with twenty percent off."

"You better hang on to them before Tara sees."

A voice comes from the back of the store. "Hello, Jordan. Hello, Stacy." It's Janelle, the owner. "We just got those in. Aren't they cool? You want me to put them in a room for you?"

"No, I'm not going to bother trying them on," Jordan says. "They'll fit."

"Of course they will," Janelle says, rather snide.

"If they don't, you can always bring them back," I remind her.

"I'm bad about that," Jordan says. "If they don't fit, or I change my mind, I'll give them to Jamie's girlfriend. And I tell 'ya, I've given that girl a wardrobe fit for a princess."

"Oh, I'm sure."

"Wish I was Jamie's girlfriend," Janelle says.

Big mistake. Jordan looks up and glares at her so evil, it would send Satan back to Hell. Jamie is Jordan's only son from her first marriage. He is twenty-six now and an established attorney in Santa Barbara, but Jordan won't relinquish her overprotective maternal instincts. Her claws come out when women show any interest. Especially… women like Janelle. She may be a successful entrepreneur, but she also has a reputation for being a major party girl.

Janelle shrinks back then quietly slinks away.

"Whore," Jordan whispers.

"Jordan, she might hear you."

"Good. She needs to hear it. I spend thousands in her store, and if she wants to keep my business, she needs to learn her place." A woman on fire, she flips through clothes on a rack.

I quickly step away. I'll be more comfortable when I'm clear of her striking distance. There's a table lined with folded T-shirts. I lean up against it and pretend to look interested. I've never seen her get this agitated before. There is more verity to her cougar title than I thought. Besides being nearly ten years older than the rest of us—I'm just sure of it—she's also in her fourth marriage, and her husband, Samuel, is twenty years her junior.

Tara and Cally come into the store. Thank God.

"Any good deals?" Tara says.

"I found these jeans, but I'm not sure I'm going to get them." Jordan directs her comment to Janelle, acting busy behind the cashier's desk.

"Ooh, I like those. I'll buy 'em if you don't."

"No. I'm getting them," Jordan says.

"Are they the only twos?"

"Yep. And they're mine." Jordan walks off toward the cash register.

"Janelle, you need to order more of the smaller sizes," Tara shouts out.

"Look at this," Cally says.

Tara moves quickly to the other side of the store. "Cute. I love it. Come and look, Stacy."

I walk over to them huddled around a rack of bright, patterned halters. "A little cool for those now, don't you think?"

"Well, yeah, but great for spring. We should all get one. Look, there are four different designs. How perfect."

"That's a great idea," Cally says.

Jordan joins us, and after glancing at the halters says, "That's a stupid idea." She cocks her head for me to follow her out.

"We'll just be a minute," Tara says in a huff.

"Take your time. We'll be outside," Jordan says.

Jordan and I walk back to the café and sit down on a couple of patio chairs out front.

"Thanks for saving me," I say. "Those tops were hideous."

"Well, hell yeah they were, but even more than that, I was thinking of the sun spots on my back and shoulders. I can't do halters anymore."

Sunspots…Patrick…I take the cell phone from my

purse. Four bars. He must have been pulling my leg. I'm sure Jordan means age spots, but I guess using sun spots doesn't make her sound so old.

"Ooh, I got a text from Jon."

"What's he say?"

"Ugh. He'll be home late. Add-on cases."

"Oh, that reminds me…I'm glad he texted you. Would it be all right if we had lunch tomorrow instead of Friday? Something's come up, and I've got to take Samuel to the airport."

"Yeah, sure, but everything's okay, right?"

"Yes, of course. It's nothing bad. The original dates he had down for his Arizona conference got switched around is all."

"I'll call The Bistro and change the reservation. Same time though?"

"Yeah, twelve's fine. Really, you don't mind do you?"

"Not at all. Don't worry about it."

Still, something doesn't feel right. She was edgy in the store. I can tell she's holding back, but unlike Cally, I won't force the issue. Maybe she'll feel more like telling me tomorrow at lunch.

Cally and Tara walk toward us empty handed.

"Didn't find anything?" Jordan says.

"You got the only thing I wanted," Tara says. "If you don't wear those jeans, you better give them to me and not Jamie's girlfriend. She's got enough clothes."

"And you don't?"

"Come on. Let's go," Tara whines. "I've got real stuff to do today."

"Like what?" Jordan says.

"I've got to give the chef the menu for Saturday's dinner party. You're coming, right?" Tara looks at Cally and me.

"We wouldn't miss it, dear," Cally says.

When we're finished with our customary air hugs and air kisses, we head our separate ways. It will take me nearly thirty minutes to get to the other side of town. Summerlin has grown exponentially in the nine years since Jon and I moved here. The entire community is adjacent to the Red Rock Canyon State Park. There is a lot of hiking to be had, for the people who enjoy that kind of thing, and cyclists come from all over the country to ride the terrain. It's a *desert* kind of beautiful that some tourists and nature lovers appreciate, but only the people who live here can truly see. Every evening, magnificent sunsets and cloud formations hover over the red clay plateaus. They are unreal—breathtaking. I'd never want to live anywhere else.

CHAPTER FIVE

The room temperature is set at over a hundred degrees Fahrenheit, melding the stale odors of sweat and earthy bamboo. Every breath singes my airway; breathing is a slow burden, and my heartbeats are lazy, bounding. My muscles expand beyond normal limits. They have become elastic bands unable to snap in the heat. They continue to stretch out, enabling me to twist back into myself like a wilting flower poised to collapse. I close my eyes, and imagine the back of my head resting between my shoulder blades. There is peace in it.

Distant bells chime, filling my head with soft celestial melodies. They are a multitude of separate symphonies playing together to create a single harmony. They extinguish the throaty drone of Tibetan chants.

I open my eyes and slowly bring myself to a standing pose. The more aware I become, the more the bell tones fade. By the time class is done, they have completely disappeared.

"Ah, thank God that's over," Cally says.

"Did the bell music mess you up too?"

"What bell music?"

"The bells in the middle of the monk chant."

She gives me a strange look.

"Hey, Burl," I speak out to the instructor.

"Namaste, ladies." He puts his prayer hands together and bows.

"Yeah Namaste. Hey, what was that bell music you played between the monk chants?" I say.

"There is no *bell music* in the Twenty-One Emanations."

"Oh. Okay. Thanks."

"See," Cally says. "You're ears were probably ringing. I thought for sure I was going to pass out during the camel pose. Come on. Let's go."

We roll up our mats then leave, bowing to Burl on our way out. "Was it me, or did he seem overly sensitive about the music?"

"It's him. He's that way about everything. Don't worry, it wasn't a big deal, but remind me never to harp on his music."

"I wasn't harping."

"Just kidding—relax—it's yoga."

"Tell that to Burl."

Cally and I spend Wednesday mornings at the appropriately named *Sweatbox*, a Bikram Yoga studio. Tara and Jordan have never been, and they never will. They refuse to sweat. Tara hates it so much, she got Botox injections under her arms to paralyze the nerves that stimulate her sweat glands. It's her cure-all for everything.

Gail was actually the one who started Cally on this type of yoga, but she stopped coming after her divorce went public. The two of them used to be a lot closer, and sometimes, I feel guilty because Cally spends more time with me now. But I'm sure when Gail is ready, she and Cally will be good friends again, and it will be like she never took a hiatus.

We get out to our cars, and put away our gear.

"So, what're your plans for today?" Cally says. "Want to go shopping?"

"Lunch with Jordan."

"I didn't get an invite."

"It's for the fundraiser."

"Ugh, boring."

"That's why I didn't ask, but you're welcome to join us."

"No thanks. I'll see you later, and don't have too much fun without me."

"I'll try. Bye."

I grab my day planner from between the seats on my way into The Bistro. I've scribbled an arrow with two ends where lunch changed from Friday to today. Between the days, there's the letter X and a really bad sketch of a light bulb. *Oh yes...Dr. Light tomorrow.*

I can see Jordan from the hostess podium. She's already seated at a corner table. She waves, and the hostess brings me over.

"You look hungry," she says, then laughs.

"Well, you look great. And hungry too."

"So how was it, sweatin' like a pig this morning? You two still doing that?"

"Yeah. It was good. Makes me feel like I'm getting rid of those bad toxins."

"A few martinis would take care of that too." She cackles. "Speaking of which…" She raises a martini glass. "What're you drinking?"

"Chardonnay sounds good."

"Waitress," Jordan calls. "Could we get a glass of chardonnay please?" Then she lowers her head and whispers. "The service here is terrible."

"But the food's good," I say.

"That it is. Now, when she comes with your wine, I think it'd be smart to order, or we might never get lunch."

"I agree."

"Two flank steak salads?" she says.

"Absolutely."

After the waitress leaves, I raise my glass to toast. "Here's to love, life, and happiness."

"Screw that. To good health." She tilts her glass, and I watch the dirty gin drain into her mouth. "Shoot. I should've ordered another one when she was here."

"She'll be back."

"Well, until she does…I think I've got an idea you're gonna like."

I lean into the table. "Let's hear it."

"What do you think of Healthy Holidays for the name of the fundraiser?"

"Love it."

"Excellent."

Our food comes before she orders her third martini and that's just since I've been here. Fortunately, we have gone over every fundraiser detail. I am so glad I brought my day planner in. At the end of the meal, I order a cappuccino, and she orders another martini.

"Will you be all right to drive?" I say.

"Don't worry honey, I'll be fine. They water down their drinks." She turns away.

"So, how's Samuel?"

She turns back with a sad look. "He's workin' me again about the prenup."

"Oh."

I don't have the subtle finesse Cally does when it comes to talking about stuff like this and definitely not when Jordan is drunk. "Maybe he just needs a little more time," I say. Things will get better." I stare down at my lap, and bite my lip. *I'm so used to her only talking about happy times with Samuel. I forget about these.*

"Well, how's Cally?" Her speech is slightly slurred.

I look up and the sun glares into my eyes. Between squinting and blinking, I can't see until I raise my hand up over my brow. Suddenly, it appears we're outdoors.

Jordan has on a wide brim hat topped with piles of feathers, flowers, and lace. Dark navy ribbons wind through the weave. They match her gown—her gown? She's wearing a gown! And it is beautiful. Beaded and trimmed with seed pearls and ornate lacework. She lifts a dainty China cup to her mouth then takes a sip. Sheer ivory fabric hangs from the fitted sleeve of her gown. I reach out, touch it. It's soft, not starchy.

"Uh-hum." Jordan clears her throat.

I pull my hand back and look up. "Oh…she's good." I respond.

She raises an eyebrow. "You're doing the *Housewives* show, right?"

My God, she doesn't see it. She doesn't see or hear any of it. We're seated at a café, next to a cobblestone street. Ambient sounds of people talking, their footsteps and horse hooves clapping, increases. Men wearing vests and dark frock coats walk by. They smile at us and tip their hats. There are horse drawn carts. Moisture in the air soaks my thirsty pores. It smells musty, a little on the pungent side of earthy, except for the occasional waft of coffee.

"Yeah—Cally talked me into it." I can't stop smiling. I want to laugh out loud. Laugh out loud and scream. *Why can't you see?*

"I'm sure Tara will give us the details Saturday."

"Great." It's hard to keep my focus and not stare out at the people—not stare at her. Jordan's complexion isn't plastic anymore. She's no longer a spiky-haired brunette. Thick plaits of shiny auburn hair cling to the bottom sides of her head. There is something familiar in her eyes.

"It'll be a hoot." Jordan stays quiet for a minute and watches me. Her eyes shadow my every move. "Hey, sugar, you all right?"

"You just sort of remind me of me, right now." *I can't believe I said that out loud.*

"What?"

This has to stop. I put my head down and close my eyes. "Nothing. I'm good."

I hear the waitress walk over, and I look up. Everything is back to normal. I hand her my credit card. I've had it out for about thirty minutes. Jordan holds up her hand to protest.

"Please," I explain. "It's the least I can do."

"You're sweet, honey. Thanks." She leans across the table to hug me and knocks over a glass of water. "I think it's time to go." She laughs.

"I think you're right."

We leave in separate cars, and I worry about her being okay to drive. Sometimes, I wonder how she ever got so far in her career. When her son Jamie went off to college, she retired as the entertainment director for the biggest hotel-casino conglomerate in town, the only woman ever chosen for that position, then and since. After her first divorce she never had to work again, but did to keep busy, I think, stay in control. No one can plan a party worth going to without her, and she does it all on a volunteer basis for the charities she likes.

Her latest husband, boy-toy Samuel, is the male version of a gold-digger. Everyone knows it, but no one would ever say anything to her. She's a woman used to getting what she wants. It's painful to watch her spiral down like this, but she is so stubborn.

I worry about myself, too. If I didn't already have that appointment with Dr. Light, I'd consider checking myself in after that flashback type of hallucination, or whatever it was. I wonder if this is related to my nightmares in some way. For God's sake, if they keep happening during the day while I'm wide awake, I don't know what I'll do. It would be awful for sure, but really, none of this can be happening to me—not now. I have too many things to get done.

There's a tap on the glass. I unlock the doors and Patrick gets in.

"Why do you lock the car when you're picking me up?"

"Robbers."

"Yeah, right—in Summerlin?" Patrick fastens his seatbelt.

"Never know…some kid might get in and want a free ride, then dinner, then college…that's just like robbery."

"So not funny."

"Totally was."

Within minutes, the area is swarming with cars crawling on top of each other to get in or out. It's unavoidable.

"Do you have a lot of homework?"

"No."

I pull away from the curb and head home. Patrick reaches over and turns on the radio.

"Not too loud." I tell him.

He leans against the passenger's side window and stares out. I watch him and keep pace with the traffic.

"Mom, the light's green."

Funny, I can still make out his baby face hidden underneath this teenager one.

"You can go now." He raises his voice. "The people behind us are honking their horn."

"Oh. Sorry." I wave in the rearview mirror to the driver behind me, and he flips me off.

"Not enough coffee today?" Patrick says.

"Maybe that's it." I swerve across two lanes and make a sharp right into a coffee shop.

"Oh my God, Mom. I was just kidding."

"Well, I wasn't." I pull into the drive-thru line and turn up the radio. It is an eighties station, only now they call it retro. Hell if that doesn't make me feel old. "Ooh, I love this song." I turn the volume up even more and hum and sing along. "Mmm, hmm a butterfly. A hmm butterfly…" Rocking my head back and forth, tapping the steering wheel.

"Knock it off. Please," Patrick says. He shrinks down into his seat.

"Come on, sing it." I pull up to the order box and Patrick turns off the radio. "I'd like a small cappuccino, please."

A loud garbled voice comes out of the box. "Drive up—Total."

When I get to the window, I hand the young girl some money, and then she gives me my drink.

"Thanks," I say. Then back into the flow of steady traffic.

"Mom, is everything okay?" Patrick says.

"Of course. Why?"

"Never mind."

"I'm fine. You just have lousy taste in music."

"Serious? That song was beyond stupid."

"Music today doesn't have lyrics half as good as those."

"Really, Mom? Wild butterfly? What butterfly isn't wild?"

"The kind they grow artificially."

"You can't *grow* a butterfly."

"Don't be so sure."

Patrick goes up to his room after dinner, leaving Jon and me to clean up.

"How was your day?" he says.

"It was good. I had lunch with Jordan."

"And?"

"We've got a good name for the fundraiser—Healthy Holidays. You like it?"

"That's great. Your idea?"

"No, Jordan's. All the food will be organic and independently raised on green farms."

"There's still going to be a bar, right? People won't come if there's no alcohol."

"Yes. There will still be bar." I stop and roll my eyes.

"Then it sounds fantastic." He kisses my cheek. "I've got office work. You mind?"

"No. Go ahead." He starts to walk away. "Oh, but wait."

"What?"

"Have you ever heard of a Dr. Light?" I say.

"No. Should I have?"

"No. But, that's a good thing." I smile wide.

He has a look of bewilderment on his face that quickly fades. "Oh. Is that the shrink?"

"Yes."

"You make an appointment?"

"Yes."

"When?"

"Tomorrow. His office is in Henderson."

"Why so far? You'll hate the traffic."

"Yeah, I know."

"Leave early. Tell me how it goes." He walks over, leans down and kisses my cheek again. "I love you," he whispers.

"I love you, too."

If my problems were medical, he'd be all over it. I don't get sick often, but when something physically goes wrong with me, he literally becomes both Dr. Jekyll *and* Mr. Hyde.

In part, I understand why he doesn't want to talk about it. I'm not the crazy distant relative everyone in the family signed off to be committed—I'm his wife. And he is a physician, and he can't mend what's wrong with me. He's always been hands on, frustrated by the unexplainable. *"Psychiatry isn't medicine,"* he used to say. *"It's merely an imbalance of chemicals in the human body. Fix that and mental disorders wouldn't exist."*

He complains sometimes about how now, more than ever, his patients are overmedicated for depression and other mental illnesses. It affects his ability to do the chemical balancing that he does, when he puts them under then wakes them up.

Life would be so easy if it were all about balancing the right ingredients. Hopefully, Dr. Light will be able to bring some equilibrium to my mind—*soon.*

CHAPTER SIX

I got three hours of uninterrupted sleep last night. The most since the nightmares began—maybe they fear Dr. Light already. This could be a sign of good things to come, or clarification that it's all in my head. Either way, I'm feeling overly anxious. I'll have to limit my caffeine today. I do *not* want to show up manic, and first impressions are everything.

After dropping Patrick off at school, I resist the urge for coffee. I head home instead to call the caterers and party rental places. Make a list for Thanksgiving dinner. Hard to believe it is next week. My parents annually drive in from Long Beach the afternoon before, and leave Sunday morning. Ever since we moved to Vegas, they visit every holiday. My dad stays home and watches sports with Jon, or they go play golf, while I become my mom's personal chauffeur, tour guide, and gambling assistant.

Thursday appointments work best for me. It's my day

off from working out. Evening soccer practice is the only thing scheduled. Maybe Dr. Light could see me regularly on Thursday mornings. It's barely nine, but I grab my purse and head out the door. Most important, I program the car's navigation system. The east side of town is not master planned like Summerlin, so the traffic is horrific. There is nothing worse than being lost someplace crowded and unfamiliar.

Thirty minutes driving and I've nearly passed every exit for Henderson. Right as I'm about to check the navigation screen, the robotic female voice speaks out. She tells me to take the next exit then continue driving on the frontier road. There is not much around, except for mounds of displaced earth and empty lots of graded land. A great deal of construction was left unfinished when the market tanked.

She guides me onto a side street and then another. When she says I have arrived at my destination, I'm in the middle of nowhere, stopped in front of a solitary office building that must have dropped from the sky.

The building has a bland exterior that fuses into the desert landscape. If it weren't for the car's navigation system, I would have driven right past it. The stucco and trim are all the same color, taupe. It is notoriously called desert brown by all the designers in town. Even the window shades match. They're all pulled down, too, making the building look closed.

I grab my purse and step out. Nothing improves on my approach. Not a single shrub lines the walkway. Vacant buildings have become a more common sight, but if Dr. Light wants patients, he's going to have to spruce it up. Then again, if he doesn't own the building, there really is no sense. Mine is the only car in the parking lot.

I swallow hard and pull open the heavy glass door. The morning sun glares off the lustrous marble floors, blinding me. When my eyes adjust, I'm disappointed by the all-around drab inside too. The lobby entrance is large, open, and empty. No décor.

Across the way is a wall of names and office numbers placed in alphabetical order. Block white letters line a black background, set into a glass frame. Near the middle, a single line spells out Dr. T. Light, MD, PsyD, with suite number one hundred next to it. First office on the first floor also spells convenient.

Next to the name board, and halfway up the wall to my right is a matte-gold placard with the numbers one hundred through one hundred and ten. A long arrow points the way.

Around the corner, I stop and stare down the narrow corridor. The far end appears to stretch back. Long bars of fluorescent lights cast a purple, artificial glow on the walls and floors. It looks more like a tunnel than a hallway.

Desert brown doors fade into desert brown walls. Chrome levers are the only indication doors even exist. Small placards indicate the suite numbers. To my left is suite one hundred and ten. A deep sigh, then I walk to the other end of the hall. When I get to the door, I stall, look down at my watch. It's nine thirty-five, which doesn't seem right. It should be later than that.

Deafening feedback fills the hall—my head! I brace my arm over the placard and press my forehead against it. Maybe I can squeeze the sound out. Brilliant colors explode like fireworks behind my eyes. Loud, off-key squeals change pitch in sporadic outbursts. The smallest of itches starts at the tip of my nose. "No." I mutter through clenched jaws. I watch a drop of blood as it falls to the floor. It spatters in front of my shoe. And shit, I've got my favorite pair of Pliner heels on today. I keep my head down and turned to the side, away from my clothes. I take my purse from around my shoulder. Fumbling through the chaos that's inside, the pouch of tissues is within fingertip's reach. Eureka—I yank them all out and push them up under my nose.

I'm not sure I saw a restroom in the lobby, but there has to be one. So, with an open purse hanging from one forearm and bloody tissues at the end of the other, I joggle back down the hall. My eyes dart around and spot nothing. Then an illuminated sign near the entrance catches my attention. I head for it. Thankful now, the lobby is empty.

When I get into the bathroom, I pull the tissues away from my face. There was more than one drop this time, but the bleeding has stopped and so have the sounds; although, I can't remember exactly when they did. I toss the red bundle into the trash canister, wash my hands then pull new tissues from the box next to the sink. When I'm all cleaned up, I fix my lipstick, check my watch again. It's nine forty-four—impossible. I shake off time's slow crawl and return to suite one hundred. Before entering, I glance down to avoid the blood droplet. It's gone. I push the lever down, then step into Dr. Light's office.

A plain laminate desk sits out front, with no one behind it. I hear a door close off to the right. In the left corner, there are two taupe chairs. A small square coffee table between them, with magazines fanned out on top. His office is as sterile as the rest of the building. I step up to the desk and lean over. A man walks toward me. I smile coyly, then lean back. He is extremely tall and gangling, with dark eyes and black hair.

"Hello, Mrs. Troy?"

"Yes. Dr. Light. Nice to meet you." I reach my hand over the desk and give him a firm shake. His hand is enormous. Feels like warm velvet, but his grip is flaccid, almost soft.

"I'm glad you're here," he says, "and on time, too."

I smile and nod my head.

"Let's head back to my office."

He leads the way, and I follow him around the front desk. Not a single piece of paper sits on top. There isn't even a phone. We walk down the hall he came from.

"This is a large office space for one physician," I say.

His pace quickens, and I fall behind. The fluorescent lights make his dark hair look blue. His whole head, periwinkle shirt, and navy pants, they all glow like an iceberg. There is something peculiar about the hallway, too. It seems longer than it should, and there is only one door at the very end.

My heels tap along the marble. The tiny clinks sound

like thunder claps in all the quiet. Strange, there's no carpet. The rent here must be a fortune. "Do you own the building, Dr. Light?" If he can afford this building, I wonder where his staff is. "Is your secretary on break?"

He gets to the door and stops. "Actually, I do own part of the building, but I don't have a secretary just yet. I've only recently opened up my practice here, and financially, I'm not able to hire someone full-time."

"Ah, I see." That's what I get for being nosy, but he was listening—I like that.

He opens the door and steps aside. My purse brushes against him as I walk past. No surprise, his office is plain, sedate. Opposite the door is a large window with the desert brown shade pulled down. Bookshelves line the wall behind his desk, an exact replica of the one out front. Everything is the same dark wood laminate. There are two, tufted brown vinyl chairs with high backs. One is in front of his desk and the other behind it. It's like an office furniture closeout exploded in here. There's another wall of bookshelves across the room and one of those black leather and chrome gravity loungers. Very shrink chic. Strange thing, though—there's no clock.

"Please, Mrs. Troy, have a seat." He pulls the chair out in front of his desk.

When I sit down, air rushes out the sides, making a hiss sound. "Nice," I whisper. "Thank you," I say out loud, as Dr. Light walks around. He sits down behind his desk and pulls out a new file with papers in it. He takes a pen from his shirt pocket and begins writing things down.

"Dr. Light, I'd like to pay on my credit card, rather than bill through my insurance. Will that work for you?"

"That'd be fine, Mrs. Troy, but please. Call me Tom."

"Thank you, Tom. Please, call me Stacy."

He stretches his arm across the desk palm up. "Would it be all right if I run your card? Then I'll have it on file and won't need to ask again."

"Oh, yes, of course." I reach into my purse, then hand him the card.

"I'll just be a minute."

When he gets up to leave, I turn around and watch him walk. He has an awkward gait. His body hunches slightly forward, and each foot seems to lift then pause, like a toddler learning how to walk. The door closes behind him.

My eyes hone in on the chaise. It doesn't intimidate like a dentist's chair or a surgical table. It looks comfortable—a newer version of *the couch*. As I start to read book titles on the shelves, Dr. Light comes back and hands me my card. I notice his fingers shaking a little. He almost seems more nervous than me. I hope we'll both be able to relax enough to make this work.

"I apologize for these minor inconveniences." He takes his seat behind the desk. "I prefer to get them out of the way before we begin."

"No problem, really."

"Good." He picks up his pen. "Stacy, have you ever had asthma?"

"No."

He makes a checkmark, jots a few words down here

and there, and this is how we spend the next ten minutes or so. Such a waste of time. I should be telling him about all the crazy things happening. Then he could write volumes. I check my watch a lot and fidget in the vinyl chair making squeaky noises. He looks up often, but he doesn't get the hint.

"Dr. Light."

He raises his head from the folder.

"Sorry. Tom, I mean. I've always been healthy. I can't remember a time when I've ever been sick. When I was young, my mom used to say I was invincible."

"That's very interesting, Stacy," he says with a grin. "I'm done with the paperwork, though. Would you like to lie down over there?" He leans to the right and looks over at the chaise.

I nod.

"You go over and make yourself comfortable, while I grab my notebook."

I'm up and heading for it before he turns around. The chair is extremely comfortable. My eyelids are starting to feel heavy when I notice Dr. Light coming toward me, carrying the vinyl chair from behind his desk. He puts it down gently then sits, opens up his notebook, and readies his pen.

Watching him bungle around has me anxious again. "Should I close my eyes?"

"If you like."

They've been closed for half a minute now, and he hasn't said a word. This is what the fine print in the back of the phonebook gets me—self-service psychiatry. "How should I begin?"

"Tell me why you're here today, why you feel you needed to see a psychiatrist."

"I've been having nightmares since the beginning of summer, but they're not normal. Each nightmare is part of a whole story. I've had them in perfect sequence from beginning to end."

"What happens in the beginning?"

"The end of the world, and then I think I go crazy, and I...I..."

"Please, continue."

"I cut up everybody in my neighborhood enclave, including my family, and then set them on fire."

"Does anything happen after the fire?"

"No. The story ends with the fire. It took about a month from start to finish. Since then, the same nightmares occur but out of sequence."

"What else can you tell me about them?"

"Some of the things that happen in my nightmares come true."

"Please, explain."

"Like, if I see a book in my nightmare and I do something to the book when I'm awake, in my nightmare, whatever I did affects the book. Does that make sense?"

"Yes. It does. You feel you can alter your nightmares."

"Yes."

"That may be useful," he says.

"How?"

"Tell me about something in your nightmare that doesn't exist when you're awake."

"I don't understand."

"It could be anything. What do you use to cut up your neighbors?"

"All kinds of things."

"Something you don't have, but you use in your dreams."

"An axe. I know we don't have an axe, but I use one a lot in the nightmares."

"Very good. Stacy, there's an exercise I'd like you to try tonight before you go to sleep. I'd like you to sit up in bed and relax. Flex all the muscles in your body, then loosen them, starting from your head down to your toes."

I take in a deep breath and try it a little now. "Okay."

"And while you're relaxing, try to think of one of your nightmares. In your mind, change an outcome that you already know happens. At any point when you're having them, are you cognizant it's merely a bad dream?"

"No. It's all real. Vivid. Everything happens in real time. Sometimes though, I wish it were just a nightmare—*in my nightmare*. Isn't that crazy? That's why I need psychiatric help."

"Crazy isn't really a term we psychiatrists like to use."

"Oh, right. Sorry."

"Don't apologize. You're not crazy. I promise. We'll find their origin."

"I hope so."

"But for now, our time is up."

"Already?" I sit up and open my eyes.

"I know. It goes by fast, but like I told you over the phone, my schedule is currently very flexible. Normally, I'd see you every day, or every other, at least until we got some resolution. Then gradually, we could decrease the visits."

"The lunch I had scheduled tomorrow cancelled. I could come in then, and we could set up some kind of appointment schedule. Would that work?"

"I'm available."

"Same time as today?"

"Yes."

"Good." I swing my legs around and stand up. "Whoa." Dizzy.

He steps up and takes my hand. "Be careful. Take your time getting up. Your body needs to adjust from lying to standing. It is called Orthostatic Hypotension." He says this as if he were a med student who just learned a new term he's excited about.

I stagger forward and trip. My face hits his chest. He smells like cotton candy. I lean back against the chaise to keep steady. "Sorry."

"I'm going to write you a prescription for a muscle relaxant. Take one before you start the exercises. It should help."

"Thanks." My hand is still in his. He pulls me forward and helps me walk to the door but more like leads. His palm feels a little cool and clammy—kind of gross.

"Here's the script." Pinched between his shaking fingers

is a piece of paper with scribbles on it. "Get it filled today. And I'll see you tomorrow at ten."

I snag the paper from him. "Kay. Bye. Thanks"

He seems hurried to get rid of me now. I hope the whole hand holding thing didn't make him uncomfortable. I certainly didn't feel weird about it, aside from the uneasy bit of moisture. I'm sure he was just nervous. He seems nice. I like him and his approach. This just might work.

Maybe he rushed me out because he has another appointment. He could actually be busy, and I could have him and his fledgling practice all wrong.

I grab the handle and push the exit door open. My palm feels tacky against the metal. When I get out into the sun, I look down and notice an iridescent glistening in my hand—the one he shook—oh, yuck. I rub it briskly on my pant leg until it's all gone.

My watch shows eleven o'clock—unbelievable. The only car in the parking lot is mine.

CHAPTER SEVEN

The prescription flutters against my purse on the passenger's seat. Dr. Light's handwriting is illegible. I'm not so sure I want to get this prescription filled in Summerlin. I usually go to the pharmacist counter inside my local grocery store, and that place is always teeming with friends and acquaintances.

I veer off at the last Henderson exit heading west. Brakes squeal and horns honk behind me. There's a shopping area I saw from the highway. It's like a parallel universe on the opposite side of the valley. The stores are all the same, but slightly off in their appearance or the way they are set up inside.

I pass my prescription through the pharmacy window to a young woman who then disappears with it. A moment later, she returns and asks, "Have you filled a prescription with us before?"

"Yes, but on the other side of town."

"You should be in our system then. It's going to be about twenty minutes."

"That's fine. I'll shop and come back."

"Pick-up is on the other side."

"Thanks."

This store is laid out identical to the one where I shop, but everything is inverse, which makes it even more confusing. It's going to be fun trying to find something for dinner. I can't believe Jon told Patrick he could have pizza tonight. Pizza is not one of my favorite foods, particularly the carnivore kind that Patrick likes, so I grab a bag of salad and get some fish. Every now and then, something sparkles past the ends of the aisles, but I ignore it. The last thing I need is for something weird to happen while I'm trying to get a prescription filled for a controlled substance.

I head back to the pharmacy after check-out. Standing there at the pick-up window in all of his sparkling glory is none other than—Elvis. An elderly woman waits in line behind him and I queue up after her. Only in Vegas is it normal to see clowns and famous dead people—probably not the best community for the mentally unstable.

Elvis steps back and salutes the pharmacist. Then he turns around with his little white pharmacy bag and can't leave without saying, "Thank you. Thank you very much." He blows a kiss.

The withered old lady in front of me swipes at the air to move him along. She's obviously been waiting a while and is in no mood for Elvis—dead or alive. When the pharmacist gets through with her, I step up and tell him my name.

"One moment please, ma'am." He thumbs through stapled bags on the counter. He is gray, balding, and keeps a thick set of bifocals resting on the top of his shiny head. He finds my little white bag then pulls his eyeglasses down. The pads come to rest on the bridge of his nose where his skin is red and sunken into kidney bean shapes. "Have you had Valium before?" he asks really loud.

"No."

"Well, it's very addictive," he says even louder. "Take it as prescribed. There's a hotline number to call on the back if you think you're getting addicted to it." He peers over his glasses at me then looks back down at the bag. "Your insurance denied payment. How would you like to pay for this?"

"Cash."

"It'll be twenty-seven, eighty, and I'll need to see your driver's license."

I palm everything through the opening under the window. A minute later, he slides back my license, some change, and the white bag of addiction. I turn around to leave, and everyone in line is staring at me. There isn't a familiar face among them. They casually look away when I make eye contact.

Humiliating as the ordeal was, coming here was still a good decision.

"Patrick! Let's go."

He rushes down the stairs, skipping two and three at a time.

"You keep that up in those knee-high soccer socks, and one of these days, you're going to slip and fall, and probably break something.

"Gross, Mom, the house smells like fish."

"Funny. I think it smells more like the delivery meat pizza you ordered. Grab your stuff, and let's head out."

I step into the garage and see Patrick in the passenger seat. He's left the trunk wide open—again. I point at him to get out and shut it. "You can't keep leaving the hatch up after you put your backpack in," I say. "I've already crashed into the garage once, and that was enough."

"That wasn't my fault."

"You should've said something, though. Did you get some water?"

"No."

"Come on, Pat." I pull two waters from the refrigerator and hand them to him.

Gail's Beemer is the only other car in the lot when we get to practice. Cally hasn't shown up yet and neither has Coach. Patrick takes his extra gear out to the field and starts setting up nets with Justin. I see Gail sitting next to the tree, so I walk over.

"Where is everybody?" I ask. "Coach didn't call you to cancel, did he?"

"No. He didn't call. Maybe they got caught in traffic." Gail looks down at her watch. "Speaking of traffic…" She looks up at me with a wry smile. "This morning, I saw you heading West on the 215 out near Henderson. Where on earth did you have to go so early?"

"Oh. I had to approve invitations for the fundraiser."

"Doesn't Jordan usually do that?"

"Yeah, she does. They had some urgent questions and needed to meet with me."

"Ah." She looks away smug.

"What were you doing there?"

"I had an appointment."

"Oh, is Dr. Goodwin's office in Henderson?"

"No. Are you kidding? I don't care how good he's supposed to be, I'd never commit to driving out there for any doctor."

"Oh."

My phone buzzes. "It's a text from Coach. Practice is cancelled."

"Great." Gail gets up and gathers her things.

My phone buzzes again. "Now it's Cally. She texts that practice is cancelled, too. How is it that she found out before us? She always seems to be the first to know."

"I doubt that." Gail whips her blanket out. "I think that *she* thinks she's the first to know."

"We should stop the boys before they put up the other goal."

Gail nods in agreement. Then together, we head for the field. She really seems to have it out for Cally lately, but she was coming after me this time, too—digging for a piece of someone else's calamity to deter the breakdown of her own marriage. I don't blame her for being bitchy, but she's headed in the wrong direction.

Out on the field, we help the boys take down what they've set up. Repack then reload everything. Gail doesn't say much while we're all working and neither does Justin.

Before stepping into the shower, I take one of the tiny blue pills and leave the plastic container out on the bathroom counter.

Jon comes in. "Lisa Fenway came in today to have her third facelift."

"Really, what happened the first two times?"

He steps in and out of the closet, talks while he undresses. "She wasn't happy with the results."

"She doesn't look like herself anymore." My jaw aches as if it were hard work to speak.

"Hey," Jon says. "Did you take one of these?"

I look through the glass and see him standing there naked, reading the Valium label.

"Yeah."

"Sweet." He puts the bottle down. "How'd the appointment go?"

"Good."

"Did you tell him I was a doc? Maybe he'll extend you a professional courtesy."

"No. And I'm not working my shrink for a discount."

"Why not?"

"He's not like a regular doctor."

"Yeah, I guess you're right. How many of these does *your shrink* have you taking a day?"

"That's confidential."

He raises an eyebrow. "Humor me."

"Just one at night, to relax me for stretching exercises."

"Stretching exercises before bed? I like this guy already."

I turn off the water then step out.

"Sure you're done? I was just coming in," he says with a deep sexy voice.

"I'm going to do my exercises."

"Don't finish before I get there."

It takes me a moment longer to respond. "Funny."

Jon steps into the shower and looks back at me with an impish smirk.

I put on my nightshirt then brush my teeth. Strange, I feel the same, but with less of an edge. When I get to bed, I pour myself between the sheets. Everything ripples like cool liquid against my skin. I lie still and close my eyes after the muscle relaxation exercise. The images of finding Patrick in my nightmares comes to mind, so, I concentrate on not finding him at all. I imagine opening his door and seeing an empty room.

Languor settles in, and a warm wave curls over me—it's Jon. His naked body soft and hard against me, I subside to the Valium undertow. His tongue is a flame licking the rim of my ear. My neck melts in his open mouth, spilling out into red fan waves. My breasts mold to his palms, his nimble thumbs teasing my nipples to peaks of ember. Every move he makes is another wave washing me down. Between my legs his mouth is a hot bath, water lapping against my folds. The laps come faster and faster until I seize and become liquid again. The weight of his body on mine anchors me down. His fire in my water—I am undulating in deep red hues.

He lies next to me and whispers, "I love you." The words resound.

The first thing I see is blood. He died in his sleep. I pull the comforter up over him and snuggle next to it. Against the cold damp of what was once his life, his fire. I put my arm around his body and sob until I have nothing left. Then it occurs to me…Patrick! I leap out of bed, throw open the double doors, and run to his room. I run faster and faster, until I'm out of breath, but I'm still so far away. Damn this big house! Damn everything! My toenail catches the carpet. The pain reels me back. My elbow bashes the wall, just before my head hits the floor. Eventually, the stars dwindle out of sight, and my bloody toenail comes into focus right before my eyes. It's being held up in a stray loop of carpet. The bright pink polish makes it look horribly unnatural.

I get up and run again, coming to a dead stop outside his door. I'm having déjà vu. There was something important

I was supposed to remember…I can't. Never mind. I turn the handle and push the door open. Between his bed and me, is a large standing pool of blood. I lean against the doorway watching crimson drip from the corner of his comforter down to the ivory Berber. Every muted drop is a hammer striking my skull. I fall to my knees then pass out.

Days have gone by, I think, when I get up again and leave, closing his door behind me. More days pass, maybe weeks. It isn't until my discovery of the shopping cart that I realize what it is I must do.

A wall of white storage cabinets, line the back of the garage. Jon's toolboxes are to the left. Since it happened, I've had the doors open, pulling out boxes and junk in order to find the right tools. To my surprise, there was a big axe hidden behind the plastic bins of Christmas decorations. Why the hell did Jon need an axe? It doesn't matter now. His naked body is laid out at the bottom of our driveway. My arm muscles are still quivering from dragging him down.

Determined as ever not to be taken aback, I step into the garage and put on the welding goggles I found. They're so old, the plastic has yellowed and the lenses are scratched, but that's a good thing. They fog my visual clarity. The welding gloves were underneath them. They're a bit clunky, but they go up past my elbows. I pull open the bottom drawer of Jon's toolbox. Inside is a hacksaw on top of a bunch of other junk. I turn my head and look at his body. He's going to be the first—because I know he would forgive me. A deep breath in, I grab the saw then head down the driveway. I'm going to cut him in half. It will be easier to put him into the shopping cart if he is in two pieces.

I kneel down and try to ignore things like the mole on his hip I used to kiss. After a minute or two, I bring the saw down over his abdomen. Another deep breath, and then I rock the blade back and forth through him. Within seconds my hands are covered with nasty goo. Not quite blood, not quite flesh, but definitely lots of foul shit. The saw has disappeared into the gaping cavity of mush. Crawling to the side of driveway, I lean my head over a dead shrub and throw up my soul. It was all I had left. When I'm done, I get up and hobble over to my neighbor's backyard and jump in his pool.

I should have known better, should have thought it through. I will not make that mistake again. When I'm completely waterlogged and starting to sink, I head home to change my clothes, ignoring Jon's body on the curb.

His old anatomy books from medical school line the top of the bookshelves. Standing like a ballerina on my tiptoes, I reach up and pull one down. This idea should have come to me sooner, but the thought never occurred to me that there could be a wrong way to cut up a body. I take my time and study the pictures, read the pages and learn how to surgically dismember. The worst place to start was where I did—go figure. On my way back out to the garage I notice an apron hanging up in the pantry. I pull it over my head and tie it in the front.

From the kitchen I gather my sharpest German knives.

In the garage I grab a hammer, a chisel and the axe. Before getting started again I take out another one of those garbage bags and a roll of packing tape. I have to keep Jon's body together while I hack off his arms and legs.

The next door neighbors on the right are the last two. I began with Jon, then Patrick, and worked my way around the cul de sac starting with my neighbor on the left. When I'm done, I wheel them down to Bishop Almeida High School and stack the pieces into a pyre.

The entire mound ignites into a roaring fire. I push the cart and jump out of the way. Flat on my back, looking up at the sky, I watch endless swirls of black smoke rise and curl upwards. Something's not right. I hear more than the usual crackling and popping of a fire. It sounds like low moans. I sit up and look at the bodies. They are writhing. My God, I'm burning them alive! I run over to the mound. "Help us." They moan. "Please!" Their screams intensify with the fire. I step closer, but the flames are too hot. They lash out and scorch the hair on my arms. Helpless, I stand back and watch their faces bubble and peel. Their loud squawks gradually lull to murmurs. Down at the bottom of the pile, a charred hand covered with open blisters stretches out. The fingers spread apart momentarily then close. The hand falls back to the ground. Jon's wedding ring glistens in the fire light. I reach down to touch it.

I reach up to darkness.

Jon lies next to me. His body's outline glows soft

shades of gray. I watch his shoulder rise and fall with the rhythmic pattern of his breathing. Tears roll across my temples, down into my hair. Three months and the nightmares remained the same—until now.

CHAPTER EIGHT

I'm not sure how I should feel about last night's dream changes. Could be my mind subliminally acting out a form of anxiety toward the psych appointments. I don't want to go there thinking things might be getting worse. I'm seeing a shrink now—they can only get better.

Jon comes into the bedroom with a cup of coffee. He has a look on his face. I think he's surprised to see me still lying in bed. Sleeping in is not something I normally do. I'm usually up, dressed, and ready to go by the time he comes back with my morning coffee. He walks over, sets the cup on my nightstand, then sits down on the edge of the mattress.

"How'd you sleep?" he says.

"Good. How about you?"

"Not bad. Hey, I think the muscle relaxer before bed is a good idea."

"Yeah, I bet."

"You didn't have a nightmare, and you said you slept well."

"Yeah, I guess."

"See." He smiles, leans over, and kisses my forehead. "Have a good day. I'll see you later." He gets up and walks away, then stops at the doorway. "Oh, almost forgot. Can you get our clothes from the dry cleaners?"

"Why? Got a hot date tonight?"

"I hope so. Red Rock Hospital's cocktail mixer…I want to wear my blue pinstripe."

"Crap, I totally forgot."

"We have to go."

"I know."

"So don't forget the dry cleaners. I want to look hot for my date." He winks then leaves.

Great, I have to be sick this morning, but good enough to attend a cocktail party this evening. If I don't let Cally know, she will stalk me all day to find out why I missed yoga. It's still early, I'll text her. Texting is a revolutionary invention for crappy liars like me.

One hand wrapped around a coffee cup, while the other fumbles with the cell phone—I'm such a multi-tasker these days. *"Stomach cramps. Skipping yoga."*

I get out of bed then get dressed. Cally texts back. *"Heal. I'll call later."*

I better have a damn good excuse by the time she calls.

When I get downstairs, Patrick is eating cereal from one of my huge pasta bowls.

"No gym today?"

"Not today. My stomach hurts."

"Oh." He picks the bowl up and slurps the milk.

"Do you have to do that so loud? It's really disgusting."

"In some countries, it lets the cook know you liked the meal."

"Here, it signifies that you're a pig."

He snorts into his bowl then laughs.

"That's enough, piggy. Let's go."

I grab my purse and keys then head out to the garage. After starting the car—while I'm waiting for the garage to open—a sudden urge comes over me. I get out and walk over to the storage cabinets.

"Mom, what're you doing? We're gonna be late."

"Just give me a sec."

I open the middle section of cabinets where the holiday stuff is stored. Neatly stacked red and green plastic bins tower up to the ceiling. I reach my hands in and slide them all forward. Low and behold, there's an axe handle propped up against the back wall. I turn the bins to see the red and silver blade.

Transfixed, I forget Patrick waiting in the car and yell at the top of my lungs. "Why is this axe here?" The shouting, the axe, and the top-heavy bins—I lose my grip, and stumble. Then bin after bin slides off the next, crashing to the cement garage floor. Some of the lids pop open, releasing holiday ceramics and glass ornaments. The collectibles shatter across Jon's empty parking space. All I can do is stand and stare at the axe.

"Dad's gonna be pissed."

His profanity snaps me back. "Watch your mouth, Patrick Troy. He'll get over it…eventually."

I'm able to steady the last few bins and slide them back into the cabinet. I tiptoe through the broken shards, then get into the car again and pull down the driveway.

"Dad uses it to cut the Christmas trees down at one of those *do-it-yourself* farms."

"What?"

"The axe. You asked why it was there. Aren't you listening?"

"Yeah. I'm listening. What about the axe?"

"Geez, Mom. Really? Dad got that axe when I was like, ten. He hid it so you wouldn't freak. Guess that didn't work out." Patrick chuckles to himself but loud enough for me to hear.

"Oh. Well, I'll clean it up later. It's not a big deal."

"How'd you know it was there anyway?"

"Just a hunch."

Drop off couldn't happen soon enough and today, I need some drive-thru coffee. When I get home, I open Jon's garage, then get to work cleaning up the mess. It's not too bad, but one of the ornaments Patrick made me in Kindergarten broke. I put the pieces in a cup then stick it back into the bin. I'll have time to glue it together over Christmas break. It was stupid of me to react the way I did in front of Patrick. The *mom* stigma is bad enough. *Psycho mom* would push him away forever.

The garage is spotless, cleaner than it was before. Amazing, the energy in a cup of coffee. All that work, and

I'm still raring to see Dr. Light. I wonder what he'll say about the new nightmare ending. It must mean something. All this time trying to figure out what my dreams are telling me, but really, more worried what they're saying about me. The recent episodes of déjà vu, they must mean something too. It seems impossible for a normal person to become all kinds of crazy at once. There's no history of mental illness in my family. If Dr. Light can't help, I'm not sure what's next.

On the way to his office, I mull over what it is I want to discuss. If I can get everything out into the open, he will be better equipped to help. Then, as if I hadn't been driving at all, I'm suddenly parked in front of Dr. Light's dismal building. Maybe I drive better when I'm not focused. I didn't even have to use the car's navigation system this time.

It's hazy outside today, and the sun isn't glaring off the marble floors. Stooping over just a bit, I take a better look. I've never seen this type of marble before. I wonder what it is. There aren't any seams either, no grout lines. It's impossible. No builder in his right mind would do marble slab floors. I walk around in circles looking for something—anything. Not only are they the cleanest floors I have ever seen, they are the most perfect. Even hand painting is out of the question. Michelangelo himself couldn't paint a floor like this without leaving some kind of evidence. On the surface, there appears to be a texture that looks like aged, tissue paper skin. Underneath, visible layers of rust-colored veins branch throughout. Glittery gold veins run in conjunction with the rust ones. The sparkles make them appear to be flowing. It's quite fascinating, beautiful.

One of the larger veins leads directly to Dr. Light's office. Just outside the door, I pause and wait for another attack with the painful sound and bloody nose, like I had the other day. Nothing happens, so I pull the lever down and enter.

He is standing in the doorway.

"Dr. Light," I gasp. "You scared me." I put my hand over my chest.

"I'm sorry. I thought I heard you in the hallway."

"Wow, you have good ears. I was outside, but…"

"Why did you do that?" he says.

"Do what?"

"Put your hand there," he points to my chest.

"Oh, that. To check my heart—make sure it was still beating."

"Interesting," he says.

"You've never seen anyone do that before?"

"No."

"Now, that's interesting."

"We should begin." Dr. Light turns and walks toward his office.

Strange, but I can't let him throw off my agenda. As soon as he opens the door I step in, walk straight to the couch, then lie down. He closes the door, grabs a notepad from his desk, then takes a seat beside me.

"You seem anxious this morning. How was your night?" he says.

"Not so good."

"What happened?"

"The end of the nightmare changed."

"Tell me about it."

"The nightmare has always ended with me setting everyone on fire. But last night, they all came back to life. They were burning alive and screaming for help. It was awful. Do you think it could be a side effect of the muscle relaxer?"

"No. Did you do the relaxation exercises I prescribed?"

"Yes."

"Did you visualize a part of your nightmare and change the outcome?"

"Yes. I did everything you told me to."

He scribbles on his notepad, but I don't think he's taking notes. I turn my head and look at him. He raises his eyes like he knows I want to examine his face. His skin is pale, nearly diaphanous, reminding me of the marble floors. It's smooth, too, unblemished. His eyes are so dark, they're one solid color. The pupils melt into the irises. This makes them look enormous, unnatural. They are set far apart and have an elliptical shape, or maybe they just look that way because his head is so big.

The more I stare, the more it makes my skin crawl. He smiles as if he's finished examining me the way I examined him.

"What frightens you the most about your nightmares?"

"That I'm alone."

"There's another exercise I'd like you to try called dream scripting."

I raise a brow.

"It's exactly how it sounds," he says. "We're going to try and eliminate your biggest fear by visually scripting something into your nightmare that might change it up again. Give you more control. Even though you were frightened by the change that took place last night, it was still a change, and that's something we can focus on. The slightest modification can lead to bigger and better ones as therapy progresses. Close your eyes, relax. Take a deep breath then release it slowly." His voice is melodious, soothing. "You fear being alone, so think of something or someone you can add into a scene. Keep it simple, a pet perhaps or a neutral acquaintance."

For some inexplicable, odd reason, Dr. Light is the first person that comes to mind. "Okay."

"Do you have it?"

"Yes."

"Now, choose a scene that terrifies you most."

That's easy. I nod my head.

"Somewhere in this scene you're going to add the change. Describe what happens."

"I jump out of bed, run to my son's room and find him dead."

"Start over, and slow it down."

"I jump out of bed and throw open my bedroom doors."

"Good. Now stop right there. When you throw open your bedroom doors, what do you see?"

"The long hallway."

"Before you take another step, add your selection here.

Visualize the person or thing in front of you, blocking the path to your son's room."

I do it. I open the doors and see Dr. Light standing there at the doorway, just like he was today. Waiting for me, wanting to help. I try to push him aside, but he puts his arms around me.

"Are you able to do it?" he says.

"Yes."

"Good."

"This just might work." He's a little strange I guess, but everything he is saying sounds right, and it's not my place to judge considering what I'm about to tell him regarding myself.

"I think it will, but there's something else I'd like you to consider."

"Yes?"

"You're the perfect candidate for hypnotherapy."

"Hypnosis? I don't know…"

"It's quite safe and would help open your mind. I'm very good at it."

"You would do it? Hmm…let me think about it, but while we're on the subject of other things. There's more going on I'd like to tell you about."

"Please."

"Do you believe in déjà vu?"

"Yes, I suppose."

"Well lately, I've been having these realistic instances occur in the middle of the day. Not too long ago, I was taking a nap, and I dreamt I was a child in a foreign country sometime in the past. When I woke up, I could still hear children laughing. I followed their laughter upstairs and was sure I heard it clearly through the office door, but when I opened it, no one was there. Then the other day, I was at lunch with a friend, and it happened again, except this time, I was wide awake. Everything around me had changed to a setting from Victorian England."

"Déjà vu is when you experience a feeling that you've seen or heard something before. What you're describing sounds more like a past life experience."

"Yes, but it's a déjà vu feeling I get when I have the past life experience."

"Interesting."

"Does it mean I'm getting worse?"

"Not at all, but it's possible the hypnotherapy could help shed some light."

"I'll still have to think about it."

"Is there anything else?"

"Before I came in this morning, I found the exact axe that I hack everybody up with in my nightmares. It was hidden in the garage behind some storage bins."

"What do you think it means?"

"That everything might already be predetermined. Could I be a late blooming psychic?"

"It would be rare. I…"

"I'm just kidding. I don't believe in psychic powers, but it would explain how I feel I know things sometimes."

"Tell me."

"We're all going to die." I gaze into his eyes. He looks

concerned. "It's morbid, I agree, but I can't escape the dread. It heightens every day. I can feel it building."

"Stacy, I have to interrupt and I apologize, but…"

"Time's up already?" I raise my wrist and check my watch. It's close to eleven. "Really, it feels like I just got here. Can't we schedule longer appointments?"

"That's not a good idea…one hour sessions are set for reasons, and we should adhere to them. But I would prefer it if you came every day. Will you arrange your schedule?"

"Every day, though? I don't know."

"It's important."

"I know it's important, I just don't know." A quick heat flushes my face. I raise my voice. "I *do* have a life outside all this craziness."

"Every day." He stares at me blankly.

"I've got to go." I swing my legs around and sit up slowly.

It's hot. I wipe my forehead, which feels cool. I'm covered with perspiration. I stand up, and high-pitched tones spear my head, driving me to the floor, forcing me to scrunch up into a ball. I press my hands over my ears and squeeze like a vice. I'm rolling around in complete agony. The marble veins flash in and out of my vision. Some areas are so translucent, I could almost fall through.

Dr. Light drops to his knees, puts one hand over my eyes, the other across the back of my neck. "Breathe," he says. It's hard to tell if I'm actually hearing him speak. His voice seems to chime with the piercing tones. Everything goes quiet.

He moves his hands around and helps me sit up. I pull him closer, hug him, and cry. He still smells sweet. "Thank you," I mumble.

"Are you all right?"

I nod my head into his chest and wipe my tears on his shirt. "What did you do?"

He doesn't answer.

I peel my face from his damp cotton shirt and ask again. "What did you do to make it stop?"

"I used a pressure point technique."

"Will you teach me?"

"I suppose...does this happen often?"

"No. It's recent. I didn't tell you. It's a hearing problem, sort of. Well, it started out that way. Now the sounds blare straight into my head as if I were a subwoofer. Usually, there's a..." I back away and glance down at his shirt. I see a circular water stain with make-up smudges on it. I drag my hand under my nose—all clear. "I get bloody noses now too, and I never did before. Do you think it's possible, I could have a brain tumor or something?"

Mortified by the stain on his shirt, I start to get up. He helps, and we rise together.

"What else do you feel when this happens?"

"I don't know. Hot, lately. Yeah, the other night I had a nightmare, and after I set the fire, my chest caught on fire too. It was burning hot. I woke up in a sweat that was cold."

"Interesting. You didn't mention that either. They don't sound like brain tumor symptoms, but if you like, I can refer you to a neurologist. They'll run a battery of tests and should be able to give you a more definitive answer than me."

"No, thanks. There's nothing I hate more than medical doctors and tests."

He smirks. "Okay then, from now on, I'd like you to keep a pen and notebook handy. If you have a nightmare, a daydream, déjà vu, whatever, I want you to write it down. And write how you feel at the time, too."

"Do you think the sounds and bloody noses are related to the nightmares?"

"I don't know, but it's important to try and find out. The human body is a puzzle that miraculously all fits together and works—even when the pieces don't perfectly match up. Then sometimes when all of the pieces are perfect, it doesn't work. There's truly more to it than we'll ever know. Shall I walk you out?" He starts to lead the way.

"Wait, you were going to show me that pressure point technique."

"It's easy, really. Put one hand over your eyes, the other across the back of your neck like this." He positions my hands for me. His skin feels a little clammy.

"Do I have to press hard?"

"Medium pressure is fine." He moves his hands away, walks to the door then opens it.

"That's it?"

"Yes."

"Okay. Thanks." Before I step out, I stop, and look in

his eyes. "Really though, I mean it. Thanks." Something seems different about his appearance.

He gently grabs my arm. "Please. Agree to the hypnotherapy. It's imperative. I'll see you tomorrow."

"No. Not tomorrow. It's Saturday. You don't work weekends do you?"

He releases my arm. "Oh, no. You're right." He makes an awkward smile. "Monday then, and remember to do all of the exercises. Keep a notebook handy." He steps back to shut the door.

"Are you okay, Tom?"

"I'm fine. Sorry, but I have to go. You have to leave now." He shuts the door.

I'm so embarrassed and flustered about rolling around on the poor doctor's floor, then perhaps ruining his shirt. I nearly twist my ankle walking faster than usual out to the car. Without even fastening my seatbelt, I start the engine and squeal out of the lot.

I wonder why he was rushing me out. Maybe he finally noticed the stain on his shirt. He could be meeting his wife for lunch. The make-up smudges…how will he explain? Oh God, I'm horrible. Yet I can't get the last image of his face out of my head—before he closed the door. He looked different. His skin was so pallid I swear I could see veins pulsing across his face. And his eyes—they were enormous black discs.

CHAPTER NINE

S tuck in the brain-dead calm of slow-moving traffic, I gather my senses and turn on my cell phone. There is a voicemail from Cally. *"Hey Hon, get well quick, I want to have lunch. Give me a call."*

I sync the car's Bluetooth with my cell, then speed-dial her number.

"Hey Sweetie," Cally answers. "Feeling better?"

"Yeah, thanks."

"The girls asked for you, and I told them you were ill. Tara was freaking out, thinking you might miss her dinner party, but I said you'd be fine, and you just ate something that didn't agree with you."

"Thanks."

"What're you doing now? Speaking of eating, you up for a quick bite?"

"Actually, I am kind of hungry. I've been out running errands. Picking stuff up for Thanksgiving."

"Oh God, don't remind me. I still haven't started. Let's meet up at Sushi Heat on Sahara in the next thirty."

"Sounds good. Bye."

I'm not so hungry, but this may be my only opportunity to get her one-on-one for a while. I need a good reason for cancelling yoga mornings. The only thing that comes to mind is how they've all been mentioning my haggard appearance. And they did witness my nosebleed at the gym the other morning. Maybe I am ill, besides mentally. It's been a while since I've had a complete physical. That's it—Jon wants me to have some tests done. I'm sure it's a better excuse than what they've already been thinking, and I prefer their minds churning on the idea there could be something wrong with my health—not my marriage.

Traffic clears up, and I make Sushi Heat in less than fifteen minutes. Cally arrives ten minutes later, fashionably dressed and looking radiant. As she walks toward me, sunbeams penetrate the window glass and cast rainbows on gilded strands of her blonde hair. Her parents were hippies and aptly named her California. She is the epitome of gold and sunshine.

"Hi, Sweetie," she says. She leans over and gives me a hug. "Have you been waiting long?"

"No. Just a couple of minutes."

"Good."

Cally has barely taken her seat, when the waitress races over with two steaming mugs of hot tea and to see if we're ready for her to take our order. As soon as she leaves, Cally whispers, "I don't know why they're always in a rush to get you fed and out. It drives me nuts."

"More customers, more money. Especially during lunch hour."

"Lunch hour, happy hour, dinner hour, it's always crazy in here." She picks up her mug and takes a sip. I can see her big blue eyes peering at me over the rim. She lowers the mug from her lips. "Well, you don't look as bad as I thought you would. Pale still, but your skin isn't all shriveled up and dehydrated."

"Gee, thanks."

"Just making an observation. How do you feel?"

"To be perfectly honest, I'm tired."

"From what?"

"I don't know. Jon thinks it might be something physical."

"I've known you nearly ten years, and you've never been sick."

"Maybe it's catching up. Anyhow, Jon's making me get a complete physical."

"Good idea."

"He also wants me to work out later in the afternoons, instead of mornings."

"What? Why?"

"To reduce my daily energy output. Just until they give me the okay."

"Oh, I'm so bummed. You could do low impact. What does Jon think it is?"

The waitress comes back carrying *all* our food. Miso soup and salads, together with long trays of sushi rolls. Our table is a gluttonous feast for the senses. It's making me nauseous.

"He doesn't have a clue, and he doesn't want to chance a guess." I sip some tea.

Cally digs right in and talks between bites. "Well, he's doing the right thing. I'll miss you, though. It's not the same when you're not there. I won't have anyone normal to chat with."

"I'll be back soon enough."

"Hmm…maybe I should take a break, too. At least from the Bikram. Then Bill and I could have lunch together more often. He's been so busy with work lately, and he hates me going to the Bikram place in that part of town, anyway. Says it's seedy."

"Jon's been asking about having dinner with you guys."

"Great idea. Let me talk to Bill. What're you doing tonight?"

"Hospital mixer."

"Oh. How droll," she says. "What're you wearing?"

"I'm not sure."

"Hey, you're not eating."

"I guess I'm not that hungry."

"That's probably why you're sick—skipping meals for a tight cocktail dress. Ugh, we ordered too much food."

"You can take it to go."

"Gross. Sushi? No way. Kyle would complain all the way home from school." Cally pinches her nose and rolls her eyes.

"I can just picture his face." We giggle so loud the waitress comes over.

"Is everything good?" she says.

"We're not done yet," Cally says.

"Okay. Thank you," she says then walks toward the kitchen.

"Have you finished *Memoirs of a Spa Junkie* yet?" Cally says.

"No, but I'll have it read by Sunday."

"Wish I could read that fast. You'll like it. I'm at the part where she's in Bali. She does some amazing shopping while she's in all of those countries."

"I bet."

"Which reminds me, I need new shoes. You'll probably want some, too—for tonight. Have you been over to Breanna's?"

"No. You want to?" I've been ready to escape this sensory overload since the food came. Even Cally is a little more Adult-ADD than usual. Breanna's is an upscale shoe boutique we frequent. They are way overpriced, but it beats going to the strip where all the high-end stores are.

"We'll drive both cars across then leave straight from there to get the boys," she says.

The waitress comes with the check. We square it away then go out to our cars. I get caught at the traffic light. Meanwhile, I'm sure Cally's already parked and in the store.

I bought a single pair of adorable, black, strappy sandals. They were the only cute ones Cally didn't buy, and simply because her size was unavailable. Shoe shopping used to be something that would take my mind off of things, but even that's not helping so much anymore.

An enormous Hummer pulls away, leaving curbside space for three cars. Patrick walks over. "Where have you been?" he asks.

"I'm not that late. Get in. We've got to hit the supermarket on the way home."

"For what?"

"Dinner."

"Do I have to go in?"

"Yes."

"But, Mom, I'm in my uniform."

"So are all the other kids. You'll fit right in."

To the left of the automated doors is a stack of plastic carry baskets. I grab one, put my arm through and let the handles rest in the crease of my elbow. Patrick mopes along behind me with his hands shoved into his pockets. The store is chock full of moms and their kids marching through the aisles in private school uniforms. They are all eerily similar, like an army of brainwashed apathetic children.

I walk over to the produce section while Patrick heads down the adjacent cereal aisle. I'm checking out some fresh corn, pulling the husks back and inspecting the kernels. An ear rolls down from its neat pile and drops to the floor. I bend over and grab it. When I stand up to put it back, there is a woman off to my side, behind a broken down cart of dirty vegetables.

"Is that all I can do for you today, ma'am?"

She is a stout woman with a strong British accent. Her wild smile exposes her neglected dentition. Her clothes are unkempt, filthy, and she has dirt smudged all over her face and hands.

"What?"

Someone else approaches the cart and she turns her attention to them. Voices fill the dank air, capturing my curiosity. Two rows of shabby carts, line both sides of a wet cobblestone alley. The smell of rain still clings to every surface. The people in the streets…it is Victorian England again, but not as nice a place as the café.

Across the way, over muddied sanguine stones, a gentleman in a long overcoat haggles with a man wearing a bloody apron. Meat carcasses hang from the grimy cart. Crimson trickles from the skinless butchered animals down the rickety wood frame, filling the grooves between the cobblestones.

The odor turns my stomach. I drop the ear of corn, pull an ivory lace handkerchief out from under my wrist, and cover my nose. I put my free arm in front of my face to take another look at my sleeve. I'm wearing the same dress Jordan had on at lunch when I envisioned the woman at the outdoor café. *I am* that woman. That's why she looked so familiar. Nearly everyone in the market turns to stare at me while I stand in mute astonishment. Inattentive young children chase one another around my dress and through the vendor's carts. Suddenly, the ear of corn is in front of me again. It's being held up by the pudgy little hand of a toddler dressed something like *Little Boy Blue.*

"Mummy, do you want the corn?"

I step back and gasp.

"Mom, do you want the corn or not," Patrick says with an irritated tone. The grocery store returns to normal.

"What?"

Patrick tosses the corn on top of the pile, puts his hands in his pockets, then walks away. Dazed and utterly lost, I rub my eyes and take a deep breath. This can't be happening. Those people saw me, they spoke to me—I was there.

At the checkout counter, and during the drive home, neither one of us brings up the incident. We get into the house, and Patrick bolts upstairs to play video games. My mind has been in a fog since the incident in the store, and before I realize it, dinner is on the table.

Patrick comes downstairs. "Can I eat now?"

"Don't you want to wait for Dad?"

"He told me he was going to a party."

"Crap, the mixer. I forgot to pick up the dry cleaning."

I grab my cell phone and text Jon. I hope he planned on leaving work early. He texts me back. *"No problem. Will stop on way home."*

"You never forget stuff," Patrick says.

"It's called getting old." *Going crazy…overanxious… preoccupied—I've got to fix this!* If something bizarre happens at the mixer it could hurt Jon's reputation. I head upstairs to get dressed, think, and try to relax. I even run a hot bath in the Jacuzzi tub. Half asleep in the steaming bath, I see the orange bottle of Valium on the bathroom counter. That'll do it.

Jon comes in with a big smile and the dry cleaning.

"Sorry. Thanks for getting it."

"Happy to be at your service. Did you forget or just got too busy?"

"Both."

"What did you do, today?"

"I had another doctor's appointment this morning."

"Really, how'd it go?"

"He gave me another exercise to try called dream scripting."

"Sounds like psych mumbo jumbo to me. How often are your visits?" Jon steps into the closet and takes the plastic off the dry cleaning.

"Uh, once a week—for an hour." Great, now I'm a liar too. It's stupid not to tell him the truth, but I don't want him to think it's more serious than it really is.

He walks out of the closet holding up two jackets. "Which one, blue or green?"

"It's navy pinstripes or moss, and I like the moss."

"What would I do without you?"

"Wear Aloha shirts all the time."

"I would, too." He laughs.

"Oh, I know."

"What are you wearing?"

"The black cocktail dress."

"Help me out, you've got a hundred black dresses in here."

"The lace number that was in with the dry cleaning."

"I got it. Nice. And you should get out of the tub. We're leaving in less than an hour."

Jon showers, gets dressed, and I'm still seated at my vanity. "You've got ten minutes. Then I'm leaving without you," he says.

"Promise?"

"You look fantastic. Now, let's go."

"I'll be ready in ten. Tell Pat we're heading out soon."

Finally, I never thought he'd go. I pop open the Valium cap and take one of the little blue pills. *Yuck.* The tap water tastes bad. It's all that reverse osmosis, saline treatment crap.

One last glance in the mirror and I'm out the door.

We arrive thirty minutes casually late, along with everyone else. Valet parking is overrun. Someone really needs to change the standard thirty-minute-late rule. Forty-five minutes seems like a better time, because that's when they finally get around to helping us.

"Are you folks guests of the hotel?"

"No. We're local. Here for a cocktail party." Jon hands the young man a twenty-dollar-bill.

"I'll keep it up front for you, sir."

"I'd appreciate that," Jon says. He reads the parking attendant's name tag. "Gus, from Idaho. They've got some great skiing there."

"Sure do, sir. Have a good night."

Jon takes my hand, and we walk into the hotel-casino through the shopping entrance. It's a long way around to the convention area, and my feet are already sore. I should have known better than to wear a new pair of shoes, but they go so well with the dress.

We pass people crowded around craps tables yelling and cheering. Cigar and cigarette smoke billows through the designated walking areas into endless rows of slot machines. It looks like fog rolling through a cemetery of marquee gravestones. My pace slows, and I lag a little.

"You okay?" Jon says.

"Want to trade shoes?"

Jon looks down and shakes his head. "They look better on you."

"If I'd remembered we'd be walking five miles, I'd have worn sneakers."

"And you'd still look good, but we're almost there."

The convention area is much quieter. Almost too quiet, until you get up close to the rooms, then you can see and hear all kinds of big parties taking place. The walls must be soundproofed, because there's a DJ in one and a wedding reception with a string quartet right next door.

It's a labyrinth of infinite doors, hideous carpeting, and numerous possibilities.

Of course our party is at the end of the hall, my feet are about to give up. The makeshift walls and doors are pushed all the way back, making the party entrance nice and open. A large buffet area is set up along the back wall. Many decorated tables are placed from the buffet to the entrance, like an obstacle course. This makes me a little nervous about my maneuvering through them on sore feet and the Valium.

The cash bar is to the right of the buffet, and the band is on the other side. Jon brings me over to an empty table toward the open front area then walks off to get a glass of wine. If I'm lucky, he'll be back in thirty minutes, carrying a warm glass of chardonnay. He's going to network, and I am *so* glad I took the Valium. It will definitely be a long night, and alcohol consumption probably isn't such a stellar idea after taking a muscle relaxer on an empty stomach. I really should eat something.

I set my crystallized clutch on the table then get up nice and slow. I feel relatively fine, other than not having a care in the world and sore feet. Taking my time, I make my way up to the buffet then steady myself up against the food carts. As the line moves along, I move with it and put easy eating food items on my plate. The line comes to a sudden stop. Food service is replenishing some of the chafing dishes ahead. I'll wait for that. While doing so, I look to the front of the room to check on my clutch. It's still there, and next to it, is a glass of chardonnay. No sign of Jon, however.

Another couple is also seated there now. Oh no, it's Jenna Rowland and her husband Adam, who Jon says is the worst surgeon in town. They're looking feverishly into the crowd. I casually turn my head and try to focus on something else. Too late, they spotted me. They simultaneously stand up and wave. Adam shouts, "Stacy! Over here!"

Jenna looks mortified. She sits down and pulls Adam down with her. Everyone in the crowd turns around and gives me the once over. It sure is good not to care. I doubt anyone else will join our table with those two there, and tonight, that suits me just fine.

The line gets moving again. Jon strolls up alongside me and rattles off everyone he has spoken to. He asks if I saw who was at our table and tells me that my wine is there. He takes food off my plate, shoves it into his mouth, then leans in and kisses my cheek. He mumbles something before walking away, leaving a trail of crumbs.

Good thing, I don't care. I brush the mess from my cheek and carry on, adding a few more pieces to my plate. Nonchalantly, I work my way back to the table, making several stops to say hello to friends and acquaintances. By the time I get to my clutch, I have no idea who I had spoken to or what I had said.

Adam and Jenna talk over each other while I eat. My occasional smile and nod abates their need for attention. Even if I wanted to say something, I'm not sure they would let me get a word in.

Now that I have a little food in my stomach, I'm

feeling better. My focus is directed to watching Adam's lips move as he talks about what—I have no idea. Then several twinkling lights slowly circle and gather in the far corner of my left eye. The moment they come together, they take off like a rocket down the hallway. My eyes move from their drug-induced gaze on Adam, to follow the light. I notice a shadow weaving swiftly through standing crowds of party people loitering outside the restrooms.

Adam stops talking and looks out at the hallway, too. "Anyone we know?" he says.

If something were about to happen, these are the last two people I would want to see me have a breakdown. "Excuse me," I say, "I've got to use the restroom." I rise from the chair, pick up my clutch, then walk out into the hall. I can hear them whispering behind me. Jenna asks Adam what I was staring at. He tells her the bathroom, obviously.

I pick up my pace, and when I get close to the women's restroom, I duck to the right, behind one of the crowds. Dr. Light walks by in a pale gray suit. No mistake. It's him. I would recognize that distinctive stride anywhere, even though he is walking really fast.

I step away from my camouflage and follow him. He turns left at the end of the open lobby. I move a little faster. The five inch heels shift my weight forward, cramming the front of my feet into the crisscrossed straps of my new shoes. The tender pain returns.

When I get to the hall, I catch a glimpse of him turning right.

"Dr. Light," I shout.

I've passed all the crowds. There is no one else in the hall. Every step becomes an explosion of pain. My feet are bulging out between the straps. Every other step, I look down and see flashes of angry red lines around the black leather bindings.

At the end of the hall, he turns down another.

"Tom!" I gasp. "Dr. Light!"

Exhausted and out of breath. The halls are an endless maze of blank walls. Blazing shades of crimson paisley carpet comes to life. Their bold patterns pop out of the floor while I run. It's dizzying. My head starts to throb. I stop and lean against the wall to take off my shoes. Pain! The strap behind my heel has burrowed into my skin. I peel it back, exposing bright pink flesh. Blood quickly seeps to the surface. Tears fill my eyes and roll down my cheeks. I bite my lower lip, look away, and then yank off my other shoe.

Dr. Light is at the end of the hall, about to turn again.

"Dr. Light?"

He stops and slowly turns his head to face me. His eyes, they're bigger. The depth they possess is abysmal. What I thought was a gray suit, now looks more like gray skin. It's pale, too—almost transparent. Dark veins pulse underneath.

My heartbeat pounds so loud I can hear it in my ears. It beats in sync with his veins. As mine gradually slows, his gradually slows.

"Who are you?" I mutter.

He slowly turns away and looks down the next hall. Then he steps out of sight. I quickly hobble after him.

"Dammit! Dr. Light!"

When I get to the corner, he's nowhere in sight. It's impossible.

An onslaught of deafening feedback seizes my head, boring into my cranium. I drop to my knees, grab my hair and pull as hard as I can. I want to tear it apart. Free the noise.

Rocking back and forth to ease the pain, casts irregular lines of blood from my dress to the floor. It beads, coalesces, then soaks into the red carpet and disappears. The taste of tears and blood are like salty nails between my lips. "Dr. Light," I whisper through them.

Him—or maybe just the thought of him—makes me remember. I put one hand over my eyes, the other across the back of my neck.

Nothing happens.

I crumple, lie down on the floor, and weep. Through watery eyes and loose strands of hair, I see a figure moving rapidly toward me from the end of the hall. A voice yells out, "Oh my God."

When Jon gets closer, he falls to his knees and slides across the carpet. I grab hold of his jacket with a death grip, giving me strength to open my mouth and scream. The sounds stop, and then I let go. My hand falls to the floor. He gently rolls me onto my back. "Jesus Christ. Were you attacked? Security!" He shouts down the hall. He takes his jacket off and lays it over me. He uses his fingers to hold my eyes open and examines my pupils. "Are you all right?"

I nod, yes.

At first, he uses his hands to wipe the blood on my face.

Then he wrestles with his tie and throws it to the side. He hurriedly strips off his collared shirt, so he can remove more of the blood from my face with his T-shirt. He quickly establishes my nose as the blood source.

"Security!" He shouts again.

I raise my hand up and cover his mouth. It felt like my hand, but in no way does it look like it now. It's smeared with blood that goes all the way up my arm.

He checks my head.

"No security. I'm all right," I moan.

He slowly pulls me up until I'm leaning against him. "What happened?"

"I got lost. My heel snagged on the carpet, and I fell into the wall, face first."

"What? Lost, how?" He gently manipulates the cartilage in my nose. "It's not broken."

"Please, take me home. Don't let anyone see me like this."

"Maybe I should swing you by the ER. No one will be there at this hour."

"No, really, I'm fine."

"Are you sure?"

"Yes, please, Jon."

"Okay. Let me think." He reaches into his pants pocket and takes out his cell phone along with the valet ticket. He dials a number. "Hello, this is Dr. Troy. I need to speak with…uh…Gus. It's urgent. Yes. I'll wait."

He combs the hair out of my face with his fingers. "Gus. Hello. Yeah, I've got a favor to ask. Could you bring the car around to the convention entrance for me? My wife's not feeling well. Yes…great. Appreciate it."

He closes his phone then puts it back in his pocket. "I'm going to stand you up and lean you against the wall. You can do that, right?"

"Yes."

I put my hands down and help him get me to my feet. Aside from being a little dizzy, I feel perfectly fine. Jon puts his shirt back on and hands me the tie. He puts his jacket around me, buttons it, then stoops over to pick up my shoes and clutch.

"Your feet," he says.

"The shoes."

His mere mention makes them sting like I'd stepped into a mound of fire ants.

"My God, woman. You're a mess."

He finds a clean spot on his bloodied T-shirt, licks it, then wipes around my nose.

"Just pull my hair back over my face."

"Good enough," he says. Then he slips his hand under a lapel and shoves his T-shirt down into one of the inner pockets. "We've got to walk down a couple of hallways." He puts his arm around my waist and holds me steady.

When we get to the exit door, I stop and look down the second hall. Sparse crowds still linger outside the restrooms.

"They couldn't have been just right there."

"What?" Jon says.

"The bathrooms—they were farther away than this. I know it. I walked through six corridors. At least!"

"Okay, honey. Calm down. The car's here."

He leads me through the exit, and I glance back to the hall. The people have dispersed. Dr. Light stands there all alone. His obsidian discs spread out and become darkness all around. He's engulfed by it—swallowed whole. Then it pervades the open hallway. Speechless and frantic, I claw at Jon until the black emptiness reaches me. All light disappears, and I feel Jon's arms tighten around me once more.

CHAPTER TEN

Jon hands Gus another twenty then gets in the driver's seat and pulls away. Once we're on the highway, he says, "I want you to see a doctor."

"Not now. Please."

"Fine, but you need blood work done as soon as possible. I'll set up the appointments, and you better not miss a single one."

"Don't talk to me that way, I'm not a child."

"This is serious, Stacy. I'm not fucking around."

"Jon," I reach my hand out and place it on his thigh. "Is there something else?"

He turns to me with a grave expression. "Not a single drop of that blood had clotted." He looks back to the road. "Have you been taking any aspirin?"

"No."

"Herbal crap? St. John's Wort, Gingko Biloba, Vitamin E, or fish oil, anything?"

"No. Nothing. Stop it, you're scaring me."

He moves his hand from the gearshift and lays it over mine. "It could've just been my imagination, but promise me you'll go to the appointments."

"I promise."

"Strange as it seems," he says, "the last time I think I saw you bleed was when you had Patrick, and there was very little then. Remember? Even the doctor had said so."

"I'm sure it's nothing." I turn my head and stare out the passenger side window. Images of my pregnancy play across the nightscape like a slide show. Jon was allowed to be a doctor to me then and only then. I was young and naïve to his obsessive way of doctoring loved ones. I gave him free reign.

I must have seen at least ten physicians, from neonatologists to geneticists. Against the opinion of my regular gynecologist, Dr. Reynolds, Jon talked me into and convinced most of the hospital staff I should have an amniocentesis. The horrible procedure was all for nothing. My pregnancy was healthy, and Patrick was born a normal baby boy. Prior to the delivery, Jon even fought with Dr. Reynolds about me having a C-Section. He was convinced that a vaginal delivery would cause undue trauma to Patrick. It was horrible, and I swore I would never let him doctor me again. The less he knows about my mental and physical problems, the less he can complicate things.

We get home and I immediately go upstairs. Jon stays close. He walks me into the closet and sets me down on the chaise. "Take your time and undress. I want to check something online. Shout if you need anything."

"I'll be fine, really. Go."

As soon as he leaves, I pull the T-shirt out of his inner jacket pocket and open it up. Blotches of bright red blood stain its entirety, and every bit is still wet—he cannot see this. I scrunch the damp fabric back together then shove it down into one of my knee length boots lining the bottom shelf of a wall. I'll have to get rid of it when he's not around.

My reflection in the standing mirror is macabre, something out of a horror story. I quickly get out of the clothes and put them into a bag for the dry cleaners. Jon comes up behind me.

"What are you doing?" he says. "I told you to sit down and undress."

"I'm fine, really. I just need a shower."

"Let me get my clothes off. I'll get in with you."

I lean against the closet cabinetry and watch him undress. His muscles flex as he hurries to get naked. He's tall, well-built, handsome, and smart—just like he was when we first met. I'm the envy of all the other wives. Women in Vegas hover like vultures waiting to swoop in. Always trying to sniff out a weakness they could sink their claws into. The relationship doesn't even have to be dead before they start circling. Lucky for him, I'm not the jealous type. I don't doubt Jon's faithfulness, and I never would. He's one hundred percent dedicated to Patrick and me, but sometimes, I wonder how things would turn out if something were ever to happen.

"Come on. You get in first." He takes my hand and helps me into the shower, then closes the door behind him and turns on the water. When it gets to temperature, he stands underneath and pulls me against his abdomen. "Shut your eyes." He whispers behind me. "I've got you."

I rest the back of my head against his shoulder and take in a deep breath. He uses a foamy bath sponge and washes me down. He's enjoying this role reversal a little too much. Jon's never had to take care of me like this before, and I'm worried he might get overbearing again.

Jon helps me to bed then disappears into the bathroom. He comes out a couple minutes later with a Valium and a glass of water. *Oh geez—I can't tell him I've already taken one.*

"Are you sure?" I say.

"It'll help you relax."

I can't imagine just one more would hurt, so I sit up and take the pill from his palm, place it on my tongue. He hands me the glass. I take a small sip and wash it down.

"Thanks." I hand back the glass. "You coming to bed?"

He sets it on my nightstand. "In a bit." Then he pulls the comforter over my shoulders and kisses my cheek. "Love you." He taps the rocker switch and the light goes out.

I roll onto my side and fight the inevitable numbness. Seeing Dr. Light as a monster when I was wide awake makes me fear how he might appear in my nightmares. It must have been my imagination or maybe the muscle relaxer. There really is no other explanation. I'm sure he would never hurt me. I don't know why, but I have strong feeling about that.

Half asleep—attempting the dream scripting, I open the bedroom doors and imagine seeing Dr. Light in front of me. After all the horrible things I thought I saw tonight. He looks perfectly normal. Maybe if I don't think too hard about it, he won't change.

The floor falls away, but I'm unafraid. Weightless, I hover amidst a luminescent fog. Neon colored laser lights roll in ribbons all around. I hear soft bell chimes, more like electronic xylophone tones. They play a harmonious duet with the colorways, creating a fantastical orgy of dancing lights and sounds.

Gathered around me in a circle, hidden within the fog, elusive shadows begin to form. There is a familiarity among us that keeps me fearless. Together, we are twenty-seven.

I speak out, "Hello." Ripples of orange light with glowing edges move away from my lips. Each wavelet shades to green as they spread further apart. They carry musical notes.

In response, rainbow waves slice through the fog from the others. They strike me all at once with a cacophony of blinding light and tones. Then it stops.

"*See.*" The word hisses out twenty-six times, echoing through every part of my being.

"**S**ee what?" Jon says.

I open my eyes and he's standing at the doorway, holding two cups of coffee.

I'm already sitting up in bed. "That I'm fine."

"Good. How'd you sleep?" He walks over and hands me a cup.

"Great. Thanks."

He sits down next to me and examines my face. "Follow my finger with your eyes."

"Really? You're doing this now?"

"Just do it." He finishes his little examination and moves his finger away.

"Well? Did I pass?" I say.

"With flying colors."

"Funny, I had a weird dream about that last night."

"About what?"

"Flying colors."

"No nightmare?"

"No."

"That's excellent."

"Yeah. I guess it is."

"Are you feeling up for Pat's game?"

"Yes, of course. What time is it—seven? We've got to get moving."

"I'll wake Pat up" He leans in and kisses my forehead. "I'm glad you're feeling better." He gets off the bed then leaves.

I flip the covers over then step out. The floor feels foreign underfoot. And ouch! I turn my head and look down. The back of my heels have partially scabbed over. After I get dressed, I slather the scabs with antibiotic ointment and rub my feet with moisturizing lotion. They're tender and sore all over. Thank God for Indian summers. It's going to be flip-flops for a while.

I step out into the hall, and it's too quiet. Patrick must still be asleep. On my way to his room, I walk by the office and see Jon sitting at his desk.

"You were supposed to wake Pat," I say.

"I did a while ago."

"No. You can't just *tell* him. You have to stay there until he's out of bed, or he'll go back to sleep."

"That's ridiculous."

"No. *That's* a teenager."

I rush around to Pat's room and throw open his door.

"Rise and shine sleepyhead, you're going to be late."

"What?" He pokes his head out from under the covers.

"You didn't get up when your dad tried to wake you, so now we're going to be late. Get up."

"Aw, Dad."

I walk over and open his shutters. His uniform is bunched up in a pile on top of his dresser. He pulls the covers over his head and groans.

"Get moving, or we'll leave without you."

He slides his feet out of the covers and plants them down onto the floor. "I'm up."

I head downstairs. Jon shouts from his office. "Do we have to get snacks?"

"Crap. I forgot to check. I'll text Cally."

When I get to the kitchen, I grab my phone off the counter and text her. Then I pour myself another cup of coffee and wait.

Ten minutes later, she texts me back. *"Oops. We're snacks. Gonna be late."*

"Well?" Jon says from the bottom of the stairs.

"It's their turn. They're running late, too."

Patrick comes barreling down the stairs. "Mom, my socks?"

"Laundry room. Then come back and grab a breakfast bar. You've got to eat something."

We canvas the parking lot no less than five times for a decent spot. Not an easy task on soccer Saturdays. No one wants to hike more than a few yards lugging chairs, sunbrellas, extra gear, and coolers.

Patrick runs out to practice with the team. Cally, Bill, and Kyle are nowhere in sight. Gail is under the tree with a huge blanket spread out. She sees us and starts straightening out the edges to make room.

"Hey, thanks for saving us a spot," Jon says.

"No problem," Gail says.

Jon drops our stuff then leans over and gives her a hug. "How have you been?" he says.

She looks up at him and smiles. "Not bad. Much better, actually."

"Well, you look great," he says.

"Yeah, you do," I say. Then I set up my chair, spear the bottom of the sunbrella through the topsoil, into the clay, and pop it open.

"I'm gonna go see if Coach needs anything," Jon says. Then he turns to me and asks. "You okay?"

"Yeah, I'm fine. Go on."

"You're so lucky," Gail says. "He always dotes on you."

"Not always, but just enough."

"Of course I'm jealous…I have a husband who's divorcing me and a son that's about to push me over the edge."

"Something happen with Justin?"

"Well, I'm sure you heard about Friday."

"No. What happened?"

"Justin was suspended for punching the lockers."

"Why would he do that?"

"He met with his therapist Thursday afternoon and finally let loose. He told her that he blames me for the divorce, that I'm a terrible mother, and that he hopes I rot in Hell. We fought all the way home in the car."

"Oh my God. How awful. I'm so sorry."

"Don't be. It's been a long time coming. He's been saying all those things since the separation. Just not so blatantly."

"Honestly though, Patrick never mentioned a thing."

"Maybe that's good, and they're actually keeping it hushed up at the school."

"What are you going to do?"

"Keep at it. Of course, I had to make an emergency visit with Dr. Goodwin. Thank God he was able to move things around and get me in. I never needed to talk with someone so bad."

"You could've called me, or any one of us."

Gail looks away. "I meant with a trained professional."

"I understand what you mean more than you think," I say in a hush.

She looks at me again and smiles sly. It's such a strange thing to have so many friends and no one to talk to. I can wholly relate to her dilemma.

"Where's Cally and Kyle?" she says.

"They're getting drinks and snacks. They'll be late."

Jon walks toward us from the field. Cally and Kyle jog up from the parking lot. Kyle goes straight out to join the team. Cally drops down to the grass and tries to catch her breath.

"Where's Bill?" I say. "I thought you said he was coming."

"I forgot the damn oranges," she says between gasps.

"Don't worry about it," Jon says.

"I sent Bill for some. You don't think the kids will mind peeling them, do you?"

"Not at all," Gail says.

"Oh, hi, Gail," Cally says. "How have you been?"

"Good," Gail says. "With all of us here to help, we'll have the oranges peeled before break."

"Great idea," Cally says. She turns to face me and rolls her eyes a bit.

I look out to the field. "They're getting ready to start," I say.

Jon points behind me. "Hey, there's Bill."

I turn around and see him running up the hill behind us. He's carrying four plastic grocery bags full of oranges and water bottles. They're swinging wildly from both hands. Before he reaches us, he trips over a sprinkler head. Two of the plastic bags tear away, and the oranges launch straight up into the air then rain back down. We cover our heads as the oranges pummel us on their way out toward the field. I watch them roll onto the grass, then look up at Kyle and Patrick. They immediately turn away. The rest of the team is laughing out loud. I can't help it, I start laughing, too. Bill dives onto the other half of Gail's blanket. "Ah…" He moans.

"That was quite an entrance," Jon says.

Bill gets up and holds his hand out. "Haven't seen you in a while, Jon. How have you been?"

"Good. Good," Jon says, shaking the proffered hand.

"Hey, let's go over and see if Coach needs us," Bill says. The two start walking off.

"Wait a minute," Cally says.

They turn back. "What?" Bill says.

"You were going to help us peel."

"The three of us can handle it," Gail says. "You guys go ahead."

Cally rolls her eyes again.

It's going to be a long game, prepping me in some twisted way for Tara's bleak dinner party this evening. I stay quiet, peel my oranges, and gaze out across the fields of families and ponder what it is my subconscious wants me to *See*.

Cally and Gail make light conversation. I do, however, notice that Gail doesn't bring up Justin's suspension again. I wonder what caused these two women to drift so far apart. Gail's divorce hardships should have made Cally more sensitive, not catty. Nine years, and I doubt I will ever understand them. I only hope I don't fall out with any of my friends the way they did.

When we get home from soccer, Jon spends the rest of the afternoon working in the yard. Doing what, I can only imagine. Most of the yard is xeriscaped—a *must* in Vegas to limit water usage. Decorative rocks replace grass and drought-resistant plants. Shrubs are used instead of big thirsty trees.

I think I did hear Jon out there a few times, talking with the neighbors. I wanted to go out and say hello, but ever since I started hacking them to pieces in my nightmares, I feel uneasy amongst them.

I'm nearly finished with *Memoirs of a Spa Junkie*. Some of the worst crap I have ever read. Honestly, if it weren't for the spa locales I don't think Cally would have picked this book. Then again, it's hard to say.

Patrick kicked the winning field goal at the game today, and against my stern opposition, Jon gave him fifty dollars. He also promised he would take him to the movies. They left a while ago.

I've showered and have since been sitting at my vanity. Everything seems to be dragging. Then Jon walks into the bathroom. "You still not dressed? You're going to be late."

"What are you doing home? Was the movie sold out?"

"No. I dropped Pat off at the Red Rock casino."

"What?"

"At the movie theatre entrance. Relax."

"By himself?"

"He's meeting some friends. He's got his cell."

"Oh."

"You feeling up to this dinner thing tonight?"

"Yeah, I'll be fine."

"Better wear some comfortable shoes."

"Why do you think I have slacks on? They'll cover my feet. God, I wish I could wear slippers."

"That would go over well."

"Okay, get out, and let me finish my makeup."

He kisses the back of my head then turns around. "Have fun," he says.

I put on my lipstick and step into the closet to get a look in the full-length mirror. I take some baubles from my jewelry armoire and put them on. Then I grab a pair of black high heel flip-flops from one of the middle shelves. Great choice, they're lined with Sherpa fleece. I forgot about that.

Jon shouts down another goodbye as I head into the garage. I put a soft jazz station on. Now that I'm running late, I don't want to rush and start sweating in my blouse. Too bad there isn't a station that plays the music I heard in my dream last night. For the most part, it was soothing, except for all twenty-six voices together and all at once. They turned it into nothing more than white noise.

Tara answers the door. "Hello, Sweetie. Come in. Did you get lost?"

"No, just running a little late. Then your guard couldn't find me on the list."

"Sorry. I know they can be a pain, but they change guys all the time—a total nightmare. I'll call tomorrow and complain. Let's get you a glass of wine. It'll make you feel better."

"It definitely couldn't hurt."

Tara puts her arm through mine and walks me to the kitchen. She's being so overly affable it's creeping me out.

And now I see why.

More of Tara's friends, Jordan among them, are standing in her kitchen sipping wine, eating, and socializing. Cally is seated on the couch in the adjacent family room with someone I've never seen before. A younger woman, in a modern dress suit. She looks like business. Something to do with that show I'm sure.

Tara lets go of my arm when we get to the kitchen. "White or red?" she says.

"White, please."

She steps over to the hired bartender, talks to the wait staff going by, then comes back with my wine.

"Thanks. Everything looks nice."

She leans in close and whispers, "Really? You think so. God, I'm so nervous."

"You'll be fine. They'd be stupid not to pick you."

"Thanks. I'm so glad you're here. The calm voice of reason."

"Who's Cally talking to?"

"That's Jennifer Adler. She's Mr. Bancroft's assistant. The executive producer I was telling you about. You're up after Cally."

"What?"

"Just be yourself and be honest. Remember, they're looking for reality."

"Lord, if that were the case we'd all be in trouble."

"This is serious Stacy. Act normal."

"Don't worry." *Acting normal has been my latest greatest achievement.*

Tara steps away and tends to her other guests. I drink down everything in my glass then head to the bar for another. Jordan approaches me while I wait for the refill.

"Hi, Sweetie," she says, while leaning in to give me air kisses. The alcohol fumes from her breath could catch fire. I hope her interview was first.

"How have you been?" I say.

"Wonderful, dear. Just wonderful. So, what do you think of all this hoopla?"

"I..."

Tara interrupts. "Stacy, this is Jennifer Adler. Jennifer, this is Stacy Troy."

I shake hands with Jennifer. "You can call me Jenny. Shall we have a seat?"

We walk together toward the family room. I sit down where Cally was. The suede underneath is warm and slightly damp. The others must be nervous. Strange, but I don't feel anxious whatsoever.

"Stacy, Tara has told me a little bit about her friends, but there are still some questions I'd like to ask."

"Please."

"How long have you lived in Vegas?"

"Almost ten years."

"So, you didn't grow up with these women?"

"No."

"And what do you think of them?"

"They're my friends. They're good people."

"Do you always get along?"

"Not always."

"Oh."

She scribbles something down on a notepad. "And Tara tells me your husband is a physician?"

"Yes."

"Would he be willing to be on camera?"

"It's something we'd have to discuss."

"Sure. Sure."

She continues to talk, and her mundane line of questioning eats away at my façade of normalcy. I can't help staring at her mouth. As she goes on and on, I imagine the words coming out as rainbow musical notes. It's Mozart's "Queen of the Night," from the *Magic Flute*, only not so lovely.

Jennifer, *you can call me Jenny*, scoots closer to me and leans in. "So what's the story with the cougar? Cally says she's a real kick." Her head tilts to the side and her eyes casually search the kitchen then fixate on something.

I turn around and see Jordan standing next to the bar.

"Ha, I think she might actually be drunk," she says.

"Jordan does a lot of great local charity work."

"Yeah, I heard…her husband Samuel, for one. I guess he landed *his* whale." Jennifer looks down at her notepad and feverishly jots away.

"I'm sorry. Are we done?" I stand up and reach my hand down. "It was nice meeting you Miss Adler." She looks up, takes my hand and shakes it. "I hope you have a good evening, but you'll have to excuse me."

"Yes, of course," she says. "Nice meeting you, too."

I head straight for the bar. Miss Adler remains seated on the couch scribbling down notes.

Cally and Tara immediately come up to me. "Well?" Cally says. "How'd it go?"

"It was fine. I answered all of her ridiculous questions."

"She looked a little shocked or flustered," Tara says. "What did you tell her?"

"What she needed to hear. That's all. Look, I'm really tired. I'm going home."

"Already?" they say in unison.

"You should eat something," Tara says. "Stay for the Botox."

"No really, but thanks for everything. We'll talk again at book club."

"Oh, I'll see you before then," Cally says. "The boys have their mandatory choir session tomorrow at early morning service. Patrick didn't tell you?"

"No. Ugh. Then I've really got to go. You don't have to walk me out, Tara."

We say our goodbyes.

All the way home I hum "The Queen of the Night." I can't get it out of my head, actually. It's as if my brain has been sequestered by an opera aficionado. I've seen it performed less than a handful of times, once in a movie. I don't own the CD, but somehow, I seem to know it.

CHAPTER ELEVEN

The entire mound ignites into a roaring fire. I push the cart and jump out of the way. Noxious fumes, the hissing and crackling become unbearable. Exhausted and out of sorts, I stumble over to an empty parcel of graded land next to the school then fall flat on my back.

Endless plumes of thick black smoke rise and swirl up high in the red sky. I lie still and try hard to distinguish familiar shapes among them. This was a game Patrick and I loved to play when he was a child, only we used fluffy white clouds with an azure background, then.

Suddenly, the ground begins to rumble. Thunderous cracks reverberate as the earth splits apart around me. It's here at last! The impending doom I knew would come. I roll onto my abdomen and attempt to cling against the shifting sands of the desert floor. Not a mile behind the school, across an open lot, terracotta-colored canyons break apart and sink down into massive fissures. The school buildings, the smoldering mound, everything is being swallowed whole. Helpless, I'm forced to watch my shopping cart of tools disappear, along with my purpose. The enormous cross in front of the school is the last thing to submerge.

Perhaps someone or something saw my human smoke signal. Within minutes, I alone lie on an endless plain with one side of my face pressed firmly against the ground. I wait for it to swallow me, too. Everything will be over soon enough, and I will be released from my lonely, tedious, and gruesome duties. I'm not sure how much more I can take picking up the dead.

Minutes pass and still, nothing happens. Maybe this is the fate I'm meant to suffer. I roll onto my back again. Cinnamon swirls of black smoke are all that's left. They begin to merge and rotate—faster and faster. They spin together, forming a massive vortex directly above me. The nose of the funnel cloud comes down as if it were a megaphone I could shout into. I'm unable to open my mouth for a breath, much less to yell for help. All I can do is gaze up through it, and the only thing I see is a void.

The tip comes even closer, until it is mere inches from my face, and then I hear it—faint—a whirring within the spinning smoke particles, almost a whisper.

See.

I look into the darkness behind my eyes. That's where they are. And before I do *See* them, I wake up knowing everything is connected somehow. The nightmares, the new ethereal dreams, and the past life déjà vu experiences, they are all related. Together they're a story, a message, a warning, which is disheartening. I'm unable to discern whether that makes things better or worse. It's like starting all over again, and more terrifying, because I don't know what's coming. Amidst all of my uncertainty, however, I sensed a familiar presence there with me. It was Dr. Light. He was in the void, but he was not alone. He was with them, a part of them. Together we were twenty-seven, and together we felt as one. Maybe the dream scripting works automatically now, Dr. Light always feels close by. Strange, though, I don't remember doing the exercise before falling asleep last night.

As for penning any of this down in a notebook, there is no way. Who is stupid enough to leave evidence of their insanity lying around? Not me. I could describe my experiences to him exactly, if that's what he wants. Everything has become so vivid.

Jon comes into the bedroom carrying two cups of coffee.

"Couldn't you just hook me up with an IV of it?" I say.

"I'm sure it's been tried. How'd you sleep?"

"Great. You?"

"I was out like a light. We were both pretty tired— probably our bodies catching up from the previous night's mishap. You joining us for church this morning?"

"You know about Patrick's mandatory service?"

"Yeah, he told me Friday."

"Well, why didn't he tell me?"

"He probably didn't want to bother you. He says you've been forgetting things lately."

"What? That's ridiculous."

"No. *That's* a teenager."

"Yeah, whatever."

"I'll get him up when you're done with the shower. If you need anything, I'm in the office." Jon turns around and walks toward the door.

"Thanks for the coffee."

Dressed and ready to go, I head downstairs and pour myself another cup before they come down. By no means are we constant churchgoers, but Patrick's Lutheran school requires we attend and Patrick participate in several services a year. The kids can choose to sing, perform in a short Bible story narrative, or assist in running stage operations. It's great for students interested in drama or film production. Patrick was ecstatic he got to help run the stage lights last year, even though he wound up with a minor second degree burn on his left hand.

These performances give the church a chance to show parents what their tuition dollars are being used for. And if the show is a success—which it usually is—it's the perfect opportunity for them to ask for more.

These occasional Sundays are the only instances Patrick is ever on time. The very thought of walking into service after it's underway puts the fear of God into him, or maybe it's more the fear of embarrassment.

Ten minutes early, Patrick takes a seat in the back row and Jon follows. This satisfies Patrick's concern we will make a scene somehow, and then he can easily hide. It also fulfills Jon's desire for a quick getaway afterward.

Service begins with everyone standing up and greeting their neighbor. This is also when I notice Cally, Bill, and Kyle coming in one of the side entrances. I nonchalantly try to wave them over, but they don't see me. They're on the complete opposite side of the church.

"Give it up, Mom," Patrick whispers. "You can talk after."

"You're not the boss of me. Besides, shouldn't you be doing something?"

"I'm ushering at the *end* of service. Telling people to have coffee and donuts."

"Does that mean we have to stay for the whole thing?" Jon says.

"Yes, Dad."

Jon pulls his cell phone from his suit pocket and puts it into *silent* mode. No doubt he'll be checking football scores all morning.

Pastor Dean starts his sermon with a prayer. He is the youngest pastor I've ever seen. Can't be much more than thirty. Tall and handsome, with brown hair and brown eyes. Very lucky to get a large congregation like this at his age. He was merely supposed to be the interim pastor, while the former one was being charged with embezzling money from the church and school, but everybody liked him, so he was voted to stay on. I'm sure it wasn't the first time a clergyman was charged for embezzling in Vegas. It's not an uncommon business practice in the *Wild West*. Temptation *is* the foundation on which this city was built.

Pastor Dean's youth gives his sermons vitality though, and he preaches current topics. The students love him and so do most of the parents. He's clever, knows he won't get donations preaching to us about living in sin. I'm sure pastors in other parts of the country would be shocked by his sermons, but that's what makes Vegas so unique. We all cater for a living here—Jon to his surgeons—and me to his career. In the end, we hope it equals success.

Seated after singing a song, we're then told to bow our heads once more in prayer. Absorbed in my own private appeals to God, I hardly notice the deepening in Pastor Dean's voice. Then all of a sudden, he is loud. Yelling and rattling the pews. His every word, harsh and intense, resonates within my chest.

I look up to the stage. A strange man stands behind the podium. He is old, gruff, dressed head to toe in heavy black. He points his finger out across the congregation. "The Wicked shall be cast into Hell!" People quiver in their seats. Then he shakes his fist like a madman. "There is no salvation for sinners!" Saliva spews from his angry mouth.

The massive stained glass cross behind the stage is gone, the towering flower arrangements, too. This is not my church. It's smaller, simpler—old—antique.

I'm in the front row, sitting on a wobbly unpadded bench. Jon and Patrick are gone! Seated next to me are two, young blue-eyed girls—identical twins. They're wearing plain clothes, a heavy navy fabric—wool. Their hair is tucked up under puffy white bonnets, but several loose ringlets of curly blonde hair have spilled out over their shoulders. They simultaneously turn their heads and smile at me. I return their gestures then calmly look down. My colonial clothing matches theirs, but underneath, something tight binds my chest, I can scarcely take in a breath. The air in the church is suddenly hot and stifling.

The child closest to me reaches her hand out across my lap. I gently take it in mine. It is tiny, fragile, and warm. Suddenly, the preacher slams his fist against the pulpit. I jump up from the bench, releasing her delicate hold.

The collection plate flies from the usher's grasp, then comes crashing down to the aisle with one hell of a clang. Envelopes, bills, and loose change scatter everywhere between the pews.

Jon gets up to help the usher retrieve the donations. All of the present day church members turn around and glare. A few others rise to assist collecting the money. Jon looks at me and mouths. "Are you okay?"

I nod yes. But I'm getting warmer, still. I have to relax. Breathe.

Patrick is lying low across the bench.

"Get up," I tell him.

He shakes his head no.

"If you don't, I'll yell," I whisper.

Patrick coolly sits up but looks away.

After the men finish gathering the last of the stray coins, Jon returns to my side, and we sing with the rest of the congregation.

"Sure you're all right?" he says.

"It was an accident. I wasn't paying attention and he startled me."

Service can't end fast enough, but then we have to stick around while Patrick encourages people to stay. Cally, Bill, and Kyle sneak out the way they came in without stopping by to say hello. Pastor Dean shakes my hand on his way out, but he keeps his eyes on Jon and avoids talking to me.

I'm done with this—ready to give Dr. Light the go-ahead—but only if he looks normal at our next appointment. Geez, why do I have to be going crazy now? Hypnosis, Shock Therapy, Acupuncture, I don't care what he wants to do. I can't let my nightmares happen in the middle of the day, and even worse, in public. He's the only one who can help. A little peace of mind is all I'm asking for, and right now, my only repose comes when I hear those bell chimes.

Patrick stays quiet and keeps to his room for most of the afternoon. Jon is outside again, but I think he snuck across the street to watch the game at the neighbors' house. When I'm done with *Memoirs of a Spa Junkie*, I go upstairs and get ready for book club.

I can't stop wondering how it will feel to be hypnotized. It could possibly be the answer to all my questions. Take me where I fear to go—show me what I fear to *See*. The excitement makes my skin tingle, and the unnerving stirs up nausea.

As I'm pulling down the driveway, Jon walks out into the street from the neighbors' garage. He motions at me to put the window down.

"Toni and George want to know if you're still planning on hosting the neighborhood Christmas party. Toni reminded me that you volunteered for it last year."

"Yeah, I guess." I look over Jon's shoulder and see them talking in their garage, pretending to watch the game. Theirs is a four-car unit they transformed into an extension of the game room. It's complete with a ping-pong table, dartboard, plasma screens, and a refrigerator stocked with an endless supply of beer—a real party palace.

"Toni said she'd be happy to help if you need any ideas or suggestions."

"Tell her I said thanks." She looks over, and I wave. "And ask her what day, evening, whatever time works best."

"Sure you want to take this on?"

"I'll have it catered. It'll be fine."

"Okay. Well, have fun, and say hello to the girls." He leans in and kisses me.

Before driving away, I wave to Toni and George again.

God, I'm tired. Now I understand why people take vacations over the holidays, but really, the thought of dealing with overcrowded airports and weather delays is just as exhausting. Normally, I would savor overbooked schedule challenges, but I guess I'm not quite the same anymore.

Cally answers the door dressed like a maharani.

"Oh wow. You look great," I say.

"Come in, Sweetie." She motions me in. Sheer, light blue fabric sways back and forth over her arms. Numerous bangles clink around her wrists with every move.

"We weren't supposed to dress up, were we?"

"No. I've had this genie costume stored in the attic, and I thought it would be fun."

"That's a relief. I was starting to feel like I'd forgotten."

We both look down at her chest bulging up from the sequined bikini top. "Okay, maybe it's a little much," she says. "Help yourself to some wine. I'm going to change."

"No, Cally. It's cute. Really, don't change."

"Thank God you said something before Tara and Jordan showed up."

"But I didn't say anything."

She shuffles down the hall barefoot with bells around her ankles jingling like keys. I'm glad she can't see me giggling. I head to the kitchen for some wine. It's going to be an interesting evening.

"Is Gail here?" I say. She's always early and usually here by now.

"No," Cally yells, from her master bedroom. "She's not coming."

"Why?"

"She wouldn't tell me."

"Hmm, that's strange," I say to myself.

"Yes it is," Cally says. She's suddenly in the kitchen.

"Hey, I didn't hear you walk by."

We simultaneously look down. She is still barefoot.

"Ugh," she growls. "Be right back."

The doorbell rings while she puts on a pair of shoes. "I'll get that."

"Thanks!"

Tara and Jordan arrive. They step into the foyer like a whirlwind of perfume, hairspray, shrill greetings, and idle chatter.

Cally joins us wearing a new pair of boots.

"Ooh, nice," Tara says.

"I got them on sale at Breanna's."

"Why didn't you call? I hate missing her sales," Tara whines.

"Get over it," Jordan says. "Let's move it. I need a glass of wine."

We all walk to the kitchen. I hang back and watch them eye each other's clothes and accessories. Strange, it's something I've never noticed them do before—maybe because I'm usually right up there with them.

"Where's Gail?" Tara says.

"She's not coming."

"Good, then we can talk," Tara says.

"About what?" Cally says with a grin.

"Don't say a word until I get some wine." Jordan hurries into the kitchen.

Everybody fills their glasses. Then we go into the family room and sit down on the couch and chairs.

"Thank God you didn't do those stupid floor pillows again," Jordan says.

"Okay, Tara. Tell us now," Cally says.

"Well…" Tara lowers her head but can't hide her wide smile. "We're in."

Cally screams, then they all bounce up and down on the cushions and exchange hugs. I watch wine swirl and bobble up to their rims, but nobody spills a single drop.

"Isn't that great news?" Jordan says.

"Yeah. Great." I smile.

"You don't seem very excited."

"Of course she's excited," Cally says. "She's so excited, she's in shock. Right, Stacy?"

"Yeah, actually, I guess I am in shock. What did Jenny say about us, Tara?"

"Well, she just *loved* you, Stacy. Said you're like the down-to-earth one among us, but we all knew that."

"Oh my God," Cally says. "This is so exciting."

"And it is, but remember." She sighs. "We still have to wait on the other group."

"Who are they? Anybody we know?"

"Some of the gals from Green Valley, *otherwise* known as Henderson," Jordan says.

Cally groans. "So it's East Valley versus West Valley. God I hope they pick us or we'll never hear the end of it."

"No kidding," Tara says. "I don't like the girls over there in *Greenless* Valley. They're so over-the-top."

"Let's not worry too much about it now. It's still fantastic news. Let's make this a mini celebration," Cally says. She gets up from the couch. "Does anybody need a refill?"

Jordan and Tara raise their empty glasses. "Hell, I'll just

put the bottles on the coffee table," Cally says. She walks into the kitchen.

"What about the book?" I say.

"To hell with that, Stacy, this is overwhelming," Jordan says.

"Which means you didn't read it," Tara says.

"Shush."

Cally comes back from the kitchen with wine and gift bags. She sets the bottles on coasters then hands out the bags.

"Here we go," Jordan says. "What'd you get?"

"Oh, how lovely," Tara says. She pulls a long silk scarf from her bag. "And what's this?" She holds up a piece of paper. "Oh yeah, spa day. Thanks Cally. Clever of you to give us massage appointments to go with the book."

"You're welcome," Cally says. "I knew you guys would like these."

"Excellent idea. Thank you," Jordan says.

"Thank you," I tell her. "This fabric is really nice."

"It's hand-spun silk," Cally says. "They were dip-dyed by hand too."

I take mine out of the bag and wrap it around my neck. It's cool to the touch and dyed in soft shades of blue—very calming.

"Beautiful," Jordan says. Hers is red, which is perfect—fiery.

Tara's is orange—spicy.

Cally wanders off then comes back to the family room with a purple one wrapped around her hip—regal.

"Hey, that's a good idea," Tara says.

Looking around the room, I can't help thinking about how much we suddenly resemble an aged, Eighties all-girl band. It makes me laugh.

"What's so funny?" Cally says.

"Nothing. I'm just tired." I rise from the couch.

"No. Don't go."

"Besides, I've got to talk to Jon about the show. I haven't said anything to him yet."

"Oh, no," Jordan says. "You don't think he'd *not* agree to do it, do you?"

"I don't know."

"Then you better go and talk to him right now," Tara says. "I want everything ready to go as soon as we hear from them again."

"Don't worry, guys. You all know Jon. He'll be perfectly fine with it."

"You're right," Cally says. "But you should talk with him." She stands and waits for me to get up. Then she walks me to the door.

"Thanks again for the gifts."

"No worries. You just get some rest, and make sure you talk to Jon. I know this week's going to be insane, but call me."

"I will. Bye."

Their obsession with this show has been both a curse and a godsend. It's great because they are totally preoccupied, and it maintains their focus away from me. It's bad only if it comes to fruition. Either way, I have to talk to Jon about it before he finds out from one of them.

I get ready for bed then take one of the Valiums and turn out the light in the bathroom. When I've finished Dr. Light's mental exercises, Jon comes into the bedroom.

"How'd it go?" he says.

"What?"

"The review."

"Oh. We didn't talk about the book."

"I knew it. It's just another excuse for you to get together with the girls and gossip."

"No. Normally, we do talk about the books. It's just that they're excited about this show they might get on."

"You mean that *Housewives* show?"

"Yeah, how'd you…?"

"Bill told me about it at the game. He doesn't think they'll get it. Stiff competition from Green Valley, I guess. He didn't seem worried."

"Really? But Cally is so excited."

"Maybe he didn't tell her."

"Why?"

"Well, if she's that excited, he probably doesn't want to let her down."

"Still, I don't think that's right."

"I don't either, but it's none of our business."

"You wouldn't hide something like that from me, would you?"

"No. Would you?"

"No."

He kisses me then turns out the light. I'm a liar, and I think he knows it, but I can't say anything yet. Maybe when it's all over and everything is okay, I will tell him what happened. We can look back on it one day and laugh. Right now, I'm not so sure if it's me that really feels this way or the Valium. Like the other night when I took one before the party. I wonder if Valium has hallucinogenic effects.

CHAPTER TWELVE

Through the nighttime hours when sleep comes to most people, I waited, and it never came for me. There were no nightmares, no lights, or bell tones. I spent most of the time contemplating the possible relationship between all of the craziness, then got out of bed this morning with no definitive answers. I also thought of Dr. Light and his wide-eyed hypnosis obsession. I dwelled on his comment about hypnosis being the key that could unlock the mysteries in my head. I worried my mind might know about his plan, be afraid, and produce the worst nightmare ever. I'm glad it didn't happen, and although the quiet night would have been cherished by most people in my condition, it left with me with only more unease—wondering why I was granted a reprieve. I wanted my thoughts clear for today, and despite the lack of sleep, there is some unexplained, newfound energy. I feel abuzz.

Jon comes into the bathroom with morning coffee and sets it on the counter next to me.

"Thanks."

He smiles then leans against the wall with his arms crossed. He appears a little tense.

"What is it?" I say.

"You still seeing that psychiatrist?"

"Yeah. Why?" I turn around. He has my full attention.

"Just wondering. It's nothing bad, really. Actually, it's good you're talking with someone. You haven't had any nightmares in a few days, and that's a good thing."

"Jon, please. I can tell something's on your mind. What is it?"

He exhales loudly. "Our marriage hasn't come up, has it?"

"What? No."

"Not that I'm worried, I mean, but sometimes it comes up, and I'd hope that you'd talk to me about it first, if there are problems."

I get up from the bench, walk over, and wrap my arms around him. "Of course I would, but there's nothing to talk about. You're one of the only normal things keeping me together."

"I'm good with that." He kisses my forehead. "I don't know what I'd do without you."

"You'd be fine."

"I'm not so sure."

"I am. You'd better go now, or you'll be late."

"Love you," he says.

"Love you, too. Have a good day. And Jon…"

"Yeah."

"Don't ever worry about us."

He smiles then leaves.

After Patrick's drop off, I stop for some coffee then head straight for Dr. Light's office. I'm sure an hour will not be enough time to say, ask, and tell, everything I must. God, I hope he is really Dr. Light this morning and not the monster I thought I saw lurking in the hallways at the party. Of course he isn't—what a ridiculous thought. Apparently, it is more difficult for me to admit I'm crazy than imagine that he's some monster. This is a dilemma. I *need* him—and I need to keep my head together, so he can help me figure out what's wrong with it.

Traffic is slow moving along the beltway, giving me time to organize my thoughts. During complete stops, I look out across the valley—distracted by the landscape. Nine years ago, this same drive was flanked by barren desert. A multitude of housing developments have filled in the empty space, many with homes available for purchase— entire neighborhoods waiting to be sold.

The desert stalks silent in the background—slowly creeping—it will inevitably retake its claim. Above ground, it appears lifeless other than the occasional Joshua tree and desert bramble, but under the surface it is teeming with organisms and underground rivers where species of fish exist nowhere else on Earth. Life clinging to the edge of survival in a hostile environment, and yet, it does. Desert is a quiet force compared to the ocean, but it's still a force. Something about it reminds me of my nightmares, like it's trying to tell me something, wants me to *See*. Maybe *I am* the only one that will be left in the end, struggling to exist.

A whirlwind of dust picks up in a vacant lot and spins sand across a roadway toward several houses. That is how the desert will take back what belongs to it—with dust devils—thousands of grains at a time.

Lost once more in random solitude while driving, I'm suddenly in front of Dr. Light's building again with no idea how I got here. These blank memory lapses can't be safe, but I have never been in an accident.

From the entryway, I follow the larger rusty vein in the marble floor to his office. It seems to remain constant, while the other branches appear to change place whenever I look down and take notice. Nature is truly amazing in what it is capable of creating.

"Stacy. How are you this morning?"

My heart stops. Dr. Light is standing in the doorway waiting. Strange, I don't remember knocking. I can't look him in the eyes. I feel myself begin to tremble. I have to stop, before I turn around and run out of here. *Remember… you need him.* I take in a deep breath, look up into his eyes. "I'm okay. Sort of…" They are big, black, and vacuous, but normal for him, like they've always been. I exhale with relief. "I've got a lot to talk about this morning."

"Good. Let's head back to my office."

He doesn't look anything like the monster I saw at the hospital cocktail party. I'm almost embarrassed to ask. I follow several steps behind him, unable to shake a sense of déjà vu. Everything is exactly as it was the first day I came. Even his clothes, they're always the same.

"Dr. Light, before I forget. Were you at the Red Rock Hospital mixer Saturday night?"

He stops dead in his tracks and I behind him. *Please, oh please…don't turn around and be the monster.*

"No," he says, without looking back. "I was on call Saturday at the University Hospital. Most of my night was spent treating a suicide patient."

Another sigh of relief escapes me. "I could've sworn I saw you."

"Perhaps it was a doppelganger." He turns to open his door then looks back at me and smiles.

I clench my fists to prevent a shudder. His smile is unnerving, unnatural, like it hurts him.

"Come in," he says. "Let's begin."

I cautiously step in, then walk directly to the chaise and lie down. For the life of me, I can't seem to gather my thoughts, or remember what it was I needed to talk about. Maybe the extra coffee stop wasn't such a good idea.

"I'd like to try the hypnosis." It's the only thing I manage to blurt out.

"Excellent." He drags his chair over and positions himself behind my head.

When I look up, his eyes are all I see. Large hypnotic pinwheels that they are, I'm halfway entranced already.

"Wait. You're going to start right now?" I say.

"Yes."

"You're a hypnotist, too?"

"Hypnotherapy is one of my specialties."

"But…I'm not ready."

"Stacy, there's nothing to fear. Soon you'll be able to see."

"Wait. What was that?"

He puts his hands on either side of my head and holds them firmly in place. "Be still. Take a deep breath. Close your eyes. If you're frightened, imagine me with you."

I already do. His touch is soothing, his voice euphonic. I close my eyes and listen.

"Good," he whispers. "Now relax and breathe. Listen to the sound of my voice, concentrate. As you listen to the sound of my voice, I want your body to sink deeper into relaxation. Visualize yourself from head to toe in the color red. Then visualize my words moving in small blue ripples that slowly and gently pass through my fingertips and enter your head. They push the red out through your toes and leave behind their blue."

His hands turn frigid. It stings and spreads like brain freeze. "It's cold."

"No matter what you feel, your eyes will remain closed until you hear me count the numbers one-two-three in that exact procession. Do you understand?"

"Yes."

"Where is the blue now?"

"My neck." I gulp, fearing saliva could freeze in the middle of my throat. "Can't breathe."

"Relax. You can breathe just fine. Slow it down. Inhale through your nose."

"My chest." I feel naked in the middle of Antarctica. Every breath is a chore, inhaling sharp crystals of ice. Stabbing cold from the inside out.

"You're doing well, Stacy. The blue relaxes your muscles, makes them feel heavy."

Numb too. By the time the Arctic chill reaches my ankles I'm nearly paralyzed. The last bit of red passes through my toes. I wiggle them one last time.

Explosive shrills penetrate the blue in thousands of arrows. I'm like an ice sheet cracking apart. My body shakes uncontrollably.

"Stop." The word comes through my gnashed teeth.

"Take a deep breath. Relax."

The violent tremors fade, but the piercing squeals go up and down as if my head were a radio trying to tune into a station. Then it finally finds a channel and settles. I hear the bell chimes from a distance, but they're not really bells. They sound electronic, like the tones in my dream.

"There's music," I say.

"Yes. Music. Does it bother you?"

"No. It's familiar."

"Good. Now I want you to think about the visions you've had recently. As you go through these visions, I want you to find the earliest past life experience you can remember. Visualize it, describe it to me. Continue listening to the sound of my voice, and picture it moving in blue ripples through you. Every one that passes relaxes you deeper, still."

"I'm playing hide and seek with the other children."

"Stacy, describe the memory to me as if you were watching a movie. You're not a participant, you're merely an observer. Do you understand?"

"Yes."

"Now continue. What do you see?"

"Stone walls, big columns, and long billowing fabric."

"Where do you think you are?"

"Egypt."

"No. Look again. What do you see on the walls?"

"Linear shadows."

"Reach out and touch one."

"It feels like sand. There are some pictographs."

"You're in early Sumer."

"Sumer?"

"One of man's earliest civilizations."

"I don't know…Sumer, but something tells me you're right. I think it's the tones."

"Yes, the tones. Listen to them. Comprehend what they tell you. What do you see now?"

"I'm running down a dimly lit corridor then suddenly, I stop. There's darkness beyond a doorway ahead. I don't want to go inside."

"Don't be afraid. Remember you're only watching this girl from a distance. Picture her in front of you, and follow her in."

"The little girl likes to hide in here. It's a cool and dry place. Little shell-shaped lamps sit on ledges everywhere in the room. The dim light flickers, and long shadows dance on the walls. Golden statues rest on shelves that have been carved out of stone."

"Yes. What else?"

"More of the pictographs, symbols."

"It's their written language."

"Tiny orbs of light whiz by. They flit all around us. They fly through her hair and dance around her head. She's not scared of them, though. She knows what they are."

"What are they?"

"Her friends."

"How do you know?"

"She's talking to them."

"What are they saying?"

"They talk in the electronic tones. I hear them. Her lips don't move, but waves of color move through the air back and forth between the orbs and the little girl."

"Listen. Focus. What do they say?"

"I don't understand."

"You can. Listen. Remember…"

"It's vital. Something's going to happen. They must all leave right now."

My heart races with their urgency. Thunderous red heartbeats pump through the blue.

"The sound of my voice continues to relax you. Slow your heart rate back down."

"I can't."

"What's happening?"

"The little girl, she's crying. She wants to go, but she doesn't know how to join them."

I cry with her. My heart still races. Warm tears stream down my temples and melt away the blue ice.

"No. Not yet. Stay with me. Tell me more."

"The lights, they close in around her. She looks up at me and smiles. My god, she sees me. She's looking directly at me."

"Stay calm. Breathe."

"She's pointing at me. Her fingertip glows with a brilliant white light. It's coming toward me—the light! My eyes! It's in my eyes!"

The impact forces my head to buck against the chaise. "One-two-three."

My eyelids pop open. Dr. Light is in his chair next to me writing in his notepad.

"What happened?" I say.

He sighs heavy. "You don't remember?"

"Yeah, I remember everything. I'm just wondering why you woke me."

"The time."

"What? But I even came early." I hold up my wrist and look at my watch. It's dead on eleven. "That can't be, and how would you know? You don't have a watch on, and there are no clocks in here."

"It doesn't matter."

"Well, it's weird—bizarre. As a matter of fact, everything seems a little off about this place. I *have* noticed. And when are we going to talk about what I saw?"

"Tomorrow. I promise. But please, you have to go. You must trust me."

"Of course I trust you. I have no other choice, even though things feel like they're getting worse. I'm crazy Dr. Light, and I need your help."

"You're not crazy. I will explain everything when we…when *I* can. I'm sorry, but…"

"Yeah, yeah, tomorrow, then." I get up slow. Still shaking off remnants of the frost. He stays close behind as I head toward the door. "There's no need to walk me out." His footsteps stop short behind me, but I continue. With my hand poised on the exit, and without looking back, I tell him. "You were there you know, Doctor. You were one of the lights."

CHAPTER THIRTEEN

'm out of my freaking mind, and Dr. Light is either humoring me for the money, or he is certifiable too. What was I thinking seeing a shrink, then letting him hypnotize me? Oh yeah…I was desperate. Still am, and even more so now, because I'm curious. During these sessions I've tried hard to ignore the unusual things, but it hasn't been easy. I guess I finally lost it today when I told him about the bizarre instances of *time* that occur whenever I'm at his office. Hopefully Dr. Light will forgive my outburst.

Even with all the craziness, the really bad nightmares don't happen as often, and yes, they've been supplanted by outlandish dreams, but at least *they* are not horrifying. Not yet, anyway.

Halfway home, I realize the faint sound of the bell tones hasn't completely disappeared. They continue playing in the background inside the car, or maybe, it's just in my ears, my head, or all three. A lightning-fast shiver runs through me, and I grip the steering wheel until my knuckles turn white. All the hairs on my arms stick straight up. I watch them lie back down, but the chill stays with me. The *imaginary* frigid blue that Dr. Light filled me with earlier comes to mind. I think it's still inside me, but it feels darker than blue and deeper than black.

My cell phone rings loud through the car speakers, startling me. I thumb the answer button on the steering wheel.

"Hello."

"Hey babe, what're you doing?" Jon says

"Driving home."

"From where?"

"The grocery store."

"Turn around and head East on Sahara."

"What for?"

"I called GenLabs and scheduled some bloodwork."

"Right now? Don't you want to be there?"

"They're just going to draw it up then give me the results. Please, you promised you'd go. I'm also working on getting you in to see Terry Swanson, today."

"Isn't that the guy you told me is a complete asshole?"

"Yeah. He is, but he's also the best ENT in town. Don't make any afternoon plans just in case I get you an appointment."

Oh geez, it's starting already—his need to be in full medical control. Every muscle in my body tenses.

"Hey, you still there?" he says.

"Yeah."

"Just do it, okay?"

"I will."

"I'll get back to you about Dr. Swanson. Keep your cell with you. GenLabs is on the corner of Sahara and Oakey, remember?"

"Yeah, fine."

"Bye. Love you."

"Bye." My thumb hangs up before I can tell him I love him back.

I exit the freeway and zigzag my way through streets heading north. There's a lot of traffic and a stoplight every fifty feet along the main roads. It's lunch hour, this will be a while.

Parking at GenLabs is awful, too. I drive around and wait for somebody to pull out. This place does one hell of a business. I wish I'd thought of it. It's an ingenious idea really, to have healthy patients get their lab work done here instead of in the hospital.

Inside, the place is small. The lobby is standing room only. The rest is sort of set up like a doctor's office, except for the pharmacy-type window hiding the rest of the lab. I step up and tell the receptionist my name.

"Please, move to your left and wait till you hear your name called. Stand away from the door. It swings open. There are chairs if you prefer to sit."

In the far corner of the room, there are four cheap plastic chairs, but they look disgusting, and I wouldn't sit down even if they weren't already taken. The swinging door is to the left of the window. Different technicians step out in short white lab coats and call people back.

A young man comes through. "Mrs. Stacy Troy?" Other patients, who have been waiting longer than me, sigh in unison.

"Yes." I walk toward him.

"Come with me, ma'am."

I suppose I am a ma'am compared to him, but it's not earning him any points with me. He doesn't look much older than Patrick.

He keeps a swift stride as he rushes me down a dingy tiled hall, lit with fluorescent lights. A surreal glow clings to everything white, radiating a *heavenly* vibe. It must frighten the really sick patients. Hell it's creeping me out, and those damn chimes in my head aren't helping one bit.

"Busy today?" I say.

"We're always busy, ma'am."

"I bet."

We round a corner, and he leads me down another hall, to a tiny room. There's an old desk in the middle, the kind from grade school where the chair is welded on.

"Have a seat there. I'll be right back."

I sit down but keep my purse on my lap. I'm sure sick germs are crawling all over this place.

The young man whips back into the room carrying a little basket filled with various items including needles, glass tubes, and a handful of paperwork. He has a pair of those clear, protective glasses resting on top of his head. Suddenly, he reminds me of the Easter Bunny—a more demented version, minus the large pink bowtie. I have a picture of Patrick when he was three, crying on the white rabbit's lap in one of those cheesy mall portraits.

He flips through the papers. "Looks like Dr. Troy's ordered several tests, Mrs. Troy. Are you related?" He digs around in his basket then puts a few things on the desk: a tourniquet, a rubber ball, five glass test tubes with different color stoppers, and this plastic thing with a long needle at the end.

Oh, and he's a genius too. "Yes. He's my husband. It's okay that he ordered the tests, right?" *Because I would be more than happy to wait for a real doctor to order them.*

"Yeah, docs do it for family members all the time."

He yanks a pair of gloves from the basket then snaps them on, filling the air with a cloud of fine powder. "Just lay your arm out across the desk." He wraps the tourniquet around it then places the rubber ball in the palm of my hand. "Squeeze that several times, please." He slaps my forearm then slides the long needle into a bulging vein. One by one, he pushes the glass tubes into the plastic end where there is another needle, filling them all.

"Jesus, that's a lot of tubes."

"It's just what the doctor ordered." He smiles, but I give him my *I'm not amused* look. "Lots of blood tests," he adds.

"Does it look normal?"

"Your blood? Yeah, I guess. I mean it doesn't look anemic or anything. Sometimes that makes the blood look orange. It's not too thick or thin. Your husband will be able to tell you more when he gets the results."

"How long will that take?"

"He'll have them before the end of the day."

"That fast?"

"Oh, yeah. We crank 'em out." He puts a wad of gauze over the needle then pulls it out of my arm. "Press firm for a minute. I'll be right back."

He comes back and pulls a piece of tape tautly over the gauze. "Keep that on for about an hour. Then you can take it off. And here's your copy of the paperwork. Just bring it up to the window on your way out, thanks." He grabs his little basket and whisks away.

I maneuver myself out of the desk then head back down the hall. After getting through the insurance paperwork and payment thirty minutes later, I finally get to leave. Hungry and lightheaded, I head to the nearest grocery store and buy a few things, including a sandwich I devour in the car still parked in the lot.

I'm cleaning up the mess of crumbs and my cell rings again. Ugh…it's Jon. I debate for a few seconds whether or not to pick it up.

"Yes," I answer.

"I got you an appointment with Dr. Swanson, but you've got to be there in an hour."

"What! What about Patrick? It's almost pick-up—"

"I'll call the school and leave a message that you might be a little late."

"This is bullshit! I've got groceries in the car."

"Calm down. You promised. You've got a few minutes to bring them home. And Pat will be fine. He can hang out in the library and do his homework till you're done. Did you make it to GenLabs?"

"Yes. And where is Dr. Swanson's office?"

"It's in the medical building directly across from Red Rock Hospital. You'll find his suite number on the wall next to the elevators."

"Fine, I better get going, and don't forget to call the school."

"I'll do it as soon as we hang up."

"That would be now." This time I'm fully aware I thumb the button and hang up on him. I'm sure it was on purpose last time, too, but a little more subconscious than now.

I scrunch up the sandwich paper and toss it out the window into a trash can, then round the parking lot and head home.

As I'm waiting for the gate to open, Toni, the neighbor from across the street, pulls up behind me and taps her horn. I wave back at her, then pull up the driveway, grab the bag of groceries from the passenger's seat and head into the garage.

"Hey Stacy," Toni yells from the curb.

I turn around and she's parked along the bottom of the driveway, waving her arm at me through the open car window.

"Hi Toni," I holler down. "Give me a sec to throw this stuff in the fridge."

Christ, there goes my pit stop. I turn back around, sigh deep, and roll my eyes Cally-style. Then I open up the garage refrigerator and toss the bag on a shelf. They're just some fresh herbs for the turkey, but still, I would like to keep them refrigerated. It's late fall and nearly seventy-six degrees outside, which means eighty plus in the garage, and ninety in my car if it's parked in the sun. They definitely would have wilted in there.

I grab a bottle of water then walk down the driveway to Toni.

"Hi Stacy, haven't seen you out in a while. How have you been?"

"Good. Busy. My parents are coming for Thanksgiving."

"Yeah, my grandparents will be visiting for a week. I just wanted to let you know that I took a census for the neighborhood Christmas party, and it looks like the evening of the seventeenth will work for nearly everybody."

"Oh, yeah. Thanks for doing that. I'll get the invitations out around the first."

"Do you need any help with the food?"

"No. I've decided to have it catered."

"By who?"

"Rosemary."

"If you do it through Tiesto's, I might be able to get you a deal. I know the owners."

"No, that's okay. But thanks. Jon prefers Rosemary."

"Oh—what about decorations?"

"Decorations?"

"Yeah, the table set up and stuff like that?"

"I'll just have my holiday decorator do it when he plans the outside, it'll be fine."

"Okay, well, if you need any help, you know where to find me."

"Thanks again, but I've got to go. I'm running late for an appointment."

"Don't let me keep you. Bye." She circles around to her own driveway.

I get back into the car and pull away. The dash and seats are warm, but my inner core remains a solid block of ice. On the outside, I feel toasty, irritated, and I can't get those fucking tones out of my head. The phone rings as I'm putting the windows down.

What now!

It's Cally.

"Hi Sweetie," she says. "Dinner tomorrow night at Chopsteaks, seven o'clock. We've got a VIP table, so don't say no."

"Uh…I don't know. Let me ask Jon."

"I need the answer by tonight. I'm sure he'll be up for it."

"You're right, but let me double check, okay. I'll call you later."

"Bye."

I slide my thumb over the hang up button. "Shit. Shit. Shit." I squeeze the steering wheel.

"Hello…Stacy? You there? It's Tara."

Crap, she must have been holding on the other line. "Hi, Tara, sorry about that."

"No problem. Everything okay? I just wanted to give you a heads up. Cally might be calling you for a dinner invite tomorrow night at Chopsteaks."

"Oh?"

"She's got a VIP table. Anthony and I were supposed to go, but he's got some important meeting he's stuck with."

"Well, thanks for the warning."

"You should do it. The food is good."

"I'll think about it. Right now, I've got to go. Enjoy the holiday. I'll call you after Thanksgiving."

"Do you guys have big plans? Both of our families are coming in, but there's plenty of room at the table if you'd like to join us."

"That's really sweet Tara, thanks, but my parents will be here."

"Well, if you change your mind just give me call. You know your folks are more than welcome to join us, too."

"Okay, thanks again. Bye." I hang up before she can say anything else.

The tones, the calls, these appointments, everything—I'm ready to scream, speed up, drive into a wall.

An icy chill grips my chest. It slowly spreads through me in rippled waves of blue. Over the music playing in my head, I hear Dr. Light's voice telling me to be calm and relax. I take in a deep breath and exhale. For a split second, I swear I see a white puff of air come out of my mouth, the way it does when it's frigid out.

CHAPTER FOURTEEN

Feeling a restrained sense of calm, I drive safely and head north on Town Center Drive. After the third roundabout, I turn off toward Red Rock Hospital Road.

The medical offices building looks exactly like the hospital. They're both vertical rectangles, built with bricks in varied shades of sienna. Everything looks the same in Summerlin. By code, all buildings must be constructed to mimic the surrounding desertscape. Also by law, no billboards are permitted. To skirt this, some idiot genius created billboard trucks. They drive around with pictures of half-naked women on them and phone numbers made up with as many sixty-nines that they can fit in. It's ludicrous. The only place allowed to have a huge lit marquee in Summerlin is the Red Rock Casino, and that was all politics.

It's later in the day, so there is a skeleton crew left for office staff. Up front, I see only one receptionist, and she looks like she's had a rough day. Her hair must have been up in a bun at some point, but most of it has fallen out around her shoulders. Several pens are stuck through what is left of the bun at different angles, making it look like an old space satellite.

"Hi, I'm Stacy Troy—here to see Dr. Swanson."

"Dr. Swanson's gone, you'll have to reschedule, but there's an order for a CAT scan. Come around and I'll get you ready."

"Are you the only one here?"

"Yeah, just call me secretary, slash, nurse, Dr. Betty."

"Sorry you had to stay."

"I've got to be here anyway, might as well keep busy."

I nonchalantly glance at the badge hanging around her neck, and her name really is Betty. She leads me to a small exam room with a short metal sitting stool and a paper-padded table. "You can leave your bra and panties on, but take off all your clothes and jewelry. Here's a patient gown for you. Put it on backwards and tie it up front. They'll be shooting your head mostly, but it's important you're comfortable."

"They?" She makes it sound as though I'll be up against a firing squad.

"Yeah, the CT & MRI techs on the first floor."

I remember seeing the sign on my way in. This is turning into a perpetual disaster. I never should have given Jon any medical leeway. As soon as Betty leaves, I get out of my clothes and into the gown. She comes back a few minutes later and lightly taps on the door.

"Come in," I say.

She walks in and opens a cabinet underneath the sink. "You can put your purse in here."

I hesitate, unsure I want to put my couture Dior in there, but she seems pretty intent.

"Don't worry," she says. "It'll be safe."

I'm more concerned about the bag, than what's inside. I place my purse away from the pipes, in a spot that looks relatively clean. Then Betty closes the cabinet door. "Now follow me," she says, as she walks back up to the reception area. "Here are the orders. Give these to the gal at the front desk. I'll see you in about an hour."

"An hour?"

"Sometimes longer. I don't know how busy they are down there today."

Furious now, and wanting to send Jon a hate text, I pat around for my cell phone.

"You left your phone in your purse, I hope," she says.

"Yeah, I did."

"You can't get a good signal down there with all those machines going, anyway." She opens the door for me. "Go back to the elevators. First floor, you can't miss it."

"Thanks," I mumble on my way out.

I look over the orders and can barely make out the word, head, possibly the word sinus. Wow, Dr. Swanson's handwriting is atrocious. I'm amazed anything right gets done without some sort of verbal affirmation as to what it is he actually wants. But I suppose his staff is used to it.

The bell rings when I get to the first floor like a loud

note and off-key, compared to the quiet symphony that continues to play in my dark mental recesses. If I were to listen carefully to the music of my subconscious mind and could understand what it means, then maybe hearing it all the time wouldn't be so bad. I'm not sure, but what I do know, is that if this continues, it is going to push me past that brink I've been clinging to these past few months. I have to ignore the tones and wait—or give up and go insane.

"Can I help you, miss?"

I look up out of a haze and focus. I'm staring at this young girl with dark wavy hair. She is cute, too, with a soft cocoa tan, most likely of Hispanic descent. Why am I here, again? Oh! She must be the gal up front, Betty told me to give the orders to. I like her already though, I'm pretty sure she called me *miss*.

"Hi. Sorry. Stacy Troy."

"Are those your orders?"

"Yes." I hand her the papers.

"Go ahead and have a seat, one of the techs will be out in a moment."

"Thanks."

I turn around and there's an entire waiting room of no less than twenty people behind me. How did I miss that? I sit down at the first empty seat and reach out to pick up a magazine.

"Mrs. Troy?" A deep voice calls out.

I stand up. "Yes."

"Come with me, please."

His voice perfectly fits his features. He's an older man in his fifties, with salt and pepper hair, longer sideburns. He looks like he's lived a little on the rough side, a biker-type, maybe. Because he's wearing navy blue scrubs, he reminds me of someone who is retired military.

"My name's Dan and I'll be your tech. How are you today, ma'am?"

Oh yeah, retired military for sure, and the USMC tattoo on his upper arm gave him away.

"Good. Thanks."

"Have you ever had a CAT scan before?"

"No."

"It's nothing. No worries. What we're going to do is go back to this room. There'll be a monster in there that looks like a giant washing machine. You're not claustrophobic are you?"

"What? No, I don't think so."

"Good. So, when we get there you're going to lie down on this narrow table, and I'm going to be in the back of the room telling you not to move around."
"That's it?"

"No, I'm teasing you. If it were that easy they wouldn't need me." He turns around and smiles. If Dan's trying to scare me, it's working. "After I'm done asking you questions and filling out my paperwork, we'll get started. We're just doing head and sinus views, so you don't have to go all the way in. The machine is going to move sometimes and make swish noises when it rotates. We'll be done in thirty minutes."

"Oh good, Betty told me an hour."

"She just says that in case we're busy and you have to wait."

Well, Dan's done his job as far as allaying my time crunch fears. I'm feeling much better about it now. The *monster*—and I'm sure that's what he called it—does look a lot like a giant washing machine but with a long tongue sticking out of the hole. The tongue is actually a table that slides in and out. He has me lie down on it then rolls a stool over and sits next to me. The paperwork does not take much time at all, and when he's done asking me a bunch of questions, he disappears behind a window. His commanding military voice comes through a speaker and tells me not to move my head around. Every time I hear a swoosh sound, the bell tones almost fade out completely. To help keep me still, I close my eyes and listen, pretend to know what they mean and communicate with them in my head. Over and over I tell them to, *"Show me."*

After the CAT scan, I go back upstairs to Dr. Swanson's office and hastily change my clothes in the small exam room. I grab my purse from under the cabinet and head for the front desk. Betty is telling me things, but all I hear are the tones and swooshes. She hands me a carbon copy of something that looks like a bill. I fold it then slip it into one of the side pockets of my purse.

"Thanks." I look down at my watch. "I'm late to pick

up my son." She was still talking as I was leaving. I hope it wasn't anything important.

Fortunately, the school is only two blocks from here, and there won't be any traffic. The drop-off and pick-up swarm only lasts for fifteen minutes, and I'm a good hour and a half late. When I've cleared the third roundabout, I glance in the rearview mirror and get a look at myself. My make-up is smeared and my hair is completely disheveled. Angry again, I reach over and dig through my purse for my cell. It's in my hand as I'm pulling through the driveway in front of the school's main office. I've got a text from Jon. *"Finished early. Got Patrick. See you at home. Love you."* Then it dawns on me. *That's what Betty was trying to tell me.*

"Fuck! Fuck! Fuck me!" I pound the steering wheel with the phone. Then I realize there's a tall man in a blue suit, standing in front of the school, staring at me. It looks like Pastor Dean.

"Shit."

I take a deep breath, toss my phone into my purse then look up at him and smile. Nice and calm, I put the car into drive and wave to him as I pull away from the curb.

Back at home we have a relatively quiet family dinner with light conversation. Jon eyes me every chance he gets. He knows something is wrong. He's waiting for it. When Patrick goes upstairs and I hear his door close, I gather up the dinner dishes and give him another few minutes to get his video game headset on. Standing in front of the sink, I grab hold of the counter's edge, take in a deep breath and arch my back like a cat about to pounce.

"Jon, what happened today, will never happen again."

"What?"

"Don't act naïve. You know exactly what I'm talking about."

"You're mad about the appointments? But you…"

"What appointments! I didn't see a single doctor. Just test after test, tube after tube."

"You promised."

"I rescind."

"You can't."

"I already have."

He steps behind me and gently rests his chin on my shoulder while I rinse and clang the silverware against the dishes. "Please, don't." He puts his arms around me and pulls me back against him. "I don't know how to explain it, it's just important."

"Nothing's wrong with me, Jon." The water on my hands drips all over me and the floor.

"I got the lab work results."

"And?"

"Everything came back normal."

"What about the CAT scan?"

"The radiologist called me. He didn't find anything abnormal either."

"Then why can't you be satisfied with that?" My voice cracks, tears begin to well.

Jon tightens his hold. "Let's wait and see what Dr. Swanson has to say. He'll want to see you in his office."

"Why do I still have to go if everything's normal?"

"Let him examine you. It could simply be adult onset allergies."

"But…"

"I need a definitive answer. If he doesn't find anything, I'll let it go."

"Promise?"

"Yeah."

"Then fine. After Dr. Swanson, I'm done."

"So, do you need help finishing up, or can I go do some office work?" He releases me and steps back.

I get back to washing the dishes in the sink. "Please. Go."

"You're not still mad at me, are you?"

"No, but I'm not real happy either."

"Well, I think I've got the cure for that."

"Yeah, I bet."

"No. Serious."

I turn around and look at him. "What?"

"I'll have to show you later."

"I knew it."

He winks and grins, then turns away and goes upstairs.

Jon is still in the office working while I lie in bed and wait for sleep or something like it. I didn't take any Valium to try out my theory that it could be what's causing the weird dreams and hallucinations. I also purposely skipped the relaxation and dream scripting exercises. Instead, I have my eyes closed, listening to the tones and concentrating. As much as I want to say that I've been ignoring them, every now and then, I hear parts that sound repetitive. It really is some epic symphony that begins again once it's finished, playing over and over. There is something to it, and I have to figure it out.

The harder I focus, the more the tones become words I can understand, a type of broken English. Random words that speak out of thin air. Their intensity suddenly increases. I open my eyes and they stop. No more words. No tones. It's dark, but the room is filled with an opaque fog, glowing from the moonlight. There's a slight chill to it, my face feels cool. I also smell the cotton candy scent of Dr. Light. I open my mouth and let the fog curl in to settle on my tongue. There is an actual sugariness in the taste.

I push the covers down, but nothing's there. My hands alone move through the dense, cool air. Blindly feeling out everything around me, I start to panic. My fingers don't touch a thing, only emptiness.

"Jon?" Rainbow-rippled waves come out of my mouth, cut through the fog, then disappear.

I sit up in bed, but I actually bend over. I'm already standing, I think. There's no sense of equilibrium. I slide my right foot forward. It feels solid underneath, but I can't tell if I'm upside down, about to walk on the ceiling, or sideways. As my heart rate increases, a red glow pulses within the fog, keeping time with the beats. I close my eyes again and take in a deep breath. While exhaling slowly, I open my eyes and examine my surroundings again.

Images begin to take shape in blocks against the fog, forming a wall that looks like flatscreen televisions directly in front of me. So many different scenes come to life with movie clips flickering as they play, the way old projectors used to run reeled films. The pictures are still obscure, gradually coming into focus. I glance around and notice nothing familiar.

The others are here, too. I sense them and Dr. Light. Twenty-six shadows in a slow drift circumvent the fog, keeping just barely out of my full view.

Their words begin as tones again, and colored waves of neon light dance around me. "*See*," they say in different voices.

It's the movies they want me to examine. At last…it is something. I look up to the screens made out of the fog. How is that even possible? The scenes are diverse. There are a multitude of people, cultures, and places, in different time periods.

My eyes study one in particular. A scene with a woman, and I'm guessing her husband, and two children. The boy looks like he's ten years old maybe and the girl around seven. They are outside, in a large backyard. Kelly green, the lawn is neatly manicured and surrounded by a short, white picket fence. The husband grills hot dogs and hamburgers, while the wife sets out a bowl of potato salad and a bottle of ketchup onto an old style picnic table—but it looks new, painted brick red. Like the kind you still see in public parks, except the wood is gray, weathered and splintering. Children play on one of those old, A-frame, metal swing sets with a slide. I'm pretty sure they stopped making those, too, because children were getting hurt. The whole thing would flip over when the kids would swing too high or something. It all looks real *Dick and Jane*, 1950's or 60's, I'm guessing. It doesn't make any sense.

I look around for another scene, trying to hone in on something I might recognize. Suddenly, I'm captivated by an image in the upper left corner. I feel the twenty-six come in around me, closer. I don't dare move my eyes away from the screen. In it, a drove of half-naked children draped in white linen run together through stone hallways chasing some sort of ball. Most of them have on gold bangles and anklets. One of the taller boys picks up the ball and runs toward a shallow, rectangular pool of water. A young girl chases after him. Their raucous laughter is loud and hauntingly familiar. They are the children from my daydream, laughing in the office. The same girl I followed down the halls under Dr. Light's hypnosis—*me*.

"Are these all images of me?" The colored waves of my words slice through the television wall in laser beams.

"Yes," I hear in tones that are intelligible to me now.

"It's not possible."

"You have lived all these lives."

They drift in, even closer.

"*See*," they say.

"No." I keep my eyes forward and shake my head. They

want me to look at them, but I can't. I find another scene. It is the woman in Victorian England. Then in another, I see the woman in a Colonial church. Why always women? Women and children…families?

"What does it mean?"

They are almost upon me. So close! I'm cold again, frigid. The screens and images disappear. All around me, the fog has turned the deepest shade of blue. My heart pumps faster. A faint red glow skirts the outer edges of the fog. Every pulse of red—a heartbeat—a pounding drum in their symphony. Yes! My heart will save me. Wake me up before I *SEE*!

"Oh, no." It's too late. They have come through the fog. I see them! My god, their faces are melting like candle wax! Dripping people—heavy, wet shadows. They wrap their icy stinging appendages around me, pulling me down. I'm sinking fast with their weight, feeling heavier than lead. There is nothing I can do. It's too hard, so cold. Maybe this is it, and I should let go. Then memories of Jon and Patrick fill my head, and I begin to flail wildly. I'm kicking up, swimming upwards—hungry for air, surrounded by water.

As everything goes black, I hear a faint whisper.

"Come back to us."

CHAPTER FIFTEEN

The cold heavy darkness does not let me go. I move around like a frog, struggling to get through dense algae. My arms and legs catch in the gooey strands, tiring my muscles.

Suddenly, Jon grabs my hand and pulls me out. "Stacy, wake up. You've wet the bed."

"What?" Oh my God, it's bright. I cover my eyes and blink until they adjust to the light. Then I realize I've been swimming in our bed, fighting sheets soaked with my own urine. "What happened?"

"You tell me. One minute I'm sound asleep then I feel a slap and a kick. I reach over, and you're soaking wet. I thought it was another bloody nose, so I hit the lights."

"This is disgusting. Sorry."

"Was it a nightmare?"

"No. I must've been in a really deep sleep."

"Well, at least *you're* getting some. Go get cleaned up. I'll change the sheets."

"Thanks." I peel the rest of the top sheet from my legs, then get out of bed and bolt to the bathroom. In the mirror, I look like a losing contestant from a wet T-shirt contest. Then the odor of pee wafts up, making me gag. I carefully roll the drenched nightshirt up my body and lift it over my head. Once it's off and I have rinsed it in the sink, I spread it out across the edge of the bathtub to dry.

The hot water in the shower feels good. I close my eyes and see flashes of the nightmare. I quickly open them again, afraid of seeing anything else.

Jon barges into the bathroom carrying the sheets a full arm's length away from his chest. He walks over to me in the shower and opens the door.

"Smell these," he says, practically shoving them into my face.

I push them back. "Jon! They stink, I get it. Shut the door. It's cold."

"No. They're not just foul. I noticed a familiar smell when I took them off the bed."

"Gross. What?"

"Sugar."

"Now, *you've* lost it. Stop sniffing the sheets and put them next to my shirt. I'll wash them tomorrow."

"Stacy, I'm being serious. I want you to go back to GenLabs for a urinalysis."

"I'm too tired to argue."

"Good. I don't know why I didn't think of it before… you could have Diabetes."

"What?"

"Sugar in your urine is a sure sign that your body's not breaking it down properly."

"You're wrong about this. I'm certain I don't have Diabetes."

"A urinalysis would prove that."

"Whatever."

Finally, he closes the shower door. I have goose bumps all over, and my nipples are so hard, they ache. I turn up the water temperature and stand directly under the shower head. Thick steam fills the shower stall, reminding me of the sweet tasting fog from the nightmare. I quickly turn off the water then step out. After drying, I put on another nightshirt and crawl back into bed.

"Goodnight again," Jon says. He leans over and kisses my cheek.

"Night. Thanks for fixing the bed." I snuggle into my pillow and pull the covers. The sheets come all the way up, exposing my feet. "You didn't tuck in the sheets?"

"It's not going to be perfect."

I kick the blankets over my toes. "Not a biggy."

Morning comes too soon, and the coffee can't come soon enough. Jon must have woken up late then rushed off to work. Funny though, I didn't hear him, and he *always* wakes me up. Maybe the whole bedwetting thing really threw him off schedule.

I get dressed then head downstairs with my nightshirt rolled into the damp sheets. Jon meets me at the landing.

"I was just coming up with your coffee."

"I thought you left already."

"Without a kiss?"

He's right. He always kisses me goodbye, even if I'm still asleep in bed. Sixteen years of marriage, and he has never once forgotten.

He steps up and pushes his lips against mine, then quickly backs off. "Phew, that stinks! Don't forget to go to GenLabs today. I'll call them on my way to work." He turns around and walks back down with me two steps behind him. "I'm going to try and get a hold of Terry Swanson again, too. I'm pretty sure he sees patients on Tuesdays and Thursdays, and this Thursday's out, because of Thanksgiving. Maybe he can work you in. Keep your cell close."

"Gee, thanks."

"Where do you want me to put your coffee?"

"Just set it on the kitchen counter. I'll get it after I start the laundry. I don't want Patrick to know. And please— don't say anything to him."

"I won't. But I think he'd get a kick out of it that *mom* wet the bed."

"No. He wouldn't."

He looks at me when we get to the kitchen, and I snarl at him on my way to the laundry room. He puts the coffee cup on the counter then follows me down the hall.

"Don't worry. I won't tell." He pulls open the hatch door of the washing machine for me.

"I know." I turn my head and look at him.

He smirks then turns around to leave.

"Wait, Jon, I almost forgot."

He stops in the doorway. "What now?"

"Why do you say it like *that*?"

"Sorry dear, what is it?"

"Cally invited us to go to Chopsteaks tonight. They have VIP table reservations."

"Excellent. What time?"

"Seven."

"I'll be done. You up for it?"

"Yeah."

"Then we should go."

"I'll confirm."

"Kay, bye." He leans in and kisses me again. "Love you, Grouchy."

"What?"

"Just kidding."

"Bye, then. Love you, too."

Grouchy? He's never called me that before. Maybe I have become a grouch, because on top of everything else, the constant background tones are really starting to get on my nerves. Now that I know they mean something, I find myself trying to decipher them. It's worse than having a bad song stuck in my head. And who do I talk to about it, Dr. Swanson or Dr. Light?

I worry about how things are going with Dr. Light. For a while the new dreams were just that—*new*, but they've turned into nightmares now, too and with him in them. That can't be good. At this rate, I'll be in therapy for the rest of my life, but that's only if Jon doesn't test me to death first.

I've finished all the coffee and am rinsing out the pot when Patrick comes downstairs. He goes straight into the pantry without saying a word and rummages around for a few minutes.

"You want me to make you some eggs?"

He steps out with a box of cereal. "I hate eggs."

"Oh, I forgot."

"By the way, I've got practice at four-thirty."

"Did you think I'd forget that, too?"

"Maybe."

"We're going out to dinner with Mr. and Mrs. Giordano tonight. Remind me to order you a pizza on the way home."

"Pizza…again?"

"I never thought I'd hear you complain about pizza. Would you prefer baked chicken?"

"No, I'm good."

I wouldn't want to show up at Dr. Light's office early again, even though somehow, I really wasn't before. After dropping Patrick off, I head home and print up the invitations for the neighborhood holiday party. I fold the cards neatly into the envelopes and put on the stamps.

It's exactly ten o'clock when I pull into the parking lot of the desolate office building. I picture Dr. Light standing on the strange marble as it changes underfoot. He knows I'm here, and he waits for me with the door open. I shake the vision from my head then make my way in.

"Good morning, Stacy." He *is* in the doorway, just as I'd imagined him.

"Dr. Light." I nod my head, step in then walk directly to his office in the back. The door is already open, so I enter and make myself comfortable on the lounger, then wait. There's no point in wasting any time, especially the way it occurs here.

"You seem eager today."

"Yes. I've got a lot to talk about. Do you mind if I start?"

"No, go ahead." He drags one of the chairs over then sits next to me.

"It seems I always have a lot to tell you, but then when I get here, my mind goes blank. Do you know why that is?"

"No. Do you?"

"Possibly…maybe I'm just crazier than I thought. What if I told you I imagine you have something to do with what's happening to me? Would you put me away?"

"No. There'll be no putting anyone away. I promise you that."

"I've been having these dreams lately."

"Yes?" He scoots his chair in, and it sends a chill up my spine. He feels almost as close as he did last night in my dream, when he and the others tried to drown me.

"I'm not sure how to tell you something without sounding completely insane."

He tenses up, looks frustrated. "Please do," he insists. He's on the edge of his seat, staring down at me with his jet black disks for eyes. "I'm here to listen, to help. Please, you must go on."

I close my eyes to keep his appearance from distracting me. "In these dreams I hear music, unearthly tones. I think they were the ear-piercing sounds I used to hear—only now, they've *tuned in*." I move my fingers around and pretend to turn knobs. "I'm sorry for the lack of a better description."

"No. That's fine. Continue."

"At first, I couldn't understand them, but then I could. It's some kind of language, a message from these things."

"What things? You only mentioned the tones."

"No. The things…they communicate in the tones, along with waves of brilliant colors. There are shadows, too. Those *are* the things—dark auras in a glowing fog."

I hear nothing above me except for the tones in my head. I don't even hear Dr. Light breathing. He must be deep in thought about something.

"I told you this would sound crazy," I say.

"It doesn't. Please, go on. What were these things doing?"

"They kept telling me to *See*, but I couldn't figure out what."

"And have you now?"

"No, not really. All I've been able to make out is that it has something to do with the nightmares and the déjà vu past life experiences. Last night, they told me that I'd lived all the lives I've been hallucinating about. Then they turned into these monsters and smothered me."

"That sounds awful."

I open my eyes to look for sincerity in his expression. There isn't any, so I close them again and continue.

"It was, but even worse than that…"

"What?"

"I always feel like there's more they want to say. And they're trying, but I can't understand them."

"What do you mean?"

"The musical tones, I told you about—they've been playing in my head ever since you hypnotized me. Is it possible something went wrong? That the hypnotherapy closed one crazy door and opened another, I mean?"

"Not likely. What you need to do, is try harder to understand them. Your subconscious is trying to tell you something. Listen."

"But I do. If I concentrate any harder, my brain's going to have a meltdown."

"I assure you, that won't happen."

"And why do you think you're always there, Dr. Light…in my dreams and nightmares? Your presence is felt, but you never help me."

"I only wish I could, but I can't interfere in your dreams."

"I'm afraid, Dr. Light."

"Of what?"

Of you… "Of what I told you before, about how everyone's going to die."

"I'm counting on you to solve your mind's puzzles before that happens."

"Yeah, me too. I guess it's a good thing that this all just an imaginary circumstance."

"How's that?"

"Well, that it's not really real."

I open my eyes again. Dr. Light's face hovers directly over mine. It's jolting how his eyes are transfixed on me. Another chill runs down my spine, and I point my toes to ward off the shiver. He doesn't move. Like he's frozen, and his mind is someplace else. Those empty black eyes look like portals left open. I blink, and suddenly, I see my own face staring back at me from the lounger, as if I were looking through his eyes. I blink again, and it's him I see. *Crazy!* He hasn't blinked once since we've been in this staring match. Come to think of it, I don't think I've ever seen him blink, but who pays attention to shit like that? It isn't until I notice he's not breathing that I get uneasy.

I reach up and gently touch the side of his face. "Dr. Light?" Ooh! His skin is like ice. My hand jerks back, and there's a slight sting at my fingertips.

He finally blinks then moves his head like he's shaking off a thought. "Yes. Sorry, I got stuck in a daze."

He's completely oblivious to what just happened.

"I'm glad I'm not the only one who does that," I tell him.

"Yes. That's perfectly normal."

Is he asking or telling? For the first time, I really want to leave. "Time's up, I think."

"You're right. I'll see you tomorrow." He makes a contorted smile, like his face was still partially frozen.

"Not Thursday or Friday, though." I sit up slow and get my bearings.

"Why?"

"Thanksgiving, Dr. Light, and Friday is considered a holiday, too. My parents will be in town. You've got plans don't you?"

"Oh, yes. I forgot."

"Goodbye, Dr. Light." I hop down from the lounger and head for the door.

"Goodbye…and Stacy?"

"Yes?" I turn around to face him.

"Please, don't ever be afraid of me." His expression looks sincere.

"I'll try, Dr. Light."

CHAPTER SIXTEEN

'm not exactly sure how I think that appointment went or any of the ones before it really, but I spoke my piece, and he didn't overreact the way I thought he might. He hardly reacted at all, as if what I told him were trite. He only seemed to get frustrated when I wasn't able to tell him more. He must think I'm holding something back, and I honestly think he means for me to work this out on my own, even though it's his job to help.

"Try harder..." Really, that was the best he could do? I wonder how much that little bit of worthless advice cost. It doesn't matter, I guess. It's priceless just to have him listen and constantly assure me that I'm *not* psychotic. Overall, I think the visits with Dr. Light are helping, but I may be subconsciously thinking about him a little too much. I imagine him to be there when he's not, and now, I even sense his presence in the abstract dreams. Although I have a feeling it's all about to change. I'll have less time to think about him, with Jon and his barrage of tests.

My phone rings as I'm turning off the exit for GenLabs. I swear Jon has ESP for these things.

"Hello."

"Hey Babe, you make it to GenLabs yet?"

"I'm on my way now."

"Kay, good. As soon as you're finished, head over to Dr. Swanson's office. He's going to see you between his scheduled patients. You might have to wait a little."

"Fine. I'll be there, but if it starts getting late, I'm walking out."

"Just show up."

"Okay, bye." There goes my darn thumb pressing the disconnect button again. It's turning into one of those bad habits I'm starting to enjoy.

The parking isn't so bad at GenLabs today, but Tuesdays are an off day for everything. It's normally the day I do the grocery shopping, but it doesn't look like I'll get to any of that. I'll have to go sometime tomorrow when it's completely insane, the day before Thanksgiving.

Once more, I go to the counter inside and give the receptionist my name. She hands me one of those plastic cups in a clear bag with directions inside on how to give a urine sample.

"You can use the bathroom over there." She points to a door hidden in a dark corner, behind the filthy chairs in the waiting area. Oh, great. I can just imagine…

No need for an imagination, the bathroom is absolutely disgusting. The same white tile used everywhere in GenLabs is in the ladies room, too, except it's grimy, black, and sticky in here. As I enter one of the two stalls, I close the door behind me and try not to lean against anything. I hang my purse across my body and swing it around behind me. Still standing, I pull my jeans and underwear down together then push the cup between my legs. I fill it about halfway then stop. I grab a wad of toilet paper, slide the cup out and replace it with the paper. Fortunately, I didn't make too much of a mess, just a couple drips. Easy to wipe up and most importantly—my pants are dry. It's one thing to wet the bed and entirely another to pee your pants. I tighten the lid on the cup then set it down on top of the toilet paper holder while I finish cleaning up and get dressed.

I wash my hands twice then head back out to the receptionist counter carrying the still warm, urine sample in my hand.

"There you are," she says. "I was just about to send someone in to see if you needed any help."

Was I gone that long? "No, I'm fine…here you go." I hand her the sample. She takes it and places a label around it. Then she turns to the same young man that drew my blood the last time. "This is for you, Jack. Routine UA, looking for glucose."

"Just keep it here," he tells her. "I'll come back for it when I'm done." He steps out from the door on the left. His left hand is wrapped in white gauze. "Come on back, Mrs. Troy."

"I have to go with you?"

"Dr. Troy ordered another blood draw. Seems he's focusing on your glucose levels now."

"Christ," I mumble, as I walk through the doorway.

He takes me to the same little desk. I sit down. He puts the ball in my hand then wraps the tourniquet around my arm. "Wow, is this the same arm I drew from yesterday?"

"Yeah, why?"

"There's no bruising. No sign I was there at all. I've never seen that before."

"Hmm…guess I'm a good healer."

"Or maybe I'm getting pretty good at this."

"I'm sure that's what it is. What happened to your hand?"

"Oh, I was being stupid and took a specimen out of the freezer without gloves on—burned it."

"Freezer burn?"

"Yeah, from the dry ice. That's how we have to store certain specimens."

"Oh. I never knew you could burn from something cold."

"Oh yeah, for sure. That ice is like minus a hundred degrees Fahrenheit."

"Did it burn when you touched it, or did it feel cold?"

"Both. It's like frostbite."

"Well, I hope it heals quickly."

"Me, too." He releases the tourniquet around my arm with his good hand. "Here's a copy of your paperwork. Just take it up front like before." Then he's off again with his little basket of clinking tubes.

"Thanks," I call out, as the tail end of his lab coat disappears around the corner.

"No problem," echoes in from the hallway.

Everything went much quicker today at GenLabs, but maybe, that's because I'm becoming a routine patient, which is not something I care to be.

I get in the car then head for Dr. Swanson's office, making a quick, necessary stop for drive-thru coffee and a muffin. I finish them both before I'm anywhere close to finding a parking spot. Tuesdays must be the *patient seeing* days for *all* the doctors. Maybe that's why everyplace else is sparse of crowds. Finally, a couple of seniors put their big Caddy in reverse. They pull out of a sweet spot and almost clip my bumper.

Nearly every seat is taken in the same office that seemed empty yesterday. I walk up to the reception desk, instantly glad when I see Betty. Her hair is wound tight in a bun. No stragglers hanging down, yet. That has to be the sign of a good day, so far.

"Hello again, Mrs. Troy. Come on back," she says in a cheery tone.

I walk around and notice several people glaring at me, while they have to keep waiting. This *cutting in line* is what Jon means by professional courtesy—and today—I'm all for taking advantage of it.

Betty leads me down the hall to a different exam room, set up exactly like the one I was in the other day.

"The doctor will be here shortly, he's finishing up with another patient."

"Thanks, Betty."

She closes the door on her way out.

A few minutes later, a young man with short, spiky, blonde hair whips into the room wearing a lab coat. Right away, he reminds me of the *Iceman* character from the movie *Top Gun*. His appearance fits the *asshole* persona Jon told me about. He grabs a folder from a rack behind the door. "Hello, Mrs. Troy. I'm Terry Swanson." He reaches his hand out, and I shake it. His grip is rudely tight.

"Please. Call me, Stacy."

He lets go then takes a seat on the rolling metal stool, opens up the folder and starts to read. He clicks the end of a pen in his hand while he talks. "Jon thinks there might be something going on…he told me you had a bad nosebleed this past weekend."

"Yes."

"Have you had any since?"

"No."

"And prior to this weekend?"

"One other time, but it wasn't as bad. Other than that, I've never had a bloody nose."

He makes checks here and there in the folder and continues nervously clicking the ballpoint pen. Then he grabs a small flashlight from his pocket and turns the top until a light comes on. He pinches and pulls the skin around my eyes as he shines the light in and tells me to follow his finger, look this way and that. He pushes back the cartilage at the tip of my nose and directs the light up there. Then he practically jumps up from the stool, reaches over to the wall and grabs a different kind of medical flashlight. He puts on a funnel-like attachment then looks into my ears and up my nose again.

"How's your hearing?"

"Good…uh, sometimes though, I hear a ringing in my ears."

"When did it start?"

"A couple days ago."

"Same time as the nosebleeds?"

"No. Later."

"Hmm…" He clicks a different attachment onto the flashlight, one with a lens. Then he examines my eyes again. His movements are quick and radical, he's making me dizzy. His bedside manner is awful, so he must be good at what he does to have an office full of patients waiting to see him.

"Everything looks perfectly normal," he says. "Have you felt dizzy at all?"

Only since I've been watching you jerk around like a crack fiend. "No."

"I don't think it's allergies, none of your mucous membranes look irritated. It's possible it was a random incident." He snaps the attachment off the flashlight then puts everything back in its place and sits down on the stool.

"I'm sure that's exactly what it was, and Jon's just being paranoid."

He snorts and nods his head. Then he puts his nose right back down into the folder, and he's clicking that goddamned pen again. "As for your blood work, clotting factors, CAT scan…they're all normal, too. He told me he sent you in for some blood sugar tests. Something about your urine," he mumbles.

Oh God, now I'm mortified. Jon must have told him I wet the bed. "Uh, I went to GenLabs before I came here."

"Good. Then I'll have the results by the end of the day, but Jon will know what to do if they're positive for spilled sugar."

"What?"

"It just means that there's too much in your system, so you pee out the extra."

Nice, layman terms—I had to ask. I'm amazed he hasn't said piss, yet. "Oh. And then what happens?"

"You'll need more tests. I'll have to refer you to an endocrinologist."

The phrase *"Whatever,"* and the attitude that accompanies it, is about to leave my mouth when Dr. Swanson looks up from the folder.

"It's an endocrine doctor—a hormone specialist."

"Ah."

Asshole! Dr's wife does not mean physician by association. Hormone specialist? How come when women get ill, it's always because of hormones? I know what he's thinking. *"I'm sure your hormones are just off balance."* If he says it, I'm going to kick him.

"Well, I've done all I can. Just waiting on the rest of the lab results. I'll call Jon and let him know my findings." He stands up and reaches his hand out again. "It was nice meeting you, Mrs. Troy, and don't worry. We'll get to the bottom of this."

I shake his hand. His grip isn't as aggressive this time around. "Thanks again for seeing me."

"Not at all. Take care."

"Bye."

He's already gone and in the adjacent exam room greeting his next patient. I hear the rack behind the door bang around as he takes the folder from it. I get up from the table, grab my purse and head up to the front desk. Betty spots me right away. I take my wallet out and open it up to get my insurance card.

"It's covered, Mrs. Troy. You can go."

"Please, thank him again for me."

"Will do. Have a nice day."

"You, too."

No charge. Of course now I feel a little crappy about my impression of him, but he really was an asshole. Or maybe that's just how he is. I guess all doctors are bizarre in their own ways. He definitely made Dr. Light seem *not-so-bad* in my eyes. I wonder what Jon's patients think about him and his bedside manner. God, I hope he doesn't joke around with them the way he does me. I imagine the worst, but I'm sure he's nothing like that.

Ha! It's miraculous. Everything is running on time today, despite the interruptions. I pull up to the high school a few minutes early and use the time to look through my day planner. It's been a while since I've opened it. My life has become so spontaneous, it is barely necessary anymore. Hard to believe not that long ago, I couldn't function on a daily basis without it.

Apparently, the only big upcoming event I thought worth planning for is the surgery center holiday party, and most of that is done. Now it's just a matter of making confirmations via phone calls. Jordan is in charge of some of the preparations, too, through her nonprofit organization, which is still based out of Dallas. That's how she gets tax breaks on her estate. Personally, I don't care where her business is, I'm just happy to have the help.

With the day planner on my lap, I lean back and look up at the sky. It seems hazy today, even through the tinted gradient of the windshield. I grab a pen from the console and start scribbling lines across the blank pages in tune with the tones. Every low note is a valley, every high, a peak. I never studied music or played an instrument, but now I wish I had. Maybe it's a type of code they use to spell out secret messages. I write the letters B-A-D, across three of the peaks. That wouldn't make any sense though, not every letter in the alphabet is a musical note—that much I do know.

I jump at a tap on the glass. My day planner shuts in my lap. It's Patrick. I unlock the door, and he gets in.

"What were you doing?"

"Going through my lists. How was your day?"

"Good. Tomorrow's only a half day."

"Why?"

"I don't know."

"When do you get out?"

"One."

"Hmm…"

"When do Grandma and Grandpa get here?"

"Not until three. I'll be able to get you."

"'Kay."

"You excited for the holiday?"

"Yeah, I guess."

"Why do you *guess*?"

"It's just turkey. Then Dad and Grandpa watch sports, and you and Grandma go out."

"But it's nice that we can all sit down together as a family, even if it's only for an hour."

"Yeah, I guess."

"It's supposed to be a time for giving thanks."

"I know…never mind." He turns his head and looks out the passenger window.

Of course, he is absolutely right about Thanksgiving. From a teenager's perspective, I guess it would be boring. I was an only child, like Jon, and Patrick is, too, so he's never had a bunch of cousins to play football with or show around town. Maybe I should have taken Tara up on her offer to join them for Thanksgiving, but it's too late now.

I'm not sure why Jon and I decided to have only one child, that's just how it worked out. Jon was busy finishing his residency and then establishing his practice. It seemed any more kids would be too much, but not having any wouldn't feel right either. The timing in my career made it the perfect opportunity. It was the easy way. Perhaps, I've always taken that route—lived it.

There was never a time I can remember when I felt wanting, sorrow, or pain. My parents were not wealthy, but we were always happy. I loved school, attended college and met Jon there. Everything seemed to follow some sort of formula for a happy life—until the nightmares began.

CHAPTER SEVENTEEN

When Patrick and I pull into the parking lot for practice, I see Gail leaning against *our* tree. Patrick hands me some stuff, then runs out to the field where Coach and a few other boys are standing. Gail waves me over.

"It's so good to see you," she says. Then with my chair in hand and Patrick's crap bunched in my arm, she steps up and gives me a really big hug. Then she lets go and steps back.

"Yeah, it's been a while. You look great, though. How's everything going?"

"Fantastic, actually."

"Excellent." I drop Patrick's things on the grass then open up the chair and sit down. "Did you forget your blanket? I keep a beach towel in the car you can use."

"No, but thanks. I'm not staying long."

"Why? If you have to go, I can bring Justin home." I shade my eyes and look out to the field. Justin is nowhere in sight. "Where is he?"

"That's why I came early. I wanted to talk to you."

"What is it?"

"Justin doesn't want to play soccer anymore. He thinks he might just stick with baseball in the spring."

"Burned out?"

"I guess."

"I'm afraid that might eventually happen with Pat, too, but it won't break my heart."

"No doubt, but anyway—there's more." She sighs. "I think Justin's a little embarrassed about being suspended at school for punching lockers. He's been talking a lot lately about transferring to Bishop Almeida."

"Oh no, Gail, you can't. The boys have all practically grown up together. People will get over what happened. It wasn't that big a deal."

"I know, but he wants a fresh start."

"I understand...I guess." Poor kid—I know he's been struggling with the whole divorce drama, but I had no idea it was this bad. Switching schools? "Patrick would freak out, but if it'll make Justin feel better, then you've got to do what brings him happiness. I'll miss seeing you guys around, though. Next year won't be the same if you're not there."

"He wants to start after Thanksgiving. We've already taken care of the paperwork."

"What? Oh my God, and you never said a thing? You should've called, or we could've met for coffee."

"I'm telling you now. Justin didn't want me to make a big scene or tell anyone. I tried to talk him out of it, but like you said...if it brings him happiness..."

"Wow. I wasn't expecting any of *this*."

"Shit happens, Stacy, you know that. I just wanted to tell you, because you've always been a good friend to me. Not like the rest of them."

"What? But they love you, too, Gail."

"No. Not really."

"Don't say that."

"It's true, though."

"I wish you would've talked to *me* about it then."

"It wouldn't have changed anything. This is how it's got to be."

"I don't understand."

"You will. I'm sure it'll all come out eventually. It always does. I just kind of wanted to say *goodbye*, sort of. Explain to you what I could and let you know I've always appreciated your friendship."

"I don't know what to say."

"There's nothing you can. What's done is done, but I want you to know I'm happy. I'm happy about everything."

She stoops down and gives me another big hug, kisses the side of my head, whispers. "Thank you." Then she walks to her car, gets in, and drives away.

I'm dumbfounded, sitting in my soccer mom chair, staring out at the parking lot with a gaping mouth. What the hell just happened? Was that my craziness, or was that real? Right now, I honestly don't know.

Patrick runs up and grabs a water bottle from his pile of stuff. He tilts his head back and gulps until the plastic caves in.

"Pat, you saw Mrs. Katz here, right?"

"Yeah," he pants. "Where's Justin?"

"Uh, he's skipping today. I'll tell you about it later."

"'Kay. Is Kyle skipping too?"

"I don't think so…Cally didn't say anything. They're probably just late again."

"Crap. I hate running extra laps. I'm gonna kill him."

"No killing of friends, today. I've got dinner plans."

"Whatever." He tosses the empty bottle down then runs back out to the field.

It was all real then, everything Gail told me. Normally, I'm quick to pick up on these things, but I don't think so clearly anymore. My thoughts are in a constant jumble, dancing around to the music that never leaves my mind. She's probably better off not telling me about her problems. I'm the worst friend to have right now, most likely incapable of giving any sane advice.

God, I feel guilty about letting her down, though. What she must be going through. When she stopped coming to yoga and then book club the other night, I should have known something was wrong. A phone call at the right time might have meant something. Then again, no one has really said anything to me since I stopped yoga. None of us want to talk about what is really happening in our lives. Not even me.

Sitting at my vanity, staring into empty eyes, "Cally and Kyle never showed up for practice today," I say.

"Hmm," Jon mumbles from the open closet. "Did you call? We're still on for dinner, right?" He leans his head out for a response.

"No. Yeah. She would've called. I'm sure everything's fine."

"If you say so. We should leave soon." He steps out buttoning his cuffs. Leans down and kisses the side of my head. "You've got ten minutes."

"I'm just about ready."

"Ready? You're not going out like that."

"What?"

"You're half-naked."

Then I realize I'm wearing just my bra and panties. "Oh, yeah. It won't take long."

"Your eyes look a little puffy, too. You should try and cover up the dark circles. Are you sure you're okay to go out?"

I smile a closed smile, holding back a show of gnashing teeth and nod my head. He turns around then leaves the bathroom.

I dab more makeup under my eyes with a wedged sponge. How is it that he points out the bags and dark circles around my eyes, but fails to notice the pot of coffee I drink every morning, or my lack of appetite? Maybe it's more normal for a doctor to recognize physical changes and natural for a husband to ignore the obvious ones.

"You *See*," I tell the tones. "You're making me look old and ugly."

I stop and listen for a moment, but there's no response. Only the same loop of tones playing the identical song in different pitches. I bet there are twenty-six in all. One singular message, yet spoken individually.

Twenty minutes or so later, I make my way downstairs. Jon is still in the office. "Are you coming?" I shout up.

"Be right down," he yells back.

I walk into the kitchen and Patrick is standing at the counter eating pizza straight out of the cardboard box.

"Why don't you sit down, and get a plate?" I say.

"Nah, I'll be done in a minute, and I don't want to dirty a dish."

"You don't want to wash one, you mean."

"That's what the dishwasher's for. Besides, I'm done. See." He lifts the lid to show me his handiwork.

The pizza was a large, too. I don't know where he puts it. He emptied the entire thing, even scraped away the melted cheese. There's nothing left, but a big grease stain. Geez, I've got to stop with the junk food, but it's just so easy. "At least throw out the box," I say.

"But you're headed that way. Would you, Mom? *Please*."

"Fine." I close the lid and carry it away with one hand, my clutch in the other. If your father comes down, tell him I'm waiting in the garage."

"'Kay. Thanks. You kids have fun," he shouts from halfway up the stairs.

"That's not funny," I yell back.

Cally and Bill are in the lobby of the restaurant sipping cocktails when we finally arrive.

"There you are," Cally says. "I was just about to text." She steps up and kisses the air at both sides of my head.

Bill and Jon shake hands. "You're not on call are you?" Bill says.

"No," Jon says. "It was all her this time."

"Thanks a lot," I say.

"Let's get our table," Cally says.

An attractive young woman approaches. "Is this the rest of your party?"

"Yes," Cally says.

The hostess grabs four menus from the counter behind the mâitre d' podium. "This way, please." Then she leads us to a glass elevator in the middle of the restaurant that goes up to a large platform. There's a thick pole in the center that appears to be holding it up. It reminds me of the acrobats who spin dishes on sticks while standing on their heads.

"The table doesn't spin around, does it?" I say, unsure I could handle it.

"No," says the hostess. "But I do get that question a lot."

"Thank God," Cally says. "Spinning, and cocktails, and dinner, *Oh my.*"

The elevator doors open to an elegantly decorated dining table with velvet high-back chairs. Down below is a perfect view of the entire restaurant.

"Good thing we're not afraid of heights," I mumble. It's not that high up, but enough to make me feel slightly off balance. A glass wall surrounds the edge of the platform, but it doesn't offer any increased sense of safety. I suppose that's the appeal, giving it a VIP status. I'm truly amazed people put their names on a long waiting list for this table. Within a year or so, it will lose its appeal, and people will move on to the next big thing.

The hostess leaves, closing a glass gate behind her. Then a few minutes later, a waiter comes up to take our drink order.

"Just water for me, please," I say. I wouldn't want to get woozy and trip over the only thing keeping us from falling—a three-foot-high, clear glass enclosure.

"The selections are on the back of the wine list, ma'am." He turns over the ridiculously large, leather bound drink menu and points them out to me.

There must be twenty different things listed for water. "Whatever you recommend," I tell him.

"Do you prefer flat or sparkling?"

"Flat, please."

"For the whole table then?"

"Yes."

After he takes our orders, he goes back down the elevator. Then a bunch of different people come up and down with our drinks, bread, and a tasting from the chef. It is completely distracting, and at one point, three people from the serving staff were on the platform with us. I thought I felt the floor give a little underneath my feet, and it made me horribly nervous.

Once our food orders are out of the way, it quiets down. Bill and Jon strike up a conversation. I lean across the table toward Cally. "Did you forget about practice?" I say.

"No. Things just got busy." She won't look me in the eyes. Instead, she stares down at her silverware. "I was running late with errands then realized we wouldn't make it on time. Kyle didn't want to be blamed for the team having to run extra laps, so we decided to skip."

"Oh."

"Were Gail and Justin there?" Her eyes move up to mine.

"What're you two talking about?" Bill interrupts.

"Nothing," Cally says. She makes a slight smile.

Something isn't right. She almost looks afraid. "Just soccer," I reply.

"How's that big party of yours coming along?" Bill says. "Cally tell you we got the invitation?"

"They're absolutely fab," Cally says.

"Wow, I can't believe Jordan sent them out already," I say.

"I was surprised, too. A little early, don't you think?" Cally says with an inquisitive tone. Her changing expressions from fear to curiosity, makes it all the more hard for me to try and decipher what exactly is going on.

Jon clears his throat. "She called me at the center not too long ago and asked about it. She didn't want to bother you, I guess. I told her to do whatever she thought would raise the most money."

"Oh," is all I can say. Between the VIP table, Cally's

strange behavior, and just the overall feeling that nothing is right—I'm in a daze.

I look at Jon, and he smiles quaintly then turns to face Bill. The men get into a new discussion about golf. Cally starts talking about Tara and news regarding the interviews for the *Housewives* show. I look at her occasionally and nod. Take a sip of water then say, yes. The conversation continues but without me. She lost me after the first sentence. Then I wonder if Jon and Bill are actually listening to one another or just wanting to hear the sound of their own voices.

Really, this is my life? It's not making any sense, and why didn't I notice it before? Is this some kind of whacky newfound awareness caused by my instability? No thanks—I prefer to remain blind and content to all these hidden comments and gestures and not give a damn. Maybe this is what the tones want me to *See*—that my life is a façade.

Too much is going on and so much still left unsaid it seems. For reprieve, I mentally orchestrate all the ambient sounds to harmonize with the tones. Bill and Jon's voices, Cally's, the ambient music sifting through speakers in the restaurant, along with the voices coming from down below, and the clinking of dinnerware—they are all a part of my escape symphony. My heart starts to race. I turn my head and look toward the elevator. I want to jump up and leave, run far away, but where?

To Dr. Light—I want to run to Dr. Light.

CHAPTER EIGHTEEN

Halfway through dinner, I'd already made the decision to take a Valium before bed. Skipping them doesn't feel like it's done me any favors. Even though I haven'tt felt like I've needed them, a little relaxation would be most welcome after this evening's emotional chaos. I played with my food most of the time, taking only small bites here and there. They all spoke incessantly, but no one commented on my lack of participation. There was a sense of gloom around us left ignored. It felt to me like they all knew something was wrong, and I wasn't necessarily the cause.

Jon didn't say much on the way home, or when he was undressing, then showering. He put on a pair of sweats and an old T-shirt, kissed my forehead as I lie in bed, then headed down to the office.

I'm trying hard to take in slow deep breaths while thinking of Dr. Light, but I keep losing focus. It's no use, so I give up and allow the Valium to do its work. I reach over then turn off the light.

The light of the fire glows beneath the hazy red sky. Flat on my back, looking up, I watch endless swirls of black smoke rise and curl. Something's not right. I hear more than the usual crackling and popping of the fire. It sounds like low moans. I sit up and look at the mound. All of the bodies are whole again, and they are writhing. My God, I'm burning them alive!

Frantic, I get up and run over. "Help," Several of them yell. "The pain," they scream. "Get us out!"

A gnarled bundle of burning flesh, they fight and struggle to free themselves from one another. Their limbs are stretched out, reaching and swaying like anchored soft corals in a strong current.

Toni, from across the street, inches her way toward me. "Help me," she cries out. Half of her face is charred, bubbling open the way pizza does when it's baking. It's drooping, coming off. Distorting her image, like a melting picture.

I panic, can't think. I'm turning around and around, looking for a way to help. Then I run to the cart. Grab the axe. Race toward the mound again and stumble over something. The axe launches forward. I look back— it's Toni. She reached her hand out and tripped me. She continues to strain and drag herself closer. Then she grabs hold of the back of my leg just above my boot.

I'm punching and kicking her, but she doesn't let go. It feels as though her hand has melted into my thigh. "Stop! It burns," I scream. Remembering the axe, I turn around, dig my elbows into the hard desert clay and inch my way over to it. The handle within arm's reach, I claw at the earth with my fingernails. Several of them crack and splinter back, a few tear away from their nail beds, but nothing hurts worse than the burning of my leg. At last, I feel the smooth handle with the tips of my fingers and pull it closer. Toni tightens her grip, and I shriek in pain. I glance at my leg and my pants are on fire. Without thinking, I sweep the axe toward her. Against the sand and rubble, the skin on my wrist peels back and bunches up under my thumb. The axe blade doesn't have enough momentum to hit her. It stops, and she reaches for the blade. I clench my teeth then scrape the axe back across the dirt. The bundled skin beneath my thumb moves over my stripped wrist embedded with sand and pebbles. I use the handle to get myself up, and when I'm standing firm on one leg, the other still on fire, I raise the blade up into the air. The skin from my wrist flaps open and hangs. Sandy blood sprinkles onto my face and into my eyes. I squint to keep them open and chop.

"No," Toni yells through sloughing lips.

The axe strikes her upper arm, but doesn't cut deep enough to sever it. Her screams are now loud gurgles and hisses. I pull and lift the axe out, then bring it down hard, splitting what was left of her scorched face. Her grip on my leg releases. I drop and wriggle my backside around in the dirt. Then everything goes silent.

Lying on the ground, I turn my head and look over to the mound, blinking constantly to clear the sand from my eyes. A face stares back at me—one I immediately recognize—it's Patrick. He is burning, screaming, and he can't get out. There are too many bodies squirming to get free. All piled on top of him. My God, what have I done? Sound comes back all at once. It's chaos.

"Mom! Help!"

I jump up and run to him. Drop to my knees then grab hold of his burning hands and pull. Flames lick my raw wrist, making it sizzle and sting. Patrick's skin slides off like a pair of gloves, exposing gooey blood on top of the flesh. He screams again, and I scream with him, holding burnt layers of his tissue in the shape of fingers and hands. I toss them away then extract the axe from Toni's face. Maniacal, I raise and swing, raise and swing, hacking at my neighbors, killing them, trying to get them off Patrick.

His screams intensify and my attempts to free him are useless. His shrill cries, I can't stand them! I look down into his eyes.

"Save me, Mom," he groans.

My knees buckle, but I stay upright. "Close your eyes," I tell him. "I'll get you out."

When his eyes are closed, I raise the axe again with shaking hands. "Love you," I whisper. Tears roll into my mouth and onto my tongue as I take in a deep breath. I exhale and bring the heavy blade down with everything I've got left. The chop is smooth, but then I hit something more solid, stopping the motion. It nearly splits his head apart. The metallic back end of the axe flickers in the firelight. I tug on the handle. It's stuck. The blade must be buried deep into the base of his skull. No energy left, I step away and fall back to the ground, crying.

My hands grip the tear-soaked pillow as if it was the handle of an axe. I let go and reach behind me for Jon. He's not there. I sit up and take a look around. He never came to bed. It's a first that makes me curious. I flip the covers off then go into the bathroom. After drying my tears and blowing my nose, I lift my robe from a hook in the closet then head down to the office.

Standing in the hall with my hand on the lever, I hesitate for a second. Last time I was in there, I heard children from one of my past-life déjà vu's laughing behind the door. I put my ear up against it and listen—nothing. The door swings open and I see Jon seated in the office chair, lying face down across the desk. I walk over to him and gently move the computer mouse from his hand. The screen lights up and he moans a little then covers his eyes with his arm.

It's an email from Jordan about the fundraiser sent directly to his account. She praises him for allowing her to have more control in the decision making. She thinks it's a good idea that *I* get some rest, too. They have obviously been collaborating.

What is she up to?

A part of me thinks I know.

Bitch.

None of this matters now for God's sake—I just killed my son in a nightmare!

I click and close the message then put my hand on Jon's shoulder. "Honey, wake up."

His head jerks back and his eyes open wide, staring at the computer screen. Nothing is there now but a picture of Patrick kicking a soccer ball. "What? Did I fall asleep?" He rubs his eyes.

"Yeah. Come to bed, okay?"

He gets up and walks to the door with me right behind him. And when he leaves the room, I look back to the shelves. His anatomy books glow electric blue in the computer light. They are the same ones that taught me how to properly dismember him. It makes me shudder as I step out, then close the door behind me. Jon walks down the hall to our bedroom, and I quietly make my way to Patrick's room. I open the door and creep up to his bed. He is sound asleep, snoring. Not quite like a man, but no longer like a little boy. I pull the covers up over his shoulders then lean down and kiss the head I cleaved—in my nightmare.

Loud rhythmic thumps jolt me from bed. I swing open the double doors and catch a glimpse of Patrick. His heavy footsteps pound the carpet as he goes downstairs. I step back and look at the clock on my nightstand. It's a little after seven! I can't believe I slept in so late. Why didn't Jon wake me? It is another first.

A cup of coffee sits on the nightstand with cream clumping on the surface. I pick it up and gulp it down in one swallow. Cold yuck, it leaves a pasty, oily texture on my tongue. I put the cup on the nightstand then dart into the bathroom.

After brushing my teeth, I splash some water on my face. Then put my hair up in a big clip, and put on a pair of yoga pants with a matching jacket.

Patrick comes charging in. "You're just getting up?"

"I'm ready. Let's go." I've got one hand crimping my eyelashes, and I'm waving him away with the other.

"Great, I'm gonna be late," he grumbles on his way out.

I put on some lip gloss then jog downstairs. I grab my purse from the laundry room and rush through the door. Patrick is in the car waiting with the garage open. I get in, start the engine, and peel out.

He's staring out the passenger window, brooding over the fact he might be late for school. It feels strange looking at him after what happened in my dream last night. When I see his face, the image of him on fire with his head split open comes to mind. Even though it wasn't real, it felt real. Glancing down at my wrist, I distinctly remember the rubbing and stinging like sandpaper. The burning of my leg was so intense—unlike any other nightmare I've ever had.

Once I pass the school zone in front of Bishop Almeida High, I push the gas pedal to the floor and haul ass down the road at fifty miles an hour. It's green lights all the way.

Patrick looks up, dumbstruck, then grabs hold of the side door and grips it tight as I zip between cars. It's kind of fun, just this once, to drive like them and cut them off. To give back a little taste of the havoc they wreak on me every day.

In half the time it normally takes, I pull up to the school and slam on the brakes. I have a big smirk on my face. We're not late at all, and he knows it. He scrambles to unbuckle his seatbelt then gets out of the car. "Don't forget I'm done at one today," he says, "and I think maybe you should lay off the caffeine a little." He shuts the door before I can respond.

I put the window down and shout after him. "Okay! Bye…Love you." The last part comes out in a whisper the way it did in my dream last night.

Without turning around, he raises his arm and waves his hand for me to drive off.

Typical.

Now, I suppose I should go home and get properly dressed, but the idea of a real cup of coffee seems to be more vital. I pull into the drive-thru and order the sixteen ounce with three extra shots of espresso. It's nearly seven dollars, but worth every damn penny. I drive away from the pick-up window, then pull off to the side and put the car in park.

The coffee is hot, and I burn my tongue, but I can't imbibe it fast enough. Hmm…molten energy, it's exactly what I need. When I'm halfway done, I put the car into drive then head toward the freeway. I'm amped up now between the coffee and the road racing I'd done earlier. To calm myself, I take in a few deep breaths and tune into the soft music of the tones.

Once again, I arrive at Dr. Light's office building on time and without remembering how. Mine is the only car ever in the parking lot, and if it weren't for the fact I knew I was in Vegas, this could all be taking place in the backlot of a movie studio in Hollywood. But it's not important now. I need a quick fix for these nightmares, a cure, before something terrible happens. The latest instance confirms my doom theory, and if I'm right, it appears I will be the one responsible for everyone's demise—burning them in some way.

I get out of the car, walk fast, and keep my eyes down. I notice something unnerving about the building I never did before—I feel like it is looking at me. Every window is a socket with the shades cracked open just enough to peek out, and *See* me.

I don't care anymore, I need him to listen, hear me out. It's easy to understand how people get caught up in these one-on-one therapy sessions. It is addicting. I have a tremendous feeling of power knowing I can tell him anything at all, and no matter what I say, he can't repeat it. Then there's the downside, where he could have me committed, but nowadays I think it would take something like a horrible psychotic episode for that to happen.

In the building, I rush to his office ignoring the glimpses of oddities my eyes see along the way. The marble floor pulsing and swirling underfoot, walls in the lobby that weren't there before. And plants—I do *not* remember seeing any of those.

From the end of the hallway, I see him leaning against the entry, keeping the door from swinging shut with his shoe. His head is down. His gaze seems to be fixated on the floor. Even when I'm sure he hears me coming he doesn't look up.

I get to the door, and he moves his foot, but neither one of us makes any eye contact. "Good morning, Dr. Light." I walk on through, head straight back to his office, throw my purse to the floor, and hop up onto the lounger.

A minute or so later, he catches up then closes the door.

"I killed my son last night."

"What?"

"Not for real. I mean, in my nightmare."

After a second or two, he sighs dramatically. "Oh. That's a relief," he says. It's as if he had to think about it first before coming up with a logical response.

"Not really though, see…I think it means I'm going to kill my family. People I love."

"And what brought you to this conclusion?"

"Nothing I can pinpoint—I just know. I'm not sure how to explain, but I'm right."

"Perhaps we could find out more with a little hypnotherapy today. What do you think?"

"What? No. The last time you hypnotized me I left hearing…music. And I still hear it."

"Interesting…maybe if I hypnotize you today, it'll stop."

"I don't know. What if it does something worse?"

"Are you worried?"

"Yes actually, I am. I think the hypnosis opened a mental gateway of some sort. Things from my dreams are free to move back and forth into my reality."

"That's impossible. I told you not to be afraid."

"If you'd seen what I have, you'd be scared, too."

"I've observed a great many things. More than you could ever imagine, unless…" He turns away and stares out at the air.

The tones seem a little louder in here. Something is different about them, too. They have changed, sound more insistent, if that's even possible. Instead of listening to a recording, the music is live. I only wish I could understand. "Unless, what?" I say.

"Nothing. Let me hypnotize you. Sometimes it can help interpret the meaning of things."

"Are you reading my mind, Dr. Light?"

He turns and looks straight into my eyes. "No."

"Seriously, I was just thinking something along the same lines, and it was like you answered. Did I say it out loud?"

"I don't know what you mean. Shall we begin?"

"You really think it will help explain last night's nightmare?"

"Yes."

"Then fine. Go ahead." I try to relax, lie back, and close my eyes, take in a deep breath then exhale. "I see the red now, Dr. Light."

"The sound of my voice is blue. As I speak, my voice moves through you in waves and gently pushes out the red. You will take in three slow breaths. With each one, the blue waves of my voice will darken until you can see only a deep indigo. Do you understand?"

He puts his icy hands on my temples again. The red disappears in a flash. Nothing is left but blue. It's an arctic darkness he's putting into me. My head feels heavy, weak. I'm already under his spell. The indigo is oppressive. I can't stop sinking into it. I concentrate and put all my energy into wiggling my big toe, but I can't. This is the first time I've felt powerless in his presence. Something seems different, not quite right.

"Tell me about your dream," he says.

Even my lips are heavy. It is nearly impossible to move them. I inhale through my mouth to force them apart. "They were burning." I sound like a drunk, slurring my words. "I killed my son."

"No. About your other dream. The one with the shadows. Do you know who they are?"

"Not people."

"What then?"

"Monsters."

"No, not monsters either. I want you to think about a time when they were near."

"Too scary."

"Please, try Stacy. Can you do that?"

"Yes."

"Where are you? What do you see?"

"Little lights…they dance around in the dark."

"Yes?"

"They fade."

"Go on."

"They're in a circle."

"Who?"

"The twenty-six. You're there, too. You're one of them." My heart starts to race. "I want to stop. I don't want to see anymore."

"It's important, Stacy. Face your fear, and tell me what you see?"

"Their eyes. Big and black…like yours. Monsters." *I have to wake up, but I can't snap out of this.*

"Focus. They're not monsters."

"Not human." *They'll try and drown me again. Oh, shit! I'm already deep in the indigo.*

"They won't hurt you. Don't be afraid. You're right, they're not human. Look closer."

"Human shapes but wet shadows."

"What are we, Stacy?"

"Not real."

"Yes. Yes, we're real. Tell me what you see!"

"Aliens." *There it is. Let it be done now. Wake me up.*

Like he's reading my mind again, he counts. "One, two, three."

Everything snaps back to red. I sit up and stare at the wall. My heart flutters while I hyperventilate, trying to catch my breath. I was drowning, smothering in cold. I put my hands over my face to help slow my respiration.

Something cool and slimy is across my forehead. I bring my hand down to take a look. It's slick, clear, and somewhat opalescent. I think it could be the same stuff that made my hand sticky before. I rub it between my fingers. It's definitely not sweat. I put it up to my nose and sniff. It has a sweet smell—Dr. Light's.

"Stacy, are you all right?"

"No. Dr. Light. I'm not. I'm fucking crazy! And you're making me worse." I've added crying to my huffing and puffing. I'm delirious now. I have to get out of here before I pass out. "I'm sorry. I've got to go!" I reach down and grab my purse.

He jumps up from his chair, lunges toward me and reaches out. His slimy cold fingertips brush across my arm as I make a run for the door. "Stacy, stop!"

I turn around and look at him. Trying hard to ignore his big black eyes, his dripping wet skin. The floor underneath me almost seems agitated, like it's alive and angry. I focus on the door again. "I can't"

"Come back." I hear him yell as I round the bare desk up front.

"I won't!"

"Come back to us…"

The sun is extremely bright. I grab a pair of sunglasses from my purse and put them on. Then I'm in the car, squealing out of the lot. Tearing down a dirt road I've never seen before. Thankful I drive a big SUV, grateful I got out of there when I did.

CHAPTER NINETEEN

'm speeding through traffic on the highway when I regain my senses enough to know where I am. I've got to slow down. Relax. The exit sign for the grocery store I'd gone to for my Valium prescription stands out like a beacon. I turn off, park in the lot, then think about what happened and what my options are now.

An eerie calm pervades the car. The desert sun shining through the windows should have me feeling warm, but I'm not. I'm chilled to the bone. No doubt Dr. Light's to blame. I wonder what that cold slime was he put on my head? It feels like it's *in* my body now. The icy goo reminds me of the gel they put on my belly for an ultrasound when I was pregnant. Maybe Dr. Light had me hooked up to some kind of brain monitor I never noticed before. I don't think so, though. I'm sure I would have seen it, those machines aren't small.

It is perfectly still in the car—a deafening quiet. The

tones, they're gone. I close my eyes, sink back, and exhale with relief. A faint whisper tickles the hairs on the back of my neck. I snap up, whip around, and check the backseat. Nothing's there. No one is nearby. In the distance, I see people walking to and from their cars, but I made sure to park far from the storefront traffic.

More whispers speak but in different voices. "Hello," I say aloud. "Who's there?"

I gasp at the thought. It's *them*. The twenty-six. Only now, their music is spoken. I listen in, concentrate. *"Come back to us,"* I hear. *"There is danger."*

"Shit!" I put my hands up over my ears, but it continues. "Stop it," I shout. Jesus, this is it. I've completely gone insane. I'm hearing voices. It's schizophrenia. I hum, turn up the radio. It helps a little, makes their words harder to distinguish. A man walks by pushing an empty shopping cart. He stares at me through the window.

I'm going to need a new shrink.

What do I do until then? Cally…someone normal has to hear me out, a person that knows me, who wouldn't consider me crazy. I dial her cell, and the phone rings, but she doesn't pick up. Neither does her voicemail. That can't be right. I hang up and try their home number. There's no answer, only more ringing.

This just doesn't happen. Maybe it's not real.

Desperate, I dial Tara. There is no way I'm calling Jordan after seeing that email she sent to Jon. She seems to be flirting with him more than a friend should and behind my back. I'm not ready to deal with that, yet.

"Hello?" Tara answers.

"It's me…Stacy."

"I know it's you, Sweetie. What is it?"

"Have you spoken to Cally lately? I can't get in touch…"

"I haven't talked to Cally since I told her the bad news."

"What bad news?"

"Not getting the show. Didn't she tell you?"

"What? No. When did you talk to her?"

"After your dinner last night. How was it by the way? Cally didn't say much about it."

"That's what I'm saying. No one's told me anything."

"Well, we didn't get the *Housewives* show. They gave it to the girls in Green Valley. It's all Jordan's fault, fucking alcoholic."

"Jordan? Is she all right?"

"I haven't called her since she told me Samuel didn't come back from his convention."

"What?"

"Samuel left her. Aren't you listening?"

"Yes!"

"Sorry. It's just that I've been down ever since I heard about the show."

"I understand, but…do you think I should call her?"

"No. She doesn't want to talk about it. I told her to get into rehab. She hung up on me."

"Ah." *But she wants to talk with Jon…*

"I've got to go, but I wouldn't worry. Everybody will be fine. We always recover."

"Okay. Bye, Tara."

Not much of that conversation made any sense. It was disjointed, somber, and got me nowhere closer to Cally. I feel like I've been struck by lightning. Nothing is right. I'm out of sorts. Instead of healing, I'm getting worse, everything is.

Jon...

If I call him though, he'll send me straight to the hospital, and I have to…oh shit, it's almost twelve-thirty. Patrick. How long have I been sitting here? Several cars have parked nearby. The store's business is picking up. In a car opposite mine, a woman is waiting in the passenger seat. She pretends like she's not looking my way, but I can see her eyes directed at me. She must think I'm nuts sitting all alone talking to Tara, talking to myself.

I exit the parking lot then head back to the highway, to Patrick's school.

"How was your day?" I say.

"Fine…" He stares out the window then turns his head and looks at me. "Mom, can you take me home first and then go get Grandma and Grandpa?"

"Yeah, I guess. Why?"

"Grandpa always has to ride up front with you, and Grandma's perfume stinks."

I laugh. "I never liked the smell of it either. Red something or other, it's really strong. And I think that's why Grandpa rides shotgun. I'm sure they won't mind if you don't greet them at the airport."

I t's a good thing Patrick stayed home, too. Holiday traffic is full on, making it a hectic mess getting to the airport via the highway. I purposely ignored it when I passed the exit for Dr. Light's office. It was hard, but I kept my hands at ten and two and studied the cars ahead.

I can't help hearing the voices, listening to them. Now and then certain words stand out. Something about the sun, communicating. I wonder if that's what they'd been repeating when they were the tones. It makes me think of the sunspots Patrick mentioned forever ago. He said they might affect cell phone signals. If that is what they mean, it still doesn't make sense to me. They don't need to call— they're already in my head.

I get damn lucky, and a car pulls out as I'm pulling into the airport parking garage. The timing couldn't be any better. According to the monitors, their flight landed early. I'm glad I gave myself plenty of time to get here.

My mom and dad are easy to spot in a crowd. She will have on a long heavy coat and he will be in a turtleneck with a cable-knit sweater over it, even though they checked the weather reports a million times before they packed and got on the plane.

"Where's Patrick?" my mom asks with her arms around me in a gentle hug.

"He wasn't feeling good."

"Boy's not sick is he?" my dad says. "I don't want your mother catching something. She always gets the flu after we leave here."

Typical dad—*Ignore the fact that she loves going to casinos and mingling with strangers from around the world.*

"No, he's not sick. He was just tired."

"Well, you should've said that first," my mom says. "And why didn't you tell us you were having such warm weather?"

I smile and grind my molars. I swear, as soon as Patrick can drive, this is going to become his responsibility.

My dad walks over to the luggage carousel and watches the bags slide down the ramp.

"You look terrible, dear. I didn't want to say anything in front of your father, but my goodness, have you been eating?"

"Yes."

"But you look so thin and frail. I've never seen you like this."

"I'm fine, Mom. Nothing's wrong."

"How do you know? Have you gone to a doctor? And I don't mean Jon."

"Yes. I have." My parents won't recognize Jon as a real doctor, because he's family.

"It's worse than I thought if you've already been to a doctor. What did they say?"

"That I'm fine. They didn't find anything. I've been having trouble sleeping is all."

"You drink too much coffee."

"I didn't use to."

"It's not good for you. You need to cut back."

My father walks up rolling their big suitcase behind him. "Stacy's been to a doctor, dear. She's sick."

So much for keeping it from him.

"What's that?" he says.

"Stacy's sick, honey."

He gives me a quick sideways glance. "She looks fine to me. Stop your worrying."

"Thanks, Dad." I stretch up and kiss him on the cheek. "I'm glad you're here."

"Me, too," he says.

Oddly enough, I'm happier about them being here than I thought I would be. I can live with them thinking I look exhausted. They know I'm busy planning parties, preparing for the holidays, and for their visits. My haggard appearance should make it all the more convincing. If they were silent and said nothing, then I would have to worry. Sometimes, I forget that my mom has nothing better to do than trouble herself about us. We are really all they've got.

Traffic has lightened up considerably for the drive home. Normally, it's a twenty to thirty minute stretch from the house to the airport, but it took me over an hour this afternoon. My mom is in the back seat complaining about the flight, and my dad stares out the window and nods in agreement, occasionally. It's his way of listening, even though he isn't. I'm sure he's busy thinking about his golf swing and whether or not Jon has been playing enough to give him a good round.

I still can't believe the musical tones have turned into words I actually understand. I catch myself listening to *them* again and turn up the radio. *Come back to us*—would have to mean that I was with them before. It's complete lunacy.

Since I'm with my parents, I decide to take the long way home, keep off the freeway. They like to look around, and to be honest, I'm perfectly good about *not* seeing the exit for Dr. Light's office again so soon. I stop at a red light on Flamingo Boulevard.

"You've never taken me to this casino," my mom says, gazing out like a kid looking into a candy store. "It looks lovely."

"A lot of the locals go there, because it's away from the strip."

"Do they win?"

"I don't know. Our friends don't gamble."

"You should ask them sometime. Maybe they're acquainted with someone who does. I'd like to know."

"We can go there, if you want."

"I'll let you surprise me."

Which really means, *yes*, take me there.

"What're we having for dinner tonight?" she says.

"Jon's bringing home take-out from that place you like."

"Oh."

I glance at her reflection in the rearview mirror. Her eyes are transfixed on the tower of beckoning lights.

"Do you feel like going out after?" she says.

"No, Mom. I've still got a lot of prep work to do for the turkey."

"What if I help you?"

"Relax, dear," my dad says. "You'll have plenty of time to get robbed by the one-armed bandits while we're here."

My mom rolls her eyes but doesn't stop staring out the window.

"This is a long light," Dad says.

"No kidding," I say.

Finally, it turns green, and I speed away. She eventually snaps out of it and asks me what needs to be done for tomorrow. My mom hardly cares whether or not I cook a turkey with the fixings. It's the time it takes to prepare everything and clean up afterwards, she worries about. Less time cooking and cleaning, means more time spent at the casinos.

Lucky me, she loves to gamble, but fortunately, I didn't inherit her genes for that. Besides, gambling in Vegas takes on a different meaning when you live here. It's actually frowned upon. People may do it but nobody ever talks about it. You learn to get over it quick or risk losing it all. I've never minded taking my mom to the casinos when she comes. She enjoys it, and we usually have a good time, especially if she's winning.

My dad doesn't like to gamble. He prefers to spend time with Jon. They have heated conversations about politics and sports, topics of which my mom and I have no interest. I'm thankful that my dad and Jon get along so well. Compromise is why my parents' marriage has endured, and they're a wonderful testament to why my own marriage continues to persevere. *Maybe.*

I get a tense feeling of unrest whenever I'm anywhere near the strip. Jon thinks it has something to with all of the electric energy it takes to keep everything lit, like living close to an electrical substation. He says it's been linked to causing cancer. That, on top of the nuclear testing they used to do, makes Nevada a real radioactive hotspot.

It's comical in a way, how Dr. Light has me seeing aliens. Area 51 is famous for them. I've never believed any of that crap, not a shred of solid evidence. Does the facility exist? Yeah, but it's secretive, I think, because they test new airplanes out there. It makes perfect sense.

When I'm finished cleaning up after dinner, I start bringing stuff in from the garage refrigerator. Then I get to work on some of the side dishes for tomorrow.

"If you don't need me for anything, I'm going to shower then go to bed," Mom says. She stands next to me at the counter and leans over to see what I'm doing.

"No. I'm fine. Get some rest." I knew she would be too tired to go out once we got home.

"Goodnight." She shuffles her way down the hall. "Don't stay up too late."

The men watch TV and talk for a while. Patrick has been hiding in his room since he scoffed his dinner. Dad eventually gets up and says he's going to check on Mom, but doesn't come back out.

Jon gets up and walks over to me. "Is there anything I can help with? It's getting late."

"No. I'm almost done, but thanks. Thanks for picking up dinner tonight, too and the turkey."

"You're welcome," he says. Then he kisses my cheek. "You coming to bed soon?"

"In a few minutes. Are you?"

"Of course, that's why I want you to come, too."

"It's just that you've been spending a lot of time in the office lately."

"I've been busy and I'm sorry, but I've got the rest of the week off for Thanksgiving. I promise to stay out of there."

I turn my head and look him square in the eyes. He means it. I move closer and kiss his warm soft lips. He puts his arms around me and pulls me against him. Then he moves his head back. "Sure you don't want to come to bed with me now?"

"Let me finish. I'll be quick."

He releases me. "Okay," he says as he walks away. "I'll wait."

When he's gone, I do my best to hurry and cover the food. I put the cranberry sauce and turkey back into the refrigerator along with everything else. Then I wash more dishes and throw out the trash. By the time I get upstairs he is sound asleep and snoring under the covers.

So much for that.

Watching the comforter rise and fall with his breath makes me jealous. It's been so long since I've slept like that. It doesn't seem fair. These past months are nothing but a blur. Before the tears in my eyes have a chance to fall, I walk into the bathroom and undress.

After a hot shower, I put on my nightshirt then take two of the tiny blue pills. "Screw you," I whisper to *their* voices. "Tomorrow is Thanksgiving." I am determined to get some sleep, because right now, I'm thankful for nothing.

CHAPTER TWENTY

A breathy whisper fills the air. *"Danger…"* The word echoes around the room then settles and stays as if it were a solid thing with weight.

"What danger?" I say. I turn over, sit up. "Jon?"

His back is to me, and he is still asleep.

It's *them—the others*. I lie back down and pull the covers up to my neck. I wonder if this is a dream or if it is just the voices. *They* are the presence I feel in the room. The danger that draws near, that encircles the bed.

"Please," I beg. "Go away."

"We have come for you."

The icy, haunting words blow across the fine hairs on my body, making my skin tingle and crawl. The phrase, their proximity, reacts with something internal—the indigo blue. It resounds to freeze the marrow in my bones.

"I don't want to leave," I whisper. Afraid Jon might wake and find me talking in my sleep, talking to myself.

My teeth are chattering, and I'm shivering almost uncontrollably.

A blast of different voices all sound off at once. *"Remember." "Come back to us." "You have been too long here." "There is danger!"*

Paralyzed with cold and fear, I can do nothing. Maybe, if I talk to them they will go away. Would it mean then, that I've accepted my madness? Does it matter, as long as they disappear? Or will I go into my head with them and lose my sanity forever? I don't care. I can't live like this anymore.

"What is the danger?"

"Come with us." "We help." "Remember." "Earth..." "Suns..." "Lost..." "See..."

"I don't understand." My voice rises with agitation. "Stop talking like that." Anger burns inside, warms me, and melts their frozen indigo.

"It is time you return...you will be with us, soon." The voice was definitely Dr. Light's. His last word hisses then drifts off and fades away.

The room is different now, though, I can tell they're gone. I'm lying in bed on my side. The digital clock reads four.

I slide out of bed then quietly go into the bathroom and get dressed.

Dad is the first one to wake up and join me in the kitchen for a cup of coffee. The turkey is already in the oven. Everything is prepared. I've even set the table and brought out the china.

"Morning," he says.

"Morning."

"Coffee on?"

"Yeah." *The second pot, actually.* "I'll get it. Just black, right?"

"You have any of that flavored cream your mom likes?"

"It's in the fridge."

"I'll take a little."

"Is this for you or Mom?"

"Your mother."

"She up already?"

"She thought you might need some help."

"Tell her I was up early and took care of everything. She can go back to sleep."

"Once she's up, she's up. You know. It'll take her over an hour to get dressed anyway."

I hand him the cup. "Thanks," he says. "I'll be back in a minute for mine." He grabs the remote and turns on the news. "When do the games start?"

"I have no idea, Dad, but I guarantee Jon will be up before then."

He disappears down the hall with my mom's coffee. It's sweet, even after all these years he gets hers first. That was surely one of the reasons I fell in love with Jon. The things he used to do—does, remind me a lot of how my dad dotes on my mom.

Jon is actually more understanding than I give him

credit for. When my parents leave, I'll get him alone, then sit down and tell him everything that's been happening to me. If it takes a battery of tests, so be it. We can get through this, and I can't do it without him. He still loves me, I know it. I've just got to be totally honest and open. If I have to spend some time at a sanctuary, *sanitarium*, I'll do it—anything now to save my marriage, our family, and my peace of mind.

The mere thought of telling Jon about everything is liberating. I feel better already, more alive—looking forward to a wonderful family meal, then later, time alone with my mom and having fun. Then I notice it…the voices, they're hardly audible anymore, only hushed mumbles now. Could it be that acceptance of a disorder and plan of resolution is enough to make their influence dissipate? Lose their power? This is really turning out to be a fantastic day.

Jon eventually comes downstairs for some coffee. "Morning, honey," he says. Then he leans down and kisses my cheek. "You're up early. What time did you come to bed?"

"Too late for you," I say.

"Sorry about that. I was tired. I'm rested now though…" He wraps his arms around me.

"Later." I wriggle free.

He changes the channel to the football game. "Are your folks up?"

And at that moment, they enter the hall. "Good morning," Mom says. "Happy Thanksgiving."

"Oh good, the game's started," Dad says. Then he makes himself comfortable on the couch with a cup of coffee in his hand.

"It's just the pregame stuff," Jon says.

"Careful not to spill that, dear," Mom says to Dad. She grabs a coaster and places it on the natural steel side table next to him.

"Mom, that table's not an antique," I say. "I think it might even be bulletproof."

"If there's a mess to be made, your father will make it."

Jon sits on the other end of the couch, casually looks over at me, then rolls his eyes. I smile back and wink.

"What?" Mom says.

"Nothing," I say. "Would you like some more coffee?"

"No. I only have one cup a day. You should follow suit. How'd you sleep last night? You look a little better this morning."

"I feel pretty good actually."

"What do you need help with?"

"Nothing. Everything's in the oven."

"My goodness we'll be eating before noon."

"Isn't that what you were hoping," my dad says from the family room.

"Never mind," she says. "Where's Patrick?"

"He'll be down when he smells the food cooking," I say.

"It's not good to let him sleep so late."

"Mom, he's a teenager. He needs it."

"You never slept in late like that. Did she, honey?"

My dad waves her off. "The game's starting." He picks up the remote and turns up the volume.

Between the TV and my mom, *the voices* have mostly become static. I'm so glad, too. I wasn't sure I would be able to make it through this next week without losing it.

Patrick comes downstairs two hours later. "What can I eat?" he says.

My mom perks up from the couch where she took a seat next to my dad. "Good morning, Patrick," she says. "I mean afternoon."

"Morning, Grandma."

"Happy Thanksgiving," she says.

"Happy Thanksgiving." Then he faces me and rolls his eyes.

"Everything's almost ready," I tell him.

"Even the turkey?" he says.

"Yeah."

"Awesome." He goes into the family room and sits down next to Jon.

During the time between games, everyone gets up, comes into the kitchen and piles food onto their plates. I was informed this would be the best time to eat, since the first game was the better match-up of the two.

No one bothered to turn the TV down. Then a local news bulletin comes on and interrupts the programming.

"I hope this is over before the game starts," Dad says.

Patrick walks into the family room with a full plate and turns the volume up another notch. We all turn around curious at what has captured his attention.

A news anchor I've never seen reporting before, talks about the recent activity of sunspots and how it has caused temporary malfunctions with some of the U.S. space satellites, resulting in disruptions with communications networks and spotty cell phone service. On a separate screen to the left of the anchor, they play old footage of an incident that occurred in Montreal, Canada in March of nineteen eighty-nine. The sunspots then had caused electrical surges in energy plants and overloaded their power grids causing them to shut down, creating citywide blackouts.

"This is what I was telling you about, Mom," Patrick says. He turns the TV up a little more. No one complains about the loudness. Everyone is fixed on the news report.

Now they're interviewing a scientist—a solar scientist to be specific. Whoever heard of such a thing? Dr. Jeff Boren, solar physicist.

"We're entering a cyclical time of increased solar activity," he says into the reporter's microphone.

"What can we expect?" asks the reporter. "Is this the end of the world portrayed in recent films?"

"It's cyclical, meaning it's happened many times before. You won't notice any direct physical changes. There will be an increase in electromagnetic radiation," he says. "These solar storms erupt with coronal mass ejections powerful enough to reach Earth's atmosphere creating an amplified aurora borealis. They can do some damage as well, like they did to the power grid in nineteen eighty-nine. More than anything else—in this electronic age we've grown to depend on—we'll be annoyed when our gadgets occasionally get out of whack. Solar science is relatively young, and we'll continue to learn more as the interest in the Sun and the effects of solar radiation grow."

"Thank you, Dr. Boren. You've heard it here first," the anchor says. "Signing off now. Everyone have a Happy Thanksgiving."

Patrick turns the TV down then heads into the dining room with his plate. The pregame show comes back on, and the rest of us finish loading our plates with food.

"Humph," Mom utters. "End of the world broadcast on Thanksgiving. Doesn't your friend's husband run the news programming?"

"Not for that channel." Jon looks at me and smiles.

"What were they thinking?" She continues on into the dining room.

When we are all seated, Patrick gives thanks for our meal and we eat.

"That was an interesting news report, huh Mom?" Patrick says.

"Not at all," my mom replies.

"It was," I say. "Why are you so into it?"

"It's cool," he says.

"Looks like you might have a scientist on your hands," my dad says.

"Absolutely not," my mom says. "You should be a doctor like your father."

Patrick slides the fork out from between his lips, and I watch his jaw muscles clench.

"So where would you like to go after dinner, Mom?"

Patrick looks at me, and I sneak him a little wink. He swallows his food then grins.

"I thought you were taking me to the place we passed yesterday."

"Oh yeah…that's right," I say.

She quiets down and finishes up her plate. A little faster now, too and with dollar signs in her eyes. It doesn't take much to put her at ease, just a casual mention of a casino.

I wonder if the sunspots have anything to do with the tones and the voices. I'm sure *they* said something about it, but I'm positive it was *suns—plural*.

CHAPTER TWENTY-ONE

Jon and my dad walk my mom and me out to the car in the garage. They kiss us and wish us luck as though we were heading off to sea.

"Drive careful," Jon says.

"I will."

"Have fun," Dad says to Mom.

"We'll have more fun than you two," she says.

They stand at the door and wave until we pull down the driveway then close the garage. No doubt they'll be heading outside to have cigars on the patio. I just hope Jon doesn't forget to close the sliding door again. Last time, they filled the kitchen with cigar smoke and set off the fire alarm. And the smell was revolting. It took months to get rid of the odor.

"You sure you want to go to the local place we passed the other day?" I say.

"Why don't you drive down to the strip? If I see a

place that gives me a good feeling, I'll tell you, and then you can stop."

"It'll take a while to drive the whole strip." I'm not sure it's even possible. I've never done it. It would take at least an hour, if not more, depending on traffic. Ugh, this little outing isn't looking to be so fun anymore.

"Just aim for that light up there." She points to the sky. *"There is danger."*

"What?" I say.

"Don't tell me you can't see that white light pointing straight through the clouds."

"We are coming." "It is time." "Come back to us…" Their voices are loud, simultaneous, and confusing.

"I'm not going anywhere," I tell them.

"Stacy, are you all right?" my mom says.

"Yes. I'm fine. I was just talking to myself."

"Well I heard you loud and clear," she says. "If you don't want to go out with me then turn this car around and take me home. I'll have your father drive."

"No. Don't be ridiculous. I didn't mean it to you."

"Then who? I'm the only one here."

"You're right. Sorry. I *do* want to go, really. I just thought I heard something, that's all."

She turns away and stares out the window. I keep my mouth shut and drive toward the beacon. It's glowing bluish-white like an iceberg. Because it is one of the older casinos at the south end of the strip, Jon and I don't frequent it. Usually when people visit or for special events, the newer, north end of the strip is more popular. Everyone wants to see magnificent fountains and the ceiling made of hand-blown glass.

As the voices in my head become more intense, I'm ready to pull into whatever place is next, but the light…I'm inescapably drawn to it. With everything that is happening, I'm not sure how I'm able to concentrate on driving, but I get to the massive pyramid of black glass. One minute I'm on the beltway, and then a minute later, the car is idling in the valet parking line. My mom practically jumps from the passenger seat, snapping me out of it. I turn off the engine and leave the keys in the ignition. Then I exit the car and stand next to her. She is complaining about the parking attendant taking too long. When he finally comes, he writes down the license plate then hands me a ticket stub.

"Wow," she says, "you've never brought me here before."

During the day, the windows on the outside are gold and reflect the sun, but at night they are shiny and black. It is a magnificent feat of engineering. The light above is so bright. "I've never been either," I tell her, "or seen it this close up. It's amazing."

"Yes, yes, it looks nice. Now let's go and see what it's like inside."

My mom grabs my arm and yanks me through the casino doors by my coat sleeve, just like when I was a little girl. I guess this means I'm forgiven. Now it's my turn to say, "Wow." The high center of the pyramid ceiling is visible all the way from the casino lobby. Everything is decorated in Ancient Egyptian, reminding me a little of my earliest past life déjà vu. I remember Dr. Light telling me I was in Sumer, but I wonder exactly how he would know that from this.

"Come on," she says, "let's go and see what kind of slot machines they have."

Too much like a mother and her child, she pulls me along by my purse while I stagger behind and stare at everything in awe. It amuses me how a modest, intelligent woman such as my mother could become so helplessly entranced by the mindless spinning reels and flashing lights of slot machines.

"Okay, okay. Just stop pulling me."

She turns back and gives me a wicked glance. The *don't push it* look.

"Which ones do you want to play?" I ask with a forced smile. "I'll help you look for the ones you like."

"I want to play the ones that win."

I guess I set myself up for that. "Mom, I don't play them enough to know which ones win. Do you want me to ask somebody in here?"

"No. Don't do that. What about those over there?" She points to a circular bank of slot machines lit up with sevens and flames.

"That looks good. Let's go." I take the lead and she follows. There aren't a lot of people around these, but I'm glad it doesn't make her leery about their winning potential. I'll be happy to get away from bumping shoulders with strangers.

"You're sure these are ones you like?" I say.

I turn around to see her wide-eyed, staring at the machines. *I guess this is it.*

"Yes. Why don't we start over there," she says, as she walks away.

Exhausted, I sit right down on a stool in front of a machine. The balls of my feet are tender, the voices in my head are louder, and now, I've got the sound of people talking and slot machines all going on at once. My head is ready to burst.

"What are you doing?" she says.

"You said this is where you wanted to play."

"Yes, but don't you want to walk around and check them all out first?"

"Check them out for what?"

"You might get a better feeling from one, more than the other." The look on her face and her tone, tell me she's completely serious. She honestly believes she's going to win because a slot machine told her so.

"No, you go ahead. This one feels pretty good to me."

"Fine, but I don't feel it. I'm going to walk around and check out the rest. I'll let you know where I am when I've found one."

"Okay, good. I'll be right here, waiting."

Last year when I took her out, she wandered off without telling me, and it took me over an hour and a half to find her. I had every security guard and change person on the lookout for her. She was embarrassed and scolded me about it when they finally found her. She had been playing at a sit-down poker machine near one of the restrooms. She had herself hunched over it, so she wasn't recognizable. It was ridiculous.

After several minutes, I sit up and look around. She waves at me from across the way. I nod, wave, and sit back down. Not five minutes later, a loud shriek comes from the other side. Afraid, I jump up and look over the top of my machine. She's already standing, almost bouncing and pointing at me.

"Come and look," she shouts. "I hit the jackpot!"

Great, now I'll have to hear about her psychic gambling mojo for the rest of my life. I get up and walk around to her. I'm glad she's happy, though.

She hit the jackpot all right. Loud, obnoxious carnival music blares from the machine. Three, red fiery sevens are perfectly aligned underneath the glass. The dollar amount she won flashes up at the top of the machine. The lucky woman who listens to machines won twelve hundred and forty dollars. People walking by, stop and stare. A few step up to congratulate her. She just stands and smiles, pointing to the jackpot like a game show model.

"What are you doing?" I say.

"I have to wait for the people to come back with my money."

"How long does that take?"

"I don't know. Why don't you ask one of the workers?"

I look away to find someone. Bright swirling colors and shapes move around the outer edges of my visual periphery. I blink a few times, close my eyes, and try to focus on something else, but nothing works. It's as if I'm looking into two different kaleidoscopes at once.

An attendant arrives with another woman wearing a polyester business suit. She has a little clipboard with a form on it for my mom to sign. I give it a quick look. Even through kaleidoscope eyes I can see that it's a tax form.

"That's not fair," my mom says, as she hurriedly pens her signature.

"Anything over eleven hundred and ninety-nine dollars, ma'am," the attendant says. She hands my mom a copy of the form then counts out the money into the palm of her hand. When they're done my mom slips some money to the attendant. "Thanks," she says, "and good luck. Hit another one."

It all seems so unreal.

"See. I told you," my mom says. "Here's a hundred dollars. Go find a different machine to play."

"No, Mom. You don't have to—"

"Just go. I'm luckier when you're not standing here."

"Thanks." I walk toward another slot machine in the same circular bank.

"Not that one," I hear her yell.

I take several more steps, careful not to stumble. Then I walk around to the exact same machine I was sitting at before. The swirling shapes and vivid colors spread into the center of my sight and blurs everything in front of me.

I hear my mom from across the way. "Did you go back to that same machine?"

"No, Mom, the one next to it."

Now she's being completely absurd, but I've got to play along until a waitress comes by. My mouth is dry, and

I'd really like some water. I put the hundred dollar bill she gave me into my wallet and pull out a twenty. I put that into the machine then press the button. I can barely see the symbols spinning in front of me. Then I feel a sharp pain as if I've been struck in the head by a bullet. An earsplitting, high-pitched tone pierces my ears and nearly knocks me off the stool.

I press my forehead against the slot machine as hard as I can to make it stop. I reach up and squeeze my head. The pain! I can't shout for help, I can hardly breathe. I close my eyes and wait. Why is this happening to me again?

When I open my eyes, I see red. I move my head back, blink, and look again. The entire front of the slot machine is covered and dripping with bright red blood. Copious amounts spout profusely from my nose, spraying over everything in front of me. I pinch off my nostrils. Then blood starts pouring out of my mouth. It splashes onto my lap, streams down my legs then onto the floor. People stop, stare and point. Some of their mouths are open. I think they're screaming, but I hear nothing. Only the blaring tone. Men in suits gather around me as I begin to fade.

A halo of darkness replaces the wild dancing colors. It spreads in from the periphery and grows so large—my eyes are open—but I am nearly blind. Gurgling to breathe, I focus on the pinpoint of light in the very center where I can still barely see. Then it disappears, and I feel my body hit the floor. The deathly tone ceases and the more familiar tones begin to play.

CHAPTER TWENTY-TWO

This must be Heaven. I wonder why it is so unbelievably cold. Surely, I must be dead.

My eyes open to an aurora borealis. Motionless, my naked body hovers within it. Illuminated ribbons furl around me in iridescent waves. The colors fluctuate with the music of the tones. It is *the others*. All twenty-six are with me. Suddenly, the cold begins to burn. My body melts away, and I become liquid light—the color red. Together we are twenty-seven. In a flash beam of luminescence, we travel through the empty darkness of space. A space in which there is no light, no stars, nothing, except for us. We come to a slow halt, surrounded by our colors which fade into a pale rainbow within a dusky background.

The volume of the tones rises, bringing with them hues of streaming brilliant light. *"Be calm,"* they say, to allay my fear. My red is much brighter than any of their colors. *"This is a sleeping dream."* They speak in music and color I fully understand now. No longer embodied, I am an abstract moving fluid of light—like them.

I sense Dr. Light by my side, but he is no longer Dr. Light, just the aura of him in indigo blue. He's not actually a *him* anymore either, he is more of an *it*. We all are. A flash of memory comes back to me…genderless alien life forms, unable to reproduce.

"*Yes,*" they say in unison.

I'm not sure where that thought came from. Remembering such a thing doesn't make any sense. Unless…unless, there's something more to the tones and the alien dreams. Dr. Light seemed to think so—even encouraged it—and he's here with me now. Hopefully, he will be able to give me the answers. I don't want to be responsible for some kind of catastrophe. I'm not sure what to think or believe. I've either completely gone off the deep end and am lost somewhere in my own mind, or there is truth to my madness.

What I thought was a gray and dusky cloud around us, has become clear and opalescent. It is changing into a solid thing—sort of. I'm in front of the others moving through this place as it forms around us. Dr. Light's indigo is right behind me. Tunnels take shape about the diameter of a human with outstretched arms and legs. But I no longer have any limbs. I'm not human.

Knowingly, I lead the others through long corridors of thick membranous tissue lined with protective layers of mucous. I'm not sure if this is what the gray turned into or if we have always been in this biological environment, and it has been invisible until now.

As we move along, any contact with the walls sends streams of neon colored lights shooting past. The moist partitions bulge and pulse around us. They fold over and collapse after we move on. We are inside a living thing, and we are also a part of it. As if traveling and living within a bioluminescent organism at the bottom of a deep, dark ocean. A subdued atmosphere settles in amongst us. My fear and anxiety begin to subside—I know this place.

"*Yes,*" they say in colored waves of light and notes. The tonal sounds of their divergent voices echo hauntingly around me. The word itself I hear in my mind or what I think is my mind. It is also theirs. They hear my thoughts. We are telepathically linked. Then I wonder again if I have died.

"*No. The human you, sleeps. It is only a part of your dark energy that is here.*"

Dark energy, like dark matter is something unknown to them on Earth, I think.

"*Yes. We are these.*"

Everything I see is clearer. The fog that always clung to the rainbow lights has lifted, but I don't think I can see—with eyes—the way I used to, because I can see *everything* and from *every* angle.

Together, we continue moving forward through living halls. Everywhere, there is the sweet scent I often smelled on Dr. Light. We glide through labyrinths that wind around in circular narrow corridors. The pathways are long and cavernous. Everything is made of a thick gelatinous substance. For the most part, it is clear, but denser in certain areas. Just below the slick surface of the gelatin, long dark branches run endlessly throughout. They resemble arteries and veins. Some of the vessels are deeper than the ones above them, giving them a layered appearance much like the marble floors in Dr. Light's office.

Yes. It is alive, pulsating on its own—as we pulsate within it. We are individual, and we are one. Everything works together as a living entity—we are a biosphere. We come from dark matter. I remember...we were created from it, feeding on dark energy.

Tones and colorful lights sound and flash all around. *"Dark energy is our source of life."*

My thoughts and theirs, move throughout in various hues and amplified tones.

An alien sucrose, a type of sugar, is what we excrete—a byproduct of the dark energy—*sweet waste.* It is the slime that covers everything here, the ooze that is our composition, and the smell of Dr. Light. And the excess...we have to get rid of it, or it becomes toxic.

"Yes."

But my mind, *our* mind is clouded. I can't see the rest of it. Then I think of Dr. Light...

Before I can finish the thought, the indigo next to me changes form. The light dims, and the liquid morphs into the human Dr. Light, clothes and all. The others change, too and me. Then the environment around us becomes his building. I look like me again, next to Dr. Light. We are standing in his office, but I can see everything in my mind from the viewpoint of everyone—I mean *everything* else.

The others have taken forms like the desk out front, the chairs and the lounger, even the bookshelves.

"Here in dark space we can keep these configurations so long as we have the dark energy as a direct resource. Our negative dark matter breaks down in the positive presence of electromagnetic radiation without the protection of our lifesource. If we were not in dark space, and back on Earth, depending on the variable intensity of the emission from that planet's star, the forms we took would begin to decompose within one planetary hour."

I see…yes. That would explain the strange occurrences I noticed, like the disappearance and odd placement of things—the times when I would see Dr. Light melting. I'm beginning to understand and remember, but…

All of a sudden, there is a loud thump, followed by a bright white light. It beams directly at me from the end of the office hall. It intensifies and with it comes a flash of pain. Then a powerful, electric shockwave blasts through me.

"No! Come back to us." Their words, tones, and colors quickly fade.

I reach out to Dr. Light, but my body falls away. I'm being pulled faster than light through empty space. The darkness is acute and so horrifying I have to close my eyes.

It stops and I hear the faint voices of people shouting— no longer the tones. My chest hurts and my head. Then I hear my name and open my eyes. Everything in front of me is blurry. I blink several times to clear my vision.

"Stacy! Stay with us."

"Not done," I gurgle. My throat is sore, full of liquid. I cough out and my head lifts up then crashes down against a hard surface. A spray of blood flies through the air across a dingy moving blue wall.

Jon's voice rings out. "Come on, Stacy, fight it!"

The wall moves in. My sight clears. People in blue scrubs stand over me.

"Must see." I reach up to the light. My hand and arm are streaked with blood. Someone grabs my wrist. A sudden chill jolts down my spine, bucking me upward. Then my body violently begins to spasm and jerk around. I sense *the others* with me again. They have come for me and I need answers. If there's going to be some kind of apocalypse, maybe they'll know when it will happen and tell me how to prevent it. So I succumb to their cold, and then the lights fade out.

"No," Jon screams. His voice gradually disappears.

In absolute darkness, I slip and slide through soft silky folds of cool, lubricated gelatinous tissue. This must be what it's like to be born and remember it. The layers of plica move away with little effort as I pass, writhing slowly to an opening. I pour out onto an area like a landing that is alive. I am fluid light again—red. The twenty-six are all positioned around me, staring. I can see in my head the image each one of them perceives.

My liquid self thickens a little. The others' forms have coagulated somewhat, too. I straighten up and take on the same shape as them. Their figures are still mostly blobs but slightly more humanoid. Their heads, or highest part of the gelatin masses, are shaped like oversized footballs. On either side, there are two large black ovals. They remind me of Dr. Light's eyes—creepy open portals. They look out of place, like they were put there merely for ornamental purposes. Soon after my thought, their eyes slide down and disappear into their bodies, which are simply in the shapes of tree trunks. At the very bottom of each being, there are two nubs. They look like blunt ankles—no feet. Maybe that's why Dr. Light always appeared to move awkwardly…he wasn't used to having feet or walking.

I'm opalescent now, too, with my red light encased within branchy veins. All over, my form also illuminates a crimson glow that pulses with the rest of the biosphere.

Curious, I think of human fingers. Then there they are but made from the jelly substance. There is no outer layer or skin, just the slime. We are sleek and moist—transparent. Inside us, there are flecks of glimmering rainbows. The suspended particles do not reflect light, they emit it. We would be in total darkness if it weren't for our own light.

The others watch me examine myself. *"See."*

Yes, I *See*. I *See* everything. It is beautiful. What happened when I went away?

"Your human body tried to die."

So, I'm not dead?

"No. You must live…live to remember."

Remember? I am remembering, and if I'm not dead, then what am I?

"It is what they call a coma. It is the only way your dark energy life force can be here and there simultaneously."

If I did die though, would I be stuck here?

"No. Your dark energy force would have to return and enter a new host."

I don't understand.

"Let us show you."

Memories come and go here. Nothing is straightforward. I can't figure out why I can remember some things and not others.

"You have been gone a while. It is a part of what we are."

What…memory loss? That's absurd. Then it comes to me—they're right. They don't know how we came into existence. They don't remember. All they recall is traveling. It has only ever been the twenty-seven, bound on an endless journey in search of life like ours. An infinite voyage to discover how we came to be…that's it! We, ours, we…I talk like I'm one of them. How is it that I know all of this? Maybe I am…

"Yes."

But how did I…forget…and so much? This could simply be an alien abduction. They're trying to brainwash me into believing I was one of them. They need me for something…

We have found no other life in the darkness in which we exist. It is infinite. And the light—the positive matter—places like Earth. Life is abundant there. So that is where we go. We travel there to study and learn. We…

Oh God, how is this possible? The things I'm remembering. They can't be.

"Yes, but there is more." "Show the rest." "No. Let it try to remember." "Perhaps it can tell us what we do not know."

This is the first time I've heard you as separate entities.

"We are twenty-seven—we are one."

It all has something to do with the sweet waste. There's something significant about it. I just can't put my finger on it.

"You do not have fingers."

Sure I do. *See.* I raise a blobby limb then simply will the fingers to take shape again. Then I lower them and they all turn back to amorphous jelly. Now let me think… the sugar…it could be what makes us forget. The build-up becomes poison in our system, the same way aluminum on Earth is thought to cause Alzheimer's or the sugar issues with diabetes.

"Yes, it knows." "See." "Remember."

Stop talking like that. It's making me nuts. I'm still partly human—I guess—or at least I think I am, so let me try and analyze like one.

"No." "Show it."

Stop!

A tidal wave of red light rolls through the soft walls around us. There is a collective feeling of fear and awe.

The sweet waste again…we throw it away. Dump the excess.

"Yes."

The others circle in to hear my epiphany. Their nubby appendages that are together legs and feet sink part way into the opalescent ooze—the sucrose gel. But the thought, it doesn't come. I can't remember. Dammit! The words rumble like thunder through the biosphere.

"Let us help." "We will show you."

How exactly, will you do that?

"*In the chambers.*" "*No. We do not know the effects it will have.*"

The last thought came from the entity that was Dr. Light—the indigo. He seems to be the more sensible one. Whatever the chamber is, it doesn't sound like someplace I want to go.

"*It is the only way.*" "*We must go.*" "*No. Not yet.*" "*The chambers.*" "*Come with us.*"

CHAPTER TWENTY-THREE

Some of the others begin to change their positions around me. Several move to the front and take the lead. The indigo Dr. Light stays with me in the middle. The rest fall in behind us. I'm thinking I do not want to move, but my nubs are gliding along the slick surface anyway. Apparently, the *lifesource* wants me to go. It is a living thing, a separate entity with its own mind, able to communicate with the others and with me. It's an organic spaceship, a transport vessel that can change shape and cloak itself with darkness. The sweet waste coats everything and protects it from the electromagnetic radiation we are sensitive to. Everything here works in harmony to survive. A simple, yet complicated organism. I wonder what drives them, us. What is our purpose, if any, for existing?

"We will show you." "To the chambers." "Yes." "No. This could be a mistake."

The indigo next to me reaches out and places some

of his slime on my blob of a body. A wave of blue enters me. It feels cool and is somewhat calming. The glowing red within me begins to lessen. It's the same thing he did when he was my psychiatrist. I see the images clearly now, like I can see what he sees—what he saw. Either that or he is showing them to me. I'm lying on the lounger in his office with my eyes closed. He places his fingertips onto my temples, but then his fingers change. They turn into dripping, wet digits of indigo. He inserts them into my head. Neon blue flows into me. I understand now that was the cold I felt—the slime.

"It was the only way to help you remember." "To bring you closer to us."

We are being led through a fleshy junction, something I imagine a sphincter would be like from the inside. We have to squeeze through it. The other side opens to a large circular area about the same size as an ice skating rink. Evenly spaced around the room, are individual compartments which line the bottom of the living breathing walls. They look like cavities roughly dug out of the opalescent gelatin. No need to count them, I know exactly how many there are. The recessed spaces are as wide and long as each one of us. These must be the chambers. And the name for something has never been more appropriate.

When the twenty-seven of us are within the circular area, waves of color flow from our forms in bands and travel up the walls like ripples across a lake. The lights illuminate the slimy sucrose that covers everything, making the iridescent flecks inside sparkle. They dance to the sounds of the different tones, which I've also come to realize, distinguishes us as individuals—the color of light we are and the specific pitch of tone. Now that I think of it, I was right all along about the tones sounding like separate voices when their symphonies played in my head.

"*Yes,*" they chime.

Then one by one, the others glide to the entrance of a cavity and wait. The indigo leads me over to the chamber I assume will be mine, then stays beside me. There is a single empty space left, next to the one I'm in front of, but I wonder why the indigo doesn't go to it. I understand immediately, when each of the others turns around then backs inside. I watch in horror as the chambers quickly fill with the sugary pearlescent ooze.

I don't think I can do this.

"*You must.*" "*You will see.*" "*We will show you.*"

No. Dr. Light, please don't make me. Anxious, I turn to him for a response and as always, there is none. His indigo may be slightly brighter, indicating he might be anxious, too but not by much.

"*I will be here. I will watch for ill effects.*" "*We are all here.*"

Ill effects? Oh, hell no! Now I'm really not getting in there.

Images of what the others see appear in my head. Their vision is clouded over except for the dancing lights. Their bodies are suspended within the gelatinous wall. They have become a part of it, like fish frozen in a winter's pond. The slime underneath my nubs moves me, spins me around. Slowly, I'm backed into the cavity. I reach out for the indigo, and it moves just out of reach. The walls inside begin to heavily secrete the sweet syrup. I panic and reach out again to the indigo. This time it extends a limb then touches mine and sends a surge of calming blue through me. I bring my extremity back and let it rest by my side. Behind me, upward along the circular wall, ringlets of neon blue rise and disappear into the iridescent gelatinous ceiling. It is beautiful—the most spectacular thing I have ever witnessed.

The chamber continues to fill. The slime is cold, wet, and heavy. The lower part of me has already melded with it and solidified. I'm suddenly frantic again, struggling to get free as the ooze seizes my limbs. The red within me begins to pulse. Soon the entire circular room throbs with a bright red glow. My tension affects the others as well. They send their colors out to help calm me. Bright rings of rainbow hues ascend the walls faster and faster. The icy gelatin spreads over what used to be my face. A cool wet sensation envelops it. Still thinking like the human me, I open what I think is my mouth and try to gasp for air.

"*No,*" they tell me.

It's too late. The sugary slime enters the hole I made. It feels like acid as it seeps into my head. Every part of what I am now is frozen, paralyzed. I try one last time to move, but it's no use. Before what I see becomes clouded, too, I notice the indigo that is Dr. Light enters its cavity then is quickly swallowed by the ooze. The circular room starts spinning around.

My head feels like it's in a vice, getting tighter and

tighter. Any moment now it will burst. And then it does. It explodes into a billion stars of rainbow colors. I'm blown against the back of the cavity and kept there by centrifugal force as if I were on a carnival ride. The wall gives way. I'm being sucked backwards by an intense unseen power—absorbed into the very *lifesource* itself. The others are with me, I can sense them. Together we are fleeting through dark space, space with matter, and time. Then a brilliant white light consumes us, devours everything.

"This is white space." "The space within time." "Forward and back."

Besides not making much sense, their voices sound strange. They don't echo and cut out.

"It is a vacuum within space." "A void."

That little bit of information doesn't help much, either. *"You will see."*

A sudden flash, then the white disappears. We come to an immediate stop and hover in the middle of space that has matter. I can tell because there are stars—billions of them. This is the space I'm more familiar with as a human.

"Yes." "Now look." "And See…"

They turn and face an open area. I follow suit. Then images begin to emerge out of the darkness. Amorphous incandescent clouds of thick gases form around an inordinate amount of floating rubble. They swirl and combine but not without pandemonium. Two bright flashes occur, creating suns. Debris takes planetary shapes around them. A massive planet, easily equaling the size of one of the suns, collides into the smaller of the two suns and causes a great explosion. When the haze clears, there is more debris. The smaller sun has moved far away from the swirling clouds of gas, and its light is dim. It looks more like a planet now. The space rubble continues to take shape, while the smaller darker sun moves further into deep space.

The planets that have formed, and debris, encircle the remaining sun. They continue bashing into each other, sometimes destroying both, sometimes making a bigger planet. In one case the planet becomes two, the smaller one orbiting the bigger. This I believe is Earth and the moon.

"Yes."

They are two balls of twisting fire and ember—hostile—spinning wild and variable on their axes, revolving around each other in a hellish, high velocity dance. They continue to spin and form. The other planets and their moons do the same under the constant bombardment of debris. The images begin to slow—cool. The Earth is surrounded by a thick cloud layer impossible to see through. And that is when they come.

"Yes."

The *lifesource*—dark and invisible, it moves toward Earth then projects an enormous amount of the sweet waste toward the planet. The comet of sugar hurls through space, smoldering and leaving behind a long trail of white smoke. It breaches the cloud layer then disappears. The sucrose substance! It is important to life and not just alien life, but all life—human life. That is how it all began—*they* did it.

"Yes." "We."

Why?

"You will see." "There is more." "We will show you." "Look." "See."

The cloud layer vanishes, revealing vast areas of milky green oceans. Then there is more fire and smoke, the Earth is twisting and churning on the inside, but then it clears again and the areas quickly change to blue, brown, green, and white. They are the familiar images of Earth as seen from space. This cycle happens repeatedly then abruptly stops. We seem to be in some kind suspended animation. Suddenly, the others and I fall straight from outer space in a blur. Then we're hovering again just a few feet over shifting sand in a vast area of high desert dunes. A wind gust carrying millions of sand grains whirls straight through us.

I don't think we are really here. This is something they are showing me.

"Yes." "See."

Just beyond the crest of dunes is a big river valley. Primitive dwellings surround the area. We speedily float toward them, dripping sugar as we go along. The slime disappears when it touches the sand, validating my theory that we are not really here. The others don't tell me one way or the other—even though I know they can hear my thoughts.

When we get close to one of the buildings, I notice two others there—like us—more than the twenty-seven. But their forms are more human than ours. They have backs, butts, arms, and legs with fingers and toes. They're not covered in the wet alien sucrose like we are; however, the outer part of their gelatinous bodies does appear to be melting. I'm not sure how long they will last out here in the scorching desert sun.

The extra two, peer through an open window. One is red like me inside, the other indigo blue. I don't understand why we are here. My slimy gelatin body glistens in hues of red to my tonal thoughts.

"Go and See."

I was already on my way.

I drift closer and closer until I'm directly behind the other two. They carry on in a conversation as though they don't see me. I speak to them and ringlets of red move through me, then away without a reaction from either one. I am just a bystander then, here to watch what happens. I move forward to get close enough to understand. Their communication seems heated—for these aliens, anyway. They are rather calm for the most part, from what I've seen, nonviolent. Then suddenly I understand or maybe, just remember…I'm not sure exactly, but the red one *is* me and the indigo, Dr. Light. I turn around and face the twenty-six behind me. I want them to know I remembered something.

They all nod yes, sort of, which makes their heads jiggle like gelatin.

I refocus my attention on what the two *See* through the window.

We were here to examine and observe life on Earth, Dr. Light and I. Our kind have never been able to procreate and we do not know why. We were created as twenty-seven, and that is all there has ever been of us. There are things about our past we cannot explain or can't remember. It could be because of the alien sucrose or because of the way we travel through space and time. To always exist and continue existing…it is not natural in light space where there is matter. Forgetting could be a way of keeping soundness in the dark. All of the life forms we have bestowed upon and observed in light space eventually evolve. We wonder if this is how we came into existence—not from dark matter, but evolving from light matter to survive in the dark. We want a successful experiment. For all of the travel we have done through dark space, we have found no other life forms like ourselves. That is what drives us—it is so rudimentary and fundamental—we want to know how it is we came to be.

"Yes."

But then something happened…

Within the dwelling there is an indigenous woman birthing a child. I remember being astounded by the whole nature and idea of birth. We have rarely had the opportunity to view live births so closely in our observations of these newer life forms. The next time we return, these life forms may no longer exist. A relentless yearning overwhelmed me. I wanted more than to watch. I longed to be a part of the experiment. Experience it firsthand. The indigo is opposed to my thoughts. He does not think it's a wise decision and makes a strong case against it. He argues that we are here as mere observers—evolutionists—sent by our kind to study in brief encounters, then return with our collective findings. His other main concern involves the possible disruption in our means of communication. Something like this has never been done before, and if I was to transfer—project my energy from a dark biological being to a light one—the outcome for the other twenty-six would be uncertain. The risks would far outweigh the benefits of any knowledge gained.

I wouldn't listen, grew furious. Didn't think, then entered the room through the window and made my presence known. The indigo tried frantically to call the others, but the Sun's solar radiation that day was at its peak, and our telepathy was discontinuous. The indigo turned away to get help, and then there was a bright white flash behind him. When he returned to the window, I was gone. I had somehow projected my dark energy life force into the female child. I do not remember how I did it, and the others don't know either. That is why I'm still here—there.

They came and spent time with me as I grew—in this place called Sumer—one of Earth's earliest civilizations. They hoped I would remember how to change back. That is how Dr. Light, the indigo, knew I was seeing Sumer in my visions and not Egypt.

Raging spots whirled on the face of the sun, and a rare cycle of intense solar storms ensued. *The others* had to go or be destroyed by the electromagnetic radiation. All communication with them was lost after that. I survived—protected within the confines of a human body. When my host died after having a child, I jumped into another and then another. By the time the twenty-six were able to return, I had forgotten what I was. They had to be near in order for the telepathy to work. Sometimes, they were able to get random images and those were the ones they remembered, like Sumer, and the Victorian woman, the Colonial woman, and the 50's woman. They were always women because I wanted to be a mother.

The others were not able to pinpoint my location until now, because the Vegas strip is such a distinct place in the middle of a desert. They searched heavily in the suburban areas, teeming with families. I *See* it. I *See* all of it. But why now, I wonder. It has been so long. They should have gone on without me. Why come back now?

"You will see." "We will show you." "Come back to us."

I leave poor indigo staring into the window alone and return to the others.

Those people—the villagers, they saw what happened. They must have known or suspected something.

"You were revered." "We taught them what we could." "They were primitive." "We helped them build."

Build?

"Places." "Cities." "Pyramids." "We would return when and where we could, to resume our search for you." "Always teaching." "Always building." "It was futile."

Futile? No, far from it. They learned quickly. They worshipped you as deities. They did evolve—are still evolving.

"Not enough." "It was all for nothing." "It will end."

And with that, we shoot straight up into the bright

white light again, moving forward into space with matter. We come to a stop and hover.

I'm guessing you're going to show me the future now. *"You are right." "See." "It knows." "It doesn't." "It will."*

Earth is far, far away. We are in a distant galaxy. Very close to the dim star that was booted out of our solar system when it was first being formed.

"Yes." "See." "Look beyond."

Look behind, is what they really mean. On the other side of the dead star there are two, enormous blue-white stars coming together in a spin. They rotate faster and faster until they collide, causing a violent explosion. Beams of light, blast from its center. One disintegrates the dim star then continues its path through space. The shaft of light—pure radiation—is headed straight for Earth!

"Yes." "Now you see."

The light passes through the Earth, stripping away layers of atmosphere. This is my nightmare, isn't it? It is real.

"Yes."

Everyone will die.

"Yes."

Including me?

"Yes."

And the alien me?

"The amount of radiation is too powerful." "You will disintegrate into nothing." "We may be destroyed with you."

That's not possible. You have the ability to go far away—deep into dark space.

"We are all connected." "Always living." "Always together." "Destroyed as one."

I understand. The possibility exists, but I don't think—

"We are most certain." "You will be our end." "You must come with us."

Yes. Now I understand, completely. You need me to go away with you to survive, but I can't. I have a life on Earth—a child that is mine.

"He is no longer a child."

He will always be my child.

"You have had many children." "Lifetimes of experiencing humanity." "It is time to go." "There are other ways."

Other ways?

"Other places." "This is not the only one." "Yes." "There are more." "Come with us." "See."

Couldn't we take some of them? You can't just leave them all to die.

"No." "Nothing of light matter survives in the dark." "We have tried."

It is always the indigo that speaks last. His words are the most heartfelt compared to the others. He comprehends what I'm thinking, better than the rest.

"We all understand." "We are twenty-seven." "We are one." "We all know."

Yeah, I guess you would, but it doesn't change my mind about anything. I can't go with you—I won't.

"Soon it will be too late." "All communication will be lost." "You will be our end."

The sun storms have been causing all the static, the

squealing in and out, and searching for the right frequency. Then I remember…the news…something about intense solar flares and disruptions in signals.

"*Yes.*"

Suddenly, in a violent rush of light, I feel a pulling sensation from inside me, like I'm being yanked back. *The others* remain still and calm, as I fall away. What is happening? Help!

"*It will be our end…*"

CHAPTER TWENTY-FOUR

'm surrounded by an electric blue haze, but it's not the cool wet indigo of Dr. Light. It is hard, warm, and not alive. The harmonic tones have been replaced by resonating mechanical ticks and swoosh sounds. They remind me of the noises a Hula-Hoop makes, only a hundred times louder. My throat feels raw, and something is inside it. It is choking me. I can't breathe! Every attempted breath leaves a raspy sting in my lungs. There's an acrid taste on my tongue and something stuck to my face. Whatever it is down my throat, it's also coming out of my mouth! I reach up to move it away, and my hand knocks a solid surface just above my face. Something catches my forearm, pulls, and there's a sharp twinge. Icy fluid trickles down and pools in my armpit. I'm trapped in a tight space—*like a coffin!* Maybe back on Earth, they thought I was dead. Tubes are coming out of me everywhere—I could be in the middle of some kind of embalming process. I panic and struggle to get out. Pitch a raucous fit by banging my feet, knees, and hands against the hard surface.

I hear shouting. "She's awake!" "Don't move!" "Turn it off!" "Get her out!"

The loud thrum and clicks come to a slow stop. Still flailing my arms and legs, I feel myself sliding down the tunnel without moving. Then suddenly, I'm blinded by bright white lights. There is a force pinning me down. I fight to break free. They won't be putting me back into that coffin. Something pierces my left thigh and then everything fades to black.

Someone or something stirs not far off to my right, but my eyes won't open. I strain to see. I'm not sure where I am anymore—or even who or what. When I finally get my eyelids to stay up for more than two seconds, the first thing I see is a hand. It's wrapped in white bandages like a mummy. There's a small patch of dried blood coming through the back about the size of a quarter. I wiggle my fingers. It's mine.

"Mom," I hear Patrick's voice, but as hard as I try, I can't turn my head. My muscles ache and feel so weak.

I hear him rise, walk over, and then he leans down so we can see each other, confirm our guesses. I try to smile, but my face hurts a little, so I blink a few times instead.

"I'm gonna go get Dad," he says.

I try and reach up to stop him, but he's already gone.

Well, I guess this means I'm back on Earth. I wonder what the hell happened. The twenty-six may have been finished telling me what they wanted me to know and let me go, but I was nowhere near done asking questions. I close my eyes and listen for them. I hear nothing.

I'm in a hospital room, I've gathered that much. It makes sense since the last thing I remember is bleeding. It's coming back to me now—I was with my mom at the casino. She had just hit a jackpot. Oh, I'm never going to hear the end of how I ruined her big win.

Maybe whatever happened to me made the tones go away. Someone comes barging through the door. It's several people actually. Jon, Patrick, Dr. Swanson, and a couple nurses, I think. This is going to be overwhelming—the mere sight of them already has me exhausted.

Jon walks up and takes my hand. "Honey, are you feeling any pain?"

I nod and then a nurse steps up with a loaded syringe. I quickly raise my bandaged hand and pinch my fingers close together to mean it hurts—*just a little bit*. Then I point to the stained dressing on my other hand.

"You pulled your IV out. Do you want some pain medicine?" Jon says.

I close my eyes then move my head slow and gently from side to side and motion *no*. Plastic tubing is draped across my face. It tugs on my nostrils when I move around. Sweet smelling air blows into my nose. It must be oxygen. I open my eyes again and see Jon keeping the nurse back— the one with the syringe. The other nurse comes forward and slides a digital thermometer in my mouth. Dr. Swanson steps up with a pen light and shines it directly into my eyes. "Follow my finger," he says.

My throat feels so raw I can't imagine what the hell was down there. It feels like they took a bottle brush and scrubbed it. I try and muster up some saliva to moisten my mouth then whisper, "water."

"I'm not sure that's a good idea just yet, Jon," Dr. Swanson says.

"You don't need to drink any water now," Jon tells me. "You've got another IV. See, here." He points to the other side of the bed. I slowly move my head that way and yeah, there's an IV all right. Strange I couldn't feel it before, but I'm feeling it now—a cold tight ache across the back of my other hand.

If I close my eyes and pretend to sleep, it's possible they might all go away.

When I wake again, the entire process is much less complicated. Right away, I notice Patrick sitting in a chair near the foot of the bed. Filtered light shines through the window blinds behind him, making him look like a shadow. He's either playing with one of his handheld gaming devices or his cell phone. I can't tell, and he has his earbuds in. He looks up and sees me watching him. "I'm gonna go get Dad," he says.

"Not yet," I squawk.

He appears rattled. I don't think either one of us expected my reaction to come out quite so loud or adamantly.

I hold up my hand and motion for him to step forward.

He pulls his earbuds out then puts his phone on the chair. There's a plastic mauve pitcher on a little rolling side table next to the bed. I see sweat beads streaming down the side, and my mouth waters with anticipation. When Patrick gets close, I point to the pitcher. "Water," I say.

"Maybe I should get Dad."

"No." I shake my head. "Water first."

He walks over to another table next to the window then comes back with a Styrofoam cup and a straw. He pours some water into the cup then holds it so I can take a sip. I put my lips around the straw and take in a big swallow.

He pulls the cup away. "Not too fast," he says.

Spittle drips from my chin and I cast him a wicked glare.

He gets the hint and puts the cup back to where I can take a few more sips. When I'm done I nod for him to take it away.

"Can I get Dad now?" he says.

"Wait a minute," I manage to say. My throat is still dry, but my voice is coming back. "What happened?"

"Dad can tell you better than me."

I shake my head no. "I want to hear what you know—what you've heard." I'm nobody's fool. I know Patrick probably has a handle on the situation better than anyone else here, including Jon and all the other doctors.

"Start from the beginning," I say. "Don't talk loud enough for them to hear." I glance at the door then focus back on Patrick. "I don't want them to interrupt you."

He drags the chair he was in over to my bedside then

sits down. "Grandma said that you passed out because you were so excited that she won. She said you must have hit your face on the slot machine before you fell on the floor because you were covered in blood when the ambulance came. I guess people were running around all over the place screaming. Then Dad says when he got to the hospital they were already giving you blood transfusions because the paramedics told the ER staff that you bled so much—*more blood than two people*, they said.

"Dad was mad because they didn't do labs first to check your blood count. 'Cause later on when they finally did do them, they were fine. Grandma and Grandpa were mad because nobody told them you were sick. I told them I didn't know either, but it didn't help. They stayed until you got quarantined, then they went home 'cause Grandpa was worried Grandma would get whatever you had."

"Quarantined?" I give him a stern look.

"None of the specialists could figure out what was going on or why you were bleeding so much and not showing blood loss. One of the doctors thought it might be some rare disease, something like Ebola, and then *I* had a bloody nose, so they put you in quarantine, and I couldn't see you for over a week, which was total bullshit, but—"

"A week? How long have I been here?"

"Two weeks, Mom. You've been in a coma. You stopped breathing like four or five days ago, and they had to put a breathing tube down your throat. Then Dad told Dr. Swanson to do an MRI 'cause he thought maybe you had a brain tumor or something. They weren't supposed to I guess, while you were in a coma anyway, and when you woke up inside there you freaked and pulled your breathing tube out, and your IV, and they got in trouble with the hospital, but Dad said he didn't give a shit if they wrote him up."

"Enough with the language, Pat, I'm not that out of it. Now tell me about your nosebleed."

"It was nothing, Mom, really. Dad had some *tool* doctor check me out, and he said it was probably just from the dry hospital air. Do you want me to finish the story or not?"

"Tool doctor? Do you mean Dr. Swanson?"

"Yeah, that's him."

I smile and nod for him to continue.

"So anyway, after that MRI thing happened, you were breathing fine on your own, so they left the breathing tube out. They also took the quarantine sign down, and we could visit you again. See, no big deal."

"So, what exactly is wrong with me?"

"That's just it. They don't know. Dad and uh, Dr. Swanson, were talking about how they sent some of your blood samples to a guy in South Africa who's supposed to be a blood scientist expert or something like that. Maybe he'll be able to figure out what's going on.

"Can I go get Dad, now?"

"In a minute." I gesture my head and eyeball the water pitcher again.

He sighs but then gets up and pours a little more into the cup. While he holds the straw to my lips I look up at him and take in several sips. I can see some relief in his expression. I don't blame him for not liking being cornered for information, but he also knows I believe he's got one up on the rest of them. As much as I nag him for being a teenager, he has more insight than most adults. We have a special type of trust, the two of us.

Tool doctor—that's funny. The door swings open, speak of the devil.

"She just woke up," Patrick tells him, "and she wanted some water."

Jon follows Dr. Swanson in through the door. "How do you feel, honey?"

"Much better, but…"

"But what?" Jon says.

"I…"

"What?" Dr. Swanson says.

"I have to pee."

"Oh, that," Jon says. "That's just a sensation. You have a bag, a Foley catheter."

"No. I want it out. I want to do it myself."

"You've got to get up and sit for a while first," Dr. Swanson says. "Show us your condition is stable, and then we'll start disconnecting things."

I nod—*Bastard.* Now I've got to do tricks to earn points.

"I'll call some of the nurses in to help sit you up," Dr. Swanson says.

"I can do it myself."

"That's their job, Stacy. I agree with Terry," Jon says.

I flash him a nasty look. "Fine then, let's get on with it."

Dr. Swanson leaves the room.

"What about Pat?" I say.

"I can help," Pat says.

"We know you can, but why don't you go down to the cafeteria vending machines and get yourself a soda or something," Jon says.

Patrick huffs.

"Get me one too, please," I beg. "Something sweet like orange or grape. Do they sell candy bars?"

"No candy bars," Jon says. "They'll want to start you on a liquid diet to see if you can keep normal food down."

I give Patrick a look before he leaves. I can tell he's going to try and sneak me candy.

Dr. Swanson comes back into the room with a female nurse and a young man in scrubs. "This is your nurse, Sally, and an orderly," he says.

The orderly speaks up, "Vince. Hi."

Jon steps out of the way and stands next to Dr. Swanson. The nurse comes forward then lowers the side rails. There's a vinyl recliner in the corner of the room, a vestige from the Seventies, I think. The orderly drags it over.

"Let's take this nice and slow," the nurse says. She picks up a controller and raises the head of the bed to a ninety degree angle. "We're going to turn you around, so your legs can dangle off the side. Sit like that for a minute, okay? We don't want to rush it and make you dizzy."

I nod my head. "Okay. I've got it."

The nurse moves out of the way, then the orderly comes up and puts one arm behind me, lifts and turns me in a single motion. My legs are dangling off the bed, but he doesn't move away. He stands right in front of me to keep me from falling face forward. He is tall and built muscularly. It's no wonder they brought him in here, they stand back and let him do everything.

The nurse pushes a button on the wall and a cuff that was already around my upper arm tightens. They all wait and stare at the digital readout panel in the wall for the results. It beeps then displays the numbers one hundred and twenty, a line, and the numbers seventy-six underneath. "Good," she says. Then she moves an IV bag from a pole to a closer one and checks and straightens out all the tubes and wires I have coming out of me. Last, she picks up a bag that was hanging on the side of my bed and puts it next to my leg. It's warm and full of light yellow urine. *Gross.*

"Her blood pressure is perfectly normal," Dr. Swanson says.

"It *has* been this whole time," Jon says.

I can tell they're about to get into some medical discourse about what is wrong or not wrong with me, so I keep looking down. My legs are pale white—too pale, actually. I move my hand from my side then reach over and touch one. It is some type of tight stocking.

"Those are TED hose," Vince says, "to prevent blood clots while you're laid up."

"Oh," I say.

"Do you feel ready to move into the chair?"

"Yes." But I wish he wouldn't say *the chair*, like it was the naughty chair, or an electric chair, or something equally dreadful.

Vince turns to the nurse for approval. "Go ahead," she tells him.

He puts his arms around me. "Put your feet on mine."

I do as he says, then he lifts me up, shuffles his feet and pivots, then sets me down gently into the chair. He slowly backs away. "There, how's that?"

"Good," I say. "Can I get something to eat now?"

"Sure," the nurse says. "What would you like?"

"Not candy," Jon says.

"It doesn't matter," I say. "Whatever it is I'm supposed to eat and keep down so I can get some candy bars and soda."

Vince laughs. The nurse types on a keyboard I didn't see before, located on the side table by the window. "I'm ordering you something now," she says.

"What's with your sudden desire for sweets?" Jon says. "I've never seen you drink soda or eat candy."

"I don't know. It's just something I'm craving."

Dr. Swanson leaves the room as soon as he and Jon finish up their strategy regarding my recovery and eventual discharge. It seems I have a lot of tricks to perform before I can get out of this place.

Vince, the orderly, is about to go as well. "Ring us when you're ready to get back in bed," he says, placing the *call* remote in my hand. "You can turn the TV on and change the channels with this, too."

"Thanks for everything," I say. "Hopefully, I'll be staying out of bed for a while."

The nurse tells me lunch is on its way and that she has notes to chart then she goes, too.

When they've all gone, Jon sits down on the edge of the bed and looks over at me in the recliner. "Are you comfortable?"

"As much as I'm going to be sitting in this antique."

He smiles. "So…what do you remember?"

"Almost everything up until I passed out at the casino. What happened after that?"

"What I want to know is what happened before?"

"Nothing, really, I remember being dizzy and seeing swirling colors."

"That's it?"

"Yeah, and why isn't Patrick in school?" The thought just occurred to me that it's lunchtime as the nurse stated, and he's not in class.

"He really wanted to be here with you. Honestly, we weren't sure how this would end up. We've been getting his assignments and the school's been more than gracious about letting him miss some time under the circumstances. The dean, you know, Ray Bloch, said he just has to come in to take his semester finals. That he can skip from Thanksgiving break until the New Year, so long as he keeps his 4.0 grade average. Ray and Pastor Dean have been really supportive about praying for you and stuff like that."

"Oh, that's nice. And what's this I hear about Patrick having a bloody nose?"

"It's just the desert air and the ventilation system in the hospital. I had Terry check him out. He's fine. It wasn't anything like what you experienced. You didn't have any bloody noses before the incident at the cocktail party did you?"

Shit, I can't tell him now. I'm sure he's right, and it's nothing to worry about. There isn't anything I can do about it in here, anyway. "No. I didn't. And what about you, have you missed a lot of work?"

"No. Not much. That's why it's been kind of nice having Pat here. If things came up at the surgery center, I could go in and take care of them."

"Ah…I see." *I can't believe he pulled Pat out of school to watch over me.*

"But how do *you* feel—really? Your prognosis has been anything but normal. You've been tested for just about everything under the sun—from Epilepsy to Hemophilia—and even the Ebola virus."

"Actually, I feel fine. I'm not sure what all these tubes are for. I just want to go home."

"Not quite yet. Like Terry said, they want to make sure your condition is stable before they let you go."

"What's your guess then?"

"A week maybe."

"That's too long."

"A lot of things happened you don't know about."

"Like what?"

"Your mom called me from the casino, hysterical. When I got to the ER they said you were bleeding to death. You coded right there in front of me."

"Coded? You mean I died?"

"Cardiac arrest—your heart stopped. They brought you back quick, but you were in a coma after that. When your lab results came back there were no signs of blood loss or a heart attack. The EKG data didn't show any cardiac muscle damage, either. No one could explain it. We tried the hospital labs, outsource labs, everything came back negative. Almost a week later, you spontaneously had a respiratory arrest."

It's obvious what he means, but I shrug my shoulders anyway.

"You stopped breathing. We had to intubate you—insert a breathing tube."

"We?"

"You were in isolation, but I was in the room at the time. They stocked a crash cart just outside your door in case you had another cardiac arrest. Like I said, nobody knew what might happen next. I had already intubated you by the time the code team got to the room."

"Is that why this is here?" I point my head toward the side table. There's a large tube labeled K-Y Jelly on top of it.

"Yeah, probably. I'm sure someone just forgot to put it away."

That's a relief. Seeing it there made me a little nervous when I noticed it a minute ago. Jelly and a breathing tube shoved down my throat, evokes the memory of the chambers and how I had taken in the slimy, acidic, sugary substance. Could the timing be? I wonder if there's a correlation.

"So, tell me exactly what I have to do to get out of here as soon as possible."

"That's up to you."

"I'll do any and every thing, just tell me."

"Eat, don't bleed, or stop breathing, and make sure your heart keeps beating." He winks. "You've got to get moving again, but don't rush. You've just been through an ordeal. We all have, and I don't want you to hasten the healing process. It could trigger another attack."

"But you said my lab results are normal, so there's really nothing to worry about."

"Yeah, but we haven't really trusted the lab work so much in your situation. Something is definitely going on. We just haven't found it yet. You came out of your coma in the middle of an MRI and pulled out your breathing tube and IV. As soon as you're up to it, they want to try it again. The images from the first one didn't turn out so well."

"Fine. I'll do whatever it takes to go home."

"Don't be in such a hurry. You're not missing anything."

"What do you mean? Of course I am. I've been out for two weeks. There's a lot to do."

"Well, Patrick's been here. Your parents arrive tomorrow. I called them and told them you were awake, by the way. And other things…that can wait."

"What other things?"

"The usual bullshit stuff, that's all."

"I want to know what you mean. Besides all this, is something else wrong? Tell me Jon, please."

He looks away. "You'll find out soon enough. For now, you need to focus on getting better and showing them you're fine if you want to get out of here."

"Then that's exactly what I'll do."

He slides off the bed then leans down and kisses my forehead. "I've missed you like crazy."

"I've missed you, too."

He straightens up, and I see tears welled up in his eyes. He sniffs a little. Then the door swings open and Patrick barges in with a woman wearing light green scrubs, carrying a big tray of covered dishes. It smells like hospital food—a blend of bland and plastic.

"Hello, Mrs. Troy. This is for you." Her name tag reads, Maria, Nurse's Aide.

Jon rolls the side table over and lowers it gently onto my lap. Maria places the tray on top then proceeds to remove the covers. Hmm…hot tea in a plastic mug, steaming broth in a plastic bowl, and red gelatin. *It seems silly now when I look at it, that not long ago, that's how I saw myself—red and jiggling.*

"Thank you," I tell her.

"Well, I'm going to step out and check on things while you eat," Jon says. "I'll be back."

"Okay," I say. "Bye."

"Doesn't this look good, Pat?" I say.

"No," he says. Then he picks up his phone, puts his earbuds in, and plops down into the chair at the foot of the bed.

"If you don't need anything else, I'm going to go," Maria says. "When you're finished you can buzz me, and I'll come back to get the tray."

I nod at her and smile. After she leaves, I examine my tray of liquids, picking up the mug of tea first. It smells like burning plastic. "Pat," I say, and wave my hand to get his attention.

He pulls an earbud out. "What?"

"Can you pour this down the sink in the bathroom? It's disgusting."

"Dad said you have to eat something."

"It's not food. I'll drink the broth but not this. Just toss it for me okay, and rinse out the sink, so they don't see we threw it away."

He gets up and does what I ask. The broth is lukewarm already, and before it gets any colder, I pick up the bowl and chug it all down. It soothes as it passes down the rough patch in my throat.

"Geez, Mom, no spoon?"

"Stuff like this, it's better to gulp."

When I'm done I wipe my chin with a paper napkin from the side of the tray then stare at the gelatin. It almost doesn't seem right to eat it, but it smells sweet, like strawberries. Pat comes back with the empty plastic cup from the bathroom and sets it down on the table.

"Are you going to eat that?" he says.

"Why, do you want it?"

"No, but it looks gross."

I pick the spoon up from the tray, and he watches me slice down into the gelatin. I scoop up half and put it in my mouth before I change my mind.

"Well?" he says, staring at me for a reaction.

"Not bad." I finish it in two bites. "I'm still hungry, though. Were you able to score anything from the vending machines?"

"I guess it would be all right, since you ate that nasty lunch." He reaches into his pocket and hands me a candy bar.

"No soda?"

"Just a sec." He huffs, then reaches into the kangaroo

pocket of his hoodie and pulls out a slick, sweaty aluminum can. He hands it to me. "I had to wait for them to go."

"I know. Thanks."

"Aren't you glad I wear these baggy sweatshirts?"

"Yeah, I guess they come in handy at times like these. You got anything else in there?"

"No. That's enough for now."

I turn the can around and take a look. "Ooh, strawberry. Perfect to wash down that Jell-O aftertaste." I snap the tab open, slide a straw from the tray down into it, and take a few sips. "Ah…" It feels good going down my throat, too." I tear the candy bar wrapper open and chomp off a bite. "Hmm…yum." I take another drink of soda.

Patrick watches me like he's seeing someone who's never had a candy bar before. Then again, I don't think he's ever seen me eat a candy bar.

"Mom?"

"Hmm?"

"When you were dead, did you see anything?"

"What do you mean, like a light at the end of a tunnel or something?"

"Yeah, I guess, or dead people you knew, like *your* Grandma and Grandpa?"

"No. I didn't see anything like that."

"Did you see *anything* at all?"

"I don't remember. Why?"

"I was just wondering."

"You shouldn't wonder about stuff like that."

"Why not?"

"I don't know…because you're too young, and it's morbid."

"What about when you were in a coma? I Googled it and some people dream about stuff they hear going on around them while they're out."

"Really? That's interesting, but no. I didn't have any dreams I can remember."

"Oh."

I'm not sure he believes me, but he seems genuinely disappointed. As insightful as he is, there's no way I'm telling him what I saw, where I thought I went, and with who. Better to change the subject altogether before he keeps on about it.

"So—I bet Dad was a real basket case, huh?"

"Yeah, but I handled him. You know, like you do when he freaks out about stuff. Calm him down by talking and suggesting good ideas."

"Thanks for doing that. I'm sure he appreciates it."

"I'm not sure he knows I did it."

"And that's the magic of it."

"Magic?"

"To do things for people and not have them realize it. They may later on, but not right away, or maybe never. There's something to be said for that. I know you did it for me, too, and I appreciate it—that you kept things together while I was away."

"If it happened again though, not that I want it to, but I think I'd be all right. I mean, I think I could handle things."

"I know you could, and it's good you learned something

about yourself. Now—don't you think it's time you went back to school?"

"What? But then who's gonna sneak you sodas and candy?"

"You've got a point, but I don't want you to miss classes for me. I'm fine now."

"Yeah, but I was getting so sick of everyone looking at me and not knowing what to say. It'll be better if I go back next year, kind of like starting from a beginning."

"All right then. I guess I understand."

"Good. Besides, I can help you with Christmas decorating and stuff."

Now there's a legitimate thought that actually could exacerbate another attack. "Hey, can you text Dad for me? Ask him to pick up a cheeseburger, some fries, and a milkshake—tell him it's for you."

"What kind of milkshake?"

"Strawberry."

My sugar rush from the soda and candy is short-lived. I'm crashing fast and beginning to wonder if they laced the broth with a sedative. I wouldn't put it past them to try and keep me down so they can run more of their tests.

Patrick is at the foot of the bed playing with his phone, and if it weren't for his occasional squeaky position shift in the vinyl chair, I wouldn't know he was there at all. My head feels like a lead balloon and my eyelids are even heavier. They close for a minute or two then open up again because it is too quiet. The roaring nothing makes it hard for me to fall asleep, so I keep my eyes shut and hum the melodies of the tones I remember. They had become lullabies, sort of. It's odd, but I miss them. I would like to be light again—graceful, moving around with little effort. I imagine myself gliding through soft rippled halls. It's all so dreamy, but solid and weighty is how I feel now. Every part of me is present and accounted for in fleshy mass. Now that I'm here, I wonder if I was really *there*—with *them*.

It could have been this unknown sickness everyone thinks I have that caused me to hallucinate. It's possible for a brain tumor or something like that to create neuroses and psychoses, I'm sure of it. Yes, I was in a coma, but where did I really go? Deep inside my own mind or into outer space—it should be easy to answer, but I still don't want to admit something is or was psychological. Who would?

They're gone now though, the tones. Whatever happened—like maybe I did hit my head on the slot machine and dislodged a tumor—it seems to have cured me. Over time, I'm confident I'll be able to forget about it, all of it, and as far as I'm concerned, Dr. Light never existed. I'll finally have the peace I've been wanting, even if I have to make it myself. It will take time, but I'll just have to be patient.

"Stacy?" someone whispers.

I'm asleep, I think, but I can hear. I can't open my eyes. It might be *them*—they're back.

"Wake up, it's me. I came to see you."

The voice is familiar. I know it well, but it sounds oceans away. In my sleep, in my head, I shout, *"I'm here. Wait for me. I'm coming."* I struggle and swim through dark blue waters to get there—get to consciousness. Then I remember the voice and who it belongs to. I emerge from the indigo darkness with a big splash and call out her name, "Cally."

"Mom, you were dreaming."

"Patrick?"

"Was Cally here?"

He turns his head and looks to the door. Jon is standing there holding two paper bags of fast food. He has a severe expression on his face. "Pat, did you leave the room?"

"Just for a minute, to get a soda."

"What is it?" I ask. "What's going on?"

"Nothing," Jon says. "Let's eat."

CHAPTER TWENTY-SIX

The aroma of cheeseburgers and fries is too overpowering to think about anything else. Jon walks over and sets the bags down on my tray table.

"How did you do with lunch?" he says.

"Fine, but I was still hungry. Thanks for bringing the food. Pat told you it was for me?" I look over at him in the corner and he shrugs his shoulders.

"At first I didn't believe him," Jon says. "It's not like you to want cheeseburgers, fries, and a *milkshake*, but since you were craving candy bars and soda earlier, I figured what the hell."

"Maybe Mom woke up a different person," Patrick says.

"You Google way too much. A lot of that information is just a bunch of crap," Jon says.

"I agree," I say.

Jon hands Patrick his food then arranges mine. As soon as everything is divvied up, he sits on the side of the bed next to me in the chair and eats his cheeseburger, talking between bites. "Looks like they came in and fixed the bed while I was gone. You'll have clean sheets tonight."

"More like clean sandpaper," I say. "I can't wait to go home and sleep in our bed."

"Soon," he says. "Did you get a nap?"

"I must have. I don't remember anyone coming in to fix the bed or taking the food tray from lunch."

"It's good that you're getting some rest."

"Yeah, I guess. After dinner, can you please have them take this urine tube out? It's driving me crazy. I feel like I have to go all the time."

"It's already taken care of. I saw the doctor's order written in your chart. If you keep eating, they're going to discontinue the IV fluids, too."

"Really, when?"

"Sometime tomorrow…"

"Fine."

"Want to go for a little stroll after dinner?"

"I'd love it. I think my butt is numb from being in this chair. Can we go outside?"

"No. I was thinking just around the hospital floor."

"What floor is this anyway?"

"The fourth floor, where post-surgical patients recover. You were in the ICU for a while, but after you pulled your breathing tube out and they were sure your respirations were normal, they transferred you here."

"Oh. I thought this was an isolation floor."

"No. They can put up signs for those precautions anywhere."

"And why did they, exactly?"

"It was just in case whatever you had was contagious. The infectious disease doc that works for the hospital thought it would be a good idea, and I was in no position to argue about it."

"Oh."

"Don't worry. It was all normal protocol."

"Did a lot of people try and visit?"

"They called me first to ask. I told them not to come."

"Why?"

"I didn't think you'd want anyone to see you like this."

He's right. I wouldn't. "Not even Cally, though?"

Patrick coughs real loud and kind of phony. He has his earbuds in, but I know he's listening. They're hiding something, the two of them. Before I can ask again, Jon scrunches his fast food papers and gets up. "I'm going to step out and talk to one of the nurses about coming in to remove your catheter, so we can take that walk," he says.

"Great," I say.

As soon as he leaves, I try Patrick. "Patrick," I snap and wave my hand. He pretends he doesn't see me for a minute then finally takes notice.

"What?"

"Is there something going on that you and your dad aren't telling me?"

He glances down at his phone. "Not that I know of."

If Patrick doesn't want to talk about it, it must be serious. I wonder what could be going on. The last thing I remember about Cally…I couldn't get in touch with her and had to call Tara. Geez, I hope nothing bad happened.

Jon comes back into the room with a nurse. He looks over at Patrick who is still staring down at his phone.

This is ridiculous.

"Hello, Mrs. Troy," the nurse says. "Dr. Troy says you're ready to get that Foley out."

"Yes, please," I say. *Everything else will have to wait.*

The nurse walks me into the bathroom and has me sit on the commode. She has a syringe in her hand. "What's that for?" I say.

"To take the saline out of the balloon that's keeping the catheter in your bladder."

"It's fine," Jon says.

There's hardly room for the three of us in here, but I know Jon won't leave. At least Patrick has the decency to hide in the corner of the room where he can't see what's happening. I can't imagine it would be something he would want to observe, anyway.

The nurse's hand is a little shaky. I'm sure Jon watching over her shoulder is making her nervous, but there's no needle on the syringe, so I'm not worried about her jabbing me on accident. She attaches the hub of the empty syringe into a port along the tubing and pulls back slowly. Clear liquid fills the chamber and the tubing slides out.

"Better?" Jon says.

I feel a little bit of a burning sensation, but it's not something I'm going to mention. "Yeah," I say. "Much. Now can I have a little privacy, so I can go on my own?"

"I'll need you to stand up for a minute so I can put the measuring hat back into the commode," the nurse says.

"What?" I say.

"It's to measure your output. Just stand up," Jon says.

I grab hold of the metal rail attached to the wall next to the commode and pull myself up. The nurse raises the toilet seat and sets in what looks like a white hat turned upside down. Then she lowers the seat again. "Okay. You're all set. You can sit back down."

I do as she says, then they both leave the bathroom and shut the door. It stings, but I imagine that's normal considering I've had the tube in there for nearly two weeks. The nurse comes back in when I'm finished and helps me up.

"Strange," she says, holding the white hat. "It smells really sweet."

Oh, great.

Jon rushes back into the bathroom. "Will you do me a favor, and test it with a glucose stick?"

"Sure," she says. "That's a good idea."

She leaves for a moment, then returns with a skinny little strip she dips into the white hat. After a minute or two, they both look down at the result. "It's perfectly normal," she says.

"Can you do me another favor, and send some to the lab?" he says.

"Yeah, I guess," she says. "Is there anything specific you want them to test it for?"

"Everything," he says.

The hallways are high and wide. A continuous metal handrail splits the walls. The bottom half is painted dark brown, the top is desert tan. Industrial carpet in the same dark brown covers the hall floors. The fluorescent lighting above makes the tan paint glow and the flooring appear darker. From one end to the other, it looks as though I will have to cross a muddy trench.

Jon walks next to me and pushes the IV pole as I shuffle over the carpet. Every now and then I reach out to use the handrail and get a static shock in my fingertips. It makes me feel like I'm part of some lab experiment because I know it's going to hurt, but I do it anyway. Jon offers me his hand, but I don't take hold of it. I have to show him I can walk on my own.

The nurses are gathered at their little station off to the side, in the middle of the hall. They watch us go by and smile. I hope they're taking notes. *See*—I'm ambulatory now, and if they don't let me out of here soon, I will walk out on my own.

After the second pass around the floor, I finally have to ask. "Jon?"

"Yes?" He stops and looks me over. "You want to head back?"

"No, no. I'm fine. Keep walking." I move ahead and he quickly comes along.

"What is it then?"

"Did you mention to anyone I was seeing a psychiatrist?"

"No way, are you kidding? With everything that's been going on, I wouldn't think of it."

Now I stop and look at him. "What do you mean?"

"It's nothing."

"I'm not stupid, Jon. I know you're hiding something. Go ahead, tell me. I can handle it."

"No. I don't want to discuss it."

"Dammit! I want to know what the hell happened. Is Cally okay?"

As we round the corner, I see a nurse standing in the hallway by their charting station. "Is everything all right?" she says.

"Yes. We're fine," Jon says. "I think she's through walking for now. Would you mind?"

I'm furious—huffing and puffing. "Yeah, I've had enough," I say. "I'm ready to go."

The nurse walks over and takes Jon's place. "Happy to help," she says. She's smiling at Jon a little too much. This is like a fucking conspiracy against me. Thank God I never talked about my sessions with Dr. Light. Jon would've had me committed for sure. No one will ever know what I saw in my nightmares. It's become a thing of the past, and I'm all alone again.

"Thanks," he says to the nurse. "Patrick and I are going to head home, now."

"What? Already?" I say.

"It'll give you time to clean up before bed. We'll be back tomorrow, sometime after breakfast."

"Fine," I say. Then I look over to the nurse. "Do you think I could take a shower?"

"If you feel up to it, I don't see why not." She glances

at Jon again and smiles. "We could wrap your IV arm in plastic. I'll have to come in and stand by though, if you don't mind."

Just like a prisoner. "Not at all," I say. "I just want a shower."

"Sounds good," Jon says. "We'll let you get to it then." He stands out in the hall and holds the door open to my room. "Come on, Pat, time to go."

Patrick gets up from his chair and walks over to the doorway where I'm standing with the nurse. He leans in and gives me a hug. "How'd your tour go?" he says.

"She did well," Jon says. "No doubt she'll be home soon."

"'Kay," Pat says. "Night, Mom."

"Goodnight. Love you," I tell him.

"See you tomorrow," Jon says.

They leave, and the nurse races around the room gathering clean hospital gowns and towels. Then she rummages through cabinets for hygiene products Jon obviously brought from home.

"Your husband is such a nice man," the nurse says. "And a good doctor, too."

"That's what I hear."

Breakfast consists of runny scrambled eggs that taste like plastic, dry toast, and thank Heaven…coffee. Plastic flavor, but it's better than nothing. The smell of it all is making me nauseous, but I have to keep it down. When I'm through, I wash up and put my robe on. There's no sign of Jon and Patrick, so I decide to take a stroll while the nursing staff clears away the breakfast tray and tidies up the room.

"Hello, Mrs. Troy," one of the nurses says from a desk at their station. "How are you feeling today?"

"Good morning," I say. "I feel good. Thanks, and please, call me Stacy."

She smiles, and I walk on. The smell of eggs permeates the entire floor. I need some fresh air. As I turn the corner at the end of the hall, I see a set of elevators and decide to step in. What the hell, nobody's looking, and it's not like I could get very far dressed like this. The elevator goes down then stops on the second floor. The doors open up and a middle-aged man in a white lab coat gets on. He has a stethoscope around his neck, and he's holding a clipboard full of papers in one hand and a cup of coffee in the other. He gives me an up and down sort of look, which makes me a little nervous, so I step out.

The doors close behind me, and I take a look around. It's exactly like the floor my room is on, but there is a hall to the left of the elevators I didn't notice on my floor. I decide to head that way and stay clear of the nurses' station. The hall slants downward and there are large viewing windows on either side instead of desert tan walls. I walk a little further down and look out through the glass.

On the other side, I see tall trees planted in boxes with flowering shrubs around their bases. Small stone benches are situated in between some of the trees. It looks like a nice little courtyard area. Then something, someone unmistakable, catches my attention—it's Cally. She's sitting on one of the benches near the corner of the courtyard. And it looks like she is smoking. That can't be her. I blink several times, sure I must be mistaken. No, I'm right. It is definitely her, unless I'm having another hallucination, which wouldn't be anything new, either.

I move farther down the hall for a better look. Then I lightly tap the glass. She doesn't look up. She's staring at the ground. "Cally," I whisper, then bang harder on the window.

Someone comes into the hall. Crap, it's a nurse. "Can I help you?" she says.

"How can I get out there?" I point to the glass window.

"The only door is through a secured area."

"Secured? Why?"

"That courtyard is for psych patients only, ma'am."

"Psych patients?"

"Yes," she says. "Are you lost? Can I help you get where you need to be?"

"No, thank you. I'm fine." I turn around and rush back toward the elevator. I look out at Cally one last time before I leave the hall. She looks up at me with a blank expression on her face. I'm not sure she recognizes me. The nurse is still standing in the hall, watching me. I turn the corner and push the UP button for the elevator. The doors open.

"Stacy?"

"Jon?" I step in and the elevator doors close behind me.

"I was just on my way to see you. What were you doing here?"

"I went for a walk to get away from the egg smell. I guess I got lost."

"Oh," he says. There's a nervous inflection in his voice. "I brought something for you." He hands me a white paper cup with a plastic lid on top.

"Ooh, coffee, thanks," I say then take a sip. "Hmm, better than the plastic flavored cup I had with breakfast this morning. Where's Pat? I thought he was coming with you?"

"He had some homework. I'll bring him by later. So, how long were you lost?"

The elevator doors open and I step out. "Not that long."

He follows me down the hall. "Did you see anything interesting?"

"No. Should I have?"

"I was just wondering. How are you feeling this morning? Everything okay?"

"I feel great, Jon. Can I go home now?"

"Not quite yet. They've rescheduled your MRI for this afternoon. Then I'm sure they'll take the IV out after everything…"

"Everything what?"

"Turns out."

"You mean if I don't lose it during the MRI?"

"Yeah."

"Are they going to drug me?"

"Yeah, but it'll just be a pill—Valium probably, to relax you. Don't worry. I'll be with you the whole time."

Valium…I wonder if it will bring back the tones? "I'm sure I'll be fine. I just want everything to be done. And would you please stop finding things for them to test me for."

"I'm not."

"Yes. You are."

"Look, what happened was a really big deal. I'm not quite sure you grasp everything that went on. You almost died for fuck's sake."

"I understand that perfectly clear, Jon, but you're not helping my chances of getting out of here any sooner if you keep finding tests for them to run."

"I'm sorry, you're right. I guess I just want to cover every base before you come home."

"They're doing everything they can and then some, I'm sure."

When we get to my room, the nurses follow us in and make the rounds with the blood pressure machine, taking my temperature, and checking my heart rate. Jon stands back and lets them do their work.

"I'm going to step out, then go and get Patrick. Do you want me to pick up lunch?"

"Oh, would you?"

"What would you like?"

"Same thing as yesterday."

"Really? A cheeseburger and a milkshake?"

"Yes, please."

"Okay. I'll be back in a while. Do you want me to bring you a book or anything?"

"No. I won't be here that long."

After Jon leaves, the nurses go on and on about how nice he is. I'm really quite over it, too. When they've all finally gone, I lie down on the bed and close my eyes. Cally is there— behind my eyelids—staring at me with that same flat expression. She puts a cigarette up to her lips then inhales deeply. The smoldering end glows bright for a moment then fades to gray. Her skin is pale and her eyes don't shine. She exhales the smoke from her mouth then forces a sheepish little smile. The image disappears from my mind.

She must have snuck out and come to my room yesterday while I was sleeping. God, why couldn't I wake up? I have to find out why she's in the secured psychiatric area. What could have possibly happened in the span of two weeks to put her into a psych ward?

I feel myself getting worked up about all the possibilities. I hope everything is all right with Kyle. Maybe she had a breakdown because Tara didn't get the *Housewives* show. I know she really wanted it but even Cally's not that extreme.

My heart is pounding and the red behind my eyes seems to throb in time. This would be the perfect moment to have some of the *indigo blue*.

Sometimes I think I can or maybe, it's more like wish I could, hear the tones. But they're just memories now, fading fast.

CHAPTER TWENTY-SEVEN

A metallic scraping noise echoes and continuously encircles my head. It sounds a lot like the little ball that spins around a roulette wheel, but it doesn't bounce then stop. I keep my eyes closed this time and wonder… maybe even hope, that the Valium they gave me will help me hear the tones again. The space is tight, claustrophobic almost. It reminds me of the time I spent in the slime-filled chamber. Wherever I was, whether it was in my mind or someplace that really exists, I don't think I'll ever be able to forget it.

I've always been creative—the right-sided brain kind of a person, but still, if I had fabricated it, not everything adds up. Most of the past life experiences I had hallucinated I can probably account for. History and architecture were subjects I studied in interior design, but Sumer? I'd never heard of the place until Dr. Light made mention of it. I suppose a program about it could have been on TV while

I was flipping through channels, but it isn't something I would have stopped to watch. Not long enough to catch all the details, anyway.

Then there are the nightmares that started everything. What normal person could dream up all those gory details? Things I had never seen or heard before. Yes, Jon is a doctor, but I have never personally seen him at work in the operating room. I don't watch any of those medical TV shows, either. Maybe the world is coming to end, and somehow, I was given the foresight to see it, like Nostradamus. But what good would that do, really? It's not like there's anything *I* could do to save the planet—according to the others. They showed me things I couldn't have known, ever wanted to know, or would have even guessed on my own. I wonder if it's even possible for a solar system to have two suns—that one could dwindle, then move away to block the view of a pair of gigantic stars on a collision course to catastrophe. With all our human technology and space telescopes, I'm sure scientists would be able to see something like that looming. Then again, maybe not. There's still so much that is unexplained.

When I left the aliens it was abrupt, and I don't think they expected it. Something must have happened—interfered—but what? Maybe the Sun had broken our communication like they told me it eventually would.

"We're almost done, Mrs. Troy," a voice comes through a speaker near my head. "Keep still for just a few minutes more."

Not exactly what I was hoping to hear, but knowing

this will be over soon is still good news. The mechanical drone finally stops, and then the long table slowly slides out. I open my eyes then squinch up at the bright lights as if it were toxic—radioactive. A sudden thought comes to mind. "What does MRI stand for?" I ask. My eyelids flittering to adjust.

"It means Magnetic Resonance Imaging," the technician says.

"Does it emit radiation?" I say.

"It won't hurt you." Jon's voice echoes in the room.

"It uses magnetic fields and radio waves to produce 3D images. Your husband's right. It's harmless."

Unless you're an alien made of dark matter, I think. I must have been in this thing when I lost contact with them. It had to be what caused our communication break. If this stupid machine is powerful enough to do that…I suppose a direct beam of magnetic radiation would be deadly for them, me, all of us.

An electric chill shoots up my spine. Taking the Valium was a good idea.

Jon and the technician come into the room, help me off the table, and back into the wheelchair I came in on. Dr. Swanson and some other doctor in a white lab coat are staring at a computer screen. They stand behind a glass window in an adjacent room. Seems like an awful lot of precaution for something that is *not* supposed to be harmful. Simultaneously, they look up and out at Jon. He's standing behind me waiting to push the wheelchair. They shake their heads to say, *no*. It doesn't take a doctor or a genius to figure out what they mean. They didn't find anything wrong.

Jon lets out a sigh behind me.

"Are the results that fast?" I say.

"Yeah," he says.

"The computer screen they were looking at shows and records all the images in real time," the technician adds. He walks into the adjacent room, leaving Jon and I alone.

"And that's the radiologist next to Terry Swanson," Jon says.

"Oh. So what now?"

"I'm not sure there *is* anything else. We'll have to wait for the results from your blood samples we sent to the hematologist in South Africa."

"And how long will that take?"

"Who knows?"

"They're not going to make me wait here until then, are they?"

"No. They may discharge you as early as tomorrow."

"Really?"

"Well, they can't find anything wrong, and you're recovering fast. Hospitals are all about getting rid of patients these days."

"Well, that's good. Can you take this IV out, now?"

"Yeah, sure." Jon's tone is somber—distant.

The technician comes back into the room and Jon asks him for some dressing sponges and tape. After he gets the supplies, Jon clamps off the IV. He puts a folded wad of the gauze over the site, gently peels the tape back then slides out the plastic needle in my arm. He presses down on it for a minute then puts a strip of tape over the gauze to hold it in place. It's a makeshift Band-Aid.

"Ah…that's a lot better," I say. "You're not going to get in trouble for taking it out are you?"

"No. There's no sense in keeping it in, and it'll save the nurses having to do it when we get back to the floor. They'll thank me."

He pushes the wheelchair forward, waves to the doctors behind the window then thanks the technician.

"Jon?"

"Yes."

"You don't seem very excited about them letting me go home."

"I am. I just wish they knew more about what's happening. That's all."

"Nothing is, anymore. I think it's over now. You can stop worrying."

"That's not likely to happen." He kisses the top of my head then pushes the wheelchair through a labyrinth of long hallways.

"I'd like to visit Cally before I go home."

He doesn't respond. I can almost feel him thinking above me. The weight of his thoughts are about to come crashing down.

"I know she's here, Jon. Please, tell me what happened. I'm fine now. I can handle it."

I sense he realizes there's no point in holding it back anymore. He takes in a deep breath then exhales some of his burden. For a moment, the air around me hangs heavy with it, but we quickly move past.

"She tried to kill herself a few days after you were

hospitalized. It had nothing to do with what happened to you, though."

Calm—I have to remain composed, or he'll stop talking, I just know it. Anyway, I'm not sure I heard him right. Cally—*my best friend, Cally*—tried to commit suicide. It makes about as much sense as me being in here because aliens needed to communicate with me.

I can't express my shock or dismay. I sense his eyes watching me close for a reaction, even a subtle one like gripping the armrest of the wheelchair. "Why, then? And how?" I keep my voice flat, unaffected. I stare ahead at the tile floors glowing in the fluorescent light. I would like to hear the tones now. But I don't.

"She took an entire bottle of sleeping pills. I'm *so* glad I never wrote her a prescription. Remember? She asked me to last year."

"Yeah, I remember." Apparently, the second question was easier to answer than the first which makes me a little nervous, and he's already trying to change the subject. "Why though, Jon? What made her do it?" I try not to sound overanxious, keep my tone steady.

Silence again. Strange, but I can feel his grip tighten on the wheelchair. I'm sure in part, it's the sound of the silicone covering the handles squeaking in his sweaty palms, but it also seems to be a nervous apprehension he's emitting. There's something more serious about this than he's leading on. But it would have to be serious—tragic even—to make Cally attempt something so awful. Most likely, he knows I'm aware of this, and after thinking about it, he probably concludes he can do nothing but tell me the truth. He starts with a sigh. "Cally found out Bill's having an affair."

There's an acute pain in my chest as if the heart muscle clamped down and decided not to pump anymore. I swallow hard but don't flinch otherwise. "Anyone we know?" I say with an empty breath. When he first told me I stopped breathing and haven't been able to breathe since.

Jon's stomach growls behind me. I picture tense acids churning and burning inside his belly. He has to tell me. He needs to get it out for his own relief. "Gail," he says. Her name came out of his mouth on an empty breath, and I'm glad. It gave no life to her—traitor.

Like two people knowing and telling the same story, we simultaneously feel free to breathe again. Even the tension I felt from his grip on the wheelchair earlier, relaxes. I slouch back, get comfortable.

"I see." My tone reflects no emotion.

"Did you know?"

"No. I didn't, but maybe in some ways I did. Gail hinted about things, and I think she even tried to tell me, but I put it out of my head. I wanted to be wrong."

"Me too, I guess. Bill seemed a little off that night we had dinner with them, but I thought maybe he and Cally had an argument before or something."

"I still want to see her, Jon. I need to talk to Cally."

"It won't be easy. She's already been caught once trying to leave."

"No. She came to see *me*. I remember."

"Uh…no, they found her on the first floor. She was on her way out the door."

"Please, Jon. It's urgent."

"It can't wait till she gets released?"

"No." I reach back and place my hand on his. "It can't."

"I'll see what I can do."

"Thank you, and what about Kyle, how is he?"

"That I don't know. Patrick hasn't said much, and to be honest, I think it's one of the reasons he didn't want to go back to school."

"Poor kid."

"Kyle?"

"No, Patrick—having his mom in the hospital and his best friend's mom, too."

"He's fine honey, really. Kids are resilient."

"You always say that…I wonder if Justin knew and that's why he was acting out so much. Gail told me she was transferring him. I should have put the pieces together. I should've known…"

He puts his hand on my shoulder and squeezes down gently. "Don't you dare blame yourself for any of this shit. Nobody wants to suspect their friends are screwing around with their other friends' husbands."

"Nothing like this would ever happen to us, right? You'd tell me if you were unhappy."

"Are you kidding? You're the only woman I love. And besides, all your friends are nuts. I've always thought so."

I laugh, hysterically almost, because *so am I*.

Off and on throughout the rest of the afternoon and into the evening, people come by to say their goodbyes after they'd heard the good news about me being cleared to leave tomorrow. It's mostly been hospital staff and people from the ER I hardly remember. I don't know what Jon told my friends, but so far Cally has been the only one to come and see me, and they locked her back up for it.

When things quiet down, Jon leaves to make his rounds thanking everyone again. Patrick sits in the corner with his earbuds in, looking out the window.

"Pat."

He looks up and pulls one of his earbuds out.

"Is Kyle okay?" I say.

He looks a little surprised. "Dad told you?"

"Yeah."

"He's okay, I guess."

"And how about you?"

"It's all good, Mom. I'm a big boy."

"You're not just being silly are you?"

"No. I'm being *serious*. I don't know why, but when bad things happen they don't bother me as much as other people….and especially girls."

"Ah, so you think girls are more sensitive."

"Think? I know they are."

"Yeah maybe, but it's probably because of hormones.

You know your dad always blames everything on hormones."

"Crazy hormones, maybe."

Yeah…maybe.

"You sure you're all right, though? It's not healthy to be so nonchalant when bad things happen. Do you want to talk about it?"

"No, Mom. I'm good, really. It's not that I don't feel bad. I do, but then it goes away."

"Well, okay. But if you change your mind let me know. You haven't had any more nosebleeds, have you?"

"Nope." He smirks then stuffs his earbud back in like there's no chance in hell he wants to discuss anything else with me. He's a tough one to crack. A lot like me in that regard. It took three whole months of hellish nightmares, hallucinations, and very little sleep until I finally had a breakdown. And still nobody knows why. No family history of it. Unless it's possible shopping and lunching with friends have become major life stressors. Event planning, holiday parties, and fundraisers aren't even that much work, but I like to say they are. No. There really isn't a reason—*unless it were all true.*

Not long ago, I prayed the tones would stop and go away. Now, I wish I could hear them once more. As if hearing them again would somehow validate my sanity, even though something tells me there's more to it than that. Maybe I could ask them about Patrick.

Only, they don't come. And there's nothing for me to do except wait. Inside, I feel changes on the way. I can't tell if they're good or bad. I just know they won't be stopped.

CHAPTER TWENTY-EIGHT

Morning sun beams through the window and overheats me. I'm still asleep, but it's that in-and-out of consciousness kind. I kick the blankets down then nuzzle my face deeper into the pillow and smell the scent of sweetness. Behind my eyelids are a multitude of colored shapes against a predominantly red background. I imagine myself there again—with the others—liquid light gliding through luminous vapors.

At last, I get my eyelids to stay open. The sun seems brighter. I squint and stretch out. Then I realize I'm soaked through. The sheets are even wet. I sit up, turn over, and put my nose down into the mattress. It's definitely not urine, which is a relief. It must be sweat—a fever. I put the back of my hand against my forehead. It feels cool and damp.

This isn't good. I jump out of bed and take off my gown then lay it on the windowsill to dry. I walk into the bathroom and look at myself in the mirror. My hair is wet, flat, and clinging to my head. Sweat beads trickle from in between and underneath my breasts, rolling down over my abdomen. I notice Jon's makeshift Band-Aid and yank the tape off with one swift motion. Not a single pinprick mars my arm. Even I know that's *not* normal. Not for as long as I've had an IV there. Jon told me they were feeding me something called TPN or PPN through it, too, so I wouldn't get malnourished when I was in a coma. It's similar to Gatorade, I guess…liquid food, but it would mean the IV was used often—enough to leave some kind of a mark. Both Patrick and Jon bruise horribly just from getting shots. I'll have to keep it covered, so he doesn't get suspicious.

I step into the shower and turn on the water. When it feels tepid against my palm, I stand underneath the spray. Thick plumes of steam rise up from everywhere on my body. I jump back and check the water again to make sure I didn't misjudge the temperature. It feels lukewarm on my fingertips. I turn my hand over and put it under the spray of water. Steam immediately billows up from my skin. With my other hand, I reach out and touch the arm that's steaming. "Whoa!" I jerk my hand back. My fingertips feel raw and numb. The arm underneath the shower is frigid like ice, maybe even colder. I don't get it. Something is *very* wrong, but this can't be happening—not now.

I move back underneath the showerhead and let the steam roll up in waves. It quickly fills the stall and then the entire bathroom. Thank God I closed the door, and the vent automatically comes on with the light. The steam is so thick I can barely see my hand in front of my face.

After about ten minutes, the thick white cloud starts to dissipate. There's a sweet smell all around. *Cold, but steaming...* Then I remember the lab tech that burned his hand on dry ice. Maybe it's something similar to that, but I have no intention of bringing it up now that I'm so close to leaving.

When the air is visibly clear, I step out and pull a towel down from a metal rack above the toilet. I pat myself dry. My skin temperature feels normal again. I wrap the towel around my body then step out of the bathroom. I rush over to the bed and look down at the sheets. They're perfectly dry. The gown I put on the windowsill is, too. *Strange*—it's as if the wetness was pure cold. Not enough to freeze into ice, but *so* extreme it simply evaporates. Something I'm excreting reacts exactly the way dry ice does when it comes in contact with water. I remember the chemical reactions from high school lab experiments. But why am I excreting it? The question gives me chills in the worse sense of the word. I wonder if there's a trigger. The more I consider it, there's a possibility all my prior incidents of night sweats revolving around the nightmares were actually cold ones. At least it doesn't leave any evidence. All those times I got up and changed my nightshirt, it was all for nothing. If I'm right, it has something to do with sleep, but I've been wrong about so many things lately. Hopefully, it doesn't happen again before Jon gets here or even worse, in front of him.

I'm swallowing my last bit of plastic-flavored coffee when Jon comes into the room. "Morning," he says. He walks up, leans down, and kisses my cheek. "You look great."

"Thanks for bringing that bag of clothes and leaving it in the closet."

"No problem. I figured you'd want the comfortable stuff."

"Nothing's more perfect than jeans and a long sleeve T-shirt."

"I didn't know it would be this warm out, though. I'm pretty sure I packed a short sleeve shirt in there, too, if you prefer it."

"No. This is good."

"Your cheek did feel a little cool. Are you warm enough?"

"Yeah, I'm fine. So—is it time to go?"

"That's the bad news."

"Oh Jon, please don't. What was the good news? You can't do this now."

"Don't worry. It all works out. They're not done clearing your discharge papers, but I was able to get you in to see Cally."

"Really? When?"

"You'll have about thirty minutes after she has lunch until her group therapy session.""Poor Cally."

"Yeah, I really had to do some serious schmoozing with the staff nurses. They told me about some pretty messed up people in there. It's also a *swing* wing for addicts overflow."

"What! She's in there with drug addicts?"

"When detox is full, they send them to the psych unit 'cause it's secured."

I can't believe he's telling me this crap. The *walking on pins and needles* phase of my recovery must be over. He's going straight for the jugular. I have to change the subject before I get worked up and show him what it really is to be *steaming* mad.

"By the way…how are my parents?" I say.

"Typical. Anxious. Still paranoid your mother might come down with something. I love them, but they've been killing me. Trying to get you home and keep you here at the same time. In a lot of ways, I think they doubt me now. I didn't know what was wrong with you. I had no answers, couldn't fix the problem."

I move the tray table away then stand up and put my arms around him. "I'm sorry, honey. I love you, and I promise to make it up to you."

"I'm holding you to that. I've missed you so much."

"I've missed you, too but soon. Just a few more hours."

"What do you want to do until then?"

"Well, if you want, you could get me a decent cup of coffee, and I can pack up my stuff while you're gone, or you can stay here and tell me exactly how it was you *schmoozed* the nurses into letting me see Cally."

"I'll be back in a bit with your coffee."

Jon leads me through a long stark hall where the floor tiles and even the handrails are desert tan. Not a single picture hangs on the walls, and there are no high rectangular windows near the ceiling to let natural sunlight in. The illumination is purely fluorescent, which makes the walk more ominous. Barricading the end of the hall is a massive solid door also painted desert tan. A tiny square window—roughly the size of a human face—is centrally positioned in the door at eye level. When we're up close, I notice a fine wire mesh woven into a pattern in between the glass panes of the window, emphasizing the feeling of no escape.

In the upper right corner of the ceiling, there's a small black video camera. A neon red dot blinks continuously as the camera lens sweeps slowly back and forth across the hall. There is a loud electronic buzz, and then Jon opens the door.

Standing in the doorway is a middle-aged woman wearing plain blue hospital scrubs. The hall behind her seems to stretch out and go on forever. I step forward then all at once feel unbearably alone. I whip around, and Jon is still standing with the door open on the other side of the hall.

"You're not coming?" I say.

"No. Just you. Don't worry, you'll be fine. The staff is all around." Then the same buzz that opened the door goes off again, but now it sounds more like an alarm. "Oops," Jon says. He steps back. "Sorry," he looks at the nurse behind me, then he lets go of the door. I leap forward, but it's too late, the door is about to close.

"Don't reach your hand in!" the nurse says.

As soon as the door shuts, a strange sound comes from all around it.

"It locks with a security seal. You could've lost your hand or fingers." She seems perturbed, but all I can think of is how I feel right now—this very minute—in this whole scenario.

This could eventually be my fate. I stare out through the little window at Jon. He has a small smile on his face. He winks then raises his hand and makes an *okay* sign. I nod my head, take a deep breath then turn around.

"I'm sorry," I tell the nurse. "I wasn't thinking."

"That's part of the reason why we don't usually bring visitors in this way, but your husband was very sweet and bought us all lunch. He's a real charmer that one is."

"Yes. He is."

"My name is Ella by the way." She reaches her hand out and I shake it.

"Stacy." Then I gasp at what I see next. Directly behind her is an old man sitting in a chair. His hair is long, gray, and tousled this way and that. He has a thick coat of stubble on the lower half of his face that looks like dirty snow.

"And this is Jerry," Ella says. "Don't mind him, he's harmless." She leans in close to me then whispers, "He likes to sit up near the nurses' station so he can listen to what's going on."

I nod my head and smile. The nurses' station behind him is a lot like the one on my floor, but it's completely sealed in by windows with more of the steel mesh between the panes and one solid door in the middle.

"This way," Ella says. "I'll take you to Cally."

Then it all coalesces, and I remember why I came. I'm not here to be left. I'm here to talk to Cally.

As we walk past, I can't help but stare at Jerry a little more. There's a blank expression on his face, and his eyes are void of emotion. He's a very pathetic-looking old man. It saddens me that this is probably someone's father, brother, husband. Then I notice his wrists strapped down to the arms of the chair with white padded bindings. *Geez, this place is fucking tragic.* I smile at him then turn my head forward and follow Ella down the hall.

We come to a glass door, and it's obviously very thick and impenetrable. Shatterproof most likely, maybe bulletproof, too, or even electrified when closed. They try and make everything *look* normal on this floor, but with a little further inspection, it becomes blatantly apparent nothing is—*normal.*

Ella punches several numbers into a keypad connected to the door handle, then slides her hospital ID badge through it as if it were one of those credit card scanners. The door buzzes open, and she steps out first. It's the same landscaped courtyard I saw Cally sitting in the one day I got lost, but now I'm looking from the inside out.

As soon as I step into the courtyard, Ella closes the door behind me and I hear that pneumatic seal sound again. From this side, the door isn't clear. It blends right into the segmented concrete walls. Incredible, I think it's faux painted. It mimics the walls right down to the small bits of river rock embedded into the makeshift slabs. Even the keypad virtually disappears. I look across the way to where the windows I stared out at Cally were. From in here, they don't look like windows at all, more like two-way mirrors reflecting the trees to make the courtyard seem bigger. How awful to have the hospital *crazies* on display like this without their knowledge of it. Cally would be mortified if she knew. Whoever the idiot is that designed this place should be fired and severely beaten.

Ella walks around a few of the potted trees to a bench in the corner. I see Cally sitting to one side, staring down at the ground. I'm so used to her expecting my visits and watching her face light up when she sees me. They must have her on something, she appears to move in slow motion as Ella approaches her. Cally's eyes are pallid and glossed over. She's definitely medicated. It's hard to believe a few weeks or so ago we met for lunch, and she was pure radiant sunshine.

Ella leans down and whispers something in her ear. Cally's eyes move over and look into mine. They immediately begin to well up. Cally nods her head then Ella turns around, walks up to me, and gently puts her hand on my shoulder. "I'll be on the other side of these trees if you need anything."

"Thanks. I'll be fine." She moves her hand away then walks on. I step up to Cally and sit down next to her on the bench.

"Oh, Stacy, it's so good to see you." She raises her arms to give me a hug and it appears to take all the energy she can muster. So, I scoot in closer and put mine around her.

"I've missed you," I whisper into the side of her head. The stale odor of cigarettes and hospital disinfectant lingers in her hair.

"Just to see you makes me feel so good, but getting to smell your sweetness now, too has really made my day." She slurs her words as if she's had one too many *Cosmos*. "That's why I've always called you *Sweetie*, you know… because you smell like gumballs."

I release her from my arms then sit back and look her over. "Cally, I'm going home today."

"You are? That's wonderful. For a while, I thought you would die."

Yeah, she's definitely, very medicated. "They didn't find anything wrong."

"I'm happy for you, then." A shadow of sadness veils her face, followed by silence. I'm not sure how or if I should even respond. All I can think of is her answering the door wearing that silly genie costume for book club. *And now…*

"Cally, I'm just so sorry."

"For what?"

"Everything. Not being a better friend."

"But you're the best."

"Not really. We should have talked more. Spoke about things that really mattered."

"That's no fun."

"But maybe we could've helped each other."

"We did."

"How?"

"To forget."

I tilt my head in confusion.

"When we were together, Sweetie, it was just *you* and *me*. I forgot about all my doubts. You made them seem less important. That was what I needed more than anything—to forget."

A sudden swell of tears blurs my image of her. I blink and they stream down from the corners of my eyes.

"Oh, don't cry," she says. "Everything's going to work out. You'll see." She puts her arms around me and holds me tight. "I'll be fine and so will you. They're going to let me out soon, and then we can go back to doing things the way we used to."

She releases me then rests her hands in her lap. Purple bruises encircle both her wrists. They must have had to tie her down like old Jerry sitting in the hall. I'm not sure she's getting out of here any time soon.

Like clockwork, Ella comes around the corner. "I'm sorry to interrupt ladies, but Cally, you've got a meeting to attend."

"That's right," Cally says. "I better get going." She stands up and I do the same.

"Sasha will be here for you shortly," Ella says to Cally.

"Aren't you coming, too?" Cally asks Ella.

"I'll be there as soon as I walk Stacy back."

"Okay. Bye Stacy," Cally says.

"Goodbye." I say, holding my breath. I'm weak in the knees, keeping back tears and gasps. I don't want her to see me break.

Ella puts her hand on my shoulder and gently guides

me over to the camouflaged door. As soon as it buzzes open I stumble in, put my face down into my hands and cry. Ella supports me with her arm and walks me to the door by the nurses' station. Poor Jerry is still seated next to it, but he has a small blanket over his legs now.

"I understand how you're feeling Stacy, but she's showing signs of improvement, and that's all I can tell you." She pulls a tissue from her pocket and hands it to me. I blow my nose and wipe my tears. From the end of the hall I can already see Jon's face peering into the small square window through the door. He smiles and I'm somewhat at ease again.

"Thanks again for all of your help today, Ella. It was very nice to meet you."

"Nice to meet you, too. I've got to go in and buzz the door open. When you hear it, go ahead and pull the handle."

"Okay."

Ella keys herself into the enclosed nurses' station through the solid door. As soon as she's inside, Jerry lunges at me from the chair. He reaches for me and I see remnants of white straps hanging from his wrists. Jerry broke free! The weight of his body throws me down against the hard tile floor. Jon is yelling and kicking the bigger door from the other side. I raise my head and look up at the little window. I get a distorted glimpse of Jon with a horrified expression on his face. Then Jerry grabs the back of my head. I turn to look for Ella, and he pushes my face into the floor. Ella is trying to get back out, but she's in a panic.

I can hear her fumbling the keys around the door handle. The code doesn't seem to be working. A siren goes off, like a fire alarm. Suddenly, blue-white lights come on. They're positioned along the ceiling every five feet. They blink in time with the blaring electronic beeps.

Within seconds, I hear and feel thunderous footsteps behind and underneath me. Jerry's dead weight is lifted from my body, but he has hold of my hair and he's pulling it up. Then there are more buzzes. Jon bolts through the door, Ella steps out into the hall. They are prying Jerry's fingers from my hair.

"Let go!" Jon says.

"They're coming," Jerry screams. "She'll kill us all! Do you hear? We're all gonna die!"

He flails wildly in the arms of two large men wearing white uniforms. Several other people are standing around in scrubs and white uniforms. They must have lifted him off me. Ella has a syringe in her hand. She quickly pulls the cap off with her teeth and stabs Jerry in the thigh. She pushes down until the clear liquid is gone. Within moments, Jerry gives up and passes out.

Jon gently turns my head in his hands and takes a look at my face. "Jesus Christ."

A warm trickle moves down from my nose and over my lip. I take the tissue Ella had given me, put it up to my nostrils, and blot. "It's nothing," I tell him. "I'm fine."

"I'm so sorry, Stacy—Dr. Troy. I've never seen Jerry lose it like this before," Ella says. "You guys take him back to his room and sheet him, please." She directs the orderlies.

"I don't know how the hell he got out of his bindings, but I've got to call Dr. Springer."

"Let's go, Jon. Please," I beg.

"Is it all right if we leave?" Jon asks Ella.

"Go ahead, but keep your cell phone on just in case."

"Okay. Thanks."

"Are you sure Stacy's all right?" she says. "Maybe you should bring her to the ER?"

"No. I'm taking her home. She's fine. I'll handle it."

"I'm really, really sorry about that, Dr. Troy. I'm still not sure what happened."

"Tell Dr. Springer to give me a call if he needs anything."

"I will." Ella slides her badge and steps into the nurses' station. She pushes a button over by one of the telephones and the alarm stops blaring through the speakers. I hardly noticed them anymore after Jerry slammed the side of my face into the floor.

"The alarm lights are still twinkling." I didn't mean to say that out loud.

"They will for about ten more minutes. Come on. Let's get you home."

After the massive door closes behind us, Jon examines my face again. The bleeding has stopped. It wasn't a nosebleed like the ones before. Then for a split second I hear a musical electronic tone.

CHAPTER TWENTY-NINE

The bells chime—it's *them*. "Do you hear that?" I say. Jon is still examining my face for injuries. Twisting my head from side to side, using my chin like a knob.

"That ringing? Yeah. It'll go away in a minute. It's from the alarm. I'll talk to administration about it. It's loud enough to wake the dead."

"Maybe that's a good thing…for this place, I mean." I giggle.

"Not funny." He releases my chin then moves in and kisses my forehead. "You're fine. Let's go." He takes my hand and leads me back the way we came. As soon as we round the corner, the tones stop. I wonder if it had something to do with my head hitting the floor. And Jerry—what the hell was his problem? I know he was tied to that chair earlier. I saw it. I've never been happier to leave a place. Poor Cally…

"Honey, is Cally going to be okay?" I say.

"Eventually…at least she's getting help."

"How long will she have to be here?"

"As long as it takes."

"That's not reassuring."

"I'm not a shrink, babe. Speaking of which, I don't want you going to anymore of those appointments. You weren't planning on it, were you?"

"No. I stopped going a while ago."

"Good. You don't need it. That's not what's wrong with you."

Yeah, right. More like, good, you don't want word to get out I've wound up like Cally.

Jon helps me into the passenger's side of my SUV then runs around and gets in. Brown paper bags with market handles line the back seat. Several small Mylar balloons stick up from some of the bags, the little round ones that come in flower arrangements. Jon backs out of a physician's parking spot.

"Where did those come from?" I say.

"What?"

"The balloons."

"Oh those—Geez, I thought you meant a car was headed straight for us or something—they came with some flowers. You got all kinds of *Get Well* stuff, but while you were quarantined they kept it all at the nurses' station."

"Oh."

Jon looks around for moving cars then exits the parking garage.

"It's gray out," I say. Not that it has anything to do with anything, but my mind seems to be jumping around a little bit. Maybe I developed Adult ADD while I was in the hospital…I wonder if that's even possible.

"Well, it is winter," Jon says. "Christmas is in a little more than a week."

"That means the fundraiser is this weekend."

"Don't think about it. Jordan finished up all of the arrangements."

"Yeah, remind me to thank her."

"Why'd you say it like that?"

"No reason—I want to go."

"I don't think that's a good idea."

"I'm fine, Jon. It's like nothing ever happened. My life should go on as planned."

"We'll see."

"Humph." I turn my head and stare out the window at the concrete sky above and desiccate earth below. In between is an area where the two meld together. That middle ground of gray and brown is where we live. A stark contrast to a place made up of gelled, liquid-color lights. When people lose their minds their distortions on reality always seem to go in the extreme opposite direction of their everyday environments. The more I look around, it makes perfect sense why.

Jon pulls up the driveway and for some reason I expect to see Patrick and my parents waiting in the garage. My side is empty though, except for some stacked trash boxes and Patrick's long skateboard shoved up against the side wall.

I get out and open the door to the back seat.

"What are you doing?" Jon says. "Go inside. I'll get this."

I shut the car door and head for the house. As soon as I step in, my mom walks up and throws her arms around me. "I'm so glad you're home, dear." Her voice cracks and she takes in a rapid sequence of quick breaths. She's crying now. My dad comes up and pries her from me. She wipes her tears while my dad leans in and gives me a peck on the cheek.

"Glad you're home," he says.

"We thought we might lose you," my mom says. Then she breaks into tears again.

Jon comes through the garage door behind me. "Why is everybody in the hallway?"

"Here, let me help." My dad steps up and takes two of the bags from Jon.

We all walk toward the family room.

"Where's Pat?" I say.

"Upstairs," my mom answers. "That boy plays video games all day and all night, nothing else. It's not right, and now that you're home *you* can talk to him about it."

Jon whisks by us in a huff. Now I feel a hundred times sorry for what he's had to endure. This is going to take some serious making up, and the mere thought of it has me exhausted.

"Mom, please, not now." Three steps into the family room and I come to a stop, suddenly exasperated. The room feels like it's caving in around me. I'm being crushed by Christmas.

"What's the matter? I bet you're tired. Come in and sit on the couch." She gestures me toward the loveseat as if I were a guest in *her* house. It feels strange, surreal almost. I look around between the family room and kitchen. Nothing looks familiar, not even the decorations. Her things are set out on the counters and on top of the end tables. Right now, I actually *do* feel *alien*, and in my own home. It's as though I've been away on another planet and have returned sometime in the future. Nothing feels right. The smell in the house isn't even the same. It reeks of my mom's perfume and cheap plastic Christmas decorations. Reality has become a nightmare, and my dreams are someplace I think I might like to get back to.

"What is it?" she says. "Have a seat."

"Nothing. I'd like to shower first, that's all."

"Oh," she says. "Well, don't take too long. I've made some food. Maybe get Patrick on your way down. I don't think he's eaten anything all day."

"Let me get rid of these, and I'll walk you up," Jon says.

"That's all right," I tell him. "I can do it."

He gives me a stern look then pushes aside some ridiculous glittery Santa figurines.

"Don't listen to her," my mom says. "She might get

weak and slip, and we can't have her falling down the stairs now, she just got home."

Jon tosses the bags on the counter then walks over to me and rolls his eyes when she can no longer see his face. I head for the stairs, and he follows me up with one hand gently placed across the small of my back. Sparkling red garland is wound around the handrail to imitate the look of a candy cane. At the landing I nearly trip over a small snowman set down on the carpet. It's wearing a cowboy hat and a red paisley 'kerchief around its neck. There's a piece of rope between both hands.

"Watch this," Jon says. He moves his foot over the base of the snowman then pushes down on a button. The snowman immediately goes into a country western song about "Lassoing Santa Claus."

"How could you let her do this to *my* house?" I whisper.

"Like I had a choice."

Then from the bottom of the stairs, we hear. "Isn't that adorable? It was on sale and I just knew you'd love it."

"Yeah, Mom, real cute. Thanks," I yell down. Then I get right back to whispering exclamations at Jon. "Good God, why didn't you call James? He's arranged our holiday decorations for the last decade. Honestly, Jon. It looks like a bargain mart Christmas aisle down there. *And* up here." I stroke the garland around the staircase, and it makes a crackling sound. Then there's a tiny snap, and the piece rolls down from its position. "You let her use tape on the cherry handrail?" I put the garland back into place, re-stick the tape to the banister and roll my eyes at Jon.

"I'm telling you, I had no choice. When James called to schedule an appointment, your mother answered the phone. She told him we wouldn't be requiring his services this year." He whisper yells back at me.

I can't help but laugh in snorts. He starts to crack up, too then quickly guides me up the rest of the stairs before my mother hears us. When we get into the master bedroom he closes the French doors behind us, grabs a hold of my hands and turns me around to face him. "You're probably wondering why you left after a homecoming like this."

"Never." I kiss him on the lips. "You're my hero. You getting in the shower with me?"

"No. This is my chance to finally get some work done. I'm behind. Your mother thinks that when I'm home I should keep your father entertained and run errands for her. She even asked me to string lights around the rooftops. I flat out refused. She was upset at first, but then it was your dad who finally convinced her it was a bad idea. One of us in the hospital was enough."

"Like I said, you're my hero."

He smiles, kisses me, and then quietly opens the door and heads toward the office.

I walk into the bathroom and undress. A hot shower anywhere else will never feel as good. It's the only place in the house that has stayed the same. I close my eyes and breathe in the rising whorls of steam. The scent they carry is lightly sweet, and then I wonder…maybe I've always smelled this way but never noticed until now.

The hot water pelting my back is nothing like the cool

slimy gel I was covered in when I was away. I'm not so sure anymore which one has better soothing powers. Living essence from *the others* seemed to flow through the ooze, and all at once I would feel safe, comforted, an integral part of something—home.

When I'm done, I step out and make good time getting dressed. Yummy, home cooked food aromas have been floating upstairs, drifting through cracks in the door. My stomach grumbles and my mouth waters. I slide into a pair of fuzzy slippers then head down to Pat's room.

I open his door, step in then close it behind me. He covers the microphone of his telemarketer-looking gamer headset. "Hey, Mom, glad you're home. What's up?"

"Not much. I just wanted to talk with you for a minute before we go downstairs."

"Hang on. Let me finish this."

I hear voices coming from his headset. "Dude, you're already dead."

"Aw, man. You ass…" Patrick glances over at me then stops. "I gotta go, guys. Catch 'ya later." He takes off his headset then powers everything down. There's a deep impression across the top of his hair like he'd been wearing a headband.

"Doesn't that thing give you a headache?"

"No."

I step up and sit down on the edge of his bed. "Pat, I don't think playing these video games all the time are good for your social skills."

"Yeah they are. I talk to people from all over the world."

"Talk or swear?"

"Depends where they're from. It's funny to hear people with different accents cuss."

"Wouldn't you like to go and hang out with *your* friends?"

"Not really."

"I could drop you off at the movie theatre or the mall."

"The mall? I think that was the Eighties. Nobody goes to the mall now. Besides, all my friends are gone on family vacations."

"You're right. You know, I didn't even think of that."

"That's 'cause Grandma's got you believing her."

"She's just looking out for you. And she's right. It's not normal to stay cooped up in here all day and night. Get out and do something. Life's too short to sit around and wait for things to happen. You never know when it might end, and if it did, would you feel as though you lived up to your potential?"

"Uh…yeah, Mom. I've got the highest score in this game so far, and soon I'll have it beat."

"Then what?"

"Next game."

"You're sure you wouldn't rather be out, though?"

"Where? You have to be twenty-one to go anywhere that's any fun. I go out and do stuff. Don't listen to Grandma, she's old school. Thinks I should go door to door and ask people to rake their leaves. No one even has any leaves, and there's no grass. I told her it wouldn't be right to put landscapers out of work in this economy. That's when she got mad."

"She doesn't remember what it was like when I was a teenager."

"All she ever talks about is how good you were. I told her times have changed. She didn't like that, either."

"I bet. Come on, let's go downstairs and eat. She cooked, and there's no reason to be rude to her because you don't agree with what she's saying."

"I guess."

"Promise me you'll try and get along."

"Yeah." He sighs.

I get up from the bed and he follows me out. On our way through the hall, I push open the office door. Jon looks up from the computer screen.

"Is it time to eat?" he says.

"Yeah, we're heading down."

"You've got Pat?"

"Uh-huh."

He circles the mouse, clicks it a couple of times then gets up from the chair. Pat and I go on ahead. My mom has set up a smorgasbord across the kitchen island.

"You've outdone yourself," I say.

"Make up a plate then have a seat. Can I get you something to drink?" she asks.

"I'd love a soda."

"Soda," she says with a quizzical look. "Really?"

"I'll get her one," Pat says. He takes off down the hall toward the garage then comes back carrying two cans.

"I see you got a soda for yourself, too," my mom says. "Did you ask anyone else if they wanted one?"

"Uh…" Patrick says.

The phone rings and my mom darts across the kitchen to answer it. Patrick lets out a sigh of relief. He was literally saved by the bell. It seems *she* is the one I have to have a talk with. She's too hard on him. Patrick needs space, not nagging, and if she keeps this up she'll alienate him forever.

"Troy residence," she answers. "Yes, she's back home. Uh-huh…well I'm afraid she's unavailable at the moment, but I'd be happy to take a message." She grabs a slip of paper and jots something down. "Okay, I'll let her know. Bye."

"Who was that?" Jon's voice booms from behind me.

"It was for Stacy," she says. "Tara says to give her call."

Jon kisses the back of my head. "See," he whispers. "She's a phone whore."

CHAPTER THIRTY

A million colored twinkles glint at the far end of a dark open space. I float toward them, disembodied. My dark energy travels transcendentally, the way *they* told me it did when I was in a coma. The brilliant flashes recede upon my approach, leaving behind a fleeting rainbow trail that goes black as my energy suddenly sinks. I stretch and reach out, but I am only darkness.

"Come back to us." "We wait." "You must See."

The tones, their voices, are one in the same. I understand. They are calling me and I have to go.

Day comes and beams white light through shutter slats. They streak across the room in elongated linear patterns and make me feel confined. To break free, I flip the covers away and accidentally smack Jon in the side of the head.

"Ouch!"

"Sorry. You okay?"

"Are you?"

"Don't be grouchy, it was an accident. I'm ready to get up. I've been in bed too long."

"How'd you sleep?"

"Fine, but it took me a while to get there."

"Really?"

"It was too quiet."

"You got used to all the bells, beeps, and buzzers… hospital sounds." He yawns.

"Ha, you're right. I don't remember them now."

"Ready for some coffee?" Jon pushes his half of the covers to the middle of the bed and sits up.

"Yes, please."

I'm in the shower when he comes into the bathroom carrying two steaming cups. "Are you going in to work today?" I ask.

"No. Not till Monday. Remember? I told you I was off for the rest of the week."

"Oh. I don't remember. So what're your plans?"

"I didn't have any, really. Thought I'd play it by ear. Wasn't sure how you'd be feeling."

"I feel really good, like I have to get out and do something. I was thinking we could go to the mall for a bit and I could look for some new shoes."

"Shoes for what?"

"For the party."

"You still determined to go?"

"Yeah."

"Positive you're up to it?"

"Yeah."

"Then fine, go shoe shopping but not with me. Take your mother."

"'Kay."

"If you start feeling unwell, come back. At least I'll get some more office work done…" He continues mumbling something on his way out.

I knew he wouldn't want to go if I said the word *shopping*, but I hadn't planned on him making me take my mother. I'll have to improvise for where I mean to go—lie and tell my mom there's a new store I want to check out. Fortunately, she's easy to convince.

When I'm dressed, I take my empty coffee cup and walk down the hall to Patrick's room. He's already up and sitting on the edge of his bed with his headset on, deep into something involving lots of rapid gunfire. Strobe light reflections from the TV flicker across his pale face in the half-dark of his room. Then I notice a bulge protruding from one of his nostrils.

"What's wrong with your nose?" I say.

His eyes don't shift from the images on the television. "I had another bloody nose."

"Did it stop? Let me see." I step up, and he holds his hand out to keep me back.

"It's fine, Mom, not now. I'm in the middle of a game." He quickly pulls the bulge from his nose and hands me the scrunched up, bloody tissue shaped like a tiny badminton shuttlecock.

"That's really disgusting, Pat."

"Will you toss that? Thanks."

I move to the corner of his room and step into his bathroom with the thing splayed across my open palm. His wastebasket is a third of the way full with bunches of bloodstained tissues.

"Are all of these from today?" I say.

"What? No. Mom…" he whines. His words are followed by a succession of quick, clickety-clack sounds. I turn my palm over and the redheaded tissue falls in with the rest. Then I walk over to the door and lean my hip against the jamb. His fingers move speedily over buttons on the game controller in his hands. His focus remains fixed on the television screen.

My mind wanders off and remembers bits and pieces of the nightmares I tried so hard to forget. The bleeding disease—the pandemic—I can't remember how it began. Suspicion followed by nightmare images and horrendous thoughts begin to wall up around me. *Impossible.* That can't be right. I have to stay calm.

"Fine, I get it. You're busy, but we *will* talk about this later. I'm going to the mall."

"'Kay. Bye, Mom. Later."

Downstairs, I put my coffee cup in the dishwasher. Odd, I don't feel the need for a refill, and good thing, too, because the empty pot is sitting in the sink. I'm thankful to have been in a coma while being weaned from caffeine. Hard to believe only a month ago, I was drinking close to two pots a day, not including my drive-thru visits.

Jon told my mom about the mall and she's just about ready. My dad is sitting outside on a patio chair reading the paper, sipping a steaming mug of coffee. So, that's where it all went.

I hear the sound of tapping echoes around the hallway before I can physically see my mom in her heels. "Which mall are we going to?" she says as she rounds the corner. A heavy cabled sweater is draped over one of her forearms and her purse is in the crook of the other.

"The one on the strip, but there's a new store I want to take you to first."

"That mall is going to be crowded today."

"It's always like that, but we'll be fine. We're starting out early." I grab my purse and keys from the counter. "You ready?"

"Well, I wanted a little more coffee."

"Dad drank it all. Let's go, and I'll hit a drive-thru on the way. We won't have to wait in long lines at the mall then."

"Let me tell your father we're leaving." She walks over to the sliding glass doors, pulls one slightly open and sticks her head out. My dad gets up, gives her a kiss and then she comes back inside and closes the door. "Okay. Let's go. Did you want to say goodbye to Jon?"

"He knows I'm leaving."

The line is five cars deep after we order our coffees. I take the time to check the car's navigation history. I scroll down the addresses, but I can't find the one for Dr. Light's building, and I don't recall the exact street names and numbers, either. Strange, I know I programmed it in the first time I went there. I guess I'll have to go on memory, which shouldn't be too much of an issue. Every time I had an appointment, I usually wound up smack dab in front of his office without remembering how I had arrived there.

"Here, Mom." I hand her coffee over.

"This is too hot," she says, nearly dropping it. Good thing I didn't let go. I set it down in the cup holder between us.

"It'll cool by the time we get to the mall." Mine on the other hand is perfect. I take several gulps then pull away and head for the 215 Beltway.

"What kind of stuff do they sell at this new store? It's not another one of your friend's boutiques is it? I'm not in the mood to be pressured."

"No. You'll like it."

She clings to her purse as if I'm the one after her shopping dollars.

After about twenty minutes, I take the exit and drive down the frontier road for a ways. Then I turn down a familiar, newly paved road that leads to nowhere.

"That's weird," I say.

"What? Are you lost?"

"No. This is where it should be." At the end of the road there's a large circular drive but nothing on the other side.

I know I'm not lost because there is zilch out here, except for miles of graded land.

"Maybe it's not built yet. How did you hear about it, anyway? What's on that sign over there?"

I pull in front of a big white billboard with two matching legs staked into the dirt. It reads, "Five Acres for Sale, zoned for commercial business park," and there's an out-of-state phone number at the bottom.

"Are you sure this is it?"

"Yeah, Mom! I know it is." Geez, between her twenty questions, a missing fucking building, and feeling ridiculous, I'm about to lose it. My hands start shaking on the steering wheel.

"Are you all right?"

"Please, Mom." I say with a calmer voice. "Just give me a minute."

She turns away and looks out the passenger side window. "Okay, but if you're not feeling up to the mall, we can go home."

I know she won't stop. I take in a deep breath then purse my lips and slowly exhale. A thin stream of icy white smoke blows out. I put my window down and cough out the rest. *Shit!*

My mom turns back around. "What is it?"

"Nothing. The coffee's hot is all."

"I told you."

Before I put the window up, I take a quick breath in and out. The air is clear. I put the car into drive then circle around and exit the way I came in. When I'm back on the highway I pick up my coffee and take another drink.

"Maybe you shouldn't have any more of that, dear."

"You're probably right." I put the coffee down. I'm a lot less shaky now.

She gently puts her hand on my arm. "I'm sorry I upset you."

"Aw, Mom, it wasn't you. I'm sorry I snapped. I was just sure…"

"A lot of things have changed since you were in the hospital. Maybe you remembered it wrong."

"Yeah…that could be. I'll look it up later."

"Maybe your friend Tara will know. You can ask her when you return her call."

"I'll do that. Thanks." I keep my eyes focused on the road ahead. I couldn't bear to look at my mom's face right now. I'm about to burst into tears, and I know if I see her expression I'll start and won't be able to stop.

She gives my arm a light squeeze then releases it, moves her hand away, and clutches her purse again. She shifts her body slightly toward the passenger door and stares out the window. Gray and brown images fleet by in continuous flashes of blah. No matter how hard I push my foot down on the gas pedal, I can't make the boring parts go by any faster, and they go on for miles—that I know from driving to Southern California for weekend getaways.

I can only imagine what she could be thinking now. Probably the same thing I am.

So, I guess this means I'm crazy. Everything about Dr. Light and his office building, *imagined*. It seems impossible I could be that far gone. Every other part of my life is normal, aside from the recent bout of bleeding and the coma. Which I guess, probably isn't so typical. I'm not so sure however, unbalanced people suspect they are disturbed. I know I heard or read that somewhere. I wonder if Cally knew she was going to try and kill herself. Depression, which is what she must be suffering through, is different though, like comparing apples to oranges. If I am crazy, it's Schizophrenia, I think, and that's about as far out there as a person can get. But Dr. Light didn't think that's what I had. But, HA! According to what just happened, he doesn't exist. And if he does, then he's an *alien*! What the hell is wrong with me?

Nothing. This is bullshit. I must have made a wrong turn somewhere, taken a different exit, but the more I think about it, there were no alternate routes. Maybe if I came without her, *they*, the building, would have been there. That would still make me crazy, though. *"They only appear to me when I'm alone."* Definitely sounds like a textbook nutcase statement.

They did call to me in my dream this morning. *They* are the ones who told me to come, that *they* were waiting, and then *they* didn't show up. I suppose something could have happened—maybe something involving the sun. If only I could get back there without a chaperone. I'll have to try again, soon.

My mom and I step through the door. Jon and my dad are standing there in the hallway to take our bags.

"Oh, I could get used to this kind of service," my mom says. She steps over to my dad.

Jon comes up, takes my bags, and kisses me. "I thought you were just buying a pair of shoes. What's all this?" he says.

"They were having a sale."

"Famous last words."

"Besides, I needed to get some holiday shopping done."

"Oh," he raises the bags and peeks in, "is there anything in here for me?"

"Knock it off."

"Not that I'd be able to see anything with all this tissue paper."

"That's exactly why it's there—to keep nosy husbands from seeing their gifts."

"I thought it was to hide all the extra stuff you bought for yourself."

"Funny. Will you bring them upstairs?"

"Yeah. You coming up?"

"I'll be right behind you."

We walk past the family room and kitchen. My parents have already gone to the guest room. No doubt my mom is whispering tales of my lunacy while she shows my dad how much money she saved him because she bought everything on sale. Fortunately, I know my dad will assume it's my mom who's crazy.

At the top of the landing, Jon heads into the master. I make a break and head down the hall to Patrick's room. Jon steps back with the bags crunching together. "Where you going?"

"I wanted to ask Pat something. Give me a minute. And no fishing around in the bags."

When I get to Pat's room, it appears he hasn't moved since I left him this morning. "Pat, please tell me you've eaten today."

"Oh, hey Mom." He rubs his eyes. "Hang on, guys." He pauses the game. "Yeah, I had a sandwich. What's up?"

"If you get anymore nosebleeds, I want you to tell me."

"Why?"

"You might have to see a specialist."

His eyes widen into bloodshot discs. "You don't think I've got what you did?"

"No. Absolutely not. I'm sure it's from the lack of humidity, but if it keeps happening, maybe there's something they can do to help."

"Oh, shit. You had me scared for a sec."

"What?"

"I mean, oh *wow*."

"Enough with the swearing, and by the way, have you heard anything else about those sunspots? Have they gotten worse?"

"I'm sure they have."

"It hasn't been on the news."

"That's because they don't want people to freak out. It would cause a worldwide panic. It's one of those conspiracy things."

"What? Are you being serious?"

"Let me put it this way…I'd be wearing fifty plus SPF sunscreen if I were you."

"Okay, I'm done. I think those video games are making you paranoid."

"I don't play spy games, Mom." He presses a button. "Hey, guys, I'm back."

CHAPTER THIRTY-ONE

Nine hours until the surgery center fundraiser and the butterflies are already having their way with my insides. One more thing I'll have to keep to myself. I came downstairs for a second cup of coffee and to build up my nerves to give Tara a call, but by the time I get around to it, I'll have finished the entire pot. I decide baking cinnamon rolls will better occupy my time.

No doubt Jordan will be at the party tonight, but I'd like to have someone else there to keep me grounded. Not that Tara is someone I would have ever thought of as being *grounded*, but right now, she's all I got.

"Morning," my dad says. He and my mom come into the kitchen like animals being led by their noses.

"Are you making breakfast?" my mom says.

"I put some cinnamon rolls in the oven. They should be ready in a few minutes."

"Homemade?" she says.

"Close enough."

"I'll have two," my dad says.

"Hungry?" I say. "Working overtime in your dreams again?"

"Maybe, how'd you sleep? Everything still hunky-dory? Your mother says you were having trouble remembering things yesterday."

"I slept fine." I'm a bad liar, too and my dad is more likely to pick up on it, where my mother won't. I was awake all night waiting to hear the tones again. I wanted to ask them about the bleeding disease but they stayed away. "I didn't have any trouble remembering anything yesterday. I simply had the wrong address."

My dad looks over at my mom as she's about to sip her coffee. "See," he says. "I told you it was nothing to worry about."

"Humph," she huffs down into her cup. She raises a brow, gives my dad an evil eye then puts the cup to her lips.

The oven buzzer goes off, and I pull out the tray of steaming cinnamon rolls. "It's a good thing Pat didn't hear you say hunky-dory, Dad. That would've made him laugh. He's always telling me I sound *old school*."

"Those look really good," he says, completely ignoring what I'd just said. He's too focused on the rolls. His body posture and facial expressions make him look like the *Big Bad Wolf* about to pounce and devour.

"They'll have to cool for a minute," I say.

When I'm done plating the rolls, I sit down with my parents and eat breakfast. It feels like a million years since it's been just the three of us. I remember being lonely sometimes growing up. I was never one of those kids that looked up at the stars and wondered if we were alone in the universe, but I did wonder why my parents never bothered to have any more kids. My dad always used to say it was because they broke the mold when they made me. And he's still goofy like that. Mom would say, *"That's just how it went."* Makes me wonder where circumstances are leading me now. *Go*, and let my mom tell Patrick the same thing when he asks her why, *or stay*, and be responsible for the demise of everything living.

"Where's Jon?" my dad says.

"I'm sure he's in the office. He said he had some work to catch up on."

"Work? He better get down here before all these rolls disappear."

"Save him one, dear," my mom says.

"Tonight's the big night for you two," he says. "He needs to start the day out right with a little breakfast."

"They're just sweet rolls, Dad. I don't think their nutritional value is worth calling him down for."

"Well in that case, I'll help myself to another."

"Go ahead. He won't mind." I get up from the table, put my dirty dish in the sink then grab the coffee pot and top off my cup. I take the phone from the counter and dial Tara's number.

"Sweetie, is it really you," she answers.

"Hi. Yeah, it's me. They set me free a couple days ago."

"And everything's good, right?"

"Yeah, great. It was just a freak incident or something."

"Freak incident? That's putting it lightly. Rumor has it you died."

"Tara, if I were dead, I wouldn't have called."

"No. Well, you know what I mean…for a minute or whatever, they lost you. Yours sounds like a case for that *House* guy on TV. He'd know what's wrong with you."

Okay, maybe even less grounded than I originally thought. "Are you coming to the party tonight?"

"I wouldn't miss it, even though Jordan will be there. God, so much has happened. There's a lot I have to tell you. It's going to have to wait, though. I was just on my way out for a manicure. Wait. You're going?"

"Of course, why wouldn't I?"

"I just thought…well…it doesn't matter. I'm so happy *you'll* be there."

"And I'm glad you will, too." I take it she and Jordan haven't made up yet.

"Come and find me as soon as you get there. We've got *some things* to discuss. Gotta go now, bye, kisses, and see you soon. Hugs. Can't wait to see you. Bye."

She truly is a Tara and *Gone with the Wind*.

"You didn't ask her about that store," my mom says from the kitchen table.

"Oh yeah, I totally forgot." *Shit. I also failed to remember not to say that I forgot.* Meanwhile, my mom looks over at my dad with an, *I told you so* expression on her face.

Jon looks as handsome as ever in his tux. "How'd I do with the bow tie?" he says from the closet.

"It's perfect. When did you get so good at tying bows?"

"Just one of many hidden talents. Stick around. I have a second performance later on, where I'll hopefully be pulling some new surgeons out of my hat." He steps out, then leans down to me sitting at the vanity and kisses the back of my head. "You're looking pretty hot."

"Pretty or hot? It's not possible to pull both looks off."

"You did."

"Aw, I love you."

"Aren't you glad you keep me around?"

"I knew there was a reason. Hey, were you being serious about getting new surgeons?"

"Yep." He adjusts his bow tie in the mirror.

"And the fundraiser hasn't even started yet. That's impressive."

"You can thank Jordan for that, too."

"Really? What did she have to do with it?"

"Don't say it like that. Jordan's done a lot for you, the fundraiser, and the surgery center. Oh, and do me a favor, don't drink tonight, okay."

"What?"

"One, I don't think it's a good idea since you were just recently discharged from the hospital, and Jordan is trying really hard to work through the Twelve-Step Program."

"Oh…*that's*…good news."

"It really is. I knew you'd be supportive." He gently pats my shoulder then steps back into the closet. "I'm heading downstairs in a minute. You about ready?"

"Yeah…almost."

"Want me to take anything down?"

"Uh…my shoes, and um, my black sequin clutch, please."

"These are more comfortable shoes?" He steps out with a wry expression on his face carrying my clutch and brand new pair of crystallized Louboutin's. "The heels must be five inches high. You'll break your neck."

Even in my state of emotional shock, they're still dazzling. "I'll be fine. They're really not that high, you're not seeing the platform under the sole. Honey, I've been wearing shoes like that for years."

"Okay, okay. It's definitely a good thing you're *not* drinking then. You'll need all your focus just to walk. Don't be long. I'll be downstairs. I think your mom and dad want to take some pictures, too. Kind of feels like prom, doesn't it?"

"Yeah…prom."

He leaves, but a wisp of his vivacious spirit lingers a moment longer. When all of him is truly gone, I turn back around, look in the mirror, and put the finishing touches on my face. I'm more confused than I've ever been in my life. I know in my heart Jon could never be unfaithful, but I feel uneasy. Like an animal sensing danger. Something that should be the least of my problems has taken center stage. Maybe it was there all along behind the curtains, and I just didn't *See* it. *And when did I become so blind?*

Jordan is greeting guests at the door when we arrive. "Oh, Stacy, you look wonderful." She puts her arms around me, careful to keep some distance between us. She kisses out at the air on either side of my head then steps back. "I can't wait to catch up on everything, but right now I've got to be up here. Jon why don't you stay with me and Stacy you go on in and get to mingling."

Jon steps forward and immediately begins shaking hands and talking to people coming through the entrance. Jordan smiles at me, then moves in next to him. *That should be me.*

I walk away in a daze, suddenly wondering if I go back out to the desert whether or not Dr. Light's building will be there. If *they* will be there…I look up and notice a bartender staring at me. I can't remember how long I've been standing next to the cash bar. I can't say exactly how it is I even got next to the bar or if I spoke to anyone along the way, but I know that if I get in my car and drive out into the open desert, I will wind up where Dr. Light's building is—was. Is it just me though, or is it *them? The others,* and their influence of forgetfulness on me. I do seem to be forgetting things lately—recent memories of the here and now. Why is it that they can't remember the past of how they came to be? It could be for some of the same reasons humans forget—something to do with chemical imbalance, like Alzheimer's. Maybe I could help them remember somehow. I wonder if the memories of the lives I had on Earth would fade away if I went with them. There could be important information contained in my memories that might be useful. Since all thoughts are shared. It should make memories last longer. Not be forgotten.

"There you are." I turn in the direction of the voice and see Tara walking toward me. "You look great!" She steps in and gives me a real hug. "Geez, what're you a zero now? Maybe a coma is the best way to lose weight."

"What?"

She lets go of me and steps back. "Just kidding, and why are you empty handed?" Tara leans up to the bar and orders two Appletinis.

"Oh no, I can't. I promised Jon I wouldn't."

"Wouldn't' what?"

"Drink."

"You've got to be shitting me. Who the hell's going to come to a party like this and not drink? Here take it. We'll have them over there in the corner next to the bar so he won't see you. He looked pretty occupied when I saw him at the door anyway."

"He did?"

"Well, not by choice. Jordan was all over him."

"She was?"

Tara faces me with a serious look. "You know she and Jon have been seen out lunching together."

"She's been helping him with the fundraiser and surgery center."

"Helped with what? You had all the work done already."

I swallow a mouthful of Appletini. "There were last minute details. Jon told me she got some surgeons to come over."

"Surgeons that have worked on her, probably. I'm sure she threatened to stop using them and referring them if they didn't go over to Jon's little surgery center."

"Really, Tara, I think you're reading more into this than there is. Especially after what happened with Cally, I just don't think it's possible they're having an affair."

"Just sayin'…" She swirls her martini glass and takes a sip.

"Then say something else, 'cause you're starting to piss me off. Tell me…did you know about Gail and Bill's affair?"

"Not straight up, not until recently, anyway."

"What do you mean?"

"Well, I've been kind of hanging out with some of the Green Valley girls. You know…the ones that *got* the show. Well, Bill's office is on that side of town and some of the girls told me that Bill and Gail have been seen out and about together for months. Maybe even close to a year. To be honest, I think that's how Gail's divorce got rolling. Her soon-to-be-ex, Steven, must have found out."

"Poor Cally."

"Yeah, but I think she kind of knew. Come on. What woman doesn't?" She gives me a funny look.

I down the rest of the Appletini in one gulp. "She should have talked to us about it. We should have talked more."

"I don't think anybody in Summerlin talked more than us."

"About serious things, though."

"Oh please, nobody wants to have meaningful conversations."

The alcohol has made my head warm and fuzzy. I walk over and put the glass down on the bar. "Would you like another?" the bartender asks with a big smile.

"No, thank you."

"I'll take one," Tara says.

The bartender grins and winks at her. His charm won't be lost there. I look at her face and she's smiling from ear to ear. I'm either drunk after only one drink, or she's flirting with a bartender. Everything seems wrong in the world, and I've either been blind, or oblivious, or both, to it all this time and just recently *awoke* when I came out of the coma.

"I'm feeling a little tired. I think I'll ask Jon to go."

"It was good seeing you again. And I was only joking about the talking serious stuff. If you have something important you want to talk about then just do it. Better that than going off and trying to kill yourself. I wouldn't want that on my conscience."

"Thanks Tara. You're *such* a good friend." But now I *See*. She's not, not really. She's too occupied with the bartender handing her another drink to notice my expression of disgust. I walk away.

Jon and Jordan are standing in the doorway talking to one another even though it's obvious everyone attending the party is already inside. I step up and interrupt them. "I'm feeling a little tired. Would it be all right if we leave?"

"Yeah…okay."

"I can take you home," Jordan says. "You should stay, Jon."

I take another step closer. "Thanks for everything, Jordan. The set-up and decorations are fabulous. You've done a great job, and I hate to leave, but *Jon* is taking me home now."

"Of course," she says. "I just thought I'd offer in case he wanted to mingle with some future prospects."

"We've been here for a while, and he hasn't done much mingling as far as I could tell."

"I'll go get the car," Jon says. "You should come wait outside and get some fresh air."

"Yeah, I think I'll do that."

"You two go on then, and don't worry about a thing. I'm glad you could make it out for a bit, Stacy." Her Texas twang has never sounded so intentionally condescending, and I want nothing more than to be far, far away. "I heard you got a chance to see Cally while you were in the hospital. It's a real shame what happened there."

"Yes, it really is. And we should all be ashamed for not speaking up. Goodbye, Jordan."

As soon as I step out, the cool air soothes my hot head. In fact, it's never felt this good—the cold. Jon pulls up in the car then gets out and runs around to open the passenger door for me. I look back and see Jordan standing in the doorway, watching us. Jon drives away and I glance at the entrance one last time. Jordan is no longer there.

"Did you see Terry Swanson and his wife at the party?" Jon says.

"What? No." I'm staring out the window. Thinking about how the cold comforts me.

"He set up another appointment for an MRI sometime next week."

"Oh."

"The party was great wasn't it? Jordan really came through."

"Yeah…great."

"I saw Tara come in. Jordan wouldn't greet her. Did you get a chance to see her?"

"I did."

"You sure you're okay?"

"Yeah, I'm fine."

It's not late when we get home, but my parents are already in bed. Jon goes down to the office while I take my shower. Strange, I wanted nothing more than to come home when I was at the party, but now that I'm here it doesn't feel right, either. Everything is different. *I* am not the same. It's up to me to make things right again.

I lie in bed and wait for Jon to get in after his shower. When he finally comes to bed, I wiggle over and put my arms around him. "Congratulations." I kiss him on the back of his neck.

"Yeah, I really think it was good this year."

"It's always good with you," I whisper heavy and move my hand down between his legs.

He reaches for my hand then moves it back up to his chest. "I'm a little tired tonight, too, and you need some rest."

I have to catch my breath. Sixteen years and he's never done this. "You're right." I exhale slowly and move away. "Goodnight."

"Goodnight."

No *I love yous*. Not tonight.

CHAPTER THIRTY-TWO

Somewhere between sleep, dreams, and consciousness, *they* come. Their music is lucid words and voices calling out—willing me to wake—desperate for me to hear. *"Come back." "You will kill us all." "You will kill* them, *too." "You will See." "It has begun."*

My eyelids pop open and I gaze out across a terrain of ruffled linen, the peaks glowing in the bright sunlight. I wonder again…could there be some truth to what they're saying? Will *I* be responsible for the extinction of two separate life-forms? And when exactly did it begin?

After a minute, I realize Jon is gone. Does it begin with?—*Jon!* I flip the covers back, leap out of bed and rush into the bathroom. The closet is open and the light is on inside. For a moment I breathe easy. Then I go in and see articles of his clothing draped over the chaise but no Jon. Where could he be? Maybe he's downstairs making coffee. But why would he need to get dressed? I find a pair of his clean slacks on the closet floor in a crumpled mess. Something must be going on. I pull on some jeans and a T-shirt, put my hair into a ponytail then leave the master bedroom.

First, I check the office. The door is open but it's empty, and I'm sure he isn't in Patrick's room, so I trot downstairs. My mom is on the couch in her robe, holding a cup of coffee and watching TV.

"Hey Mom, have you seen Jon?"

She jumps a little and the cup bumbles in her hands. "You startled me."

"Sorry. Did you spill?"

"No."

"Where's Jon?"

"He and your father went golfing."

"Really?"

"He didn't tell you?"

"No. When did they leave?"

"Early. I think your father said they were playing eighteen holes."

"Oh."

"You two came home early last night. You weren't arguing were you?"

"No. Why?"

"I guess Jon has seemed, well, out of sorts to me lately. That's all."

"Which is understandable considering the circumstances."

"Not in the way that you're thinking, dear. A mother

just knows these things, but if you say you haven't been fighting then I'll have to believe you."

"I promise. We haven't. A mom knows what kind of things?"

"I'm sure it's nothing."

"No really, what? Tell me."

"How was the party?"

"It was fine. Nice."

"Are you going somewhere dressed like that?"

"Nowhere…"

"Come back." "Please!" "Now!" "No time!"

"Mom, do you hear that?"

"Hear what?"

Suddenly, their tones become high-pitched squeals, forcing my eyelids and jaw to clamp shut. I clench my hands into tight fists not wanting to cover my ears in front my mom.

"Stacy, what is it? Are you okay?"

It stops, and the muscles in my face immediately release their grimace. "Yes. I'm fine." I open my hands then raise them up to my head and tuck loose strands of hair behind my ears. All the while, a faint static noise tunes in and out of my head. "Actually, I think I might step out before the guys come home and finish up some shopping."

"What? Oh no, I don't think that's a good idea at all. Maybe I should give Jon a call. What just happened?"

"Nothing, I told you, I'm fine. Don't interrupt them. I won't be gone long."

"Well, in that case, I think I better go along. Give me a minute to get dressed."

"No Mom, really, I'd like to go by myself. I'll be okay."

"But Jon told me not to let you go out alone."

"He did?"

"Don't be upset with him. They still don't know what's wrong, and he's worried."

"Fine, then. You've got thirty minutes."

She gets up from the couch and heads for the guest room. "What are you going to do while I get dressed?" She watches me from her doorway.

"I'm going upstairs to wake Pat."

"That's a good idea."

Her eyes follow me as I go up and disappear from view—unbelievable. Now I'm most definitely a prisoner in a home that no longer feels like mine.

When I get to the end of the hall, I open Pat's door quietly then tiptoe in. I walk across his room and step into his bathroom. Even in the daylight shuttered darkness, I see bloodied tissues flowing over his little bathroom garbage can. They're spilling out onto the floor. Icy daggers stab me all over, and I quiver uncontrollably in response. *No!*

I rush over to him lying in bed and rest my hand across the top of his blanket. Underneath, his chest moves slowly, rhythmically, up and down. He's still breathing—good. I lean over him and move away a pillow he has covering his head, exposing one side of his face. He's still sound asleep. I hunch over and kiss his temple, mouthing, "I love you… I'm so sorry," into his head. I know somewhere in there he hears me. I sniffle and then inhale deep. I fill my lungs with his *human* smell that is always strongest in the morning. I kiss his temple again then sit up before my tears roll onto his face and wake him. Maybe there's still something I can do to stop this.

I leave his room and head straight into the office thinking I can Google Dr. Light's address. I move the mouse and Jon's email account is open on the screen. There's a sealed email envelope from Jordan in his inbox. I move the mouse over it and click. It says, "If you don't tell her about us, I will." My sinking heart bottoms out. I know Jordan intended for me to read that, and maybe Jon did, too. What Tara said at the party last night hits me now. Even my own mother suspects something. I leave the office and creep down the stairs. Along the way, my right shoulder swipes family pictures hanging on the wall. They're black and white photos I took of us on our European vacation. I had them custom framed in natural carbon steel. One swings back and forth, making a scraping noise. I put my hand out and stop it. It's a photo of Patrick when he was five. His smile was radiant—infectious. *I have to save him!*

When I get downstairs, I grab my car keys off the counter and sneak out of the house through the garage. To keep the noise minimal, I simultaneously open the garage and start the car. It seems to work, there's no sign of my mom. I pull down the driveway and head out.

As I'm waiting for the gates to open, I see her in the rearview mirror. She's jumping up and down the middle of the driveway, frantically waving a phone in her hand. She starts coming toward me, and I push my foot down on the accelerator and crash past the edges of the opening gates. *There's no time!*

I peel out of the neighborhood and get onto the beltway, confident I know where I'm going. It wasn't that I was lost the other day. *They* just weren't there or wouldn't show *themselves*. *They* will be there today—waiting for me—I know it.

I can't remember if I stopped at any of the STOP signs before I made it onto the beltway, but I do notice something strange about the brown ceiling of pollution that usually hovers over the surrounding mountains. It is gone. The sky is the sharpest hue of azure I have ever seen, and knowing what I know makes it the most dangerous kind of beautiful. It's early still, so there's no traffic. I'm not sure I've seen any other cars at all. A shudder moves through me and I grip the steering wheel to hold it back. Everything looks post-apocalyptic already.

—*My son.* He's dying. I know this, too. Maybe I've known it for a while. It's the bleeding disease from my nightmares, and if it is real, then *they* are real, too. *They* have to tell me how to fix it—*they* have to tell me the cure! If I promise to go with *them*…*they* will know how.

As soon as I turn onto the paved circular drive, the office building stands tall against the backdrop of nothing else for miles. It is only the building. No parking lot, none of the shrubs or sidewalks. It looks weak and sickly. The image flashes in and out like a hologram run from an old projector.

I put the car into park in front of the building and stare through the windshield. "Help me. Help my son. Please."

"There is nothing." "Come back to us." "Remember now."

"That can't be. Find a way. Save him."

"It is." "We are."

"No! No! No!" I slam my fists against the steering wheel. Tears and snot trickle over my lips. I look up in the rearview mirror. It's not just tears—it's blood. Streaming from my eyes and dripping from my nose. It's running down the side of my neck. I turn my head and look in the mirror. My ears are bleeding, too. I hack into the air. The taste of salt and metal erupts from my mouth, spewing blood spray across the dashboard and windshield. A white whorl of vapor billows out in front of my face. I reach up and my hand passes right through it. I exhale again and another cloud, thicker than the first one, rolls out. In a matter of minutes, the car is filled with a dry white fog.

"It has begun." "Come back to us." "See."

"No, goddammit! Listen to me!" I grab the steering wheel and bang my head against it. Something on my face shatters into a thousand pieces. Frantic, I unbuckle my seatbelt, and wave the fog off. I move my head an inch from the rearview mirror so I can see what broke. It was the blood, the mucus, and the tears. It had all frozen. I move my hands over my skin and slap away the rest of the fractured ice. "What is this? What's happening? Help me!"

I'm crying hysterically, blabbering, and I can't tell if I'm talking out loud or talking in my mind anymore. Every sign shows it's freezing in the car but inside, I'm on fire—searing—my lungs are on the verge of combustion. My God, the burning!

"Yes."

"No!" My mouth roars open. Bright white light launches straight out into the building. The next moment, I'm in the light—I am the light—in the building. The marbled veins in the floor pulse and the walls fold and collapse around me. Once again I'm moving through folds of slimy plasma, but it's mostly clear. I can see through it. I push my way to the bottom and peer out.

Down below I see my car. A body is hunched over the steering wheel—my body. "Am I dead?" I say.

"Only in that form which was never yours to live through." It's his voice all around in rippled waves of blue—Dr. Light.

"No! How can I save him if I'm dead? Please! Help my son!"

A profound deafening stillness surrounds me. It encroaches and pervades. Then all at once, sound, lights, and fragmented remembrance come down in a viscous tidal wave of multicolored ooze. It takes me under and rattles my existence. At long last, I finally *See*.

"He, they, all, will die peacefully in their sleep to avoid suffering slow burning deaths," I think.

"Yes."

"What is it—an illness—a disease?"

"A viral form of radiation poisoning." "We yield to the radioactive emissions of their light." "They succumb to the radiation emanating from our darkness."

From where I am in the slimy plasma bubble, the view of my car gets smaller and smaller. We are moving up. We are leaving, and I am seeing the entire valley through what seems to be the rounded end of a water droplet. I reach out into opalescent liquid light—afraid. My fear travels in ringlet hues of brilliant purple.

"I will miss it," I think.

"What will you miss most?"

"Being human."

I sense their confusion at my answer. I forget they don't know what it means, so I explain. "I was an individual with my own thoughts, and I used them to make my own future. Humans are all separate beings in a vast sea of choices. Make the right ones and rise, breathe to survive. Survive to procreate. And the children…I will miss the children.

"Will I—I mean we…forget?"

Together we answer, "We do not know."

ACKNOWLEDGMENTS

I'd like to thank my parents for VHS horror rental weekends in the 80s. A special thanks to my dad, L.J. Esterly Jr. for showing me that science and science-fiction are cool. David-Matthew Barnes for encouraging me not to give up. Greg Herren for motivation. Gehret, Parker, Chris Marrs, JG Faherty, Mindy Morgan, and Seth Scranton for their love and support.

ABOUT THE AUTHOR

Rena Mason was born in Nakhon Sawan, Thailand. She is a first-generation American horror and dark speculative fiction author of Thai Chinese descent and a three-time winner of the Bram Stoker Award®. Her co-written screenplay RIPPERS was a 2014 Stage 32/ The Blood List Presents®: The Search for New Blood Screenwriting Contest Quarterfinalist. She is a member of the Horror Writers Association, Mystery Writers of America, International Thriller Writers, The International Screenwriters Association, Science Fiction & Fantasy Writers Association, and the Public Safety Writers Association. She is a retired operating room RN and currently resides in the Great Lakes State of Michigan. For more information visit: www.RenaMason.Ink